HOMECOMING

Books by Cynthia Voigt

THE BAD GIRLS SERIES

Bad Girls
Bad, Badder, Baddest
It's Not Easy Being Bad
Bad Girls in Love
Bad Girls, Bad Girls, Whatcha Gonna Do?

THE TILLERMAN SERIES

Homecoming
Dicey's Song
A Solitary Blue
The Runner
Come a Stranger
Sons from Afar
Seventeen Against the Dealer

THE KINGDOM SERIES

Jackaroo
On Fortune's Wheel
The Wings of a Falcon
Elske

OTHER BOOKS

Building Blocks
The Callender Papers
David and Jonathan
Izzy, Willy-Nilly
Orfe
Tell Me if the Lovers Are Losers
Tree by Leaf
The Vandemark Mummy
When She Hollers

HOMECOMING

CYNTHIA VOIGT

ATHENEUM BOOKS FOR YOUNG READERS
New York London Toronto Sydney New Delhi

ATHENEUM BOOKS FOR YOUNG READERS
An imprint of Simon & Schuster Children's Publishing Division
1230 Avenue of the Americas, New York, New York 10020
This book is a work of fiction. Any references to historical events, real people, or real locales are used fictitiously. Other names, characters, places, and incidents are products of the author's imagination, and any resemblance to actual events or locales or persons, living or dead, is entirely coincidental.

For information about special discounts for bulk purchases, please contact
Simon & Schuster Special Sales at 1-866-506-1949 or business@simonandschuster.com.
The Simon & Schuster Speakers Bureau can bring authors to your live event.
For more information or to book an event, contact the Simon & Schuster Speakers Bureau
at 1-866-248-3049 or visit our website at www.simonspeakers.com.
Also available in an Atheneum Books for Young Readers hardcover edition
Book design by Debra Sfetsios-Conover
The text for this book is set in Baskerville.
Manufactured in the United States of America
This Atheneum Books for Young Readers paperback edition March 2012
12 14 16 18 20 19 17 15 13
The Library of Congress has cataloged the hardcover edition as follows:
Voigt, Cynthia.
Homecoming.
Summary: Abandoned by their mother, four children begin
a search for a home and an identity.
ISBN 978-0-689-30833-8
[1. Survival—Fiction. 2. Family Life—Fiction] I. Title.
PZ7.V874Ho
[Fic] 80-36723
ISBN 978-1-4424-5061-5 (hc)
ISBN 978-1-4424-2878-2 (pbk)

To Jessica & Walter

HOMECOMING

PART ONE

CHAPTER 1

The woman put her sad moon-face in at the window of the car. "You be good," she said. "You hear me? You little ones, mind what Dicey tells you. You hear?"

"Yes, Momma," they said.

"That's all right then." She slung her purse over her shoulder and walked away, her stride made uneven by broken sandal thongs, thin elbows showing through holes in the oversized sweater, her jeans faded and baggy. When she had disappeared into the crowd of Saturday morning shoppers entering the side doors of the mall, the three younger children leaned forward onto the front seat. Dicey sat in front. She was thirteen and she read the maps.

"Why'd we stop?" asked James. "We're not there yet. We've got food. There's no reason to stop." James was ten and wanted everything to have a reason. "Dicey?"

"I dunno. You heard everything she said, same as I did. You tell me."

"All she said was, *We gotta stop here.* She didn't say why. She never says why, you know that. Are we out of gas?"

"I didn't look." Dicey wanted some quiet for thinking. There was something odd about this whole trip. She couldn't put her finger on it, not yet. "Why don't you tell them a story?"

"What story?"

"Cripes, James, you're the one with the famous brain."

"Yeah, well I can't think of any stories right now."

"Tell them anything. Tell them Hansel and Gretel."

"I want HanselnGretel. And the witch. And the candy house with peppermint sticks," Sammy said, from the backseat. James gave in without a quarrel. It was easier to give in to Sammy than to fight him. Dicey turned around to look at them. Maybeth sat hunched in a corner, big-eyed. Dicey smiled at her and Maybeth smiled back. "Once upon a time," James began. Maybeth turned to him.

Dicey closed her eyes and leaned her head back. She put her feet on the dashboard. She was tired. She'd had to stay awake and read maps, to find roads without tolls. She'd been up since three in the morning. But Dicey couldn't go to sleep. She gnawed away at what was bothering her.

For one thing, they never took trips. Momma always said the car couldn't run more than ten miles at a stretch. And here they were in Connecticut, heading down to Bridgeport. For one thing.

But that might make sense. All her life, Dicey had been hearing about Momma's aunt Cilla and her big house in Bridgeport that Momma had never seen, and her rich husband who died. Aunt Cilla sent Christmas cards year after year, with pictures of baby Jesus on them and long notes inside, on paper so thin it could have been tissue paper. Only Momma could decipher the lacy handwriting with its long, tall letters all bunched together and the lines running into one another because of the long-tailed, fancy z's and f's and g's. Aunt Cilla kept in touch. So it made sense for Momma to go to her for help.

But driving off like that in the middle of the night didn't make sense. That was the second thing. Momma woke them all up and told them to pack paper bags of clothing while she made sandwiches. She got them all into the old car and headed for Bridgeport.

For a third—things had been happening, all at once. Things were always bad with them, but lately worse than ever. Momma lost her checker's job. Maybeth's teacher had wanted a meeting with Momma that Momma wouldn't go to. Maybeth would be held back another year. Momma said she didn't want to hear about it, and she had ripped up every note, without reading any of them. Maybeth didn't worry her family, but she worried her teachers. She was nine and still in the second grade. She never said much, that was the trouble, so everybody thought she was stupid. Dicey knew she wasn't. Sometimes she'd come out and say something that showed she'd been watching and listening and taking things in. Dicey knew her sister could read and do sums, but Maybeth always sat quiet around strangers. For Maybeth, everyone in the world was a stranger, except Momma and Dicey and James and Sammy.

Momma herself was the fourth thing. Lately she'd go to the store for bread and come back with a can of tuna and just put her hands over her face, sitting at the table. Sometimes she'd be gone for a couple of hours and then she wouldn't say where she had been, with her face blank as if she couldn't say. As if she didn't know. Momma didn't talk to them anymore, not even to scold, or sing, or make up games the way she used to. Except Sammy. She talked to Sammy, but even then they sounded like two six-year-olds talking, not one six-year-old and his mother.

Dicey kept her feet on the dash, and her body slouched down. She looked out through the windshield, over the rows of parked cars, to where the sky hung like a bleached-out sheet over the top of the mall buildings. Bugs were spattered all over the windshield and the sky promised a heavy, hot day. Dicey slid still further down on the seat. Her skin stuck to the blue plastic seat covers.

James was describing the witch's house, listing the kinds of candy used for various parts of the building. This was the part James liked best in Hansel and Gretel, and he always did it a little differently from the time before. Picturing the almond Hershey bar roof and the shutters made of cinnamon licorice sticks, Dicey did fall asleep.

She woke covered with sweat from the hot sun pouring in through the windshield. She woke hungry. Maybeth was singing softly, one of Momma's songs, about making her love a baby with no crying. "I fell asleep," Dicey said. "What time's it?"

"I dunno," James said. "You've been asleep a long time. I'm hungry."

"Where's Momma?"

"I dunno. I'm hungry."

"You're always hungry. Go ask someone what time it is, okay?"

James climbed out of the car. He crossed to the walkway and stopped a man in a business suit. "Twelve thirty," James reported.

"But that means I slept for more than two hours," Dicey protested.

"I'm going to eat," Sammy announced from the backseat. He opened the bag of food and pulled out a sandwich before Dicey could say anything.

"What do you want me to do?" James asked, looking into Dicey's face. His narrow little face wore a worried expression. "Want me to go look for her?"

"No," Dicey said. (*Now* what had Momma gone and done.) "Sammy, give Maybeth a sandwich too. Let her choose for herself. Then pass the bag up here."

When everyone had a sandwich, and James had two, Dicey reached a decision. "We have to wait here for a while more," she said. "Then we'll do something. I'm going to take a walk and see if I can find her."

"Don't you go away too," Maybeth said softly.

"I'll be right where you can see me," Dicey said. "I'll stay on the sidewalk—see?—just like a path in front of the stores. Then maybe later we can all go into the mall and look in the stores. You'd like that, wouldn't you?" Maybeth smiled and nodded her golden head.

Dicey did her best thinking when she walked. On this warm June afternoon, she walked so fast and thought so hard, she didn't even see the people going past her. If Momma went past she'd say something, so Dicey wasn't worried about that.

She was worried that Momma had wandered off. And would not come back.

("You always look for the worst," Momma had often told her. "I like to be ready," Dicey answered.)

If Momma was gone . . . But that wasn't possible. Was it? But if she was, what could they do? Ask for help, probably from a policeman. (Would he put them in homes or orphanages? Wouldn't that be just what the police or some social worker would do?) Go back to Provincetown, they could go back home. (Momma hadn't paid the rent, not for weeks, and it was almost summertime, when even their old cabin, set off alone in the dunes, could bring in a lot of money. Mr. Martinez wasn't sympathetic, not when it came to money, not when it came to giving something away for free. He'd never let them stay there to wait for Momma.) They could go on to Bridgeport. Dicey had never seen Aunt Cilla—Great-Aunt Cilla. She knew the name and address, because Momma had made her write it down four times, on each paper bag, in case something happened: Mrs. Cilla Logan, 1724 Ocean Drive, Bridgeport, Connecticut. Aunt Cilla was family, the only family Dicey knew about.

The sun beat down on the parking lot and heated up the air so even in the shaded walkway Dicey was hot. The kids must be hot too, she thought, and turned to get them.

Momma must have gone away on purpose. (But she loved them, loved them all.) Why else the addresses on the bags? Why else tell them to mind Dicey? (Mothers didn't do things like going off. It was crazy. Was Momma crazy?) How did she expect Dicey to take care of them? What did she expect Dicey to do? Take them to Bridgeport, of course. (Dump it all on Dicey, that was what Momma did, she always did, because Dicey was the determined sort. "It's in your blood," Momma said, and then wouldn't explain.)

Anger welled up in Dicey, flooded her eyes with tears, and now she was swept away with the determination to get the kids to Bridgeport. Well, she'd do it somehow, if she had to.

Momma wasn't at the car when Dicey returned, so Dicey said they'd wait for her until the next morning.

"Where'll we sleep?" Sammy asked.

"Right here—and no complaints," Dicey said.

"Then Momma will come back and we'll go on tomorrow?" Sammy asked.

Dicey nodded.

"Where is Momma? Why's she taking so long?" James asked.

"I dunno, James," Dicey answered. Maybeth was silent, staring.

After a few minutes, Dicey hustled them all out of the car and trailed after them as they entered the mall.

The mall was built like a fortress around a huge, two-story enclosed street, where store succeeded store, as far as you could see. At one end of the central section was a cage of live birds in a little park of plastic trees and shrubs. The floor of their cage was littered with pieces of popcorn and gum wrappers. At the other end, the builders had made a waterfall through which shone different colored lights. Outside, beyond the covered sidewalk that ran like a moat around the huge building, lay the huge, gray parking lot, a no-man's-land of empty cars.

But here inside was a fairyland of colors and sounds, crowded with people on this Saturday afternoon, artificially lit and planted. Inside was a miniature city where endless diversions from the work-day world offered everything delightful. If you had money, of course. And even without money, you could still stare and be amazed.

They spent a long time wandering through stores, looking at toys and records and pianos and birthday cards. They were drawn to restaurants that exuded the smell of spaghetti and pizza or fried chicken, bakeries with trays of golden doughnuts lined up behind glass windows, candy stores, where the countertop was crowded with large jars of jelly beans and sourballs and little foil-covered chocolates and peppermints dipped in crunchy white frosting; cheese shops (they each had two free samples), where the rich smell of aged cheeses mingled with fresh-ground coffee, and hot dog stands, where they stood back in a silent row. After this, they sat on a backless bench before the waterfall, tired and hungry. Altogether, they had eleven dollars and fifty cents, more than any one of them had ever had at one time before, even Dicey who contributed all of her babysitting money, seven dollars.

They spent almost four dollars on supper at the mall, and none of them had dessert. They had hamburgers and french fries and, after Dicey thought it over, milkshakes. At that rate, they could have one more meal before they ran out of money, or maybe two more. It was still light when they returned to the car. The little ones horsed around in the back, teasing, wrestling, tickling, quarreling and laughing, while Dicey studied the map. People walked by their car, vehicles came and went, and nobody paid any attention to them. In parking lots, it's not unusual to see a car full of kids waiting.

At half-past eight, Dicey herded everybody back into the mall, to use the bathrooms they had found earlier. Later, Sammy and Maybeth fell asleep easily, curled up along the backseat. James moved up to the front with Dicey. Dicey couldn't see how they were both to sleep in the front seat, but she supposed they would manage it. James sat stiffly, gripping the wheel. James had a narrow head and sharp features, a nose that pointed out, pencil-thin eyebrows, a narrow chin. Dicey studied him in the darkening car. They were parked so far from the nearest lamppost that they were in deep shadows.

With her brothers and sister near, with the two youngest asleep in the backseat, sitting as they were in a cocoon of darkness, she should feel safe. But she didn't. Though it was standing still, the car seemed to be flying down a highway, going too fast. Even the dark inside of it was not deep enough to hide them. Faces might appear in the windows at any time, asking angry questions.

"Where's Momma gone?" James asked, looking out at the night.

"I just don't know," Dicey said. "Here's what I think, I think if she isn't back by morning we ought to go on to Bridgeport."

"On our own?"

"Yes."

"How'll we get there? You can't drive. Momma took the keys."

"We could take a bus, if we have enough money. If we don't, we'll walk."

James stared at her. Finally he spoke. "Dicey? I'm scared. I feel all jiggly in my stomach. Why doesn't Momma come back?"

"If I knew, James, I'd know what to do."

"Do you know the way?"

"To Bridgeport? I can read a map. Once we get there, we can ask directions to Aunt Cilla's house."

James nodded. "Do you think she's been killed? Or kidnapped?"

"Rich people get kidnapped; not Momma. I'm not going to think about what might have happened to her, and I don't think you should, either."

"I can't help thinking about it," James said in a small voice.

"Don't tell Sammy or Maybeth," Dicey warned.

"I wouldn't. I know better. You should know I'd know better than that."

Dicey reached out and patted him on the shoulder. "I do know," she said.

James grabbed her hand. "Dicey? Do you think Momma meant to leave us here?"

"I think Momma meant to take us to Bridgeport, but—"

"Is Momma crazy?"

Dicey turned her head to look at him.

"The kids said so, at school. And the way the teachers looked at me and loaned me their own books and talked to me. And Maybeth. Craziness can run in families."

Dicey felt a great weight settle on her shoulders. She tried to shrug it off, but it wouldn't move.

"Dicey?"

"She loves us," Dicey muttered.

"But that's the only reason I can think of that might be true."

"There's nothing wrong with Maybeth. You know that."

"It runs in families. Hereditary craziness."

"Well, you don't have to worry about it, do you? You're the smart one, with A's in school and the science projects that get entered in the state contest."

"Yeah," James said. He settled his head back on the seat.

"Listen, I'm going to go to a phone and see where the bus station is and call them up to find out how much tickets cost. You lay low."

"Why?"

Dicey decided to tell him the truth. "Just in case. I mean, three kids in a car in a parking lot at night . . . See, James, I think we've got to get to Bridgeport and I just don't know what would happen if a policeman saw us. Foster homes or something, I dunno. I don't want to risk it. But one kid . . . and I'm pretty old so it doesn't look funny."

"Okay. That sounds okay."

"We've got to get to Bridgeport."

James thought about that, then nodded his head. "I never listened much to Momma's talk about her. What will she be like, Aunt Cilla?"

"Rich," Dicey said.

"It would be a long walk," James said.

"Long enough," Dicey agreed. She got out of the car fast.

It was full dark, an overcast night. The parking lot was nearly empty; only two cars besides theirs remained. Dicey wondered how many cars were left in the other three parking lots that spread out from the other sides of the building. It felt as empty as all of space must be. She hoped there were cars in each lot. The more cars there were, the safer their car was for them.

Dicey headed confidently for the walkway, as if she had every right to be where she was, as if she had an important errand to run, as if she knew just where she was going. She remembered a telephone at the far end of the building. It wasn't a real phone booth, but a kind of cubicle hung up on the wall, with an open shelf underneath to hold the directory. James could probably see her from the car, if he looked for her. From that distance, she would look small.

The walkway was lit up, and the store windows were lit, so she moved through patches of sharp light. At the phone, she took out the directory to look up bus companies in the yellow pages. She ran her finger down the names, selected one that sounded local and reached into her pocket for change.

She heard footsteps. A man approached her, in a uniform like a policeman's, but tan not blue, and without the badge. He took his time getting to her, as if he was sure she'd wait, sure of his own strength to hold her, even at that distance. He moved like he thought she was afraid of him, too afraid to run.

"Hey," the man said. His shirt had the word "Security" sewn onto it. Where his belly sagged, the shirt hung out over his pants. He carried a long-handled flashlight. He wore a pistol at his belt.

Dicey didn't answer, but she didn't look away.

"Hey kid," he said, as if she had shown signs of running and he needed to halt her. He was heavy, out of shape. He had a pig-person face, a coarse skin that sagged at the jowls, little blue eyes and pale eyebrows, and a fat, pushed-back nose. When he came up next to her, Dicey stepped back a pace, but kept her finger on the number in the book.

"You lost?"

"Naw. I'm making a phone call."

"Where do you live?"

"Just over there," Dicey said, pointing vaguely with her free hand.

"Go home and call from there. Run along now. If you were a girl, I'd walk you over, but—"

"Our phone's broken," Dicey said. "That's why my mom sent me here."

The guard shifted his flashlight, holding it like a club. "Phones don't break. How's a phone break?"

"We've got this dog that chews things up. Slippers, papers, you know. He chewed the phone. The cord, actually, but it's all the same—the phone's broken."

"Are you bulling me?"

"I wish I was."

"What's your name, kid?"

"Danny."

She felt funny, strange, making up lies as quickly and smoothly as if she'd been doing it all her life.

The man took a piece of gum out of his pocket, unwrapped it, folded it in half and stuck it into his mouth, chewing on it a couple of times.

"Danny what?"

"Tillerman." Dicey couldn't make up a new last name, except Smith, and nobody would believe that even if it was true.

"You don't look more than ten. Isn't it late to be out?"

Dicey shrugged.

The guard grew suspicious. "Who're you calling?"

"The bus company. My sisters and me are going down to Bridgeport some time soon, to stay with my aunt."

He chewed and thought. "Sometime soon wouldn't send you out after ten at night to phone. What's the rush?"

"My mom just got back from the clinic and she's gonna have her baby, any day now the doctor said, and my aunt needs to know what time the buses arrive so she can meet us on Monday. So's we can take a bus it's good for her to meet. My mom asked me to come find out so's she can call first thing in the morning, before my aunt goes to church. It's hard for my mom to get around now—you know."

"Where's your father?"

"Gone."

"Gone where?"

"Dunno. He just up and went, way back, last winter."

The guard nodded. He reached in his pocket and pulled out the pack of gum. He offered a piece to Dicey, but she shook her head.

"Can I call now, mister?"

"Sure thing," he said. "I wouldn't have bothered you except

that there've been some windows broken around here. We think it's kids. I'm the security guard. I've got to be careful."

Dicey nodded. She inserted the coins and slowly dialed the numbers, hoping he'd go away. But he stood there and listened. Behind him lay the parking lot, a vast open space where occasional clumps of planted bushes spread long shadows over the ground.

An impersonal voice answered. Dicey asked about tickets to Bridgeport, how much they cost.

"From where to Bridgeport."

Dicey grabbed at a name. "Peewauket." That was what the map said. She pronounced it Pee-Walk-It. The guard, listening narrowed his eyes.

"From Peewauket?" the voice asked, saying it Pwuk-it.

"Yeah."

"Two dollars and forty-five cents a person."

"What's the rate for children?"

"The same. The charge is for the seat. Unless you've got a child under two."

"What time do buses run?"

"Every other hour, from eight to eight."

Dicey thanked the voice and hung up the phone. She stood with her arms hanging down at her sides, waiting for the guard to leave.

He was studying her with his little piggly eyes. He held his flashlight now in one hand and slapped it into the palm of the other. "You better get back now," he said and then added, "You didn't write anything down."

"I've got a good memory."

"Yeah? I'll give you a test." His body blocked the way to the safe darkness of the parking lot. "You don't remember anything about broken windows in the mall, do you? For instance, just one for instance, at Record City."

"I don't know what you're talking about."

"I wonder about that. I really wonder, Danny. You said Danny, didn't you? Tillerman, wasn't it? You see, we figure it was probably kids did it, account of nothing's been stolen. Or maybe just one kid did it, that's what I'm thinking."

Dicey glared at him. "I said I don't know anything about that."

He put one arm out to bar her in, resting his hand against the side of the phone. "I can't think of why I should believe you. Nope, now I come to think of it, I don't think I do believe you. The only question in my mind is, what do I do with you?"

Dicey thought fast, then acted just as fast. She lifted her right knee as if to hit him in the groin where she knew it would hurt bad. He lowered his arm and stepped back, to protect himself. In that one second while he was off balance, Dicey took off. She sprinted into the darkness of the parking lot. As soon as she was in the cover of the shadows, she turned left around the corner of the building, away from their car. He thundered after her.

Dicey ran smoothly. She was used to running on beaches, where the sand gave way under your feet and each thrust of your legs was hindered. Running over asphalt was easier. Dicey pulled away from her pursuer. His steps were heavy and his breathing was heavy. He was out of shape and too fat to catch up with her. She had time to crouch behind one of the little islands of green that decorated the parking lot. She had on a dark shirt and jeans, her face was tanned and her hair brown; she was confident nothing would give her away.

He stopped by the front entrance shining his flashlight out over the parking lot, like one bright eye. Dicey watched him. He listened, but his chest was heaving so much that she was sure he couldn't hear anything but the blood pounding in his ears. She smiled to herself.

"You haven't got a chance," he called. "You better come out now, kid. You're only making it worse."

Dicey covered her mouth with her hand.

"I know you now. We'll find you out," he said. He turned quickly away from the parking lot and looked farther along the front of the mall. He hunched behind the flashlight. He used the beam like a giant eye, to peer into the shadows. "There you are! I can see you!" he cried.

But he was looking the wrong way. Dicey giggled, and the sound escaped her even though she bit on her hand to stop it.

He turned back to the parking lot, listening. Then he swore. His light swooped over the dark lot, trying to search out her hiding place. "Danny? I'm gonna find you."

Dicey moved softly away on soundless sneakers through the covering shadows. He continued to call: "I'll remember your face, you hear? You hear me? Hear me?"

From halfway across the parking lot, safe in her own speed and in shadows, Dicey stopped. Her heart swelled in victory. "I hear you," she called softly back, as she ran toward the empty road and the patch of woods beyond.

Much later, when she returned to the car, James awoke briefly. "Everything's okay," Dicey whispered, curling down onto the cold seat to sleep.

CHAPTER 2

Dicey awoke at the first light. A chilly dew beaded the windshield. James's body leaning against her side was the only warmth in the car. He still slept, so she didn't move, even though her stiff muscles ached to be stretched. She watched the sun rise into a cold gray sky that turned warmer and brighter as the first peach-colored beams of light grew golden, then yellow, then white. Surrounded by sleepers, Dicey sat content. The car was a cave within which they were safe. It held them together; and it protected them from outside forces, the cold, the damp, people.

At last James stirred, and his eyes opened. All four of them had the same hazel eyes, although Dicey and James had their father's dark hair, not the yellow hair their mother had passed on to Maybeth and Sammy.

James's hazel eyes looked at Dicey for a minute before he spoke. "It's still true." His voice was hollow and sad. Their momma was really gone.

Dicey nodded. Sammy surged over from the backseat. "I gotta go to the bathroom. Bad."

Dicey turned her head and a muscle protested all the way down her back. "Maybeth? You awake?"

Maybeth was awake.

"Okay, then. Let's take our clothes bags and change. And the food bag too, if you'd like to eat breakfast outside." Dicey took the map of Connecticut and jammed it into her clothes bag.

It was Sunday and nothing moved in the parking lot, the same few cars stood empty. The air was clear, clean, lucid, lying lightly upon the world that morning. The children scrambled out of the car and Dicey led them across the highway to the woodsy patch where she had hidden the night before. She led them into the thickest clustering of trees, then they separated to go to the bathroom.

They ate the last peanut butter sandwiches sitting on a low stone wall, listening to a few birds and watching the sunlight fall in bright, moving patterns onto the leafy floor of the woods. The air grew warmer.

Dicey finished her sandwich and crumpled the wax paper up. She tossed it into the food bag. Then she stripped down to her underpants and put on a pair of cutoff jeans and a T-shirt. She also put on a pair of socks. The others changed too. Dicey insisted that they wear socks.

"Why?" James asked. "It's hotter with socks on."

"If we're going to walk they'll keep us from getting blisters."

"Is that true?" James demanded. "I never had a blister."

"Of course, it's true," Dicey answered. "Now let me look at the map and think, all of you."

The little ones explored the little patch of woods while Dicey studied the map. Route 1 was the road they'd been driving on. They could follow it for a while, then they'd have to go on the Turnpike to get over the Thames River, to New London. After that, they'd have to switch to a road that followed the coastline, because Route 1 turned into the Turnpike for a long while. There was the Connecticut River to cross, then Route 1 again, or maybe they could take a coastal road, to New Haven. After New Haven, the map showed a yellow patch connecting the cities, all the way down to Bridgeport. That meant heavily populated areas. But Route 1 ran the whole distance.

Dicey looked at the map. Maybe two or three days, she judged. They had about seven dollars, so they could spend about two dollars a day on food. Half what they'd spent on one meal yesterday. But that was okay, because you didn't starve in two or three days. You could get awfully hungry, but you wouldn't starve.

"James?" she called. "Maybeth. Sammy. Come here now."

They ran up and sat in a circle around the map. Dicey showed them where Bridgeport was and about where they were. Then she made her announcement: "We're going to walk down to Bridgeport." The idea was so factual in her mind that she was unprepared for questions.

"What about Momma?" Sammy asked.

"I don't know where she's got to," Dicey said.

"We can wait for her here," Sammy said. His mouth puckered up.

"No we can't," Dicey said, and she told them about the guard. "Momma will know we went on to Aunt Cilla's," Dicey said. Sammy's mouth set in a firm line. "We can't go back," Dicey said, "and we've got to go somewhere."

"That's all right," James spoke, "but why don't we take the bus?"

"Because we don't have enough money. Each ticket is two forty-five. That makes nine dollars and eighty cents all together and we've only got seven dollars."

"If we hadn't had supper last night," James said.

Dicey had already been over that in her own mind. "But we did," she cut him off. "So it's no good thinking, if we didn't. We're going to have to walk. Maybeth?"

Maybeth looked up from a pile of stones she was making into a long circle around herself. "That's fine, Dicey," she said. No questions, no worries in her round hazel eyes, just *that's fine.* Dicey felt like hugging her.

"How far is it?" James asked.

"I don't know for sure," Dicey said.

"How far can we walk in a day?" James asked.

"There's only one way to find out, isn't there?" Dicey asked. Only Sammy didn't smile in return.

"It'll be hard," she added. "We have to carry as little as possible. Just one bag for all of us."

They sorted through their bags. Sammy refused to speak or help, just sat cross-legged with his jaw set, picking at the dirt with his finger. Dicey took out two changes of underwear and two clean shirts for each, then she added a pair of extra socks and one comb. Toothbrushes they could get at Aunt Cilla's. There was about half a bag full when she was through. It felt light enough in the cool morning, but she knew that it would get heavier as the day went on. She inhaled the sun-sweetened air and looked around her.

"I'm not going," Sammy said. He glared up at Dicey.

"What'll you do?" James asked him, perfectly reasonably.

"Wait here for Momma. Not here exactly, in the car."

"Sammy, you've got to come with us," Dicey said. "First we're going to stash these other three bags in the car, then we start walking. So get up."

Sammy shook his head.

"Don't you understand?" Dicey asked. "Momma's not coming back, not here."

Sammy didn't answer her. Sammy's stubbornness was beyond measure. When he made his mind up, there was nothing you could do to move him. Threats didn't work. He didn't mind being spanked or slapped. Explaining was no good; it was as if he didn't even hear what you were saying to him. Even Momma couldn't bully him into doing something. Even James couldn't trick him into it.

But you couldn't go off and leave a six-year-old alone, in the woods, in a strange place.

Dicey crouched down beside him. The other two stood silent behind her. "Sammy? Momma's not coming back here. That's what I think. I think she's forgotten."

"Momma wouldn't forget me."

"No, she wouldn't. But she's forgotten where we are, I think. So if we go to Aunt Cilla's that's where she'll probably be. We have to go find her."

"I don't want to," Sammy said. But he was thinking about what she'd said.

"I don't want to, either," Dicey said. "But we have to."

"No, we don't," Sammy said.

Dicey stood up in frustration and stamped her foot on the ground. "Then I'll carry you," she announced.

"I'll kick you." He stood up.

Maybeth stepped forward. "No, you won't," she said to Sammy. "Momma said to do as Dicey tells us. You heard her."

The two stared at one another. They were both sturdy little blond figures, with round bellies. Sammy shorter than Maybeth, but almost as heavy.

"Please, Sammy," Maybeth said.

"Okay," Sammy said.

At the edge of the woods, where the grassy roadside banked above the macadam, they stopped to wait for an opening in the traffic. It was Sunday morning. People were driving to church, or to the beach. The children could look back and see their own car, green and lonely, in the middle of the parking lot.

It was kind of like a home, the car, Dicey thought. She understood why Sammy wanted to stay there.

They crossed the road, but stopped at the edge of the parking lot. A blue police car was driving around the lot. It stopped by their car. A policeman got out and opened the door. He stuck his head in. He opened the glove compartment and went through the maps, as if he was looking for something. He walked all around the car. He wrote something down in a little notebook. Then he looked toward the mall.

"Walk." Dicey gave the order. She took Sammy's hand. "Don't anybody look at our car."

They walked on, away from the mall and the parking lot and the car. Dicey led them back to Route 1. There they turned south. They dumped the three grocery bags in the first trash can they saw. Nobody said a word.

Route 1 was mostly garages and small shopping centers and discount stores and quick food places. There were no green patches and few sidewalks. They walked along concrete or asphalt, or on roadside gravel. Soon their feet hurt. Dicey walked at half her normal speed, because of Sammy's short legs. Trucks roared by and the sun grew hotter. The air smelled of oil and gas and nothing else. After an hour and a half, Sammy began to complain. It was the first time any of them had spoken.

At the next McDonald's that had outside tables, Dicey let them sit down. One at a time, they went inside to the bathroom. They had to go through a room that smelled of hamburgers and french fries, and they all became aware of how hungry they were. Dicey ordered two large Cokes, which they all four shared.

That refreshed them. Sitting still also refreshed them.

"How much longer is it?" Sammy asked.

"A long way," Dicey said. "We'll have to sleep outside tonight."

"Good-o," Sammy said. "Can we have a fire?"

"I don't know. It depends on where we get to. This road is awful."

"That's for sure," James agreed. "Dicey? When do we get lunch?"

"I've been thinking," she answered. "If we walk for a while, then rest a little, that's the best way. So we'll walk another hour or so and I'll go into a supermarket. We should have fruit every day, and maybe some doughnuts and milk. I'll see what they have. We've got to make our money last."

It was hard to start off again. Sammy lagged back on Dicey's hand and she snapped at him time and again to keep up. He didn't like being snapped at, so he pulled back a little more, while pretending to be hurrying as fast as he could. Dicey turned her head and saw Maybeth and James trudging along. Traffic passed them, roaring and honking. They passed building after building, and an occasional vacant stretch where wispy trees looked like weeds grown up. Dicey's fingers cramped from holding on to the bag, so she moved it under her armpit, holding it by a hand across the base.

The minutes stretched out. Dicey checked the time at every garage they passed. At noon, she began looking for a place to buy lunch, and at the next shopping center they turned off the highway and walked to the front of a supermarket that was open for business on Sundays. Dicey left the little ones with James, sitting on a curb off around to one side, and entered the market alone.

The electric eye door swung open before her. Dicey headed for the produce aisle, not even bothering to take a cart. If she could spend just fifty cents for lunch, they'd have a dollar fifty for dinner. She picked out four apples, then searched for the kind of rack they have in every supermarket, a place where they offered items that were damaged or old. She found it back by the meat department. She stood before it a minute, selecting a box of doughnuts at half price. That would be three doughnuts and an apple apiece.

It cost eighty-eight cents.

They ate sitting on the curb, with the sun hot overhead. Sammy couldn't eat his third doughnut but he didn't want to give it away, so Dicey put it into their bag. They trooped by pairs into the market, first James and Sammy, then Dicey and Maybeth, to drink water from the fountain and use the toilets. The pair waiting outside watched the bag while the other pair was inside.

"Now we rest," Dicey said.

"How much longer is it?" asked Sammy.

"I told you. More than today."

"Where are we going to camp?" he asked.

"I'll tell you when we get there," she said.

"I haven't seen any place that looks good for sleeping," James said.

"I figure we'll have to get off this road to find something, otherwise the cars would keep us awake. I figure we'll turn off the road and see what we find. There was that woods this morning. That would have been all right. So there are bound to be others. Don't you think?"

"Walking is no fun," Sammy said.

"Think about the soldiers who had to march everywhere," Dicey said.

"We could pretend to be soldiers," James said. His eyes lit up. "You could be the general and I could be the major, and Sammy and Maybeth could be the army. And we could sing songs while we walk, so it would be like marching, and maybe give drill orders. We could be Revolutionary soldiers, going to Concord."

Dicey didn't say that wouldn't make any difference, they'd still be walking. She agreed to go along with it.

"Everybody who talks to you has to say sir." James elaborated the plan. "And you two have to say sir to me. We should have a drum."

When they set off again, they sang a song about marching to Pretoria and pretty Peggy-O running down the stairs, letting down her golden hair. It was a song Momma sang. It even had a line in it, "What will your momma think," because in the song Pretty Peggy-O ran away with the captain.

The afternoon wore on, wore away. Each rest period got longer, each walking period got shorter. At midafternoon they lay back in an overgrown lot next to two tiny houses, the only houses they'd seen that afternoon.

"I wouldn't want to live on this road, would you?" Dicey said, to nobody in particular.

"I bet it wasn't always like this," James answered. "It might have been a nice road once. A country road. And these people might be old people, or poor people, who can't afford to move. Like us."

"Yeah, but our house was out in the dunes. We had the ocean. Our house was nicer than the ones other people wanted."

"The bathtub was in the kitchen," James reminded her. "It was small, even smaller than these houses."

"So what?"

"Nobody else would have lived in it. Only us. Some of the kids said their parents thought it should be torn down."

"What do I care what people say?" Dicey asked.

"They called it a shack," James went on.

"I liked it," Dicey said. "The ocean's better than fancy bathrooms, any day."

In the little one-story house next door, a door slammed. They turned their heads to watch as an energetic old woman came out, waving a broom over her head and shouting something.

She was shouting at them. Dicey couldn't hear the words, but she understood the expression of fierce anger on the woman's face. As she came closer, they could hear her voice. "Get out of here, get out. Go on, get! I'm counting to ten and then I'm calling the police. I've had it with you kids hanging around and taking down clean laundry and dumping it in the dirt and tossing your trash and bottles into my lawn and throwing rocks at my door and your cars and your noise. One—" She shrieked, her chin wagging up and down.

The four children sprang to their feet. "Here we go," Dicey said.

"I can't," Sammy said. "I'm tired."

"You've got to," James said.

"No, I can't."

Dicey tried to persuade him. "We're soldiers, remember?"

"No, we're not. That's just pretend. You have to carry me. Piggyback."

Dicey also was tired. "I'll just leave you here," she said.

"Okay." Sammy sat down.

The old woman shrieked anew.

"I've got to carry the bag," Dicey pleaded.

His eyes regarded her calmly.

"Okay, okay." She gave in. James took the paper bag. Sammy jumped up onto Dicey's back. They set off, to the accompaniment of the old woman's voice: "And don't come back. Ever!"

"We won't," Dicey muttered. "Don't worry."

The afternoon was bleached hot white, hotter and whiter for Dicey with Sammy on her back. The air tasted bad in her mouth, as she gasped for breath. The raucous cars roared past, unheeding. Dicey forced her feet to move, and her legs, and her hands to hold tight on to Sammy's feet, and her back to stay straight because in the long run that would hurt less.

It was only four when they stopped at a light, waiting for it to turn green, so they could cross the road. "Off," Dicey said to Sammy. He slid down.

There were at least three more hours of daylight. But Dicey could go no farther. She turned around and saw Maybeth's eyes big with unshed tears.

The light changed and they crossed. Dicey stopped on the other side. "Okay," she said. "The next grocery store I'll get food. Then, we'll have to get off this road to find a place to sleep. It'll be hard, because it's got to be private enough."

Three faces nodded at her, eyes blank with exhaustion.

It was a small market where Dicey stopped next. Again she went in alone. She bought bananas (they were cheapest by pound) and a package of hot dogs and a loaf of bread (you could wrap a slice of bread around a hotdog, like a roll) and a half-gallon of milk (it was a little cheaper that way). It cost almost three dollars, but she couldn't think of what to do about the expense. They were running out of money.

When a narrow road ran off of Route 1, marked by a sign that said: PHILLIP'S BEACH 6 MILES, Dicey led them across the four-lane highway and onto it. She chose the road because of the Dead End sign, which, she reasoned, meant that there wouldn't be many cars on the road. It turned out to have been good thinking. The blacktop twisted through a wooded area like a river and soon the sound of the highway had faded away behind them.

The road made two sweeping curves before Dicey saw a ramshackle house with a "For Sale" sign in front of it. The house had such a small front lawn it sat almost on the road. It looked abandoned, its clapboard siding faded to splintery gray. "Stay here," Dicey said.

She walked across the front of the house, where tall grass on the short driveway told her no car had driven, not for a long time. She walked around to the back, alert to run should a face appear in the empty windows.

The yard, overgrown and long neglected, stretched out behind the house to a large tree, and beyond that to woods. The quiet stretched out, over the long grass and distant trees. An unscreened porch opened along the back of the worn house. That meant they could have some shelter.

Dicey trotted back and called her family to join her.

The yard was like a private park, without swings of course, but green, and scattered with trees. Dicey sat down in the middle of it between two brown bags, one holding clothes, one food. The others sat facing her.

"Feels good, doesn't it?" James asked, but didn't wait for an answer. "Maybe we should just stay here and live here. It wouldn't be too bad. I bet we can find a way into the house."

"That's trespassing," Dicey said severely.

"It's empty," Sammy pointed out.

"I'm just daydreaming," James said. He lay back on the long grass and spread out his arms and legs. He closed his eyes. A lazy smile floated over his narrow face. "It's a bed. Better than a bed. A cloud."

They all fell asleep. When they woke, long bars of sunlight lay across the lawn. Sammy woke up first and roused the rest of them by calling back from the far end of the yard, "Hey! It's a brook back here! James! Wake up and come see." Dicey, her back too stiff to jump up as the others had, stayed put and rolled over on her stomach to watch them run to join Sammy. They'd be okay for a while. She didn't have to worry about water. They could all swim, and they had good sense about water. Living next to the ocean, they had to.

She wondered what time it was, and how much daylight was left. The sun was still above the horizon. Maybe seven? That seemed about right. But she wanted to look at her map to see where they were before the light got bad, and they would need to gather some wood. She listened to the splashing and calls while she traced her finger down the map.

One day should put them about halfway there. She started at a dot named Madison and began moving her finger backward. She saw no marking for Phillip's Beach.

She called to James. He had noticed a sign saying they were near Stonington. "What?" she called back. He spelled it for her.

But Stonington was almost next to Peewauket and they hadn't gone any distance at all. She called to James again. He was quite sure. Stonington. Then they had traveled maybe—Dicey measured with her finger from the legend at the bottom corner of the map—eight miles? Maybe ten. At that rate—she walked off sections of road with her fingers—it would be days. More than a week. Two weeks.

They'd have to conserve money, and food. Quickly she calculated a way to eat only half of the food tonight and the rest for their next dinner. No more Cokes, either; they'd cost sixty cents. No more small markets; they were more expensive. They could fish in Long Island Sound or the rivers (string and a hook, they'd have to buy those), and why didn't she have a knife? None of them did, not even a jackknife.

They hadn't planned this properly. They hadn't planned it at all. Dicey couldn't see how they'd make it to Bridgeport, and a cold panic settled in her stomach. There was nothing for it though, was there? Just going ahead. People might give them food. She might be able to earn food or money, somehow. She couldn't think how they'd manage it. But they would have to manage it, somehow. Then she didn't think any more about it. She couldn't.

They gathered wood, some twigs, and handfuls of dried leaves. Accustomed to building fires on the beach, they found it easy to light the small starting pile of leaves and twigs with the matches Dicey had taken from the counter in the store. They skewered hot dogs on green branches, and when they were cooked wrapped them in slices of bread. They passed the milk container around and around. Each had a half a banana for dessert, and a quarter of Sammy's doughnut. The fire, fed with the bigger branches, burned brightly in the darkening air. Dicey wanted them to sleep on the porch. "It's more hidden away," she explained.

"I'm going to sleep by the fire where it's warm," Sammy said.

"We're not going to put any more wood on the fire," Dicey told him.

"Why not?"

"Dangerous. It could spread. It could burn you."

"I'd wake up first," Sammy said. "It couldn't burn me."

"Well I'm not going to take a chance," Dicey said.

"Well I'm going to sleep here anyway," Sammy said. He lay on his stomach facing the fire, with the light drifting over his stubborn face.

"We've gotta sleep together," Dicey said.

"I don't see why," he answered and yawned.

"We've gotta stick together," she repeated.

"Momma didn't," he said.

"Well, we have to," Dicey said.

"Well, I don't care," he said. He refused to speak again and was soon asleep.

Maybeth curled up next to Dicey, resting her head against her sister's thigh. "It's all right, Dicey," she said. "I'm going to sing. Doesn't the fire make you feel like singing?"

Dicey would have said no, but after Maybeth had sung through one verse of Momma's song about the cherry that has no stone, she joined in, and James did too. The song put Maybeth to sleep.

"You tired?" Dicey asked James.

"Yeah, but not tired enough to sleep yet," he said.

"We'll let the fire go out, then carry them to the porch."

"If you say so, but I don't see why," James said.

"It'll be safer out of sight."

The fire crackled and spat. Its light made a hemisphere of warmth across which Dicey looked to see her small sleeping brother. "James? Do you remember Sammy at the beach?"

James grinned. "I do. That was some fun, wasn't it?"

They gathered up the two sleepers and carried them back to the porch. Sammy half-awoke, to protest, but slept again. He was too tired even to quarrel. Poor kid, Dicey thought. James lay down with them, but Dicey returned to the dying fire, to be sure it burned out entirely.

. . . Sammy at the beach, when he was only a year and a half old, and running. Summer days, eight-year-old Dicey was responsible for taking them all down to the beach. Sammy wore an old bathing suit of James's over his diapers. The first thing he'd do, every time, was take off his clothes. Then he'd turn to see their expressions and laugh and clap his hands together with a smile spread all over his face. He had a little noise he made, to go with the clapping: "Aaayy." He'd learned that from them, because they would applaud his mistakes and his learnings and cry, "Yeaayy," as they clapped.

Dicey could still remember his short, plump little body, sturdy legs and round blond head, and his tiny penis that bobbled up and down as he ran. He had a game he played with the waves, of going down to them, then turning to run back. Usually he tripped and fell, and the tip of the wave would wet him as it washed up the beach. He would raise a dripping face and laugh, then elevate his fanny, put his feet under him, and totter erect again. He would clap and cry, "Aaayy," and they all giggled and clapped back at him.

Sammy had been such a cheerful baby. He had been able to bring laughter even to Momma's face. They would watch him move around and explore, the way other people watched television. When had Sammy changed?

His first words were "hot" (he would grab out for anything) and "no" ("Doe," he would cry, waving his arms, his face dreadfully earnest). He emptied cupboards and drawers, he unmade his bed, he grabbed homework papers and ran away, laughing. He was naughty, but not mean. Not selfish. And he was stubborn, even then when he was a baby. Dicey had watched him learn to turn around in a circle, patiently practicing, tumbling over his own feet, falling in a heap, sitting down in surprise. It took him days to do it, but he learned.

He was no less stubborn now, no less determined to have his own way—but what had happened to that happiness? Could anyone change that much? It must have been gradual, or they would have noticed. Dicey tried to remember the last time she heard Sammy laugh, and that had been laughing at Maybeth because a doll she made out of sea grass had been washed away by a wave. But Dicey also remembered Sammy's merry eyes, and his mouth with only ten teeth, opened wide in the kind of laughter that took over his whole body and made him stumble and fall down laughing.

The fire was out. She stamped on it, just to be safe, and retired to the porch.

CHAPTER 3

Dicey woke from a dream about a big white house that faced the ocean. Aunt Cilla's house.

The sun was rising over the trees behind the brook, rising in waves of molten pink. James lay sprawled on his back. Sammy was curled up into a ball, and Maybeth had thrown one of her arms over him. Dicey tiptoed off the porch and down to the brook for a quiet wash.

Maybeth and James woke up immediately when she spoke their names. "It's still true then," James said.

Sammy moaned and turned away, burying his head under his arms. "It's time to get up, Sammy," Dicey said.

"'Tisn't," he answered, squinching his eyes closed.

"You all go down and wash now. I'm going to check the map. We'll eat when you're ready."

Dicey tried to look at the map realistically. She considered the lines that were roads, the green patches that were parks, and the flat blue of the sound, so different from the tumultuous, gray-faced ocean, where she had grown up.

They ate half a banana apiece and finished the milk. Afterward, prepared to set out but reluctant to leave their sanctuary, they sat in a row on the porch.

"There's a park, maybe two or three days down the road. We'll stay there for a couple of nights," Dicey offered. She showed them where it was marked on the map, Rockland State Park, with a tent to show there was camping. "It'll have a beach. We've got three dollars and eighty cents left. We're gonna have to think up some ways of getting money."

"Maybe we can find some on the ground," James suggested. "If we look."

"Anyway, we've already got dinner for tonight."

James studied the map. "Where were we yesterday?" he asked. Dicey showed him. "Only there? We'll never get to Bridgeport."

"Yes, we will. We've just got to keep moving, that's all."

"Why?" James asked.

"Because that's where Aunt Cilla is," Dicey said. "And Momma might be there too."

"What if she's not there?" James asked.

"She will be," Sammy said. "Don't say that. She knows we're going there."

"That's how much you know," James said.

Sammy attacked James. He hurtled his little body at his brother, using his feet to kick as fast as his hands pummeled. Dicey pulled him off.

"Cut that out, Sammy. You hear me? Do that again and I'll whip you for sure."

Sammy stood, sullen and silent.

Maybeth had watched this. "Momma said to do what Dicey tells us," she reminded Sammy.

"Anyway, it's time to go," Dicey said. She took Sammy's hand and pulled him, none too gently, after her. In her other hand she carried the grocery bag that held their clothes and food.

It was another hot day. The white pavement of Route 1 shimmered in the heat and in the fumes from gas and oil. The noise of traffic pounded in Dicey's ears. Her feet marched beneath her, step, step, step, plodding. As repetitive, as relentless, her mind marched over the same problems: money, food, distance, where to sleep, Momma: step, step, step.

They marched, rested, marched, lunched on water and a box of stale doughnuts, walked, rested, and once again on the final lap, Dicey carried Sammy on her back.

They were more tired at the end of the second day than they had been the day before. They had spoken little all day. Once again, Dicey led them off Route 1 toward the water to find a place to sleep. This second night they sheltered in a small stand of pines, a few yards from the road, and within sight of a big brick house. They couldn't risk a fire, so they ate the hot dogs uncooked.

The one bright spot in the day had occurred in the afternoon, when Sammy spied a dime on the sidewalk outside of the supermarket where Dicey bought the doughnuts. Added to the two pennies Maybeth and James had picked up earlier, Dicey figured that they were only twenty-one cents out of pocket for food. That left her with three dollars and fifty-nine cents. Still enough.

On the morning of the third day, the sky was overcast. James awoke with his usual observation, "It's still true." He was the only one with the energy to speak. The others were too hungry and thirsty. They assembled themselves quickly to return to Route 1.

A breakfast of milk and bananas (fifty cents) gave them energy. As they came closer to New London and the busy Thames River, Route 1 became increasingly cluttered with restaurants, bars, quick food chains and shopping plazas. Sammy found a quarter on the roadside.

"I'm tired of doughnuts," Sammy said, as they approached a supermarket.

"What do you want then?" Dicey asked. "Doughnuts are cheap, that's why I get them."

"I want a hamburger and french fries. I want a Coke."

"Not possible," Dicey said. "How about peanut butter sandwiches? We could spread the peanut butter with our fingers. And if I get a whole loaf of bread, we could have them again for dinner, so that would be okay."

The younger children agreed without enthusiasm. She found a loaf of bread on sale for fifteen cents and a jar of peanut butter for seventy-one cents. That totaled eighty-six cents, for lunch and dinner. That would leave them with two dollars and forty-eight cents. Still enough?

Dicey didn't say to herself, *enough for what.* She couldn't have. Neither could she have said what amount of money would not be enough.

Before going to the checkout line, Dicey drifted by the meat counter. Hamburger was expensive. Chicken, on the other hand, wasn't too expensive, not by the pound. But would they be able to cook it? She lingered by a package of chicken wings, which, at twenty-nine cents a pound, held some interest for her. Then she wandered over to the fruit and vegetable counter and discovered potatoes. Potatoes were cheap. You could eat all of a potato. If they could just build a fire.

That night it was in an unfinished house in a new development that they slept. Dicey picked out the house, but would not let them go into it until dark. Until then, they wandered around the maze of roads in the development, watching the children at evening play. At last it was dark and Dicey let them return to the half-built house. Only the joists had been put in for walls, but the rough floors were down. They lay on plywood. Dicey gave Sammy and Maybeth the extra clothes from the bag to make pillows. Dicey lay on her back and looked up, past the roof frame to the sky. Low clouds reflected light from the ground, which blurred softly as she fell asleep.

Fear of being caught woke Dicey before dawn. She knew that construction work began early in the day. It was one thing to be seen camping in the woods; that might be kids having a night out with their parents' permission. But four kids sleeping in an unfinished house—that would be police business.

She woke them all at the first gray light. "It's still true," James said. But he seemed to expect no response.

After a skimpy breakfast of milk, they started out and soon were crossing the Thames River on a bridge that arched like a rainbow, high enough to allow huge cargo ships to travel under it. The river, seen from the height of the bridge, seemed blue and sparkling clean. They knew better, because they had seen it close up. But the look of it refreshed Dicey. It reminded her of the sea, and it reminded her that they were heading for the water.

Sammy, cranky since the time he'd gotten up, had to be dragged away from the railing of the bridge. He had to be scolded every few steps to keep up. He never answered, just kept his eyes fixed to the ground. His jaw muscles worked. Dicey ground her teeth and stamped her feet in anger, still walking.

Step, step, step, on hard concrete sidewalks that made their feet hurt. Stop at the lights, then start again. Horns blared. Engines roared.

They ate lunch sitting on a bench at a bus stop on Route 1, finishing the bread and peanut butter, scooping it out with their fingers and licking it off. It was not really enough for lunch, none of them was satisfied, but Dicey pushed them on, to get out of the city.

When the smaller, quieter Beach Road turned off of Route 1, she told them to go on it. Immediately, even though the sky hung low and heavy with moisture, even though James protested and Maybeth's eyes glistened, even though Sammy lagged behind and her voice was hoarse with nagging at him, Dicey felt better. They were heading toward the water.

At a small supermarket, she purchased two pounds of chicken wings and four potatoes. Instead of starting right off, she pulled out her map and showed the younger children where they were. "It'll be less populated," she pointed out. "We'll be able to have a fire and—"

Rain began to fall, in fat drops that slapped the ground.

Dicey's heart sank. You couldn't build a fire outside in the rain. She hoped maybe the rain would stop, but she didn't think it would. She had never eaten a raw potato. She couldn't imagine eating uncooked chicken. She didn't know what to do.

So she urged them up and on.

"It's raining," Sammy said.

"I know that," Dicey said.

"It's like a bath," James said. "It'll clean us off."

"It's cold," Sammy said.

"Not that bad," Dicey answered.

"I'm not going anywhere," Sammy said. "And you can't make me anymore. You can't."

Dicey's patience was at an end. She spoke bitterly. "No I can't. And maybe I don't even want to. You've been a pill all day. I'll tell you what, you don't think I'll leave you, but I will. I'll be glad to leave you behind."

"I know." Sammy's voice was low. "So go ahead. Go on, because nobody cares about me except Momma, and Momma will come find me but she won't find you, so go ahead."

"All right, I will. Come on, you two." Dicey stood up and strode off. James followed hesitantly. Maybeth waited.

"He's been holding us up all day long," Dicey called back. "And now he's doing it again. It's not fair to the rest of us."

She saw Sammy bend over and pick up something. She saw

Maybeth go back to Sammy and hold out her hand to the little boy. Sammy put his hand in hers and came trudging after.

Dicey walked ahead of the others through a rain that resolved itself into drifting mist. It was gray, cool, chilling. She clutched a grocery bag in each hand and then, as the brown paper grew sodden, under each arm. She didn't allow an afternoon rest, just kept moving ahead.

They came to marshlands, tall grasses and cattails, shadowy in the gray afternoon. They passed bigger houses that had larger lawns. Then Dicey saw water on the right, a large inland pond. You couldn't sleep near it though; it was surrounded by sharp-edged marsh grass that grew only on muddy ground. However, opposite it a sign pointed to a dirt road running off into sparse, piney woods. PUBLIC BEACH, the sign said.

Dicey turned and waited for the others to catch up with her. Rain had plastered their hair down over their foreheads. Beads of moisture hung from their eyelashes, and their faces glimmered with water.

"Let's go there," she said.

"How far is it?" James asked.

"I don't know," Dicey answered. "But it's sure to be deserted, isn't it?"

The growth of pines was not thick enough to do more than interfere with the rain, and the needle-carpeted ground underfoot was damp. Their feet squished in their sneakers.

The beach at the end of this road was backed by low, rolling dunes, which flattened out to a narrow belt of sand before giving way to the placid gray water. The four children stood atop the dunes and looked down over the empty sand. Three picnic shelters had been erected for the pleasure of the people of Noank, three open-sided structures with shingled roofs, tables, and in each shelter a stone fireplace for cooking.

"It's going to be all right here," Dicey said softly.

"Look," Sammy said, coming up beside her. "Look what I found, all together. Somebody must have had a hole in their pocket." He held out a little square hand to show Dicey a cluster of pennies and nickels.

"Good for you, Sammy," she said. Her relief at finding shelter and a way to build a fire had washed away the anger of the day. She smiled down at him. "And look what I have for us."

She pulled gently at the top of the smaller grocery bag. The bag split, but she caught it from the bottom. "Chicken. And potatoes."

All together they ran down toward the nearest shelter, through the gentle rain. Halfway down the incline, Sammy tripped. He rolled the rest of the way, not trying to stop himself. When he came to join them under the roof of the picnic shelter, he was a sight. Dicey giggled. Then she laughed helplessly. Sand coated his wet hair and face and clothing. He looked like a cookie rolled in sugar.

At first, she thought Sammy was going to get angry. Even so, she couldn't stop laughing; and James and Maybeth joined in with her. But instead, Sammy smiled, threw up his arms and executed a stiff little jig, joining in their laughter. For just that moment he was again the little boy Dicey remembered, who loved to wrestle and tickle and never asked you to stop, who made games out of everything and anything.

The younger children scoured the beach for pieces of wood. Dicey went back to the woods to get needles and dry branches of quick-burning pine.

When the fire had burned down to coals, Dicey spread the potatoes out on the grate. Then they all went back down the beach to find more driftwood. They returned with arms laden, and Dicey turned the potatoes, rinsed in rain drops, over and then arranged the chicken wings near to the edge of the fire so they wouldn't scorch. Rain padded softly on the beach and water. The fire spat when chicken fat dripped into it. The smell of cooking chicken rose faintly on the air. The four children stood watching by the stone hearth. Their skin dried, then their hair and finally their clothing.

They tried to pull one of the tables over nearer to the fire, but it was bolted to the cement floor, as was every bench, so they ate in the chilly air beyond the fire's heat. The food was hot enough to warm them from within.

They ate without speaking, first wolfing it down, then savoring each bite, chewing on the narrow bones, eating every scrap of potato. There was more than enough chicken. Everyone was stuffed full by the time the food was gone, even James.

"I wish we had some butter," Sammy said.

"Or salt," Dicey added.

"Barbecue sauce is what I want," James said, "and some corn on the cob and some watermelon for dessert or a sundae, a chocolate sundae. I wish we had that."

"I wish we had Momma," Maybeth said.

Silence fell again.

Dicey got up and put two fat pieces of wood on the fire. She sat down in front of it. James gathered up the bones, put them into the trash can and came to sit with her. Sammy and Maybeth followed him. The fire glowed feverish on their faces. While the early evening light was still adequate, Dicey spread her map out.

"We'll go there tomorrow," she decided quickly, pointing her finger at a green square labeled "State Park." "It's the one I told you about. We'll rest a day there. How does that sound to you? We've been walking for four days now."

"It sounds great," James said. His finger traced the red Thruway markings down to Bridgeport. "It's a long way," he said. "Why is it all yellow there?"

"Densely populated area," Dicey said.

"Like yesterday?"

"Yeah."

"Where'll we sleep?"

"How should I know, James? We'll just have to worry about that when we come to it."

Dicey put her hand in her pocket and took out her money. She asked Sammy to give her the money he'd shown her. He didn't want to but she insisted, and he retreated to a sulky silence. They had one dollar and fifty-six cents left now. Still enough.

Dicey folded up the map and put it on top of a table. She went down to the water's edge and came back with a heavy rock, which she dried on her shirt and then placed on top of the map. Over the water, the air turned purple with twilight. She rejoined the others before the fire, sitting between Maybeth and Sammy. Maybeth moved closer to her and began to hum.

"I know an old lady who swallowed a fly," Dicey sang.

"I don't know why she swallowed a fly," James answered her.

Dicey leaned over toward Sammy. She pointed her finger at him.

"Perhaps she'll die," he sang out, his eyes lighting up.

They sang the whole song through until Dicey spoke the last line. She waited, just long enough, before saying, in a solemn voice, "She died, of course."

Contentment blanketed them. Full bellies, the warm crackling fire, the rain pattering on the roof and falling gently on the sand pulled them together and held them close.

"Sometimes," Dicey remarked, "I feel as if we could do just about anything. Because we're the Tillermans."

"And I am too," Sammy said.

"Yes, you are," Dicey answered.

James spoke quietly. "Dicey? Do you know where Momma is? For sure?"

"No."

"Why did she go?"

Maybeth spoke when Dicey didn't. "Momma's gotten lost. That's what I think."

"How could she get lost?" Sammy asked. "She knew where we were."

"Not lost from us," Maybeth said.

"Lost from who?" Sammy asked.

"Not lost from anyone," Maybeth said. "Just lost. But we have Dicey to take care of us."

"Dicey's not our momma," Sammy said.

"Lucky for us she isn't," James remarked.

Sammy turned on him. "Don't you say that. That's not nice."

"But it's true," James insisted. "Dicey wouldn't ever go off and leave us. You wouldn't, would you, Dicey?"

"No," Dicey said.

"See?" James asked Sammy.

"Momma loves me," Sammy said.

"You know what?" James asked. "We're the kind that people go off from. First our father and now Momma. I never thought of that before. Whadda you think, Dicey? Is there something wrong about us?"

"I don't know and I don't care."

"No, but think about it. We were always alone out there in our house; nobody came to see us. And Momma talked different from other people, sort of more slow. I can't think of anybody else like us in Provincetown. Did Momma ever talk to you about our father? Did she say where he went?"

"No," Dicey said.

"Do you remember him?" James insisted.

"A little."

"Tell," Maybeth asked.

Dicey gathered together her few memories, like scattered marbles. "He was tall and dark-haired, with hazel eyes like Momma's. We all have eyes like theirs. James reminds me of him, and I guess I do too. You little ones look more like Momma. He had a skinny head, like James and me. He had a big, loud laugh. He built our beds for us."

"I know that," James said.

"I remember him picking me up and sitting me on his shoulders. He'd call me his little only. I don't know why." This was vivid to her, the masculine voice crooning, *"the little only, only in the world, only only."* "He could pick Momma up too, when he was excited, and swing her around in a circle. They'd sing, sometimes, when just the two of them were home. But most of the time he had friends who'd come to see him, and Momma would take us to the beach—me and James and Maybeth. Once he bought Momma a bright red sweater and I saw her kiss him."

Dicey stared into the fire, trying to piece together something whole from her few vague memories.

"He knew about cars. During the summer, he'd work as a bartender. They had fights sometimes. Real fights."

"Is that why he left us?" James asked. "I don't blame him if it was, because Momma sometimes was—you know."

"Sometimes what?"

"Sometimes so drifty and moony she could drive you crazy."

"I don't think that's why. I don't know why he left. I remember when he did and Momma trying to explain something and crying." But she remembered more than that, she remembered that Momma was pregnant with Sammy and that made her father angry. Then, sometime, after he'd gone but before Sammy was born, two policemen had come into their house and didn't sit down but asked Momma questions, and Momma just said, "*I don't know, I didn't know*," over and over, when they asked her. One of them had knelt down to ask Dicey something, but Dicey wouldn't talk to him, just looked up at Momma and held her hand tight. So, the older Dicey reasoned, her father had probably broken the law. What law? How could she know? And then he'd run away.

"I never had a father," Sammy declared.

"You did so," James answered. "Everybody has a mother and father."

"Not me," Sammy said. "I never want to have one."

"Well, you can't do anything about it," James answered.

"We all have the same father," Maybeth said.

"And I don't even know his name," James said. "Dicey, do you remember his name?"

"No."

"But it wasn't Tillerman," James said. "That's Momma's own name, not his. You know what that means, don't you?"

"What?"

"We're bastards."

"I am not!" Sammy cried, leaping to his feet. "I'll fight you if you say that. I'll make your nose bleed."

"Don't you remember?" Dicey asked James, who held Sammy at arm's length.

"Remember what?"

"When Maybeth was little, still a baby. There was a big party at our house. Momma wore her yellow dress with the flounces, and she had flowers in her hair. They got married, right outside. There was a man in a blue suit, and they stood together in front of him and said the words. Don't you remember?"

James struggled to find the memory in his mind. "No, no I don't."

How could he, Dicey thought, since she was making it up.

"Somebody had a guitar and Momma danced with you and everybody watched and applauded."

"Maybe," James said. His eyebrows were squeezed together with the effort. "But why *do* we still have Momma's name and not his?"

"Because it's the best name," Dicey said. "It's a good, strong name. Momma said."

"Is that real?" Sammy asked. Dicey nodded. "And we can let the fire burn all night?"

"Sure. It'll be safe here."

Sammy lay down and put his head on his forearms. "I'm going to sleep now," he announced.

Soon Maybeth too was asleep, her head in Dicey's lap.

James emerged from a reverie. "I didn't know they got married," he said.

"You never asked."

"I won't say it again in front of Sammy, but I don't blame him for going. Now I won't mind as much."

"What does it matter?" Dicey asked.

"It wouldn't matter to you. You always knew how to fight. You'd fight anyone who said anything to you—like Sammy does. But I can't fight. And the kids—said things about Momma, bad things, about not being married."

"Nobody ever did to me."

"They wouldn't dare."

That was true, and the thought made Dicey proud.

"Would they say things to Sammy?" she asked.

"Yeah. Especially after Maybeth. I think Sammy really got it at school."

Dicey fell asleep before the fire that evening, thinking of Sammy and how he must have hated to go to school every morning and then come home, and if Momma was there she would talk to him—but less and less like a mother, and if she wasn't there he would wonder. That could change a person.

CHAPTER 4

Sometime during the night the rain stopped. They awoke to a sun already risen in the sky. They awoke to the last traces of mist floating above the water. They awoke to thirst. "It's still true," James said.

One by one, the little ones first, they went off behind the dunes to go to the bathroom. Waiting her turn, Dicey stared at the water. It seemed to stretch off endlessly, in shallow blue wavelets. The waves here didn't crash on the shore with a steady sound like muted thunder the way they did in Provincetown. Here, the little waves murmured and gurgled, like contented children. A light breeze came off the water, smelling of salt and marshlands.

They set off eagerly, to find something to drink, and in the knowledge that they would have to walk only a few miles to the park. They could wait to eat, after last night's dinner.

"What's the name of this park?" James asked.

"Rockland," Dicey said. They were walking abreast on the untraveled road.

"Why?" asked James. "What do you think? Named after somebody called Rockland? Or because the land is rocky there?"

"How should I know?" Dicey said.

"Most of the land so far has been flat down by the water," James continued. Dicey stopped listening.

They drank from a water hose at a gas station. The attendant, busy and incurious, barely looked at them, so they walked off, Dicey turning to look over her shoulder.

"He's not watching us," Maybeth said to Dicey.

"I don't want anyone to know who we are, or that we're alone."

"We're not alone," Maybeth answered.

"She means without adults," James said.

"But he let us drink the water. He didn't seem to notice us much."

"You can't tell," Dicey said. "You can't tell who to trust."

"Yes I can," Maybeth said, but not to quarrel. She said it simply, as if it was her name.

Dicey smiled at her and took her hand. "Well I can't," she said.

The road wound between occasional houses. It was hedged in low stone fences and went up hills and down hills and around hills. They saw few cars and no stores. Trees were in full leaf, the bright green of early summer. The sun warmed them, the shadows of trees cooled them. The houses they passed had smooth green lawns and long white stone driveways. Just before the road into the park, there was a small general store, its one plate glass window cluttered with signs for circuses, garage sales, and church suppers. Dicey went in alone.

Inside was a young man with red hair that sprang up all over his head in spurts. He had freckles and wore overalls over a plaid shirt. Dicey wandered over to the fresh produce counter. He came to watch her.

She picked out four potatoes and a bag of apples. She put these down on the counter by the cash register. Then, she got a half-gallon of milk. She went to the hardware shelves and looked at the knives, pans, fishing rods and nets.

"Can I get you something?" the young man asked.

"How much are hooks?" Dicey asked.

"You going fishing?"

Dicey nodded.

"There's not much to catch around here. The clamming's better. You ever been clamming?"

Dicey shook her head.

"You take one of these"—he pulled down a long-handled, claw-fingered rake—"and drag in the sandbars for clams. The clams dig in, just below the sand, and you can see their air holes. Or you can dig for them with your fingers. The rake is more efficient."

"But how much are hooks?"

"Ten cents each."

"I'll take one please. Do you have any fishing line?"

He offered her a spool, for $1.50. Dicey shook her head. They'd unravel some clothes, or something.

"What're you doing, anyway?" he asked as he rang up her purchases.

"We're going to the park, my brothers and sister and me. We're going to cook out. And fish. And maybe dig some clams."

"Your folks with you?"

"Naw. We're going on our own."

He looked at her. "Sounds like fun. Look"—he unrolled a long piece of fishing line from the spool, cut it off, wound it around three fingers to make a tight coil—"you'll need this if you want to try fishing. You got a map of the park?"

"Is there one? We just found the park on a state map and decided to come over and see what it's like."

He reached under the counter and pulled out a small folded brown map. "You'll have it pretty much to yourselves. People only come on weekends, this time of year. Take care now," he said, ringing up her money.

"We will. Thanks an awful lot."

"If you like the service, you come back." He smiled. Dicey hefted the bag and left quickly. They had twenty-six cents left. Not enough for anything.

Just inside the entrance to the park, the road turned to dirt. Woods grew up on both sides, pines and hardwoods, with none of the stone fences the children had come to expect. They walked down the entrance road a way, then Dicey led them off into the trees, out of sight of the road. They sat down and she gave each an apple to munch while she studied the map of the park.

Rockland State Park was the same general shape as the state of Connecticut, except in miniature. The two long sides of the rectangle were a little over three miles. The short sides measured a mile and a half. The eastern length ran along the Sound in an uneven line. One large cove made what the map called LONG BEACH. There was also a small cove further north, called just BEACH. The rest of the shore front seemed to be headlands and rocky promontories. The high land began at the southwest corner of the park and ran down to the water, which it met up with about halfway along the length of waterfront. In the southeast section the map showed marshlands, labeled BIRD SANCTUARY.

"It's four and a half square miles," James said. "Can I have another apple? Is this all there is for lunch?"

"I thought we'd fish," Dicey said.

The road they were on led through the center of the park until it branched apart about halfway through and went as two roads to the two different beaches. The map showed picnic areas and a playground off to the left, near the inland border. Opposite that, a small campground lay in the highlands on a path that branched off to the right. A larger campground, with six camping sites marked on it, was on a road that turned off the left fork. This campground lay on the headlands that overlooked the water, near the small beach. The picnic area had "Facilities" marked on it. "What do you think that means?" Dicey asked, pointing.

"Toilets I guess," James answered. "Do you think they have showers too?"

Dicey had been hoping for a kitchen house of some sort, with pans and a stove. Where you could make a soup. James didn't think that was likely.

"Okay," Dicey announced. "I say we walk down to here"—she pointed to the large campground—"and put our stuff at this site." The site nearest to the water. That would feel more like their own home. "Then we better get down to the shore and see if we can find some clams. When we've solved the food problem for the day, we can take it easy."

Once again they set off, walking four abreast. Perhaps it was the deep silence around them, perhaps the salty wind off the water, perhaps the sense of forest and solitude; for whatever reason, this walk was a pleasure. Dicey's legs swung out and she began to sing the song about pretty Peggy-O. The others joined in. They sang softly, though, so that their music would contribute to the quiet, not destroy it.

They passed the playground area to their left. It had tennis courts, parking lots and a children's section with swings and slide and sandbox and seesaws.

They continued past to the campsites, which had fireplaces, water faucets and flat dirt spaces, where a tent could be pitched or a car pulled in. They put the two bags down and looked about them. It was high land, and trees soared above them. Hulking gray rocks broke through the earth at irregular intervals, some so large you could climb to the top and sit looking down. A faint path led off to the east. One behind the other, they followed the path. Soon they were standing on top of a rocky bluff, looking down to shallow water. The path ran on for several more yards along the front of the bluff, then descended to a small beach. The children ran down that section of path, slipping, tumbling, jumping from rock to rock.

The beach was nestled into the rocks, as if after hundreds of years of work the waves had succeeded in making themselves a little room to rest in. It was high tide. Dicey knew that by the closeness of the waves to the line of seaweed that etched the sand. There would be no clams for lunch—you clammed at low tide, on the sandbars. There would be no lunch then, and they'd just have to stand it. They could drink some milk.

She explained this to the others and they did not complain. Sammy took off his sneakers and waded in the water, which he reported as cold. "Not as cold as ours, but too cold for swimming." Maybeth gathered the fragments of shells that nestled among the grassy seaweed. James went off to climb the rocks at the water's edge. Dicey stood, looking out over the water.

You could see no land across the Sound, just unending, restless dark water. A couple of white sails skimmed along in the distance, bellied out in the wind. The sun toasted her face. She breathed deeply.

Somehow, they had to get some more money. Maybe she could go back to that store and offer to work. She could sweep and straighten out shelves. She could fetch things. But then she'd have to think up stories to tell the young red-headed man, and she was tired of making up stories, tired.

James called out, then came running back. "Dicey? There're mussels on the rocks." He held out two of the black, bearded mollusks. "You can eat mussels, can't you?"

"We sure can," Dicey said. "We can eat them right here."

Dicey and James pulled mussels from the rocks and washed them off in the water, while Maybeth and Sammy climbed back up the hill for twigs and larger pieces of wood. Soon they had a large mound of mussels waiting beside a crackling fire. Dicey gathered an armload of damp seaweed from the water's edge. When the fire was ready, she placed a layer of wet seaweed right on top of it. Steam hissed its way up through to the air. Quickly, Sammy dropped the mussels onto this bed, and Dicey covered them with another layer of seaweed.

"It's like a pie," she said.

"Or a sandwich," James said.

"It looks awful," Sammy said, poking at the fire with a stick.

"But they'll taste good," James answered. "Anything would taste good. It's funny, you know? When I thought there wasn't anything for lunch I wasn't that hungry. But now—"

"Now I'm staaaarr-ving!" Sammy shrieked. He jumped up, did two cartwheels, which took him to the water's edge, and landed on his feet with his arms out. "And we're gonna eat!"

They ate the rich, meaty mussels for lunch. That evening, when the tide was low and the muddy sandbars appeared among puddles of water, as far as a hundred yards out, they gathered clams. These they steamed as they had the mussels. With supper, they drank part of the milk and had an apple apiece. They buried the fire in sand and tossed the shells into the water. Then they climbed back up the steep hill, to hurl apple cores into the woods and go to bed.

They slept behind the campsite rather than in it, in the woods nearer the water. Dicey couldn't relax. When she saw that the others were all soundly sleeping, she quietly got up and went back down to the little beach. For a while she just sat in the sand, hearing and seeing the dark waters. Then she walked back and forth along the water's edge. The stars burned high overhead. Silence and solitude: she might have been alone in the world.

If she had been sitting when the voices approached, she would have kept still and tried to remain unnoticed. But she was standing by the water, clearly silhouetted there, and she could hear a woman's voice saying, "There's someone here."

Two figures approached, descending the hill cautiously, hand in hand.

"Hey, man," the man called.

Warily, Dicey nodded to him.

"Don't be afraid of us, we're harmless," the woman said. Only she was a girl, really. They were both young, in their teens.

"So am I," Dicey answered.

"Are your folks camping here?" the boy asked.

"No," Dicey said.

"We are," the girl said. She looked up at the boy's face. "We've been here for two weeks already, haven't we? Was that your fire we saw earlier?"

"Probably," Dicey said. "I had some clams."

"You live near here?" the boy asked.

"Yeah," Dicey said. Well, right now they were living about fifty yards from where she stood.

"We always come to this beach," the girl said. "It feels like our own private beach by now. Doesn't it, Lou? It does to me. Except for weekends, it's empty. You're the first person we've met on it during the week."

Dicey made a grunting noise in answer.

"What's your name, kid?" the boy asked.

"Danny."

"Danny what?"

"Don't pry, Lou. Leave him be," the girl interrupted. "I'm Edie. This is Lou, short for Louis. You'll scare him," she said to the boy.

"Naw I won't. Will I?"

"I dunno," Dicey said.

"I know about him and it's okay," Lou said. Dicey looked up in alarm. She couldn't see his face clearly. "You ran away, didn't you? It all got to be too much for you, and you cut out. Isn't that about it?"

"So what?" Dicey asked.

"So we're in the same boat, on the same trip. So you haven't got any reason to worry about us squealing on you, or laying a heavy go-home message on you. So, relax."

Dicey grinned. "Okay," she said.

"Are you alone?"

"Not exactly."

"That's relaxed? I've seen people who thought they were about to be mugged more relaxed. Okay, I won't bug you. We'll all enjoy the scenery together here and talk about cabbages and kings."

"I gotta go now."

"If you stick around here," the girl said, "we'll see you again. I'd like that, Danny. We're easy to find, at the small campground. We'll be there, or at the playground, or down here."

"Okay," Dicey said. "Well—see you."

They had forgotten her by the time she reached the top of the bluff. They stood where she had left them, their arms around each other, facing out over the water. She returned quickly to her family and fell asleep easily.

First thing the next morning, while they munched apples and passed the milk carton around, Dicey told the others about her encounter of the night before. "I told them I was a boy," she said. "Named Danny. Can you remember that?" They nodded. "Maybeth? You too."

"But why?" James asked. "What does it matter?"

"It's safer to be a boy than a girl," Dicey said. "People leave boys alone more. Anyway, if we meet them again don't tell our last name. I told them I was a runaway. We'll all be runaways."

"Are we runaways?" Sammy asked.

"Sort of," Dicey said.

"We were running away with Momma." James worked it out. "But then Momma ran away from us. And now we're running away from everybody. But we're running to Aunt Cilla's house, and that makes it different. And Momma may be there. That's another difference. We're runaways *to*, not just runaways."

Dicey gave her orders for the morning. James and Sammy were to fish, while she and Maybeth washed out the clothes they had been wearing. They wouldn't wash the shorts, just the underwear and socks and shirts. She had seen a movie at school once, where the village women washed out the clothes and dried them in the sun.

Dicey carried the clothes down to the beach. James and Sammy came down later with some worms they had dug. The boys sat out on a rock surrounded by water, while the girls stood knee-deep in the waves, dipping and rubbing the clothing.

Half an hour later, James waded out to stand beside Dicey. "There are no fish here," he said.

"The map said there was fishing. That means there must be fish."

"Well, nothing's happening."

"Go back and wait."

"Why? Sammy's there."

"Sammy is only six years old. How do you know he'll know what to do if he gets a bite?"

"He won't get a bite."

"James, do as I say," Dicey ordered sternly. He shuffled off, picking up stones and throwing them out into the water, loitering by the base of the bluff, and finally Dicey saw him climb back up by Sammy.

In another few minutes he was back where Dicey and Maybeth were spreading clothes out on the sand.

"It's no use," James said. "Why are you putting them out here? They'll get sandy."

"That'll blow away once they're dry."

"I don't want sand in my underpants," James said.

"Our job is laundry, yours is fishing," Dicey said, and she sent him back.

He was beside her again in another few minutes. "It's boring," he said.

"We've got to eat," Dicey muttered.

"We can eat mussels and clams."

"I need to know if there are fish."

"I know that already—there aren't."

"All right," she cried, exasperated. "Never mind. Just stop pestering me. I don't care what you do, but let me get on with my work."

James wandered to the far end of the beach. He scratched at the rocks with his nails. Dicey looked to be sure Sammy was all right. The little boy sat patiently, the line hanging down from his finger into the water.

When all the clothes had been soaked and scrubbed, then wrung out and laid on the sand, Dicey waded out to the rock where Sammy sat. She scrambled up to sit with him. "Hey, Sammy," she said, "catch anything?"

Sammy shook his head. His mouth was set in a stubborn line. He glared down at the water.

"Tide's almost high," Dicey observed.

Sammy nodded.

"Maybe you should give up."

"Hush up, Dicey." Sammy spoke in a whisper. "Fish don't like noise."

"But James says there aren't any fish here," Dicey whispered.

"James is wrong. Look." He pulled up the string and showed Dicey a half-eaten worm still impaled on the hook. "I've lost two other worms. Something is down there eating them. I'll catch it."

Dicey left him there and went back to the beach. She started a small fire, more to let Sammy know she had faith in him than because she thought he would actually catch anything. Then she skipped stones across the water.

Maybeth stood swaying in a half-dance by the water's edge, singing to herself. James was climbing up among the big rocks that had tumbled down to the water. Dicey watched him scramble to the top of a rounded boulder and stand up. He saw her watching and waved his arm at her. Then, in a continuation of that motion, he began to fall over.

Dicey didn't see James fall, because when he lost his balance she had taken off down the beach. She didn't know what she would do when she got there, but she would be as close as possible in case there was something she could do. She climbed over the small boulders at the bottom of the pile before she looked for James. He had disappeared—except for one foot, which stuck up over a rock above her head.

Dicey found James cradled in among rocks. His eyes were closed. His face looked pale. "James?"

He didn't answer.

Was he dead? That couldn't happen, could it? And why not, considering the other things that had happened.

James's eyes fluttered and opened. He stared around, as if he couldn't see her. "Dicey? What happened?" he asked. He hunkered his body up.

So, she thought, no bones were broken.

"You fell," she said. "Are you okay?"

"I fell?"

"You were waving and you fell off the rock."

"Oh. Let me think. I don't—" he said. "My foot slipped, I remember. I shouldn't have been climbing with wet sneakers."

"But are you okay?" Maybeth was standing at the bottom of the rocks, looking up. "It's okay," Dicey yelled down. Sammy still concentrated on the water below the rock. He hadn't seen James fall. "Are you?" Dicey asked James.

"I think so." James moved his arms first, then his legs. "I guess my back's not broken," he remarked.

"How do you know?"

"If you move someone with a broken back, the spine separates and the person dies, right away," James stated. "Boy was that scary." He sat up beside Dicey. "Oooh . . ." He bent his head and covered the back of it with his hands. "Dizzy. I must have banged my head."

Dicey helped James make his slow, sliding way back down over the rocks. He leaned against her as they walked back to the fire. She sat him down beside the little blaze and examined the back of his head. "There's no blood, but it's swelling." She pushed the place. "Here."

"Don't, Dicey!" James cried. "That hurts!"

Maybeth brought James a T-shirt soaked in the cool water. Dicey wrapped that around his head and told him to lie down. James said it felt better when he was sitting up and he thought he might have a concussion. Dicey asked him what that was and he told her the symptoms. "And I do have a headache," he said hopefully.

"Bad?"

"Pretty bad, not terrible," he said. "But if I fall asleep within about half an hour, you better call an ambulance. The danger is lapsing into a coma."

Sammy pushed through the shallow water to them, his hands

behind his back. "Look!" he called, holding out three small fish. "I told you. Is something the matter with James?"

"I dunno," Dicey answered. "He fell off those rocks."

Sammy wasn't interested. While James sat aside, silent, they roasted the fish as they had the hot dogs and peeled off the hot meat with their fingers. James refused any. "It makes me sick to look at them," he said.

Dicey studied him while she chewed. He looked sort of bad. He was the one who knew what the symptoms of concussion were, so he could fake it. But she couldn't imagine James faking nausea and missing a meal. Should she take him to a doctor? How could she explain their situation to a doctor? How could she pay a doctor?

"Just as well you're not hungry," she commented. "There wouldn't be enough to go around."

James didn't respond.

They cleaned up the bones and innards and tossed them into the water. Dicey praised Sammy absentmindedly for catching the fish. Then they gathered up the sunbaked clothes and shook the sand from them. "Let's get back to the campsite," Dicey said. "James should be out of the sun. Don't you think, James?" James nodded, but cut the movement short, as if it hurt his head to move it.

Back at their camp they all sat around and stared at James. Dicey was pretty sure more than a half-hour had passed. Sammy wandered around, tossing stones, hitting bushes with sticks. "What can we do?" he finally demanded.

"Nothing," Dicey said.

Sammy kicked at some stones. "Why not?"

"You could take them to the playground," James told Dicey. "My headache's not that bad, if I don't move. I'm not sleepy. If I could just sit quiet. You know?"

"Are you sure I can leave you alone?" Dicey asked. "What about concussions, how long do they last?"

"You're supposed to keep the patient quiet for a few days, until the headaches stop," James told her.

"So we can't travel tomorrow," Dicey said.

James started to shake his head, but winced.

"Or until you get better," Dicey continued.

"That's probably right," James said. "I'm sorry."

Dicey swallowed back her crossness and impatience. "It's okay, I guess. I mean, it'll have to be, won't it."

She scratched with her finger in the dirt. How long would they have to stay? Days and days?

"I'm sorry," James repeated. "I'll tell you when it stops, Dicey."

"Okay," she said. "Then we *will* go over to the playground. You won't go wandering off, will you?"

"What do you think?" James asked. He was leaning back against a rock, his face still pale.

"Then we're off. First stop the bathrooms. James, don't you have to go to the bathroom?"

"No," he said. "All I want is some quiet."

They cut through the woods rather than going down the road. Dicey picked up a long stick and swung it at tree trunks, trying to work things out. They would have to stay another day, at least. She would have to keep an eye on James too, to be sure he was all right. But she wanted to get going tomorrow morning. She broke her stick against a trunk and picked up another one. But she couldn't get going because it wouldn't be safe for James.

The longer they stayed in a place, the greater their danger of being noticed.

As they emerged from the woods, Dicey saw the boy and the girl who had talked to her on the beach. Louis and Edie. They looked at her. "Remember," she whispered to Sammy and Maybeth, "I'm Danny. Remember."

"Yes, Dicey," they said.

The boy and girl were even younger than they had seemed at night, maybe even sixteen. Edie had long heavy brown hair and protruding brown eyes. Louis had wildly curling brown hair and wore heavy-rimmed glasses, which he continually pushed up on his nose. His teeth were crooked, which made him look friendly.

"Hi, Danny," Edie called.

"Hi," Dicey answered, approaching them. "Meet Maybeth and Sammy."

"I want to swing," Sammy said.

"First the bathrooms, then you can play."

"You coming with me?" Sammy asked.

"Of course," Dicey said, then remembered who she was, or, rather, who she wasn't. Sammy just grinned.

The men's bathroom was like a girls' except there were three urinals in a row, and only one toilet. The toilet had no door on it. It wasn't so bad. All the same, she hurried and her heart was beating fast when she pulled the clumsy wooden door closed behind her. Sammy was inside washing his hands and face, giggling, but Dicey didn't want to risk hanging around any longer than she had to.

Louis and Edie were standing around Maybeth when Dicey came out. She sent Maybeth and Sammy over to the swings.

"Not exactly alone," Louis said, facing Dicey.

"Not exactly."

"And there's another one," Louis said. "Maybeth shook her head when I asked was this all of you."

Dicey nodded.

"He's not with you now," Louis observed.

Dicey sighed. "He had a fall so he's resting."

"Is he all right?" Edie sounded worried. "What happened?"

"He fell," Dicey said. "He says he's okay."

"So—where you heading?" Louis asked.

"Up to Provincetown, on the Cape," Dicey told him. "We used to have some family there. It's a neat place in summer."

"Edie, want to go with them?" Louis asked. "It would be a good cover, in case your old man has the cops out."

Edie shook her head. She looked at Dicey with frightened eyes.

"Provincetown's a good place, from all I've heard," Louis went on. "Some jobs. Lots of people. Cops don't look too close."

"You said we'd stay here until our money ran out," Edie said.

"You scared?" Louis challenged her.

"You know I'm not. I proved it, didn't I?"

"Sure. You got ahold of the money just fine. You can relax, Edie—Danny here isn't about to tell anybody anything. Are you, kid?"

Dicey just stared at him.

"It's not as if she really robbed him," Louis went on explaining. He was talking to Dicey, but he was watching the effect of his words on Edie. "I mean, *I* wrote the checks. She just took the checkbook. Besides, the way I figure, I'm saving him a lot of money—on her college education. So he should be grateful to me. Right, Edie?"

"Sure."

"So—whaddayou say? Want to travel with these kids?"

Edie shook her head. "I like it here," she said.

"And if I decide I don't?" Louis asked.

Edie looked up at him. Her eyes had tears in them. "Hey," Louis said. He threw his arm around her. "Hey, I'm just kidding. Can't you take a joke?"

Dicey sidled away from them and went to the swings. Let it go on being a joke, she thought. She didn't know what to do if Louis and Edie tried to go with them.

She couldn't wait there long for worry about James, and for worry about when they'd be able to get moving again. Sammy complained, but she hurried the two little ones back to their campsite. James greeted them in his normal voice. His head, he said, was better now. His appetite, he said, was huge—he'd missed lunch, after all. They all went down to the little cove. James moved his body slowly and cautiously, as if he was afraid it might break.

They gathered clams for dinner while James watched the fire. Dicey wrapped the potatoes in seaweed, too, and baked them in the fire. They had brought the milk carton down with them. They picnicked in tired solitude, eating as much as they wanted. Behind them, the sun went quietly down. Twilight crept over the water toward them, dainty as a mouse.

CHAPTER 5

Dicey awoke to the beginning of a bright day. She lay still for a long time, looking at the cloudless sky through the branches and leaves of green maples and sycamores. The leaves made designs on the background of the sky, intricate patterns that shifted with any slightest breeze. She heard James stir and rolled over on her side to watch him.

James's eyes opened. He yawned and stretched. Dicey waited for him to say what he always said first thing, about it still being true. Then everything would be back to normal.

He caught her eye. "I wish I'd seen you going into the boys' bathroom," he said. "I thought I'd split when Sammy told me."

"I noticed," Dicey said. "How's your head?"

James rolled it back and forth. "Almost okay," he said.

"What do you mean, almost? Does it hurt?"

James thought. "It feels tender. As if it could hurt. It doesn't exactly *hurt,* but it feels like it will."

Dicey sat up. "We can't go until James is better," she said sternly to herself, "that's the most important thing." So, they'd have to wait another day.

They had only apples left in their food supply, and Dicey wanted to save them, in case. So they went down to the little beach, leaving James behind. Three or four families already crowded the beach, and the Tillermans had to eat the apples for breakfast after all.

"It's a weekend," James explained. "That means a lot of people around, especially on the beaches, I bet."

"But what'll we do?" Dicey asked him. She answered herself. "We'll try fishing in the marsh. You'll have to stay here alone," she cautioned James.

"Danny?" a voice called from the road. "Is that you?" It was Edie, and Dicey stood up to show the girl where they were. Louis was with her. They had come, they said, to see how the third brother was and to warn the children that it was a weekend, so lots of people would be in the park.

Edie was carrying something bulky, an instrument. She sat down beside James and played on it a little, leaning it back against her shoulder. The sound was part banjo, part harp. "You like that?" she asked James.

"What is it?"

"An autoharp. Here," she said, and sang a song for them about a girl who wanted to follow her boyfriend to war.

"I like that," Maybeth said, when Edie finished.

"I do too, honey," Edie said. "Do you know any songs you'd like me to sing?"

Maybeth shook her head.

Dicey looked at Edie over James's head and asked, "Do you know Pretty Peggy-O?"

"Sure," Edie said. She bent her head over the autoharp and her long hair fell down like a curtain. She strummed a couple of chords, then raised her face. But this wasn't their song. This song was about William the false lover and how he tricked pretty Peggy-O into running away with him but then murdered her. Edie sang the song quick and cruel, with sharp metallic sounds from her instrument.

"You're a good singer," James said.

"I thought we were going," Sammy said.

"Going where?" Edie asked.

"Fishing," Dicey told her.

"Do you have the hook and line?" James asked. Dicey nodded. "And worms?" She hadn't thought of bait. Count on James to think things through, Dicey thought, and forgave him for his lack of persistence the day before and for being careless and falling.

"Shall we stay with James?" Edie asked. Dicey didn't object.

When they had gotten out of earshot of the campsite, Sammy said he wasn't going fishing with them, he was going to the playground. He didn't want to walk anymore, ever. He didn't want to explore. He wouldn't get into any trouble. He didn't mind being left alone. And he would not go with them, no matter what Dicey said or did.

Dicey decided she could probably leave him safely at the playground. She instructed him to go back to the campsite if he got bored, not to go wandering about. "And don't talk to anyone."

"Why not?" Sammy demanded.

"Well, you know, don't talk about us."

"I wouldn't do that. I'm not stupid."

Maybeth and Dicey crossed the dirt road from the playground and found the path to the small campground. Another path led to a bluff overlooking the marshes. They walked without speaking through the warm morning. The only sounds were the rustling of the leaves above them and the rustling of their feet on the leafy ground. They emerged from the woods on top of a low bluff that marked the border of the marshlands. Below, the heavy grasses swayed. Narrow canals of water moved gently. The scene could have been painted in watercolors, so pale was the green of the grass, so subdued was the blue of the water.

They climbed down a short path and stood on the muddy ground of the lowlands. A heron looked up at them, curious but not afraid, before he flew to a more secluded spot. Clusters of gnats hovered in the air.

"It's so quiet," Dicey said. Maybeth nodded. "Think there are any fish?" Dicey asked, feeling her hunger. Maybeth didn't answer. Dicey walked out along the mudflat until she found a spot she liked. There she baited the hook with a worm from her pocket, put it into the water, and waited.

Maybeth sat beside her, braiding sea grass into long and useless lines. Dicey caught a fish almost right away, six or seven inches long. She rebaited the hook and caught another, even larger. She couldn't believe her luck. Every few minutes she could feel the tentative, jerking nibble on the end of her line.

When she had enough, Dicey took off her shirt and piled her catch into it. As long as they could fish, they wouldn't go hungry. She smiled at Maybeth. "Let's go back and eat," she said. It would be okay. They could wait for James to get well.

They stopped by the playground to pick up Sammy, but he wasn't there. Dicey hurried back to their camp. James sat alone, scratching at the ground with a stick. Fear clutched at Dicey's stomach. "Sammy?" she called. She shouldn't have left him alone for so long. "James, have you seen Sammy?"

Sammy stepped out from behind a boulder. Dicey let out a little snort of relief.

"Look." Dicey held up the fish she had caught. "Anybody hungry?"

"Why were you hiding?" Maybeth asked Sammy.

"We heard somebody coming. I didn't know who it was." His hazel eyes searched out Dicey's face: "I found something."

"What? Bring it over. We need some wood, too, to cook the fish."

Sammy went behind the boulder and came out holding a big grocery bag, which he set down before the fireplace. "Look at this," he said.

Egg salad sandwiches, a bag of potato chips, ham sandwiches, pieces of celery stuffed with peanut butter, a bag of cookies, paper plates, paper cups, paper napkins.

James sat silent, watching. "Where'd you find it?" Dicey asked.

"Left in the woods behind the bathrooms," Sammy said. "And some people gave me a hot dog too, but I ate it with them. They had catsup. I was so hungry," he said.

"Sammy," Dicey spoke slowly. "This looks like somebody's picnic."

"They might have forgotten it," Sammy said.

"That's not the truth," Dicey said.

"Is too," Sammy said.

"What's it matter?" James asked. "I mean, we're the hungry ones. They could probably go back to the store and buy food, whoever this belonged to. Or just go home and eat. We need it."

Dicey couldn't entirely disagree with him. "But it's stealing," she said.

"Just food," James argued. "Louis said it should be a natural right for everybody to have enough food."

"Does Louis know?"

"No. Sammy wasn't back."

"Sammy? Tell the truth," Dicey said.

"They left it on one of those tables. I don't know who they were. They left two bags on the table and I could see there was nobody watching, so I took one. I wanted you all to have something to eat. Dicey?" He made himself look straight at her. "I wanted to help out."

Dicey understood. "Well, you surely did that. But stealing—we don't steal." Not unless they had to, not unless they were starving, and then it should be Dicey herself to do it. Not a little boy six years old.

"I think it was pretty smart of him," James said. "And brave."

"I ran," Sammy boasted, "I ran so fast—it's hard to run with a big bag. Nobody caught me."

"I'm glad of that," Dicey said, reaching to pat his tangled hair. "I don't know how we would have gotten you back if you'd been caught."

"Would you get me back?" Sammy asked.

"Of course. What do you think?"

"I don't know," Sammy said.

"We're all together, aren't we?" Dicey asked him. "We'd just have to get you back. But it would be hard, really hard—so I'm glad."

They ate the celery and the egg salad sandwiches right away, because mayonnaise could spoil. The rest of Sammy's food they put away for some other time. Meanwhile, they built a fire and roasted Dicey's fish over it. Even James was full when they finished. They stayed put for the rest of that long, early summer afternoon, but when the evening cool came into the air and the families on the beach left, the Tillermans went down by the water. James sat quietly by the water's edge, while the rest played tag until dark. James wanted quiet; the heat had given him a headache. But he told Dicey she didn't have to worry about him.

When they returned to the campsite, Louis and Edie were waiting for them. "James? We got you something," Edie said. "It's convalescent food." She handed him a small grocery bag. It held two oranges.

"Thanks," James said. "They look terrific." He peeled an orange and ate it.

Dicey grabbed the other one from him, peeled it and split it in half. She gave half to Maybeth and half to Sammy. James looked like he wanted to say something to her, but he didn't.

"Guess what?" Edie said. Her voice came out of the dark.

"What?"

"When we went to get the oranges, there was some man in there buying food, who said his lunch had been stolen."

Louis took over the story. "He was a big, fat guy. Asking what the country was coming to when a family's picnic lunch was stolen in a public park. He said it was probably dope addicts. He was all for calling in the police. But the guy who runs the store said it was probably somebody's idea of a joke. The big guy said that if he could get his hands on the joker, he'd show him what he thought of it. He reminded me of your father, didn't he, Edie? Isn't that just what your father would do? Then, he pulls out a wallet a foot thick, crammed with bills. He peels off a couple and goes out, still complaining about his bad luck. I say good luck to whoever walked off with his lunch."

"Why?" James asked.

"Big guys like that, with thick bankrolls—they've got so much that they don't know what to do with it. And they're always the first ones to call in the police on little guys. Like us. Like you."

Dicey went over to the trash barrel to throw out the orange peels. Edie went with her. "Danny? I wondered if you kids had taken it."

"No," Dicey said. "No, how could we? We were fishing at the marsh."

"I thought—you know—if you were hungry enough," Edie said.

"We're not hungry," Dicey said. "We've got plenty."

"If you say so," Edie said.

Louis called over: "Hey Danny, James says you caught a mess of fish."

Glad at the change of subject, Dicey told him about the marsh and how easy it was to catch fish there. Louis said it was illegal to fish in the marsh, because that area was a game sanctuary. "So you better be careful. You don't want to get caught at it."

How were they supposed to eat then, Dicey asked herself. By buying food, she answered. The whole world was arranged for people who had money—for *adults* who had money. The whole world was arranged against kids. Well, she could handle it. Somehow.

"If you were caught," Louis said. "Kids have no legal rights at all. That's one reason I took off. What about you kids, Danny? How come you're on the road?"

"Huh?" Dicey asked, pretending she hadn't been listening.

"You're about the most secretive bunch I've ever met," Louis said. "I don't even know where you're from. Where are you from?"

"Nowhere special," Dicey said.

"You don't trust me." Louis' voice hovered in the darkness. He waited for an answer.

"Don't tease him, Lou."

"I don't trust anyone," Dicey said. "It's what you said, kids have no rights. So we have to be extra careful."

"Why don't kids have any rights?" James asked.

"Because parents own them," Louis answered quickly. "Your parents can beat you, steal your money, decide not to take you to a doctor—anything they want."

"There's a law I have to go to school," James said. "That's a right, isn't it?"

"If you look at it that way."

"They couldn't kill me," James continued. "That would be murder."

"If it could be proved."

James thought about this. "Then the only person who will look out for me is myself."

"You got it. And you better learn how to do that, learn quick and learn good. Look out for yourself and let the rest go hang—

because they're out to hang you, you can be sure of it."

"What about love?" Edie asked.

"You tell us all about it, tell us all about your old man; and then talk about love," Louis said. "Danny here knows what's what—he doesn't trust anyone."

"What do you two do when you're not camping here?" Dicey asked them.

She saw the two heads turn toward one another, and the look they exchanged.

"I can't remember," Edie said, in a soft voice. "Nothing before now seems real to me anymore. Nothing before is worth remembering."

"So I guess you'd say we didn't do anything. And now we do something—we pluck the lotus. Right, honey?"

Then they got up to leave. Edie said she'd come by tomorrow and bring James some soup. "That sounds good," James said. The two young people stole silently away. Dicey was listening, but she couldn't hear their footsteps. For a little while she wondered if they were hanging around, to overhear something.

The next morning, Sunday morning, dawned warm. Morning spread a haze of golden heat over the trees and boulders. James said it wasn't a good day for him to travel, it was too hot, it was too far, he just wasn't feeling right. So Dicey took her family across the top of the highland to the long beach. She guessed, correctly as it turned out, that that beach would be a favorite spot, that it would be crowded on this hot Sunday. She planned for the Tillermans to lose themselves among the mob of people there. James protested, saying he wanted to wait for Edie, but Dicey told him he had to come with them. The sun would give him a headache, he said. She said she thought he could stand that. "How much longer are we going to have to wait, anyway?" she demanded.

"I don't know. I told you, I'll say when I feel okay again," James said. "It's not my fault I'm sick."

Dicey didn't answer.

The long beach was a flat crescent that marked the edge of a shallow cove. Children straddled the water's edge and a few bolder ones were actually swimming. Towels crowded the sand, like bright pieces of confetti. On the towels lay people in bathing suits, surrounded by picnic baskets, paper bags, canvas totes, blaring radios and coolers full of ice and drinks.

The Tillermans walked about, unnoticed, and later returned to their camp for a quick lunch of ham sandwiches and potato chips, which finished off the food in Sammy's bag. Then they went back to the long beach. Dicey was glad not to meet Louis and Edie.

Later in the afternoon, when the beach began to empty, Dicey looked around, to gather James and Maybeth and Sammy together. They could leave tomorrow: she had watched James and she was pretty sure he was fine. Sammy was nowhere to be seen. Neither James nor Maybeth had spoken with him, not for a long time.

Dicey looked out over the low sandbars, not yet covered by the incoming tide. She knew she didn't have to worry about Sammy having drowned. She decided to wait a few minutes. He might, after all, just have slipped away to the woods to pee.

Sure enough, within ten minutes, she saw his sturdy body trudging down the path from the highlands. They went to meet him. As they walked along the cliff that fronted the Sound, Dicey asked him where he'd been. Sammy turned his head to look behind them, and then announced with swelling pride, "I got us another one."

"Another what?"

"Another food bag. It was all the leftovers a family couldn't finish. I watched them eat, then pack up the bag. Then they all went down to rinse off sand in the water, and I grabbed the bag, and I ran. It's at the camp."

"Good job, Sammy," James said.

"No it isn't," Dicey said. She knelt down in front of him. "And Sammy knows that," she said, looking straight in his eyes. His mouth grew stubborn and he would not look at her. "Stealing isn't right," Dicey said.

"Not even if you're hungry?" Sammy argued.

"You're not hungry, not really hungry," Dicey said. "We never stole things. Tillermans don't have to steal."

"Well, maybe we should," James interrupted. "It's like a war, isn't it? Us against everyone so we can get to Bridgeport. Otherwise, you'd have asked a policeman for help right away, when there was one hanging around our car. Remember?" Dicey remembered. "So if it's like that, what's wrong with Sammy taking somebody's leftovers?"

"And more too," Sammy grinned up at James. "There's money. A wallet."

"Oh no." Dicey groaned. "Sammy, you can't take a wallet the way you can food. You just can't get away with that. We have to take it back."

"No!" Sammy cried.

"Yes," Dicey said firmly. "And on the double. I'm right, aren't I, James?"

Even James agreed.

Dicey sent James and Maybeth on to gather mussels and clams and firewood. She hurried Sammy back to the camp, and he showed her where he'd hidden the stolen bag. "But they're gone home," he protested. "Their towel was gone when I came back."

Worse and worse. Dicey thought hard and fast. She took the wallet out of the bag—it was a man's wallet, brown leather—

and grabbing Sammy by the hand, ran back to the long beach. She wanted to make him give it back himself and apologize. But she couldn't, not at the risk.

The long beach was empty under shadows that fell from the cliff out toward the water. But Dicey heard voices coming from somewhere. She stood halfway down the steep hill and made Sammy point to where he had found the bag. She lifted her arm and hurled the wallet at that spot. She didn't wait to see where it landed, but turned and ran back laboriously, uphill. She didn't wait for Sammy.

Safe again under cover of the trees, Sammy spoke sullenly, "It had almost twenty dollars in it."

Dicey didn't answer. She couldn't think of what to say. Finally she said, "You have got to do what I tell you. What *I* tell you, not anybody else."

Sammy nodded as if he understood.

They had a fire on the beach that evening and steamed mussels so hot and chewy they burned their tongues on the tawny meat. The smell of damp seaweed, richer than the smell of wet wood, rose with the smoke from the fire and lingered over their faces. They were salty after the day at the water. They were together. The light dimmed, melting into early twilight. Stars became visible, pinpricks of light on the silken sky. If they hadn't known better, they would have thought that when the fire died out and the moon shone bright in the sky, they could turn and trudge slowly up over familiar dunes to their own home. Where Momma would look up absentmindedly to greet them and ask if they had a good day.

Sammy dug wells for the water to run into. Maybeth arranged shells and water-polished stones into an intricate design. James skimmed rocks out over the water.

"We'll get going again tomorrow," Dicey said.

"I'm not sure, Dicey," James protested. "I don't think I should, yet." Dicey looked at him. He looked like he meant what he said.

"We could stay here," Sammy added. "It's okay here."

Dicey sat down beside the fire, her knees drawn up under her chin, poking at the blaze with a long stick and thinking. They had to go. But what if James wasn't better and it hurt him? Should she wait another day?

Louis and Edie came up silently behind her and surprised her with some chords on the autoharp. Dicey welcomed the music, but she had wanted to avoid any further contact with them.

Edie played and sang. Louis took Maybeth by the hand and led her in a galloping dance up and down the beach. Sammy trailed them in a jig of his own, while James clapped time energetically. Dicey watched him—some brother! He was no more sick than she was. They were leaving tomorrow, if she had to drag them out of the park herself.

The dance over, they all relaxed around the fire while Edie continued to sing. Louis held Maybeth at his side. Sammy curled up against Dicey. The sky turned black velvet. Deep satin water curled against the sand.

"We gotta go to sleep," Dicey said, after a while.

"Don't go yet, Danny," Edie said, putting down the autoharp. "I don't know when I've had a better time."

Dicey stood up and dusted sand from her fanny. Barely awake, Sammy waited beside her. James stayed seated, his eyes reproachful.

"Maybeth?" Dicey spoke gently.

Maybeth came over.

"Goodnight, honey," Louis said.

Maybeth didn't answer.

"Doesn't she ever say anything?" Louis asked.

"Sure. Sometimes."

"Wait," Edie said, "we'll come with you."

They climbed up the steep path. At the top of the hill, Dicey turned to say good night, so they would go away, but Louis was holding on to Edie's arm and pointing.

Between the trees they saw a bright light that rhythmically flashed red.

"What is it?" Dicey asked.

"Shut up," Louis said. "Move it, Edie." They slipped away into the darkness.

He was right, Dicey realized. It was a police car going along the road that ran past the campsites. She pulled her family into the bushes and told them to lie down.

"It's a police car," James said quietly. "Heading toward our camp."

"I dumped the bag in the trash," Dicey said.

"That's where they'll look," James said.

"I can't see what's going on," Dicey said. "Lie quiet, everyone."

Darkness rustled through the trees. Faintly, the water lapped at the shore. Dicey thought. "We're going up to the woods past the playground, long way around," she said. "We'll sleep there and get out of here at first morning."

"But . . . ," James said.

Dicey felt Maybeth's small hand on her arm. "But nothing. You've been fine all day today, and you know it. Don't lie to me, not anymore. I won't believe you."

They waited a long time, then began a silent journey across the dark park. They made a wide circle around their campsite. They saw nothing, they heard nothing, only the insects and the noise of the wind. Dicey was sure of her direction, but she wasn't sure just where they were until she saw the pale emptiness of the playground before her. They were so tired by then that they just stumbled into the woods beyond and slept there, slept uneasily.

CHAPTER 6

They awoke in pale, predawn light. Mist lay in patches along the ground. The wet, black trunks of trees loomed out of the foggy half-light.

"It's still true," James said.

It was damp, and their clothes were sodden. Dicey wanted to get moving, right away. "Ready? Let's use the bathrooms and then get out of here."

Dawn gilded the sky when they arrived at the park entrance. The fear, which had stayed beside them since the night before, retreated at the promise of a bright morning. The sound of a car motor gave Dicey warning. She drew her family back into the cover of the woods.

"Why?" James asked.

"Shut *up*," Dicey whispered fiercely. "Lie down. Lie still. I don't know, but I don't want anyone to see us."

A police car, followed by another police car, roared along the main road. Both slowed down and turned onto the dirt road. They stopped, just inside the gates, one behind the other. Leaving his motor running, a policeman got out of the first car and walked to the car behind him. His leather boots shone. He wore dark glasses and had a gun at his belt. He leaned into the window by the driver's side and unfolded a map that Dicey recognized as a map of the park. He pointed to parts of it.

Dicey strained to hear what they were saying, but the motors drowned out their voices.

The policeman nodded his head sharply, twice, and strode back to his own car. The flashing lights on top of the police cars were turned on. The two cars roared down the road.

"Let's go," Dicey said. "On the double."

They hurried down the road.

"What was it?" James said.

"I don't know," Dicey said.

"Were they after us?" James asked.

"I don't know," Dicey said.

"Or Louis and Edie," James said. "Nobody knew we were there. People knew Louis and Edie were there—they bought food every day."

"We bought food, too."

"Only that first day. How long ago was that?"

"I can't remember. But we did take those lunches."

"Sammy did that. That wasn't us."

Dicey thought aloud: "Louis and Edie are runaways; and maybe more. Anyway, we got away in time."

The children walked the long morning through. Conditioned by the earlier hard days, refreshed by the days at the park, both their muscles and spirits were in good tone. The road wound south, following the coastline.

At noon, they rested by the roadside, leaning back against one of the low stone fences that ran all over this countryside.

"I'm hungry," James said. "Aren't you?"

"We haven't passed a store of any kind since that one town," Dicey answered. "And no garages." Then, like a black fist punching at her head, she realized: "My map! I don't even know where we are. How could I forget the map?"

"Should we turn around?" James asked. "That town had a grocery store."

"That was miles back. Besides, you might as well know. We don't have much money left, just twenty-six cents. I was going to try to get work at the store by the park, but I was afraid we'd get too conspicuous when we had to stay. So now, we have to keep going," Dicey said. "We've seen railroad tracks, right? That means there must be more towns ahead."

"But what'll we eat?" James asked.

"For now, nothing. We can't. We'll just have to keep going and see what happens. If I had my map I could see where the water is and we could fish or clam or find mussels. I need a map."

They were tired when they stood up, more tired than when they had sat down. The folds of the hills and the symmetry of the trees no longer had the power to please them. They walked more slowly than before. The feeling that she did not know what to expect, or when to expect it, made Dicey jumpy.

In an hour they passed a sign marking the limits of a town called Sound View. Dicey felt better. Soon the houses sat closer together and the welcome sight of a small shopping center placed on two sides of a crossroads greeted them. Shopping centers on this road were quite different from those on Route 1. These were small, fancier. They had no huge parking lots, just a row of parking places right up against the sidewalk. Instead of large glass windows plastered with sale signs, these stores had small panes, like house windows. Everything looked clean.

Dicey instructed the other three to stay where they were, while she crossed the street and went into a Texaco station. The office was occupied by one man with a fringe of hair around his shiny head who was dozing with his feet up on a wooden desk. He snored gently.

His head snapped up as Dicey closed the door loudly. His blue eyes studied her. "What can I do for you?"

"I'd like a map, please, of Connecticut."

He pulled out a drawer and selected one map from several file folders there. "That'll be fifty cents," he said.

"But I don't have any money," Dicey said.

"Okay," he said. He replaced the map in its folder, closed the drawer, and once again raised his feet to the top of the desk.

"I have to have a map," Dicey said.

"Paper's expensive, kid. We don't give maps away anymore."

"Who does?"

"Nobody." He closed his eyes.

Dicey stood, chewing on her lip. Money, money, money, always money. And she couldn't get into the drawer, find the right map, and get out the door—not fast enough to make it. "Mister?" He opened his eyes. "I really want one."

"That's tough on you, kid. I'm sorry."

"Could I work for one?"

"Doing what?"

"I dunno. There must be some chore—something. Sweeping? Washing? Are the bathrooms clean?"

"My bathrooms are always sparkling clean," he said. He closed his eyes. Dicey stood thinking. She wondered if she could pump gas. It didn't look hard.

"That window," the man said. The office had a large plate glass window that faced the pumps and the street. "That window needs washing. You know how to use a squeegee?"

Dicey didn't even know what a squeegee was. "Sure," she said.

"I didn't get to it yesterday," the man said, lumbering into a closet and pulling out a bucket, a rag and a long-armed utensil that had to be the squeegee.

"Inside and out," he said.

Dicey nodded.

"All over and no streaks."

Dicey nodded. If he would just let her get to work on it.

"I'll give you the map and a quarter too. Fair enough?"

"Fair enough."

Dicey began on the outside of the window. She signaled her family to wait, and James nodded to show he understood. The three sat down on the curb, facing Dicey. Dicey filled the bucket, added some cleanser from a bottle she found in it, sloshed the mixture together and began spreading the water over the window. She did it in four sections, wetting the glass, pulling the squeegee down over it firmly, squeezing the squeegee out and repeating the last step twice. The glass gleamed. Then she went inside and did the same thing. A few cars pulled in, were filled with gas and pulled out again. Every time a car pulled away, Dicey looked to be sure her three were still there.

She finished, emptied the bucket and put it away. The man came in from filling a car. He handed her a map and a quarter. "You got an audience," he said.

"They're friends."

"Well, that's a good job. If you're around later in the week . . ."

"Thanks, mister," Dicey said.

"You earned it, kid."

Dicey returned to her family, the map in her hand.

"You were hours," James said. "I'm so hungry my stomach hurts."

"The map cost fifty cents. So I washed the window. And got a quarter more, too."

"Let's eat," Sammy said.

They walked along the front of the first section of the shopping center, but saw only a restaurant and some clothing stores.

They crossed the street and entered a small market filled with specialty goods, delicatessen items and huge, fancy pieces of fruit. Everything on the shelves cost much more than fifty-one cents. The people who worked in the store stared at the Tillermans suspiciously, and Dicey hurried them out.

"But I want to eat," Sammy protested. "I'll die if I don't eat."

Dicey pulled him firmly out the door. "Hush up—you don't know what people will think," she whispered fiercely in his ear. He snuffled. "Look, you won't die, not in one day. Starvation takes days and days."

A small bakery, its windows filled with decorated cakes and layered pastries, also did business in the second part of the shopping center. Dicey would not let them linger before its windows, but she sat them down around her on the curb just beyond it. Their knees were up against the fenders of a blue Cadillac car.

"Okay," Dicey said. "We've got to do this smart."

"What do you mean?" asked James.

"We've only got fifty-one cents, and around here that won't buy enough to feed even one of us. This is a ritzy area. So—we want some bakery goods, because they're cheapest, but not at full price. So, we've got to make that lady in there feel like giving us a lot for our money. So, we've got to make her feel sorry for us."

James nodded.

"I'll go tell her how hungry I am," Sammy volunteered.

"No, you won't and have her start asking questions." Dicey snapped. Her own stomach was taut within her, and she was having trouble thinking well. "It's got to be done right. By the right person."

"That's you, isn't it?" James asked.

"Not this time, it isn't. Nor you, either. People don't take to us the right way, not at first. Maybeth would be the best one."

Maybeth shook her head mutely. Her eyes grew large and stared at Dicey.

"I know." Dicey sighed. "So Sammy, it's you, after all."

"Good-o," Sammy said. "Give me the money."

"Not so fast. If she asks you, we're staying in a summer house—where?" Dicey searched her memory. "In Old Lyme and we went for a walk and got lost, and there's nobody home this afternoon to come and get us in the car. Do you have that? And we're hungry. That's if she asks you."

"What if she doesn't?"

"We need enough food for lunch, and maybe dinner too. For just fifty-one cents. So, unless she'll give you two loaves of bread for it, sort of hem and haw. Say that's too much. Tell her you've only got fifty-one cents. Ask her if this road will get us home. Be sort of brave and pitiful—do you know what I mean, Sammy? But whatever happens, don't tell her the truth."

He stood up, his legs sturdy and brown. He held out a dirty hand and Dicey put the money into it.

"Can you do it, Sammy?"

"I think so."

"If there isn't anything right to buy, don't buy anything."

"Dicey—I wouldn't do that."

No, he wouldn't. He couldn't be bullied. They watched him walk back and enter the bakery. They heard a jingle of bells as he closed the door. Then they waited, silently, for what seemed a very long time, studying the front of the big car. It stared back at them with empty glass eyes.

Dicey turned her head when she heard the shop door open with a jingling of bells. Sammy had a big white bakery bag in one hand. In the other, he had a round cookie, half-eaten. His eyes met Dicey's, and he quickly shoved the rest of the cookie into his mouth.

"It's fine," he said. "She had a couple of old doughnuts, and some rolls and a pie she said she couldn't sell after two days. She said she'd call our parents, but I said I didn't remember the phone number yet. She said maybe my sister would. So I said I'd come out and you'd tell her the number after you ate because I thought you were pretty hungry."

Dicey jumped to her feet. "Good job, Sammy," she said. "Okay, let's go. I don't want to answer any more questions. We'll eat as soon as we're out of sight. We'll eat the pie—that's worth waiting a little for, isn't it?"

They trotted down the road and around a corner. Once out of sight, they sat on the grass to eat, breaking pieces of apple pie off with their fingers and licking all the sticky sauce before seizing another portion. They were too hungry to save much for later; only two rolls were left in the white bag when Dicey put her map into it, rolled down the top and led them off again. She wanted to get to a creek she had seen on the map. It was a little creek that fed into the mouth of the Connecticut River. There might be fish in it. If they could fish, then they could have breakfast before they set off. And then it wouldn't matter so much that they didn't have any money left.

They didn't have one penny left. Not one.

Four miles up the road they found the creek. Dicey led them up it, away from the road. The creek was bordered with marshes, but if you went a few yards back the land got higher, dryer. It was posted: NO HUNTING. NO FISHING. NO TRESPASSING. But Dicey figured they had to risk it. A small fire, during daylight hours, that wouldn't be so noticeable.

She set James and Sammy fishing down by the creek and took Maybeth back into the trees. Together they cleared a place for a fire, surrounded it with stones, then gathered twigs, leaves and branches to burn, plus four slim branches on which they could thread the fish.

For all their patient waiting, James and Sammy caught only two fish. Those Dicey cooked and shared out among them, dividing the fish and the two rolls evenly. It was not enough, not after a long day's walk. They went silent to sleep hungry, thirsty, huddled together to keep warm.

Dicey woke early and dug up some worms. She took the line and hook down to the creek and tried to catch breakfast. Fish bit in the early morning. The fishing boats that went out from Provincetown went out when night was still dark, so that as the first light brought out the fish they could be there, nets down and ready.

Birds awoke. The sun came up, although you couldn't see it through overhanging clouds. The water gurgled quietly at Dicey's feet. She heard an occasional motorboat, far off, but no cars. However, off in the distance there was a humming that suggested heavy traffic. This noise was carried to her on a steady wind that blew from off the land toward the water.

No fish were biting. Not that morning.

She heard James calling her with panic in his voice. Slowly, she trudged back to her family.

"I told you," Sammy said to James, "because the fishing line was gone."

"I didn't know where you were," James said. "Why didn't you say where you were going?"

"You were asleep," Dicey answered. "Let's get going."

She did not say a word about eating. They did not ask her.

It was a subdued four children who returned to the road, walked over the little bridge and through a tiny town that didn't even have its own post office building, just one section of the laundromat set aside, and a small flag flying outside to show where the post office was. They walked through town and on, north along the Connecticut River. It was a low, gray morning, and Dicey thought someday soon it would rain again. She didn't have the energy to care about that. Besides, you could drink rain water.

By noon they were at the town of Old Lyme and Dicey had identified the distant rumble, grown louder now, as the Thruway. Here Route 1 joined the Thruway to cross over the broad river.

They passed the Thruway entry ramp and a shopping center backed up against the fast-moving highway. They cut through to the river's bank and stood looking up at the soaring metal that arched overhead to cross the river.

When Dicey realized that the bridge had no walkway, she stared out over the river. It wasn't terribly broad, but it was much too broad to swim.

If there was no walkway, they would have to walk on the shoulder of the road. Someone would be sure to stop them. If they didn't get run over first. Cars and trucks and buses—all hurtled over that bridge as if the devil himself was chasing them. He'd be chasing them from both directions then, Dicey thought; he'd catch you either way.

Dicey crouched down where she was and buried her face in her knees. How could they go forward from here? The railroad bridge downriver had a draw section in the middle that was raised up. They couldn't cross there. It was miles and miles upriver to the next bridge. Tears welled up behind her eyes and the corners of her mouth pulled sharply down.

You don't cry, she said to herself. Not you.

No money, no food, no way to go forward. The silence behind her told her that her brothers and sister were watching her. Maybe they could just all stay right here, without moving, and turn to stone. Then her troubles would be over. Dicey opened her eyes and studied the darkness of her knees. There was nothing more she could do. Nothing. She had done her best and that wasn't good enough and now she could do no more. That was it. The end.

She sighed and felt a small hand on her shoulder. Maybeth. She raised her head to look out again over the impassable river.

At least it was beautiful, with curves and marshy islands and yachts moored along the edges. At least the trees that crowded up to the top of the bluff spread above them, proud and growing. A solitary, two-masted sailboat glided down the river. She watched it.

"Dicey?" Maybeth said.

"Yes, Maybeth," Dicey answered, without turning her head. Food, money, a way forward. They had none.

"What's wrong?"

Dicey almost laughed. "What's right?" is what she wanted to answer, but she didn't speak. Never mind even the way forward, you couldn't get food without money and they had none.

Kids just couldn't earn money.

She had, yesterday. She had earned seventy-five cents in all. They could eat something today, if they had seventy-five cents now.

James asked, "What're we going to do now?"

"I dunno," Dicey said. So, she had to earn some money. But how? There was that shopping center. It had a big parking lot, and a supermarket. She pictured it carefully, and then pictured herself coming out of the market with two big bags filled with groceries after she had earned money somehow, bags filled with fruit and meat and breads and cans of vegetables and a pan to cook things in. And a can opener; it would be just her luck to forget the can opener.

In her daydream, the Dicey she saw walking out of the store with enough food for her family to eat for days, with her eyes smiling and a big grin stretching her mouth, that Dicey tripped and fell. The food scattered over the ground. The wheels of cars squashed the scattered oranges and bananas. A dog took the package of hamburger meat and ran away with it. The people around went off on their own ways, carrying their own heavy bags of groceries.

Was this how Momma felt? Was this why Momma ran away? Because she couldn't think of anything more to do and couldn't stand anymore to try to take care of her children.

Dicey said to herself, I'm getting as bad as Momma. Imagination doesn't do any good. Then her mind flicked back to the people with their heavy bags.

That might be a way. If they all did it. They might earn something.

She turned her head and ran fingers through her hair. They had to look neat or people wouldn't trust them.

"Listen, we could carry groceries to cars out at that shopping center. People might tip us."

"I wanna eat first," Sammy said.

"We can't." Dicey looked directly into his eyes. "We don't have any money left, you know that. All we've got is this," and she held up the white bag in which she was carrying the map.

"Dicey? Is everything going to be all right?" Sammy looked scared.

Momma always reassured him, whenever he was afraid or when she'd been angry because she was worried. She always smiled at him and said everything would be all right. And somehow, it always was.

"I hope so," Dicey said. "I don't know. I'll tell you, if this idea works and we can earn some money, the first thing we'll do is buy a quart of milk. The first forty cents we have. That's a promise."

The fear stayed in Sammy's eyes, but he nodded his head.

Dicey tidied them up as much as possible. She had not noticed how dirty they'd become. Maybeth's hair was a tangled mess. James's hands were brown with dirt and his nails were black. And Sammy looked—well, Sammy looked like most six-year-olds, so that might be okay. Her own shorts were grubby, her knees stained. But her dark hair was always kept short, so that must look all right. They'd just have to try it.

They stationed themselves outside of the entrance doors, where the paper bags were brought out on a rolling belt. Maybeth looked at the people going in and coming out and shook her head. Her eyes grew big and pleading. Dicey understood. She told Maybeth to sit quiet at the far end of the belt. Maybeth nodded and ran off. She sat and didn't move a muscle, just sat quiet as if she was waiting for her mother to come and take her home.

Most of the people the children approached said, "No, thank you," with a kind of puzzled look, as if it didn't often happen that someone offered to carry their grocery bags. Some, especially ladies with babies, said yes, with a grateful look, and Dicey or James or Sammy would carry huge bags out to large station wagons. The people would give them a dime, or some nickels.

True to her word, at the end of the first half-hour, when they had forty cents, Dicey went inside to buy milk. They ducked around the corner of the building to drink it, careful not to spill any as they poured it into their mouths. The cool, rich liquid flowed down Dicey's throat and settled gently into her stomach. The carton was soon empty. "Better?" Dicey asked. "Better," they said. They returned to work.

All afternoon they went up to strangers and asked if they would like their bags carried. Dicey learned to read the no or yes in people's eyes before they spoke it. Then, unexpectedly, the way good luck always surprises you, they had a piece of very good luck.

An older man and a little girl came out of the busy store. They stood waiting for their bags to emerge from the metal doors the rolling belt used.

Soon, the man moved to a group of three grocery bags. The little girl followed beside him. Dicey stepped up to him. "Would you like me to carry those bags?"

He looked at her. "We've got three," he said hesitantly.

"My brother could help too," Dicey said.

"The car is across the lot, by the restaurant," he said.

"That's okay," Dicey said.

The man waited, hesitating, maybe, for her to say more, to ask again. When she didn't speak, that seemed to decide him and his eyes twinkled at her. "Why not?" he said to the little girl. "Sure," he said to Dicey, "you and your brother carry these two and I'll take the third. Be careful—there are some eggs in there somewhere. We did remember the eggs, didn't we?"

"Grandpa," the girl spoke. "You keep asking that. Stop teasing. But Grandpa"—her mouth puffed out sulky—"you said I could carry a bag. You said."

He shook his head at her.

"You said I could because I'm your helper on the boat."

He ignored her. Dicey ignored her too, not liking the tone of her voice.

"But I'm bigger than him," the little girl said, pointing at Sammy. "It's not fair."

They walked along to the car. Sammy carried the lightest bag. The man and Dicey carried the heavier ones. The little girl trailed behind. To make conversation, the man asked Dicey how much money they'd earned, and she answered that they hadn't counted yet. He asked her how long they'd been at it, and when she answered all afternoon he said she must like working. Dicey shrugged. He said he himself liked working, but he wasn't sure if he didn't like it because it made vacations so much more pleasant.

Dicey smiled at this.

"So you're all in it together," the man said. He didn't say it nosy, but as if he was really interested in her, Dicey.

Dicey wanted to answer, even though she couldn't tell him the truth. "We want to get our mother a birthday present," she said.

"What are you thinking of getting her?" he asked.

"She needs a new ironing board," Dicey answered.

"Your father can help you out a little, can't he?" the man said. Dicey knew that was the way this man would do it.

"He's not around," she said shortly.

The man just nodded. They had come to the car. It had Pennsylvania license plates. He held the rear door open while she and Sammy put the bags inside, and then he put his own bag in. He put his hand in his pocket. "How many of you are there?" he asked.

"Four," Dicey said.

He took out his wallet and gave her two dollars. "That's fifty cents apiece," he said.

"It's too much," Dicey protested. She would not take the money.

He folded the bills and stuffed them into the pocket of her shorts. "That, young lady, is for me to say. Now scoot and good luck to you."

Dicey thanked him and turned to go. By then the little girl had scuffed her way to the car. She stood up on tiptoe to speak to her grandfather, and he lifted her firmly into the car, talking to her. He was angry with her, but not rough. He plunked her down on the seat by the steering wheel.

Dicey and Sammy walked away. "How much did he give you?" Sammy asked, as soon as they were out of earshot.

Before Dicey could answer, she heard running feet and the little girl caught at her arm. "Wait," she said. She held another dollar in her hand. "This is from me. Grandpa said I could. Mommy gave it to me to buy her a present while I was spending the night with Grandpa on his boat, but everything was plastic and she doesn't like plastic. She says it's tack-y. She'd rather I wrote her a story anyway, and I can do that tonight. Grandpa got me some paper and crayons. To keep me quiet, that's what he said. I talk a lot. Maybe I'll write her a poem because that would be shorter. So this is for your mother. I'm sorry I got mad."

Dicey hesitated again. "Take it, Dicey," Sammy urged.

"Please take it." The little girl smiled. "I want you to, I do. Mommy likes my poems better than anything. She says they're *stu*pendous. I'm going to write one about fish, because we're on a boat. Do you think fish would eat flowers, because I write good poems about flowers."

Dicey could barely keep up with the stream of chatter. She grinned and took the dollar. "Okay," she said.

"Okay," the little girl said happily. She ran back to the car where her grandfather waited. Dicey did not watch them drive away.

"Good-o," was all Sammy said, but he strutted back to his post by the supermarket doors.

Shortly thereafter, Dicey called James and Sammy together, and they counted the money they had earned. Five dollars and fifteen cents. Dicey nodded in satisfaction.

"That sure is an improvement," she said. She went inside to buy peanut butter, bread and milk. She still had $3.85 when she came out. "And we got a good heavy bag too."

They returned to their wooded post looking over the winding river. They could see only two houses, one on each side of where they sat, both built low to the bluff and designed to face out over the river, both with those walls of windows that modern houses have. After they had eaten, Dicey explained the next difficulty, that they couldn't walk over the river on the bridge. She no longer felt so hopeless, so she could say it without sounding defeated. They had earned money, more than enough money. And that grandfather and the little girl—Dicey didn't know why they had made her feel better, but they had, even though it wasn't going to get any easier.

The Tillermans sat in a row and looked down at the river flowing below. They looked at boats moored close together in marinas, or alone at the ends of long docks. Overhead, cars roared across the bridge.

"We could go upriver to the next bridge," James suggested.

"That'll take days," Dicey said. "But we may have to." She was reluctant to journey away from the water; she didn't want to go far from the Sound that was part of the sea.

"Does the river get narrow enough to swim across?"

"I don't know," Dicey said. "It would be too risky to light a fire, wouldn't it? I feel like sitting by a fire, don't you?"

Maybeth snuggled up to Dicey and hummed tunelessly. Dicey sat looking down, not thinking or worrying, just feeling her full belly and her sister's warm body, watching the river water shimmer in the sun, remembering with pride how James and Sammy had worked that afternoon, wondering which boat the little girl was sleeping on and thinking those two would remember her. A melody came into her head and she sang one of Momma's old, sad songs: "'The water is wide, I cannot get o'er. Neither have I wings to fly.'"

The melody floated out over the water, where she could not go.

"'Give me a boat that will carry two, and two shall row—my love and I.'"

The setting sun floated gold along the surface of the water.

"'"Oh, love is bonny, when it is young,"'" Dicey sang. "'Fair as a flower when first it is new.'" Then she stopped. "We'll take a boat," she said.

"Good-o," Sammy said.

"Where will we get a boat?" asked James. "Where could we get a boat?"

"All these yachts have little dinghys that go with them, so the people on the yachts can get to and from their moorings. We'll take a dinghy and row across and tie it up on the other side. I can row and so can you, James, if you have to."

She led them down the steep bluff, clutching the bag with left-over food and the map in it. She wouldn't leave food or map behind again, no matter what. They slid most of the way down, bouncing on their fannies, giggling. At the foot of the bluff, Dicey turned upriver.

They found a rowboat easily. It was upended on the ground beside a long private dock. Waiting for dark, they watched nervously up the cliff to the house whose lighted windows looked out over the silver river. When full dark came, somebody inside pulled curtains over the long windows. Then the children stealthily approached the boat.

James and Dicey carried it down to the end of the dock and lowered it noiselessly into the water. James held the painter while Dicey went back for the bag, the oars and Maybeth and Sammy. They were accustomed to boats, so they had no trouble getting into it quietly. Maybeth sat at the bow, Sammy and James at the stern. Dicey shipped the oars and James pushed off. The boat slid away from the dock.

Dicey lifted the oars in their oarlocks. She brought them down cautiously, unused to their weight. The oars bit into the black water, and the boat shot ahead.

The current carried them slightly downstream, Dicey's strokes carried them across, the smooth water eased their passage. The bridge loomed overhead. Its thick pilings caused races in the current that could trap a small boat and maybe even overturn it. Dicey knew enough to simply follow these races until the boat had floated out of their currents. Then she dipped the oars once again into the dark water.

The sky was dark. The air was dark, so dark that they could barely make out one another's faces. The water flowed beneath them, black and bottomless.

Dicey headed for the lights on the opposite shore. It felt good to stretch the muscles in her back and arms, to lean back and then pull forward against the oars.

In the middle of the river the current eased and the boat shot straight ahead. Then, as they drew near the far bank, Dicey felt the twists and eddies begin again. James directed her to a huge marina, where lights burned in many buildings and in many of the small windows of the boats tied in rows along the docks. It looked sort of like a parking lot. They pulled up beside a boat that was dark and empty and tied their dinghy to its stern. Dicey thought that if she left the dinghy there it had a good chance of being claimed or returned.

They had come down close to the mouth of the river, where its water flowed out into the Sound. A small town lay on the low flatlands. They walked through the town, to the south. It was late at night and the houses became fewer, but there was no safe place to sleep. After an hour, they were all tired, and Sammy stumbled with every third step. Dicey put him on her back, giving James the grocery bag. She discovered then how much the long rowing had strained her muscles.

They came to a church, shining white in the dark air. Behind it stretched a graveyard, with groves of trees planted among the tombstones. Dicey turned toward the graveyard.

Behind her, James drew in his breath.

At the first grove of trees, Dicey put Sammy down. He was already half-asleep and just curled up on the ground. Maybeth settled beside him without a word. Dicey stood, looking at James.

"It's a graveyard, Dicey," James said.

"I know," she said. "But we're tired."

"Do you believe in ghosts?" he asked.

"I never saw one," Dicey said. She sat down. James sat down right beside her. They could see tombstones placed in neat rows. Some of them had statues on top.

"I don't believe in ghosts," James said. "All the same, I don't like this place. It's—too quiet."

Indeed, the silence was thick as fog around them. The silence vibrated, as if with things beneath it struggling to break through.

Dicey yawned. She was too tired, the day had been too long, for this kind of worrying. "I like quiet."

James flicked his eyes over the cemetery. "We're all gonna die, you know."

Dicey nodded. "Not for a long time."

"Do you think Momma's dead?"

"I don't know. How could I know that?"

"No matter what, we're all gonna die," James remarked. "So it doesn't matter what we do, does it?"

Dicey was thinking about other things, about maps and food. She didn't answer.

"Unless there's a Hell, to punish us. But I don't think there is. I really don't. Or Heaven. Or anything. Dicey?"

"Yeah?"

"You know the only thing you can count on, the only thing that's always true? It's the speed of light. Louis told me Einstein figured it out, 186,000 miles per second. That's the only sure thing. Everything else—changes. I was proud of Sammy for stealing that food, you know that?"

"So was I."

"You were? You sure didn't act it. You acted angry."

"Well, I was."

"Dicey, that doesn't make sense."

"I'm too tired to make sense, James. I'm trying to figure out where we might be. We came way downriver. We'll have sandwiches for breakfast and finish the food up so we don't have to carry it." Dicey let her mind wander. "Did you ever hear Momma talk about her father, James? We had to have a grandfather, you know."

"Probably dead," James said. "Everyone's either dead or dying."

"Go to *sleep,* James," Dicey said. "That's just morbid. You'll make yourself crazy."

"I make myself crazy when I try to figure out a good reason why I *shouldn't* be morbid," James answered.

"Go to sleep."

"I don't want to."

"Go to sleep, please. You're not crazy. You'll never be crazy. You're just too smart for your own good. Anyone who stays awake so he can have ideas like that . . . well, he ought to be going to sleep."

Dicey lay back and closed her eyes resolutely. James sighed.

CHAPTER 7

Morning broke low and cloudy. Streaks of smudged gray clouds covered the sky. "It's still true," James said. He looked out over the cemetery, where bright green grass contrasted with the faded marble of tombstones, and the tombstones reflected the cold gray of the sky.

"Some of them are bent over," James said. "I bet they're old, really old. Hundreds of years."

After breakfast, while Dicey gathered together their litter and packed it into the paper bag to be discarded at the first trash can they saw, the little ones explored the graveyard. Sammy stayed with James, because James could read everything to him. Maybeth wandered among the rows, studying the statues of angels and lambs.

Dicey had a sudden fear that she had forgotten where they were going, so she recited Aunt Cilla's address to herself. Mrs. Cilla Logan, 1724 Ocean Drive, Bridgeport. She ought to make the others memorize it. She made a mental note to do that as they walked that day.

Then she studied the map and admitted that they would have to go back to Route 1. She didn't want to. She wanted to stay among big houses and tall trees, on the shore road that would keep her close to the water. But Route 1 was the shorter way, even though it looped up north of the Thruway before entering New Haven.

Those decisions made, Dicey went to call the others. They had to start. They had money and a map, their stomachs were full—it wasn't a bad way to begin.

While she waited for Maybeth to return and for James and Sammy to finish working out what was written on a cracked stone that slanted back toward the earth, Dicey looked at the gravestones about her. She read an inscription: *Home is the hunter, home from the hill, and the sailor home from the sea.*

What a thing to put on a grave.

As if to say that being dead was home. Home, for Dicey, was their house in Provincetown, where the wind made the boards creak in a way that was almost music. Or Aunt Cilla's big white house that faced over the water, the one she had dreamed about. Being dead wasn't going home, was it? Unless—and she remembered what James had been saying last night—home was the place where you finally stayed, forever and ever. Then this person was home, and nobody would be truly home until he, or she, died. It was an awful thought.

Only living people had homes. That was the difference.

(If Momma was dead, where was her grave? What was written on it? Nobody would even know her name or who she was or when she was born.)

If you took home to mean where you rested content and never wanted to go anywhere else, then Dicey had never had a home. The ocean always made her restless; so even Provincetown, even their own remembered kitchen, wasn't home. That was why Dicey always ran along the sand beside the ocean, as if she had to race the waves. The ocean wasn't home, then, and neither was anyplace else. Nobody could be home, really, until he was in his grave. Nobody could rest, really, until then.

It was a cold, hard thought written on that cold, hard stone. But maybe true.

If Dicey died, she guessed she wouldn't mind having this poem on her tombstone, now that she thought about it. She was the hunter and the sailor, and she guessed dead people did lie quietly in their graves.

"James," she said when he came back. "You know what you were saying last night?"

"Yeah?"

"You're pretty smart," Dicey said.

"I know," he said.

A pale sun showed behind the clouds. It looked like there were two layers of clouds now, one layer lower, like a gray veil spread before the other. Where the veil broke, you could see silvery islands of clouds on which tall angels might stand. Not cute little Christmas angels, but high, stern angels in white robes, whose faces were sad and serious from being near God all day and hearing His decisions about the world. Dicey was hypnotized by the molten silver of the cloudy islands and not until the veil of fuzzy gray blew across it again did she begin their march of the day.

Route 1 had not changed in their absence. Stores, shopping centers, garages, furniture outlets, restaurants, quick-food stands: the cement procession marched on, broken only by traffic lights dangling from heavy wires over the roadway. Traffic was heavier, and the exhaust and the diesel fumes could not rise into the sky on that first gray day, but hung over everything. Their faces and hands felt grimy all the time. Day by day, their money dwindled away.

When she thought back on this part of their journey, Dicey found that she could remember very little of it, that it all blurred together in her memory, all the long days, all the strange nights. They spent a night on a shaly beach, with no shelter and no fire. They spent a night in a grove of pines that stood at the entrance to an estate, where Dicey woke frequently with the fear that they would be discovered by the owners of the big stone house that lay at the end of the driveway. They spent a night by the entrance to another state park. As Route 1 looped north, they crossed under the Thruway and spent a miserable night huddled at the back of a shopping center. They slept sitting together on the concrete walkway, against the concrete wall. As they approached the large city of New Haven, the buildings were closer together and there were no more open spaces.

In all these days, the sun had come out only twice, once for an hour early in the morning, and once late in the evening to give them a fine sunset. Slowly, rain had been building. The rain finally began to fall during the night they spent in a tiny playground beside the Branford River. The next day they spent the last of their money, standing in the rain to eat cold doughnuts. The rain continued, steady and gentle, all that day. Dicey led them under the shelter of an empty car wash for that night and roused them early so they would be gone before anybody arrived to open the business or to wash a car. She roused them early even though nobody in his right mind would wash his car on a rainy day. You couldn't expect people to act as if they were in their right minds. Dicey was taking no chances.

They approached New Haven and Dicey took out the map, which she carried under her shirt, where the cloth and her arm would protect it. She planned their way through the city. She wanted to get across it before dark. She didn't like cities and didn't want to have to spend the night in one.

That they had nothing to eat and no money to buy food with, these facts she refused to think of. They would cross the city first, and then get some money. They would cross the city hungry because they had to.

James, Maybeth and Sammy greeted this announcement

without a change in expression. They did not speak or sing anymore, just followed Dicey meekly. If she had food to give them, they ate it. If there was no food, then they said nothing. Dicey thought she might prefer to have them complain, but that was another worry she could not deal with until they had crossed the city. That was a worry that went along with the limp James had developed from a hole worn into the sole of his left sneaker; with the gray under Maybeth's eyes and not having heard her voice for days; with Sammy's new habit of clinging to her hand and doing whatever she told him, right away, not even the start of a quarrel.

James, Maybeth and Sammy listened quietly while she recited the streets they would take to cross the city. "We have to get off Route One to cross the rivers," she said. "So we'll follow the train tracks for a while, then take a couple of blocks on a street named Quinnipiac, up to Ferry Street. That will take us over one branch of the river. When Ferry meets with Chapel Street, we'll turn left and start walking across the city. We'll go over a river, then by a big college. There, we'll be about halfway. Okay?"

They nodded, three pale faces.

"Then, we're going to have to get back to Route One, so we'll turn left onto a cross-street to meet up with it. It doesn't matter which street we take. We can follow Route One the rest of the way out of the city."

They nodded, six blank eyes.

"So let's go. Or we won't get across before dark."

Dicey walked with Maybeth and James took Sammy's hand. At first, most of the buildings were low, four or five stories of soiled brick. They walked beside the railroad tracks and saw only the backs of buildings, houses with no grass in the yards, ripped curtains in dirty windows, fences that looked like some giant rat had been gnawing at them. The empty windows of factories stared down. Rain fell steadily. Sometimes they would glimpse a face through an open window. Most often, except for the people looking out of train windows, they saw no one.

They crossed a small river, walking on a narrow, fenced-over walkway that was built to run beside the road. Rain showered down and made miniature puddles on the turgid river water. Green and oily slime floated on the river and gathered in stringy islands by its banks.

Chapel Street was wide, lined with stores. Groceries, five-and-dimes, an occasional movie theater, army-navy surplus stores, liquor stores with metal gates across the windows. The street passed a small park before it crossed another river. On the other side of the river, tall modern buildings, with whole walls of windows, lifted up out above the squat brick constructions.

The Tillermans walked on, over the Thruway. They passed hotels, clothing stores, jewelers and bookstores; then old brick churches, with signs out front saying what sermon would be given the next Sunday, and a few large old city homes. As evening thickened and lights were turned on, you could see inside where large mirrors hung on ivory-white walls and long curtains framed polished wood tables.

Dicey did not look in the store windows as the others did, or in the windows of the houses. She looked in the unsmiling faces of the people walking past her.

Night, hurrying down upon them, was not in their favor, nor was the rain, falling steadily. But they were all past hunger, she thought—she knew she wasn't hungry anymore. Just tired.

It was after ten when they came to the college and the square park that lay at the center of the city, bordered by the college on one side, a chapel on the opposite and the city on the others.

Dicey finally admitted that they would have to sleep the night in the city. This park would have to do, even though it was too open. She chose a cluster of bushes far from any street lamp. "Look, you all go in there," she pointed to a kind of nest made by the low branches of the piny bushes. "You curl up there, as covered as you can. I'll stay out here and keep watch."

Without a word, they obeyed.

The rain pattered down. People hurried across the park, their heads bent. Dicey sat on a bench near her family's hiding place and looked across the park to a long wall of college dormitories. Some of the windows had lights in them. One had someone sitting in it.

Dicey sat and stared into the night without seeing, without thinking. Lights shone all around her. The streetlight cast puddles of light on the wet sidewalks. The raindrops caught the light from the lamps and glowed, falling, like yellow pebbles. Bright red neon light shone hazily on top of a building in the distance. The arch-topped windows of the dormitories showed like yellow cutouts. The water on the roads and sidewalks reflected light with a silvery sheen.

Dicey sat and kept the watch. Three little children, alone in a city: she couldn't sleep.

How many more days until Bridgeport? And Aunt Cilla's big white house.

How would they get money? Why had she thrown away the twenty dollars Sammy found? How would they eat all those days until Bridgeport?

How was she going to see to it that they got there, when she didn't even know where it was?

Dicey thought the rain had grown warm, until a stuffiness in her nose and an ache in her throat (like she was trying to swallow an apple whole) told her she was crying. But she never cried! And now she couldn't stop.

She heard footsteps approaching, the first in a long time. Just one person. She bowed her chin down and folded her arms across her chest, trying to look as if she was asleep. She held her breath against a sob that was swelling in her throat. But she kept an eye out. If she needed to, she could break and run, away from the bushes where her family slept. They all knew Aunt Cilla's address.

Somebody—a man she guessed from his pants legs and loafers—sat down at the other end of her bench. His pant legs were wet, as if he had been walking for a long time. They clung against his calves. Dicey didn't move.

But the sob moved. It swelled up and broke through her clenched teenth. Dicey's panicked eyes moved to the face of the person beside her.

He had turned to look at her. He was young. He wore a yellow raincoat and his hands were jammed into the pockets. In the dim light, his eyes were dark and serious. His hair was plastered down over his forehead.

When he spoke, his voice was flat. "You looked like a girl crying. I thought you were a girl crying. Can I help?"

Dicey bit her lip and shook her head.

"You lost?"

Dicey shook her head again.

"Okay." He seemed to believe her. "Can you walk home from here?"

This made Dicey feel like smiling, but not from laughter. She shook her head.

"Cat got your tongue?"

"Nope."

"Okay. I'll tell you what I think. I think you don't have a place to sleep, you're probably hungry, you're frightened and worried, and you don't want to tell me anything. So far, am I right?"

"Yeah."

He shifted on the bench and turned to face Dicey. "Okay. Now. You don't have to believe this, but you can trust me. I've been in your kind of jam myself, more than once. If it helps, I'm studying at the college, if that tells you anything about me."

"Schools are closed in summer."

"Not colleges. They have summer session. I'm taking a geology course because I flunked it this year and I have to pass it to graduate. I want to graduate next June."

"You don't sound stupid," Dicey said.

"Oh, I'm not. I just didn't work at it, so it's my own fault. Look, I have an idea for you."

"Yeah?"

"Yeah. Don't say no right away. Okay? Okay. Why don't you come with me and get some food and camp out in my rooms tonight. It's better than the Green—it's dry at least. I've got a roommate so you won't have to worry about being alone with me."

"I've got roommates too," Dicey said.

He smiled.

"No, three—over there."

He looked at her carefully. "Okay then, we'll all go. All your age?"

"No. Younger. They're my brothers and my sister."

His jaw fell a little, and then he pulled it up sharply. His eyebrows twitched, as if he were keeping them from shooting up in surprise. "Will wonders never cease?" he asked. He stood up briskly. "Let's see the worst. I've made up my mind anyway and I guess four kids can sleep on our floor. You've made up your mind to trust me, haven't you?"

"I'm afraid so," Dicey said. That made him laugh, but she didn't know why. "Wait here," she said.

He stood absolutely still, as if to show that he would do exactly what she told him, and a smile played around his lips. He wasn't serious. He was teasing her. Dicey looked up at him through the rainy light, still trying to decide. He made his mouth still, and then she nodded at him. "Okay," she said. "But we don't have any money."

"I do," he said.

Dicey roused her family. They woke easily, even Sammy, who usually slept deeply.

They rose up out of the bushes, Maybeth first, then James, then Sammy. Their eyes were surprised, but they didn't question her. She felt suddenly very sorry for them. She wondered if she had done the right thing, when she began this whole journey. Was she doing the right thing now?

With one arm around Maybeth's shoulders, holding Sammy's hand tight, Dicey led her family back to where the young man stood waiting. James tagged behind, limping slightly.

The smile went out of the young man's eyes when he saw them. Dicey was briefly worried, but he crouched down on his heels, ignoring the puddles, and looked up at them all.

"You don't have to feel sorry for us," Dicey said. "You can back out."

"Not on your life. That's not it. I'm curious—intensely curious—about you. What are your names? Mine's Windy . . . well, Windy's what they call me here because they say I talk too much. How did you get here? Where are your parents? Are you hungry?"

"Yes," Sammy said fiercely.

"When's the last time you ate?"

"Yesterday, I think," Dicey said.

"Then what are we hanging around here for?" the young man asked. He stood up and took James's hand. James was too tired to protest this extraordinary gesture. "I know just the place," Windy said. He led them to one of the city sides of the Green and into a small diner that had a long counter and four booths. The clock read 1:30. Windy herded them into a booth, then brought over menus. He called the waitress before they had even opened the menus and ordered each of them a large glass of milk. He asked for a cup of coffee for himself.

Dicey could barely see the words and prices. Food smells filled the diner, and she was out of the rain. It was warm and bright. The words on the menu swam before her eyes. She looked at their rescuer.

He sat with James beside him. He had dark curly hair and a black mustache and black eyebrows that moved up and down or wrinkled as if they had a life all their own.

"Who'd believe this?" he asked, meeting Dicey's eyes. "I ask you."

The waitress put his coffee down before him and gave each child a tall glass of milk. "Y'want straws?"

Dicey shook her head and grabbed for the glass. They drank, in large gulps at first, and then, when their stomachs had welcomed the first eager swallows, more slowly. All four glasses were empty when the children put them down.

"What can I getcha?" the waitress asked.

Windy looked at them. They had forgotten the menus. He grinned. "Four hamburgers. No, make that eight. Four large orders of fries. That's all for now, but we'll probably have dessert. Do you have any apple pie?"

"Yeah."

"Give me a piece of pie now, please," he said. "And save four pieces for the kids."

She shuffled away, writing on her order pad. "Is that okay?" Windy asked Dicey. "We can change it if it's not okay. It wouldn't be any trouble. But I thought maybe it would be hard for you to decide, and the little one doesn't look old enough to read yet."

"I can too," Sammy said.

"Apologies for insulting you," Windy said, and his eyebrows waggled, as if they were laughing.

"I wanted hamburgers," Sammy said. "Anyway. And french fries. That's what I wanted."

"Ah," Windy said. "And what is your name?"

Sammy looked at Dicey. She nodded.

"Sammy," he said.

"How old are you?"

"Six. How old are you?"

"Twenty-one. Really very old."

Dicey remembered her manners. It was easier to remember manners with milk in her stomach and food on the way. "I'm Dicey and this is Maybeth and that's James." She answered the question in his eyes before he asked it: "I'm thirteen, Maybeth is nine, James is ten."

His dark eyes studied her. "I once ran away, when I was James's age," he said. He told them a long story about running away one morning when he was afraid to go to school because he was short and skinny and somebody was waiting there to beat him up. In the middle of the story their food was set before them. Dicey stopped listening. Windy could eat and talk at the same time. But the Tillermans ate in absolute silence, in huge bites, barely tasting what they chewed before they swallowed it. They all had apple pie for dessert. Throughout the meal, Windy's voice blew over them, smooth and steady. It didn't matter what he was saying.

Windy paid the bill and left a dollar on the table for the waitress. Dicey, warmed from within, tried to thank him, but he shrugged it off. He took them back to the Green, saying he wished he could stop the rain because he, for one, had had enough of it and he suspected they had too. He led them across the Green to the long dormitory building. There, the hallways were narrow and brown, like tunnels. They climbed up four flights of stairs, twisting past closed doors. Finally, Windy threw open a door and ushered them into a room.

It was a mess. Ashtrays overflowed with cigarette ashes and butts. A newspaper had been left scattered on the floor around one armchair. Books were piled on the three desks and on the low table before the sofa and along the mantelpiece. Beer cans lay around a wastebasket that was so full it looked as if it wanted to erupt like a volcano and spew trash all over the room. It was warm and messy and comfortable, and filled with yellow light. Outside, dark rain fell. But they were inside.

Windy went through a door and turned on a light in the next room. Dicey caught a glimpse of bunk beds and dressers. He returned with an armload of clothing, mostly T-shirts and sweatshirts. "The bathroom's through that door." He pointed to the door beside the one they'd entered through. "Go get off your wet clothes and put some of these on. I guess you might want to go to the bathroom too."

"I do," Sammy said, so definitely that Dicey smiled.

"Meanwhile, I'll see if anyone's around."

When they had gone to the bathroom, they covered themselves with Windy's dry shirts, which, if none too fresh, were dry and warm. They hung their own clothes on the towel racks to dry. Dicey washed out all of their underwear, using the cake of soap on the sink. They returned to the living room. Windy waited there and another young man was with him.

"Stewart," Windy said, "let me introduce my findlings." He remembered all of their names and ages. "This is Stewart, my roommate," he said.

Stewart smoked on his pipe and looked at them. He was tall, taller than Windy, and skinny like Windy. He had blond hair, so pale it was almost white, hanging fine and straight down to his ears. He had a strong, square jaw and a mustache as blond as the hair on his head. His eyes, as he looked at the Tillermans, might have been gray or blue, Dicey couldn't decide which. It was as if his eyes changed back and forth between gray and blue, but she wasn't sure if that was possible.

"What's going on?" he asked Windy.

"I found them, as I said. Dicey first, and then the others. They need a place to sleep and it's raining cats and dogs, and mice and pterodactyls, and God knows what else out there—so I thought to myself, why not here with us?"

Stewart smiled quietly. "Why not indeed? I'll come in with you and they can have my bunks."

James grinned at Dicey. Real beds.

Stewart took them into his room. He cleared books and papers off the top bunk, and James climbed up onto it. Sammy and Maybeth lay down on opposite ends of the bottom bunk. Dicey thought they looked like two little dolls in a dollhouse, lying there. James was half-asleep before she turned out the light and closed the door behind her.

She thought she would go back and sleep on the floor in that room, but Windy said she should take the sofa in the living room for her bed. He brought a pillow and blanket from his own room. "What do I need those for?" Dicey asked. "You keep them. I'll be fine."

Windy passed her the armload of linen. "Go ahead. Live it up. I can do without for one night."

"*You* can do without," Stewart said. "Listen, he took them off the bed where I'm going to sleep. And if you really don't want them, I'd be glad to have them." Dicey passed them over.

"Can we talk a little before you go to sleep, Dicey?" Windy asked. "Are you too tired?"

Dicey was so comfortable that she would have been glad to talk all night. She didn't want to go to sleep, because then she wouldn't be able to enjoy being comfortable. But she wasn't sure she wanted to answer any questions. She was too brain-tired to be as careful as she ought.

They all sat down. Dicey sat alone in the middle of the sofa, and the young men took two arm chairs.

Stewart started. "Windy says you're not lost."

"No. I know where we are."

"A fundamentalist," Windy said to Stewart. His eyebrows moved. He asked Dicey, "What about your family? Do they know where you are?"

Dicey shook her head. "But that doesn't matter."

"Why not?" Windy asked. Dicey didn't answer that.

"Are you in trouble?" Windy asked.

"I don't think so," Dicey said. "I hope not."

"Okay," Windy said. He leaned forward and rested his chin on his hands. His eyebrows were temporarily still. "What *will* you tell us? We'd like to help if we can. Do you believe that?"

"Yeah," Dicey said. "Yeah, I do." She thought. "I mean, you already did, didn't you?"

"How about your parents?" Stewart asked. He was resting his head against the back of the chair, looking at her.

It wasn't that she couldn't lie to him. She could lie to anyone and make it good, if she had to—she'd certainly discovered that. But she didn't want to, not to him or to Windy. She wasn't going to lie to them, she decided.

"We don't have parents. We're on our own," she said. Stewart's eyes did not change, but waited, quiet as water.

"Wait a minute," Dicey said. "Let me think a minute, okay?" He nodded. "We come from Provincetown, in Massachusetts. On the Cape." He nodded his head, just a little. She heard

Windy swallow back a question. "My father walked out on us when I was about seven. Just before Sammy was born. We were okay until lately, when things happened wrong. My mother lost her job. And things. So she told us we were going to Bridgeport, where she has an aunt, and we all packed into our car."

Stewart held her eyes with his.

"We were in Peewauket and she left us to wait in the car while she went into a big mall. But she didn't come out, and we couldn't find her. So I decided that we should go ahead to Bridgeport and hope she'll meet us there."

Stewart asked, "How long did you wait for her?"

"All day and all night," Dicey said. "We waited in the car. She didn't come back. I'm hoping . . . I don't know. The only place I know she might be is Bridgeport."

"What if she isn't there?"" Windy asked.

"There's this aunt Cilla," Dicey explained.

"Do you know her?" Stewart asked.

"No. But she sends us cards every Christmas."

"You didn't ask anyone for help?" Stewart asked. "The police?"

Dicey shook her head firmly. "I don't know for sure what they would do. They might send us to a foster home. Or split us up. I don't know what Momma—she didn't say anything, she just disappeared . . . I have no idea what happened. No idea. I couldn't risk telling the police. And that's all true," Dicey said.

"How long ago was this?" Windy asked.

"In June. Maybe two weeks, maybe three."

"And you've been walking from Peewauket all this time?"

"We stayed at a park once. The little kids can't go very fast."

"Is that all you want to tell?" Windy asked.

"Please," Dicey answered.

He nodded his head and his eyebrows arched as he smiled at her. "Then I say we get some sleep. What do you say, Stew?"

"Just thinking about all that walking makes me tired," Stewart said.

"You okay here, Dicey?" Windy asked.

Dicey nodded. She hoped she hadn't made a mistake in telling them.

Windy turned off the lights and Dicey stretched out on the sofa. She didn't even hear the door close behind them.

CHAPTER 8

Dicey opened her eyes to the gray ceiling of the living room. She opened her ears to city noises floating in on warm air that came through the open windows. She sat up, alarmed at finding herself alone. Then the events of the night before came back to her, and she relaxed, stretched, bounced on the sofa and smiled to herself. She went to the window and looked out.

The rain had been swept away with the darkness. Everything on the green below sparkled in the early morning air. It even smelled fresh outside.

Dicey remembered that in the bathroom she had seen a stall shower. She went in quietly. She folded up their clothes hanging on the rack, except for her own, and put them in a pile on the sofa. Then she went back and turned on the hot water, so it would be hot when she had gone to the bathroom. When she was ready, she stripped off Windy's T-shirt and stepped into the warm water, pulling the curtain closed behind her. The warm water beat down on her back and her chest and her hips and her arms. She revolved slowly, her eyes closed, like a wind-up toy that was running down. She had forgotten just how it felt to take a bath or a shower. It felt gentle and warm, like somebody's arms around you.

Dicey took a cake of soap and washed herself, head to foot, hair and ears, toes and fingers, face, torso. The soap slid onto the floor. She bent over to pick it up and the water tattooed on her fanny.

She took one last slow turn under the water that turned into five last slow turns. Then she turned both handles off and stepped out.

As she rubbed herself dry and dressed, she thought: I can do anything. Anything. We're going to be all right. It's all going to be all right.

She squeezed some toothpaste onto her finger and brushed her teeth. Her teeth squeaked and her mouth tasted minty. She grinned at herself in the mirror and ran her fingers through her damp hair.

She opened wide the door of the bathroom and saw, not only her brothers and sister, sleep still in their dazed eyes, but also wild-haired Windy, and Stewart. Maybeth came to take Dicey's hand.

Dicey asked Windy if they could all have showers. She turned on the water for Maybeth and returned to the living room.

"So. What's next?" Windy was asking. Stewart had sat down in the same chair he occupied the last night. He looked around, but didn't speak. His face looked fuzzy and confused, not quite awake. Windy answered himself:

"Breakfast is next. And then we have to see about getting these kids to Bridgeport."

"Really?" Dicey asked.

"Really," Windy said. "Stew has a car and it's only—an hour from here? You'll do it, won't you, Stew?"

The gray-blue eyes rested on Dicey. "I've got an eleven o'clock class."

"Then after the class," Windy said.

"Okay. Sure. Do you mind waiting?" Stewart asked Dicey.

Dicey shook her head at his foolishness. "Do you know how

long it would take us to walk it? Three days. Maybe four. I'd be a jerk to mind waiting a couple of hours," she said.

"And you're not a jerk," Windy said. He was leaning against the mantelpiece, looking down at her.

"Nope," Dicey said. Maybe she should have been more polite, but she felt too happy for that. "Other things. Bossy. And I lie and I fight, but I'm not a jerk."

Windy looked amused. He exchanged a glance with Stewart.

The little children paraded in and out of the bathroom, putting their clothes on in their bedroom. At last, everybody was dressed.

"Can you lend me some cash?" Windy asked. "Stewart?"

"I've got a twenty," Stewart said. He went into his bedroom.

The living room was filled with warm air and sunlight from the windows. The Tillermans were all fresh and clean and not starving. They would have breakfast. They would get a ride to Bridgeport.

It was almost over.

Stewart stood in the doorway of his room. Dicey looked at him and smiled, but he did not smile back at her. He waited there, silent, and looked over the small group of people standing between the sofa and the fireplace. His eyes were gray now, a distant wintry gray. "I can't find it," he said. He looked at Windy over the heads of the children.

"You sure?" Windy asked. "It's not like you to keep good track of your money." His eyebrows made dark arches over his eyes.

"I'm sure this time," Stewart said, still not looking at the children. "I just cashed the check yesterday and put the money in my wallet. I didn't spend any. My wallet was in the top drawer."

Despite the warmth of the day and the brightness of the room, Dicey felt a chill spread out from her stomach and everything grew shades darker, as if a big black cloud had just covered the sun. She looked at Sammy.

Sammy shook his head decisively.

James's eyes were on the floor and his hands were clenched in his pockets. "James," Dicey said.

"Whyn'cha ask Sammy," James said. His eyes were hot and angry.

"Sammy said he didn't," Dicey answered. She held on to her temper.

"Then neither did I," James said.

Dicey looked at Stewart, who still stood in the doorway to his room where the little kids had slept last night. He looked back at her and she was ashamed.

"Give it to me, James," she said quietly.

James pulled one hand out of his pocket and opened it wide. A crumpled bill fell to the floor. "Get it yourself."

Dicey exploded. "I told you we don't steal and you just go ahead and do it. And then you try to lie to me about it. I could kill you, James. You hear me? You're so smart, but you can't even figure out—" She was so angry the words got jammed up in her throat. "Look what you've done!"

James stood with his head bowed. Silence filled the room, a cold silence.

The crumpled bill lay there on the floor. Dicey couldn't look at the faces of the young men.

"You've ruined everything," she said. She strode to the window and looked out, pounding with her fist on the windowsill. She tried to find something to say to James that would make him fall down onto the floor, that would knock him over and hurt him.

Finally James spoke. "You didn't yell at Sammy, you didn't say you wished he was dead."

"Sammy's six!" Dicey turned around. "And Sammy didn't take money, he took food. And Sammy didn't take it from someone who'd helped us. Even you can see the difference."

"He"—James kept his eyes on the floor but he jerked his head toward Stewart—"doesn't need the money like we do. He's got sweaters and guitars."

"So what!" Dicey hissed. "And who are you to say, anyhow? All I asked you was to do what I say, only that—and now—"

Maybeth went to James and looked up at him for a minute. Then she took hold of the hand he had out of his pocket.

"You're a thief," Dicey spat the words at James. His hazel eyes flicked up to hers. "You steal."

"Big deal," James answered, from deep within his own anger. "It doesn't matter."

"Okay." Dicey matched anger to anger. "Okay, if that's the way you want it. But until we get to Aunt Cilla's you will do exactly what I say to do—or I'll leave you behind. Do you understand?" James nodded. "Then we better get out of here."

James nodded.

"Apologize, James," Dicey ordered.

He had to obey her, so he apologized, looking into the empty fireplace. "I'm sorry."

"Okay. Let's go," Dicey said to her family. She felt sick inside.

"Why?" Windy unexpectedly spoke. He bent down and picked up the bill, smoothed it with his fingers and held it out to Stewart, who came forward to take it. "As far as I'm concerned, we found Stew's money. Right, Stew?"

"No," Stewart said. "But you did want to borrow it, didn't you?" He handed it back to Windy.

Dicey wished they were out of the room and on their way again, on their own.

"Dicey?" Stewart said her name. She looked at him. "What did Sammy steal?"

"Some lunchbags at a park," Dicey said. "Two. It was different. We needed food, sort of. He thought we did, anyway. He doesn't understand. He did it to help. There was a wallet in one bag, but we took that back. Sort of. Not just because it was stealing money though. Really because we didn't want to have police coming in. I guess James doesn't understand either. He's not bad."

Stewart looked at her and she looked right back at him. James was her brother and she would have to stick by him; and she wanted to stick by him. How could Stewart know James? He couldn't, but Dicey could.

"It does matter, James," said Stewart.

"Why? We all die anyway," James said.

"Sure, but you can see to it that you like yourself when you die," Stewart answered. "You can be sure you don't hurt anybody while you're alive. Especially, you can be sure you don't hurt yourself. Are you a thief?"

James shook his head.

"But you stole," Stewart said. "Who did you hurt? You're right about me; I'm not rich but I can go to the bank and take out another twenty. So you didn't hurt me very much. You hurt yourself. More than anyone you hurt yourself."

"That doesn't make sense. Nothing matters. There's nothing you can count on—except the speed of light. And dying," James said.

"So that's what it is," Stewart said. He studied James's face. "Well that may be true but it's not a big enough truth to contain me. I plan to be a man when I get through. Not only a man, I plan to be a good man."

"Why?" James asked.

"Because I owe it to myself," Stewart said.

"Is that all?"

"No," Stewart said, but he didn't add anything to it.

"I don't understand," James said.

Stewart didn't answer him.

"Can I learn to understand?"

"Maybe," Stewart said.

"I'm smart," James said. "Will that help?"

"Maybe," Stewart said. "Maybe not."

James nodded.

Dicey waited for the conversation to continue, but it didn't, and James just stood there looking at Stewart as if Stewart were a mountain or something terribly large. So she began to move toward the door, pulling Sammy with her.

"Hold it," Windy said. "Where are you going? Dicey? We've got breakfast to get and then Stew's going to drive you to Bridgeport. That's right, isn't it, Stew?" His eyebrows moved as he spoke, emphasizing his words.

"Of course," Stewart answered. "Get me some doughnuts and coffee, will you?"

Windy took the Tillermans to the diner they had eaten at the night before. Dicey followed along, as quiet as Maybeth. She felt as if she was no longer in charge. In a way, she was relieved to let somebody else give directions and make decisions. In another way she was angry at these young men for taking over their lives, for telling them when and where to eat, for leaving her out of the conversation with James.

In the diner, which looked dingy by daylight, Dicey had fried eggs, while the others had pancakes. She had time now to enjoy the taste of her food. When she had eaten both eggs, she took one piece of toast and mopped up some yolk onto it.

Never had she enjoyed a meal more. She said so to Windy and he told her she looked like she'd like to climb onto the plate and roll around in the eggs. Dicey giggled and said she guessed she might. Windy finished his own breakfast and Maybeth's. Dicey took part of Sammy's pancakes and gave the rest to James, who was never full. They all drank milk.

When they returned to the room and Windy had given Stewart his coffee and doughnuts, he said good-bye to the Tillermans. "I've got a lab this morning and you'll probably be gone when I return," he said, shaking hands solemnly with each of them.

They thanked him, but he waved the words aside. "Any time," he said. "It was fun." He grinned at them and his eyebrows arched.

Stewart quickly wolfed down the four doughnuts and while he was sipping coffee he pulled out a guitar and played. The Tillermans sat quietly and listened.

His was not an ordinary guitar, although it looked like one; it had a belly and neck and six strings like ordinary guitars, but instead of cradling it against his arm, Stewart laid it on his lap. He held a metal bar to the strings of the neck and plucked the strings over the belly. The sound this odd guitar made was metallic and round and slidy. When he reached over for his coffee cup, Dicey asked him what it was.

"A Dobro," he answered. He explained how it was made and how he played it. Then he played a slow, mournful melody on it, concentrating hard, biting his lip, leaning over the instrument and moving his shoulders with the rhythm.

Maybeth stood beside him and watched. "That's 'Greensleeves,'" she said.

Stewart nodded. "Do you know it? You want to sing it?"

Maybeth sang the old song in her clear voice. "'Alas, my love, you do me wrong, to cast me off discourteously.'"

At the conclusion, Stewart smiled at her. "You do know it."

"Momma sang to us," Maybeth said. "We know a lot of songs."

"What else do you sing?" Stewart asked. He looked around at all of them.

"Play something you like," Dicey answered him.

"I play blue grass," Stewart said. "You know what that is?"

They didn't, so he played a song about a miner's child who dreamed her daddy would die if he went to the mines that day, but he went anyway.

"That's silly," Maybeth said, when he had finished.

"Okay, then, what about this?" Stewart asked. "'Oft I sing for my friends,'" he sang. His voice was soft as clouds and clear as the sky could be. "'When death's dark form I see. When I reach my journey's end, who will sing for me?'"

It was a short song, and Maybeth asked him to sing it again, and she joined in with him.

When that was finished, he looked at them. "Do you all sing? Like that?"

Dicey nodded.

Then Stewart put down the Dobro and said he had to go to class, but as soon as he got back he'd take them to Bridgeport. He went into his room and came back with a guitar case, out of which he took a regular guitar. "You can mess around on these if you like," he said. Even after he left, the room was filled with the harmony they had made, and the singing.

James picked up the Dobro and plucked at it with his fingers. "Dicey? I'm sorry. Really. I won't ever do anything like that again."

"I know," Dicey said. Her anger was entirely forgotten. "I didn't mean most of what I said."

"You think Stewart is smarter than Louis?" James asked. "I do," he said.

"How should I know that?" Dicey asked. "I like him a lot better. I like Windy too. Maybeth?"

Maybeth nodded. She was looking at a book of pictures.

"Sammy?"

Sammy stared out the window. "How long do you think it'll be? Until we get there?"

"Not long. They said an hour."

"What's it like there?"

"I dunno, Sammy. Why?"

"Will Momma be there?"

Dicey looked at the back of his round little head, where the yellow hair stood out at crazy angles. *No,* her heart said inside her. "I dunno, Sammy," she said aloud. He didn't answer, just stood looking out.

Stewart's car was a battered old black VW bug. The three little ones sat in the backseat, crowded together. James sat in the middle because he could see out easiest. Dicey was in the front seat. "It's a good thing you don't have luggage," Stewart said. "We'd never fit it in."

The day had grown hot and muggy. City smells hung heavy on the air. The little car clattered, like a giant sewing machine.

They made their way onto the Thruway and joined the cars hurtling along there. Stewart stayed in the middle lane. Cars passed them on both sides.

"I left my map," Dicey said.

"We'll get another," Stewart answered her, without moving his eyes from the road. "I don't know Bridgeport at all. Do you?"

"How could we?"

They drove with the windows open. The air roared in their ears. Things went by so fast when you were in a car, you could barely look at anything before it was gone. But this area, all concrete and sad little houses, was the kind you liked to pass by quickly.

Dicey leaned over and said loudly: "I don't know where we would have slept along this road."

"Where'd you sleep when you came to New Haven?" Stewart glanced quickly in the rearview mirror.

"Behind some stores. In a little park. Once in a carwash," Dicey told him.

"Then you'd have found someplace along here," Stewart said.

They went through a toll booth where Stewart paid a quarter, and then after a while saw signs saying: BRIDGEPORT. Stewart kept to the middle lane.

"Aren't we going to get off?" Dicey asked.

"Not yet. I'm hungry, aren't you?"

"Yes," Dicey said, "but—"

"I thought we'd go down to Fairfield—it's only ten or twenty miles on—and eat at McDonald's there. I know where that is, and I like going someplace that I know where it is. We can pick up a map of Bridgeport too, so we can see how to get there, to your aunt's house."

Ten or twenty miles, two days' walk. Four days there and back. Dicey just nodded. "If you want to," she said.

"What I don't want to do is drive into a strange city without a map," Stewart said. He studied the traffic behind him in the rearview mirror and turned on his signal blinker. "Besides, Fairfield's pretty."

"Do you live there?" Dicey asked.

He shook his head. They pulled off the Thruway and onto a four-lane road lined with low buildings, hung over with stoplights, bleached white by the heat.

"This is Route One," Dicey said.

"You know it?"

"We've been on it most of the time."

"That's too bad."

Stewart stopped at a gas station and came back with a map. He pulled into the nearby McDonald's and they all ordered lunch. He carried their tray to a big table back in a corner. Dicey handed out the wrapped hamburgers and the parcels of french fries. She jammed straws into the Cokes.

Stewart had ordered two Big Macs. He ate them as if he were starving. When Dicey told him this, he said he felt like he was starving, most of the time. "But I'll outgrow it," he said. "It used to be worse. I used to eat much more—a whole large pizza—and still not be full. Now I'm sometimes full. When I was in high school, I felt like I could eat all day long and never fill up."

James nodded at him, chewing.

After they had cleared the table and thrown out the wrapping papers, Stewart unfolded his map. Dicey told him the address and he found the street easily. It was one of many little streets running across the map of the city.

"But it's not near the water," Dicey said.

"Why should it be?"

"It's called Ocean Drive. I thought it would be near the water. A big white house."

"Ocean Drive runs through the heart of town, a few blocks from the downtown section. But the street goes down to a main street that ends up at the harbor," Stewart pointed out. Dicey was unreasonably disappointed. "Maybe it was a joke," he suggested.

"Some joke."

"You like being near the water."

"In Provincetown, we were right next to it. Behind the dunes, but next to it. I'm used to it. Yeah, I like it. I don't feel right unless I'm near the ocean."

"You feel that way and you're going to Bridgeport? You're in trouble," Stewart said. "Listen, are you in a big hurry? Do you want to go to a beach for a while before you go to your aunt's?"

"Yes," James and Dicey said.

"No," Sammy said. "I want to see Momma. Right away."

"We don't even know whether she's there, Sammy," James argued. "You can wait an hour, can't you?"

"I don't want to wait anymore," Sammy said. "Dicey?"

"Just for an hour, Sammy. Please?" she said. His face grew stubborn. "I've decided," Dicey said. "For an hour. No more."

Once they got off Route 1 in Fairfield, everything was clean and neat. The houses all looked freshly painted. The lawns all looked freshly mown. The cars all looked just washed. It was the kind of place where all the door handles shone with polishing.

They drove through a little village and then down by some big houses around some curves—and then Dicey could see the water. At first she only glimpsed it in the spaces between the large trees that grew around the houses; then she could see a long narrow beach ahead, with marshlands on the other side of the road.

Sammy wanted to stay in the car, but Dicey insisted that he come out with them at least to begin with. "Then you can go back and wait in the car if you want," she said. "That's fair, isn't it?"

They spent an hour at the beach, no more. Sammy kept track of the time on Stewart's watch. They waded and dug. The children wandered up and down while Stewart and Dicey sat watching the little waves that meandered up onto the smooth sand. Dicey stared out over the quiet blue water, knowing that although the surface was calm, the great tides were moving underneath. She listened to the rippling waves mingled with the voices of the other people at the beach. They didn't talk much. Stewart didn't seem to be a talkative person, and Dicey didn't mind. He only asked her one question:

"What'll you do if things don't work out at your aunt's?"

He could have been reading Dicey's mind. She turned quickly to look at his face, but he was looking out over the water, his gray-blue eyes glinting in its reflections.

"I don't expect Momma to be there, you know," she said. He

nodded. "Aunt Cilla must be pretty old now. She's really Momma's aunt, not ours. So she might not want a mess of kids. Is that what you mean?" He nodded. "I don't know what I'll do. Or if she's not even there. I guess I'll have to go to the police then, won't I? Or somebody. For help." He nodded. "What do you think I should do if—"

His eyes turned to her. "I honestly don't know. Except stick together, all of you. That's the most important thing."

Dicey agreed.

"If you can," he said. "If you are able to. You might not be able to."

"You and Windy—you were a big help to us," Dicey said.

"That's okay," Stewart said.

"Especially Windy."

"Windy had a good time. You brightened up his life."

"Especially you, too."

"I didn't do anything. Sang you a couple of songs. Got you some bad hamburgers."

"And took us to the beach, don't forget that."

They found 1724 Ocean Drive without any trouble. It was one of a long row of houses that stretched down treeless streets. It was a small house, shingled with gray asphalt. Three concrete steps led up to the plain front door. On one side of the door, two windows faced the street. There were thin curtains on the windows and you couldn't see in. The house looked flat-faced and empty. Dicey sat in the car and studied it before she got out. Was this going to be their home?

They clambered out of the car and said good-bye to Stewart. He left the motor running while he climbed out himself to shake hands with each one of them, James last, and wish them good luck.

Then he drove off, down the street, away, the little black car clattering busily. Dicey waved to him, but he must not have seen her because he didn't wave back. She turned to the closed door. She was nervous, but not in any way she had been nervous before. She looked at James and Maybeth and Sammy standing in a silent row and tried to smile at them. Then she went up the steps, hoping she looked more confident than she felt. At least they were all freshly washed. Dicey knocked on the door.

CHAPTER 9

Nobody answered Dicey's knock. She could hear the echoes of her knockings inside, so she knew that she would have heard footsteps if someone had been hurrying to answer the door.

She knocked again, louder. While she waited, to be sure no one was at home, she studied the brown paint on the door. It was a thick reddish-brown color and in the inset panels you could see brush strokes.

Nobody was there. Dicey swallowed, as much in relief as in disappointment, and turned to face her family. "I guess we wait," she said. She sat on the bottom step. They sat behind her and beside her.

They had nothing other than what they wore. Even Dicey's map, rain-soaked and ripped, had been lost. Stewart had taken his with him.

"I thought Aunt Cilla was rich," James said. "This isn't a rich person's house."

"I must have been wrong about that," Dicey said.

"Momma said she was," James insisted.

"Then Momma was wrong."

"Do you think Momma's here?" Sammy asked. "If she's here why isn't she here?"

"I dunno," Dicey said. "It's Thursday, a working day, isn't it? So if she's got a job she'd be there, wouldn't she?"

"What about Aunt Cilla? Is she too old to work?" James asked.

"I don't know anything about her except what she wrote in her letters—and that wasn't true."

"Why would she lie?" James asked.

"I dunno," Dicey said.

"Dicey?"

"Yeah, Maybeth."

"Why did Momma go?"

Dicey looked at Maybeth's round and worried face. She looked down the quiet street, where no cars were parked, where all the houses were the same and had the same closed and empty faces.

"I don't know, Maybeth, but I can tell you what I think."

Maybeth waited.

"I think she got so worried about so many things, about money and us, about what she could do to take care of us, about not being able to do anything to make things better—I think it all piled up inside her so that she just quit. She felt so sad and sorry then, and lost—remember how she'd go out and not come back for hours? I think she got lost outside those times, the way she was lost inside."

"Amnesia," James suggested.

"Maybe. So she decided that she'd ask Aunt Cilla to help us, because she couldn't help us anymore. And maybe, when she went off into the Mall, maybe she'd run out of money and she couldn't take us any farther and all the things that had piled up inside her head sort of exploded there. And she just forgot us. Like amnesia, where you forget everything, even who you are. She couldn't stand to think and worry anymore. Everything she thought of, every place she went to, it all looked so sad and hopeless and she couldn't do anything about it—so it all exploded and left her brain empty." Empty. That was the way

Momma had looked those last months. As if she were far away from them.

"Will she be better now?" Sammy asked. "Do you think?"

"Maybe she's not even here," James said.

"She has to be," Sammy said.

"Why?" James asked. Dicey thought of stopping the conversation, but decided not to.

"Because," Sammy said.

"Because is no reason," James said.

"Because, if she isn't here, then I don't know where she is. And she doesn't know where I am. And how can she find me?"

"Maybe she doesn't want to find you, or any of us," James said. "That's what Dicey said, that she had to get away from us."

"Momma loves me," Sammy said. His chin stuck out in the stubborn way.

"Yes, she does," Dicey said. "And so do I."

Because she did, she loved all of them. That had kind of sneaked up on her over their journey.

"See?" Sammy said to James. "I told you."

"But that doesn't prove anything," James protested.

Sammy didn't pay any attention to him.

The sun moved slowly across a white sky. At the end of the long summer afternoon, or at the beginning of the long summer evening, the street gradually filled up with traffic, and the sidewalk became crowded with people. One after another, buses stopped at the corner and a short parade of men and women climbed off. Some carried briefcases, some grocery bags. They walked on, down the street or up the street. Some went up the stoops of the gray houses, pulled out keys, unlocked doors and went in. Others walked on, around corners, out of sight. No children lived on these streets.

The Tillermans silently watched the people move to and fro

past them. Nobody looked at them. Most of the men and women walked with their eyes toward the ground, or fixed blankly ahead. Sammy moved closer to Dicey and held on to her forearm with his small, tense hand. He did not say a word, but his eyes flicked back and forth. He was looking for Momma.

Dicey just watched the people, with no particular thought in her mind. She could not do any more. From now on, things would happen to them.

She saw men in workshirts with tired shoulders, carrying plain black lunchboxes. She saw women in brightly flowered summer dresses, the dresses wilted by the heat as if they were real flowers, the women's faces sagging after the work-day.

A short round woman wearing high-heeled shoes walked toward the steps where they sat. She actually looked at them and seemed surprised, but she walked on past them. A man in a green khaki suit, carrying a scuffed briefcase, stared at them for a minute before he let himself into the house next door.

A few minutes later, a woman of the same age as the man, about fifty Dicey guessed, struggled up the steps to the next-door house, carrying two huge bags of groceries. She noticed the Tillermans just as she pulled the door closed behind her and her eyes widened.

The little round woman in high heels walked past again, from the opposite direction and on the opposite side of the street. She stared at them. She was wearing a plain black cotton dress and had short gray hair that was permanented into sausagelike curls that bounced and jiggled on her round head. She walked as if her feet hurt her, as if she had been standing and walking in the high-heeled shoes all day long. Dicey wondered where she was going.

The people coming home from work had filled the street for a while; now they thinned out, melted away into houses, out of sight. All the sounds were faint ones from distant traffic or from the humming of air-conditioners up and down the block. A solitary man wearing shorts and sneakers walked his dog on the opposite side of the street.

The round woman came toward them again. This time, as at first, she was on their side of the street and looking at the ground. She held her purse in both hands, protectively close against her side. Dicey thought she must be old.

She stopped about three feet away and looked at them. At first only Dicey was looking back at her, into pale blue eyes that blinked behind plastic-framed glasses sitting high up on her nose. She wasn't that old after all, close up.

"What do you want?" the woman asked. "What are you doing here? What do you want here?" Her voice was high and a little scared. Her lips pursed.

Dicey stood up. "We're the Tillermans," she said. She named them all. The woman's expression did not change.

Dicey knew then that Momma was not here.

Dicey kept on talking. "I'm hoping you're our aunt, our great-aunt, Mrs. Cilla Logan."

Then the woman's expression did change. A little half-smile, a silly helpless smile, fluttered her mouth. "That is Mother," she said. "Not me. I'm her daughter. That is, I was her daughter." She fumbled around in her purse and took out keys. "Mother passed on this last March," she said. Dicey had a sinking feeling in her stomach. "But do come in. There's no need to stand talking on the front stoop."

The woman unlocked the door and stepped inside. The Tillermans followed. It was dark and stuffy after the summer evening sunlight. They entered a narrow hallway that led to the rear of the house, passed a room with thin curtains, passed a narrow dark staircase going up and went into a kitchen.

The kitchen was large enough for all five of them, but not big. Sunlight made it brighter than the rest of the house. It was shiny clean. The gray linoleum floor gleamed, the refrigerator shone, the windows, looking over a tiny yard, were polished. There was a formica-topped table in the center of the room, and the woman told the Tillermans to sit at the four chairs that surrounded it. She opened the windows and the back door, then fetched herself a chair from the front room, putting it beside Maybeth. Before she sat down, she put some water into a kettle, put the kettle on the stove and took a mug out of a cupboard. As she did all this, she spoke to them in starts and stops. "Yes, Mother passed away. You couldn't have known. It was her heart. Her heart was always weak, but we never knew. She wouldn't complain, you see. She was only in her seventies. Seventy-two. A wonderful person—everybody said how wonderful she was. It was a shock to me. I found her, when I came back from work. Sitting in her chair by the window. A Wednesday it was. We had a high mass for her." She sighed, the kettle whistled, and she poured water into her mug. She dunked a teabag, in and out, in and out. "I have been—not quite the same since Mother went away. People have said that to me. It has been hard for me."

She turned to face them, and Dicey saw little tears gathering in her little eyes. She took off her glasses and polished them on a paper towel.

The Tillermans sat silent, their mouths clamped shut, not knowing what to say. The woman sat down at the table with them. She sipped at her tea. James looked at Dicey and raised and lowered his eyebrows, as Windy had. Dicey smothered a giggle.

"And then, of course, to see four children on my doorstep. Well, I had no idea. You don't mind, do you? You aren't offended? I was afraid. You hear of such strange things happening these days. Especially to women who live alone. I live alone now. I hoped you would go away. If Mother were here, of course . . ." Her voice drifted off, her eyes drifted away from them and out to the windows.

Nobody spoke.

Finally, the woman gathered herself together with a kind of shake over her whole body. "But what am I thinking of? Are you thirsty? I don't know what I have for children to drink. Living alone, I don't keep much food in the house."

"Please," Maybeth said, "I would like a glass of water."

The woman looked at her. She smiled at Maybeth and said, "Of course, you all would like a drink of water, wouldn't you? What a pretty child you are. Really, like an angel. I was a pretty child too. Everyone said so—and we have photographs."

She got them each a little jelly glass full of water. They drank quickly and then Dicey refilled them once, twice, three times. The woman smiled absently.

"What are you doing here?" the woman asked, as if the question had just occurred to her. "Where are your parents? Who did you say you were?"

"We are the Tillermans," Dicey said again. She announced all of their names again, "James, Maybeth, Sammy, and I'm Dicey."

The woman repeated their names softly to herself. "My mother's maiden name was Hackett," she said.

"Our mother," Dicey began. She looked sharply at Sammy in case he might be about to interrupt, "is your mother's niece. We used to get a card and letter from your mother every Christmas, and Momma would read it to us. That's how we knew about Aunt Cilla, and her address. But I don't even know your name."

"Eunice Logan," the woman said. "Miss Eunice Logan. That makes us cousins, you know."

"Does it?"

"Yes, because your grandmother was my mother's sister. That means your mother and I are first cousins. Does that make us second cousins?"

"I don't know," Dicey said.

"Your grandmother would be Abigail Tillerman. Abigail Hackett she was before she married. Priscilla Hackett was my mother, you see. Before she married."

"Do we have a grandmother?" Dicey asked.

"Of course. Everyone does. But where are your parents? Are they visiting in Bridgeport?"

Dicey found herself ready to lie again. She could say they were visiting and the children had come to meet Aunt Cilla, and then later the Tillermans could go off and—and do what? If she lied, then she would get herself into a box. They had come such a long way. They had to have some kind of help from this cousin she'd never even heard of before. (That was strange too, that Aunt Cilla had never mentioned a daughter.) If Cousin Eunice didn't help them, they would have to go to the police. Dicey had to tell the truth.

But first she had to say it to Sammy. Say it out loud. "Momma's not here, Sammy," Dicey said.

He nodded, and tears welled up in his eyes. Dicey reached over and put her hand on top of his. He laid his forehead on her hand and closed his eyes.

"You don't know where your mother is?"

"No," Dicey said. "She ran away, I think. Anyway, she disappeared. We were on our way here to find Aunt Cilla, so we just came along. We hoped she'd be here."

"Where's your father?"

"He's been gone for years," James said, his voice sharp.

"You're alone?" Cousin Eunice asked. They nodded. "Oh

dear. Oh dear, oh dear. You poor, sweet little things. I don't know what to think. I have to ask advice. Will you excuse me to make a phone call? You're absolutely alone? I don't know what should be done."

She hurried out of the room, swinging the door closed behind her. Sammy raised his head and Dicey retrieved her hand, now a little wet. "I don't understand," Sammy said.

"Neither do I," Dicey answered. "She'd never heard of us, you know that? And we'd never heard of her. But Momma answered those letters, every year."

"What should we do?" James asked.

"Tell the truth and see what happens," Dicey said. "We can't do anything else. Can we? James?"

"We could take off again, and look out for ourselves until—"

"Until what?" Dicey asked.

"Until we grow up?"

"We could," Dicey agreed. "We always might do that and we'd figure a way out, I guess. But for now I think we shouldn't, unless we have to. We don't have any idea where Momma is, and I want to find out. Maybe this Cousin Eunice will take care of us—I could work later and pay her back. That's what I'm hoping will happen. Just so we're together."

"Is Momma gone for always?" Maybeth asked.

"I don't know," Dicey said. "She might as well be."

"Don't say that!" Sammy cried. "Don't you ever!"

Cousin Eunice returned. "My friend—he's an advisor really, he's my spiritual counselor—he'll be by after supper. We have to get some more food—I have only two dinners in the freezer. Dicey? Can you go to a store and get three TV dinners? I don't know what kind you children prefer. Is that all right?"

"Of course," Dicey said. She flushed and said, "We don't have any money."

"None?"

"None. I'm sorry."

"Don't be sorry—I feel so sorry for you—I don't understand what has happened—"

"Neither do we," Dicey answered.

"How could you? You're only children." She reached for her purse and took out ten dollars. "This will be enough. You must want milk, children should drink milk. And fruit? Can you decide what you need? Will this be enough?"

Dicey nodded.

"The grocer is two blocks away, just around a corner. You go up the street, turn right, and you'll see it. But don't talk to strangers."

Dicey nodded, lowering her head to hide her smile.

"And you should call me 'Eunice.' Cousin Eunice. Because we're cousins. And could you pick out a cake from the frozen foods? Something light, perhaps lemon; something that will sit well with tea."

Dicey walked to the store, not thinking about anything in particular, just taking it slow. There was a kind of pool of sadness in her heart, she thought, and she wondered why it should be so. Not only for Momma, because she had not expected to find Momma here. She didn't ever expect to see Momma again, she realized. The sadness was for themselves, even though they were much better off now than they had been, say, just last night at this time. Dicey picked out three chicken TV dinners and went to the fruit counter.

Once again, everything had changed on them. Perhaps it was all this changing that made her sad. Or perhaps the disappointment, after finally arriving at Aunt Cilla's house, and finding only Eunice there, whom they had never heard of. A stranger. Who pitied them.

Probably, they could never go back to New Haven. She wished they could have stayed there longer. She wished she knew something more about those two young men. She didn't even know their last names. Or phone numbers. Or address. Stewart hadn't even stayed to find out if the Tillermans would be all right. The Tillermans had just drifted through his life, touch in, touch out, and gone without a thought.

Dicey paid for her purchases and walked slowly back to the little gray house. Maybe it was just that she was away from the ocean, the salt water with its tides and turbulence, that made her sad.

Father Joseph, Cousin Eunice's friend, was a priest, a slender, restless man with thick gray hair and deep lines in his forehead. He had cool, thoughtful light-brown eyes, deep set, and a thin mouth. He wore shiny black trousers and jacket, a black shirt-front, and the band of white, crisp and stiff, around his neck. Cousin Eunice introduced him and fluttered nervously around him on her high-heeled shoes, bringing him a cup of tea and offering him a tray with a little china pitcher of milk and a little china bowl of sugar cubes.

Father Joseph did not show pity for the Tillermans as Eunice had. They sat together in the living room, on the chairs and the floor. He asked them about their home in Provincetown and their school, about Momma, about living in a summer resort area, about the fishing fleet and about books. After a while, he suggested that the younger children go to bed, while he and Cousin Eunice and Dicey made some plans.

"But they have no nightclothes," Cousin Eunice said.

"We can sleep in our underwear," Dicey said. "We washed everything out last night."

The priest remarked, "You did? You do seem to have managed well."

Dicey took the younger ones upstairs. James protested, but she told him: “We’re guests. We’re strangers here. She didn’t even know we existed, and she’s trying to help us. Let’s just do as we’re told, okay?”

James and Sammy were to sleep in the small back bedroom that looked out over the yard, in a double bed. Maybeth would sleep in the other twin bed in Cousin Eunice’s room. Maybeth looked small lying there, her curls spread behind her on the pillow, her hands folded over the clean sheets. “You okay, Maybeth?” Dicey asked.

The little girl nodded.

“I think I liked it better when we all slept in the same place,” Dicey said, smiling at her. “Like that first night.”

Maybeth nodded.

“I expect I’ll be sleeping in with James and Sammy, on the floor, or downstairs on the sofa,” Dicey said. “If you want me.”

“It’s okay, Dicey,” Maybeth said. “I won’t be lonely.”

“Lonely? All cramped together here in this little house? Why I’ll hear you if you roll over. I’ll hear you if you sneeze—and come running.”

Maybeth smiled at Dicey and closed her hazel eyes.

Dicey went back downstairs, where the adults awaited her in the living room, which was cluttered with the kinds of things collected over a lifetime, pictures and little china figurines and pillows stuffed with pine needles.

Father Joseph greeted her. “Sit down, Dicey, we have to get to business now. That’s an odd name, Dicey. What is your real name?”

Dicey sat cross-legged on the floor, between the two in their chairs, looking up at them. “Dicey’s my name,” she said. “I don’t have another one.”

“You just don’t know it,” the priest assured her. Dicey didn’t argue. After all, maybe he was right.

He studied her, as if he wanted to see her thoughts. He made her uncomfortable.

"Your cousin has agreed to make you welcome here, until we can make inquiries about your mother, and your father."

Dicey looked at Cousin Eunice, who smiled foolishly at her and said, "It must be temporary, I'm afraid, but—"

"Your cousin has—certain plans, of which she may tell you later," Father Joseph said. He smiled at Cousin Eunice across the top of Dicey's head, and she blushed like a little girl. "However, the Church has summer activities in which your younger siblings can participate. A day camp for the little boy and the young girl. James will attend a school-camp. Will he object to that?"

"He likes school," Dicey said. "He's awfully smart."

"I thought so," Father Joseph said. "I'm one of the teachers there, so I can see that he gets into the proper classes. And of course there will be more active things to do in the afternoon."

"That sounds fine," Dicey said. "Thank you. Thank you both. I know we've just sort of fallen on you," she said to Cousin Eunice. "I'm sorry."

"Oh, don't be sorry," Cousin Eunice said, leaning forward, pushing her glasses back up her nose. "We are family, aren't we? And when I think of you, all alone—abandoned—like myself really, in a way. Why, I couldn't do anything else, could I? Only, I work, you see, so I have to be gone all day, and there will be so much to do with four children in the house. Cleaning and shopping, laundry."

"But I can do that, can't I?" Dicey asked her.

"That is what we hoped," Father Joseph said. "And the Church, Eunice, can give you clothing, as well as all the support we can offer, and counsel. Have the children no other relatives?"

"None that I know of," Dicey said. She knew she had interrupted, but she didn't like him talking about them as if she weren't there.

"Mother had just one sister," Cousin Eunice said. "Abigail. She would be their grandmother. But I don't know much about her. She was much younger than Mother, twelve years, and then they never were close. I've never met her. They might have had a falling out. I did write to her when Mother passed away, but I received no answer."

"Was the letter returned to you?"

"No."

"So it must have been received. By someone."

Dicey was listening hard.

Cousin Eunice waved her little hands. "Let me see. Abigail married a man named John Tillerman."

"Where does she live?" Father Joseph asked.

"In Maryland, down south, on the Eastern Shore. A town called Crisfield. I don't know anything about it. It is where Mother lived as a girl."

Father Joseph nodded.

"This John Tillerman farmed, I think I remember." Cousin Eunice wrinkled her brows with the effort. "They had children." Dicey nodded her head. "I don't know how many, but one daughter would be Dicey's mother. I don't know where they are now."

Crisfield, Eastern Shore, Maryland, Dicey said to herself, to fix it in her memory.

"By that time, Mother had been in the north for years and married to Father, and they lived here. Mother didn't like her sister. She didn't like to be reminded of her family. I don't know—she wouldn't speak of them. She became a part of Father's family. These are the first Hackett relations I've met. I'll try to remember more, Father Joseph. We have photograph albums."

"That would be most helpful. I myself will see what I can find out about the Tillerman family. Sometimes the Church can make the more sensitive personal inquiries, that the police authorities can't." He turned to Dicey. "What is your religion?"

"I don't know," Dicey said. "We never went to church." He frowned slightly.

"There is another question that I'm afraid I have to ask. The matter of your name. Tillerman. That would be your mother's name. Your parents were not married?"

Dicey shook her head. "I don't think so," she said. Cousin Eunice sucked in a noisy breath. Dicey did not look at her. She pulled at the laces of her sneakers, as if she had just noticed they were coming loose.

"Had you the same father, all of you? Would you know that?"

"Yes," Dicey said. Her head snapped up and her eyes met his. He did not seem surprised at her anger. "Sammy and Maybeth look like Momma, but James and me, we look like our father. I remember him, a little. Because I'm the oldest."

"Yes, yes," the priest said, smiling a little. "I'm sure you're right." He didn't sound sure.

"No, you're not," Dicey said, "but I am. And I know. Aren't there birth certificates? There have to be, don't there? We were all born in Provincetown—why don't you call the hospital there? They'll tell you. Momma wasn't—" She couldn't find the polite word. "She didn't have boyfriends, she didn't even go out on dates. She's nice. She's good. She loves us—and you probably don't believe that either, but she does. We'd know and you wouldn't."

He held up his hands. A smile lifted the corners of his mouth. Cousin Eunice fluttered in the background making little protests to tell Dicey she shouldn't talk like that to a priest.

"No, no, Eunice. The child is probably right. She would know better than we."

"Then why did she abandon them?" Eunice asked. "Oh, I'm sorry, I didn't mean to say that," she apologized to Dicey. Dicey didn't respond.

"That is what we'll try to find out," Father Joseph said. "I think, Dicey, if you can, I'd like you to speak to the Missing Persons Department."

"The police?" Dicey asked.

"The police."

Dicey thought. She didn't want to talk to the police. But how else could they find where Momma went? And what if something bad had happened to Momma and the police could help her? And if by not talking to them Dicey could hurt her? She had a sudden memory of Momma's sad moon-face and her sad moon smile in the car window; and then of Momma running to comfort Sammy when he had fallen off a chair and was frightened, pulling the little boy onto her knees and wrapping her arms around him, saying crooning comforting things. The two round yellow heads bent toward each other, and Momma's strong hands cradled the back of Sammy's little head.

"Okay," Dicey said. "They can't put us into foster homes when we're here with Cousin Eunice, can they? We're not runaways, are we? I don't want us to be separated," she explained to the priest.

"Neither do we, if it can be helped," he answered. "I'll contact the police and someone will come here to see you. Shall I come with him?"

"Okay," Dicey said again. She was thinking furiously, trying to see if there was a trap in this, or danger.

"You really have no choice," the priest said.

Dicey nodded, with her eyes on his, but she was reciting to herself: *Crisfield. Eastern Shore. Maryland.*

Father Joseph left, then, and Cousin Eunice brought Dicey a cot that she kept in the cellar. Dicey put it into the last of the floor space in the boys' bedroom. Cousin Eunice wanted to object to having Dicey in with the boys, but she didn't want her own room to be crowded, so she didn't say much.

Dicey looked in on the sleeping Maybeth before she made her final stop in the bathroom and lay down on her cot. She could hear James breathing softly. Sammy turned and rustled in the sheets.

Dicey lay on her back with her arms under her head, staring at the blank, black ceiling. They had come here, had come here safely. If this was to be their home, then she could learn to get along here. She would have to. Stewart was right, they had to stay together. That was the only important thing.

She was lulled to sleep by the words repeating in her head: *Crisfield, Eastern Shore, Maryland.*

CHAPTER 10

A sharp knock on the door woke Dicey. She opened her eyes wide. The window was dark. Dicey had slept and awakened in so many unknown places that she never had that first, morning feeling of being lost, or not knowing where she was. She knew where she was, or rather, where she wasn't.

The knock came again. Dicey jumped off the cot and squeezed around the corner of the bed where her brothers slept to open the door.

Cousin Eunice stood there, wearing the same black cotton dress, or its twin sister, and the same high-heeled shoes. "I am about to leave," she whispered. "Can you come downstairs for a word before I go?"

Dicey nodded. She closed the door and searched through the darkness for her shorts and her shirt.

A rustling noise in the bed made her turn her head as she was about to leave. James sat up. "It's still true," he said.

"Go back to sleep, James," Dicey said. He lay down obediently, and his eyes closed.

Dicey found Cousin Eunice in the kitchen, drinking a cup of tea. Beside her on the table lay a black purse, black gloves, and a little round black hat with a brim that tilted up.

"Good morning," Dicey said.

"I'm sorry to wake you so early," Cousin Eunice said. Her

face was pale above all the black around her. "But I am going to six-thirty mass. I always do that," she said. "I get breakfast on my way to work. There's a diner on the way, quite clean. Mother didn't like making breakfast. And I've always gone to early mass."

Dicey nodded. She sat down facing her cousin.

"I pray for Mother, and for myself, and for the world," Cousin Eunice said. "This morning, I shall pray for you, and for your poor mother."

Dicey felt uncomfortable. "Thank you," she said. Was that what you were supposed to say to somebody who was praying for you?

"I thought of staying home today," Cousin Eunice went on. She talked without looking at Dicey. "But I've never missed a day of work, not for any reason. Not in twenty-one years. Somehow, I didn't want to miss today."

Dicey nodded.

"Father Joseph said he would come by this morning and bring some clothing for you. He will register the younger children at camp, so that they can begin right away. So you must be sure to be here when he arrives."

"We will."

"But there is shopping that needs to be done, and usually on Thursday evenings I clean the living room, dust and vacuum, wash the windows, damp mop the floors. I couldn't get that done last night."

"I can do that," Dicey said.

"Do be careful not to break anything," Cousin Eunice urged.

"I will," Dicey said.

"Here is some money. Try not to spend it all." Cousin Eunice handed her twenty dollars. "We'll need something for supper, I suppose. Can you cook?"

Dicey nodded.

"It has to be fish," Cousin Eunice said. "Today is Friday."

"I've cooked fish," Dicey said. Well, that was true. She had just never cooked fish on a stove, in a pan. What did Friday have to do with fish?

"I get home at five forty. Will you be all right?"

"We'll be all right," Dicey said. "You don't need to worry about us."

"I don't know how you've managed it," Cousin Eunice said. "You must be a very resourceful child."

Dicey didn't know what to say.

"But you're here now, and I'll take care of you," Cousin Eunice said.

"That's awfully nice of you," Dicey answered. It sounded so flat. But she felt flat, flat and—she admitted it to herself—disappointed.

"How could a Christian do less?" Cousin Eunice asked. Then she got up and put her hat on her head. She drew her gloves on over her plump hands and picked up her purse. "Until this evening then. You're sure you'll be all right?" Dicey nodded. "Don't forget Father Joseph."

"I won't."

"And the living room."

"I won't. I mean, I'll do it."

"And the shopping."

Dicey nodded.

"Fish, remember. Why don't we have a tuna casserole?"

Dicey nodded. She hoped she could find a cookbook in this neat and tidy kitchen, maybe behind a cupboard door.

Cousin Eunice left, drawing the door quietly closed behind her. Dicey breathed a sigh of relief, but the door opened immediately. "Don't leave the house empty," Cousin Eunice said. "There must be someone home, at all times. Thieves come, even in broad daylight these days."

"All right," Dicey said.

"It's not as if I have anything valuable," Cousin Eunice said. "But they steal anything. And murder—and other things—I don't know—the world has gone crazy. I'll have a key made for you, just one. Until then, don't leave the house unlocked."

"I won't," Dicey said. "Don't worry about us. We'll be fine."

"How can I help worrying?" Cousin Eunice asked. She did not give Dicey time to answer.

Dicey looked at the clock hanging on the kitchen wall. It was shaped like a cat, with a long, curled tail that twitched the seconds. Six fifteen. Dicey familiarized herself with the kitchen, cupboards (no cookbook), drawers, refrigerator and freezer. She took a dustcloth and the vacuum and went into the living room.

The room was cluttered, but not messy. Dicey didn't think it needed cleaning, but if Cousin Eunice wanted it cleaned then she would clean it. She dusted the wooden-backed chairs, the table tops, the windowsills, the one bookcase, which held a Bible and two rows of photograph albums. Dicey thought she should ask permission before she looked through the albums. She dusted the pictures on the walls, of Jesus and Mary, like the ones that she used to see on Aunt Cilla's Christmas cards, of Jesus being crucified, and photographs, of a round-faced man standing beside a round-fendered car, of a sharp-eyed woman with a fur around her neck, of a little girl with curly hair and a flouncy white dress and a bouquet of flowers held in her white-gloved hands. Dicey dusted the row of china cats on top of the bookcase. She dusted the lamps and the doorhandles. Then she ran the vacuum over the pale blue rug, careful to clean under tables and chairs.

When she finished, it was seven thirty. She set out bowls and spoons and glasses of milk. Cousin Eunice had two kinds of cold cereal, cornflakes with sugar frosting, and a fruit cereal that said it had fifteen flavors in its different-colored little balls. Dicey put both boxes in the middle of the table. She wished she could find some flowers to put in a glass in the middle, but there were none in the backyard. Nothing grew there except a straggly, neglected cover of grass.

Dicey enjoyed getting ready for this meal. The morning sun brightened the living room beyond. Light made things cheerful.

They ate a quick breakfast and then Dicey washed and dried the bowls and glasses and spoons. Maybeth helped her put them away. Sammy and Maybeth went out to the backyard. Dicey took James upstairs and made him help her make their beds. Cousin Eunice had made her own.

She left James in charge while she went to the store. There she purchased bread and milk and fruit, tuna fish and noodles and (after reading the instructions on the back of the bag of noodles) a can of mushroom soup, peanut butter, jelly. She also bought a dozen eggs, a box of pancake mix, a jar of syrup and a cheap red rubber ball (because if Sammy was going to spend most of the day waiting around, he'd need something to play with).

Returning, unpacking the groceries, piling the dollars and change beside the toaster, washing the apples before putting them in the refrigerator, Dicey heard herself humming the song about Peggy-O. It was like playing house.

James wandered in and took an apple. "There aren't any books in the house. Are we going to stay here?"

"I don't think we can do anything else," Dicey said. "So we've got to please Cousin Eunice, you know? And that Father Joseph too, I guess. We've got to be on best behavior all the time. Can you do that, James?"

"Sure," he said. "But it's an awful small house for four kids."

"Bigger than ours was."

"Yeah, but there we had the dunes and the beach."

Dicey went out into the tiny yard and called Sammy and Maybeth to her. To them she repeated what she had just said to James. They nodded solemnly at her, then she pulled out her hand from behind her back and tossed the red ball to Sammy.

He grabbed for it, missed, ran after it and caught it in two hands. He bounced it high. He turned and grinned at Dicey. Then he ran up to her and nearly knocked her over, hugging her. He called Maybeth to play catch.

Dicey watched them playing, proud that she had thought to get the ball. Glad in her heart that she had been able to give it to them.

They had finished lunch and washed and dried the plates and glasses by the time Father Joseph arrived. He carried two large shopping bags, which he passed to Dicey. "Clothes," he told her.

He gathered up the younger children and walked off down the street with them. James walked beside him. Sammy ran ahead. Maybeth trotted behind.

Dicey was alone in the house. It felt strange to be alone. Being alone inside was very different from being alone outside. Inside, there was nothing to do. And she felt full of energy.

She wanted to take a walk but she couldn't leave the house empty. So she sorted through the bags of clothes.

The clothes were worn, but clean and pressed. Their own clothes were worn out, but that was somehow different. Other people's old clothes—Dicey quelled the thought. She must remember to be grateful. For Dicey and Maybeth there were dresses, for the boys shirts and trousers. Dicey didn't like dresses. There was no underwear. No blue jeans. Two pairs of shoes, heavy leather shoes that tied with laces. She would have to tell Father Joseph what they needed. Or maybe Cousin Eunice could give them the money for shoes and underwear.

In an hour, Father Joseph returned. The children were not

with him, but another man was. He wore a business suit of olive green and had a round face and yellow-brown eyes that protruded. Goggle eyes. He had round fat fingers, and he jingled the money in his pocket. He peered at Dicey.

They all went to sit at the kitchen table. "The children are staying at camp for the afternoon," Father Joseph said to Dicey. "You and I will go pick them up, so that you can learn the way. Is that all right?"

Dicey nodded. She wondered if she should have changed into one of the dresses.

"This is Sergeant Gordo. He works with the Missing Persons Bureau of the Police Department, and he is also a personal friend of mine."

"How do you do," Dicey said.

"How do. Hot enough for you?" Sergeant Gordo asked. He laughed at his own joke. "Well. I understand you've got a missing mother."

Dicey nodded.

He took a pad out of his rear pants pocket and prepared to write with a ball-point pen. "Give me her particulars," he said.

Dicey didn't understand.

"Name, age, weight, description, any distinguishing marks, last seen."

"Liza Tillerman, thirty-six," Dicey said. "I don't know how much she weighs."

"How's she built? Fat? Thin?"

"She's regular," Dicey said. "Sort of thin, I guess, but she has a regular shape."

"Height?"

"Two or three inches taller than I am."

"How tall are you?"

"I don't know."

"Stand up, will you?" His eyes measured her. "She'd be about five-six or seven. Any scars or moles?"

"She's got a big mole on her chin, and one at the back of her neck, under her hair. There are more, but those are the big ones. She's got blonde hair, long blonde hair. Hazel eyes, like mine. A round face, with high cheekbones."

"What was she wearing when she took off?"

"Blue jeans. A sweater—a big, red, man's sweater, with holes in the elbows. Sandals. A purse over her shoulder."

"Rings? Watch?"

Dicey shook her head. Momma didn't have jewelry.

"Wedding ring?"

Dicey shook her head. The two men exchanged a glance.

"When did you last see her?"

"I'm not exactly sure. It was early in June."

"Where was it?"

Dicey told him about the mall in Peewauket. She told him about the car and how they had left it there.

He snapped his notebook shut. "I'll see what I can do for you," he said.

Dicey swallowed. "Do you think she's dead?"

He pursed his lips. "I can't say that, not now. If she is, we'll find out soon enough. Dead bodies stink, so we find them."

Dicey nodded. She didn't trust herself to speak.

Father Joseph seemed to understand that and he changed the subject. "I've put in a call to the church in Maryland."

"Crisfield," Dicey said. His eyes studied her briefly.

"Yes. The priest there will see what he can find out. Your people aren't Catholic."

"No," Dicey said. "We aren't anything. At least, I don't think we are."

His eyebrows went up. "Your cousin Eunice is a devout

Catholic," he said. "She was raised in the Church. But of course it was her father who was a Catholic—her mother converted when they married. She herself is very traditional in her devotion—she still chooses to keep meatless Fridays, for example."

But none of this interested Dicey. Her attention remained with the officer.

"How long will it take you?" she asked Sergeant Gordo.

"I can't say now, can I? Maybe a day. Maybe a year."

"No, I mean if she's dead."

"That'll take less time. If there's any possibilities I'll show you some pictures—oh, within a week."

"So if you don't tell me anything in a week—"

"Then we can be reasonably sure she's alive. Father Joseph tells me you don't have any idea what made her leave you."

"She didn't say," Dicey said. She looked at him. She didn't like him, but he could help her. "Do you want to know what I think?"

He took out his pad again. "Anything might be useful."

"I think she ran out of money and didn't know what to do, so she just—forgot about us. Her mind just erased us. Because she was so worried about us. Does that make sense?"

"The kind of people we deal with? Anything makes sense. Was she worried about anything in particular?"

"Everything. Always. She lost her job. That was why we were coming to Aunt Cilla's house—here."

"What about welfare? Or unemployment compensation?"

Dicey shook her head. "Momma said she couldn't do that. She wouldn't even go talk to anyone. She said charity was not for the Tillermans."

"I wish more people felt that way," Sergeant Gordo said. He folded his notebook and put it away again. "Well, I've got work to do."

Father Joseph stood up too. "And we have some children to pick up."

"But I can't leave the house. Cousin Eunice said not to leave the house empty and unlocked, and I don't have a key. Can't you get James first and then the other two? James can show me the way on Monday morning."

Father Joseph looked doubtful.

"James will remember all right. He's smart."

"Oh yes, that's very clear. I guess we can do it that way."

Dicey saw them out, and when they had gone she sat waiting on the hall staircase for her family to return to her. It seemed like a long time, waiting there in the dim, silent hallway.

At last they were at the door, James thin and thoughtful, Maybeth, who hurried up to take Dicey's hand, and Sammy, who stood grinning by the doorway. Dicey thanked Father Joseph and said good-bye to him. She took her family to the kitchen. She gave them fruit and then they all went out to the backyard. Sammy wanted to play catch with Dicey, but she wanted to talk.

"What did you do? What was it like?"

"I talked with the teachers," James said. "It's a school building and they have arts and crafts and games in the afternoons. All the teachers are priests," he said, taking a huge bite of banana and chewing it. "They've got a library just for the school and labs with Bunsen burners and chemicals in cupboards. I knew almost all the answers to their questions," he reported proudly. "I think I'll like it."

Dicey was glad to hear that.

"They talked to me as if I was a high school student," James added.

"What about you Sammy? What did you do?"

"Played."

"Played what?"

"Blocks, sandbox. We had running races and I came in second. Some of the boys I beat were in third grade."

"What about the girls?"

"No girls in my camp. All the girls are in one, all the boys in another."

"So yours was all girls?" Dicey asked Maybeth. She nodded. "What did you play?" Maybeth didn't answer. "Did you stand with the teacher all the time?" Dicey guessed.

"Yes," Maybeth said in a small voice, with a small smile.

Dicey rumpled her hair. She wanted to know more about what they had been doing. Each of them had had an entirely separate afternoon. "Did anybody look friendly?" she asked.

"I didn't see any of the guys," James said. "They were figuring out what classes to put me in. They asked me what prayers I knew, and what about the Gospels and the saints. I don't know anything about any of those. Catechism," he pronounced the new word. "They'll teach me."

"You sound glad about going to school."

"Boy, am I." James smiled at her, his hazel eyes smiling too. "These fathers, they're all so smart. Really smart. I never had a teacher like that, not even one. These guys know so much. And they really want to teach me what they know. You can tell that. Yeah, I guess I am glad. So would you be."

"I doubt it," Dicey said. "It takes different things to make me glad."

"Like what?"

"Like knowing we've got food."

"Be serious, Dicey."

"The ocean," Dicey said. "And lots of room outdoors. But mostly the ocean. And the food too, that was serious."

"Father Joseph said to tell you we're all enrolled. He said you should take us on Monday."

"What was it like where Sammy and Maybeth were?"

James shrugged. "Playgrounds mostly, next to schools. Blacktop. Lots of jungle gyms and swings. The teachers for the girls, where Maybeth is, are nuns."

"Did you like the nuns?" Dicey asked Maybeth.

Maybeth didn't answer.

"All the other girls were wearing dresses," James reported.

"We have some dresses," Dicey said to Maybeth. "Father Joseph brought them today. Do you want to go try them on? And see how they look?"

Maybeth nodded. Dicey took her upstairs and she tried on the dresses. Cousin Eunice had come home before they got back downstairs.

Dicey found Cousin Eunice sitting again in the kitchen, waiting for the kettle to come to a boil. The little woman looked tired. She had taken off her glasses and was resting her forehead on her hands, rubbing her eyes. Dicey sent the children outside to play in the backyard and cautioned James to keep them out there. She sat down facing Cousin Eunice. "Are you tired? Can I get you something?"

At that moment the kettle whistled. "I'll make the tea," Dicey said, hopping up. She poured the water and dipped the tea bag in.

"Thanks," Cousin Eunice said. "Yes, I am tired. And I have an instruction class tonight—"

"An instruction class?"

"Religious instruction. I am studying to . . . I am studying. But my feet hurt so, I don't know if I can go tonight. Well of course I can, but—"

"What kind of work do you do?" Dicey asked. The woman was almost curled over onto the tabletop. Her face was pale and her eyes lacked expression. Dicey couldn't imagine what kind of work would make a person look like that.

"I'm a junior foreman. We attach the lace insets to lingerie, my girls and I. You know, on slips and nighties there are lace panels, or the cups of brassieres." Dicey didn't know, but she nodded anyway. "I've been quite successful in my work. There are only half a dozen junior foremen who are women, and only one senior foreman. But it's tiring—the supervising and the sewing and the quality control. It's a responsibility. You wouldn't believe some of the pieces of lace they expect us to set. We have to mend some of the pieces before we can even baste them in. And I'm on my feet most of the day, what with one thing and another. When Mother was here, she knew how tired I was." Her small, high voice droned on. "She'd always have a cup of hot tea waiting for me when I came in the door. And dinner on the table at six. I do get so hungry."

"Do you always get home at the same time?"

"Oh yes, at twenty to six, precisely." Dicey made a mental note. "But I have to begin dinner if we're to eat before my class." Cousin Eunice replaced her glasses and pushed herself up from the table, tottering a little in her high heels. She put a pot of water on to boil. She opened the can of tuna and the can of soup. Dicey tried to help, but she felt clumsy—as if she was interfering, not helping. So she set the table and found the noodles for Cousin Eunice.

"And did you get the living room done?"

"Yes I did."

"Good. You washed the windows?"

"Oh no. I forgot that. I'll do it in the morning."

"Oh dear, in the morning we'll do the upstairs. And take the sheets and towels to the laundromat. And do our personal laundry. I think we'll have to let the windows go until next week. Although they get so dirty."

"I'll do them," Dicey assured her.

"And the floor. Did you damp mop?"

"No, no I'm sorry, I didn't. I didn't know what you meant by that."

"We'll just have to do the living room as well, tomorrow. Somehow."

"I'll do it, don't you worry about it."

Cousin Eunice poured the noodles into the boiling water.

"But Cousin Eunice?"

"Yes, Dicey."

"You know that Father Joseph brought us some clothes."

"That's nice."

"Yes, it was nice. We are grateful. You'll tell him, won't you?"

"Yes I will."

"But—we need underwear, and there wasn't any. And blue jeans or shorts, just one more each, so that when we play we won't ruin good clothes. And sneakers. At least, the others need sneakers. I can still wear mine for a long time. I guess I don't have to have a second pair of shorts."

"Oh dear."

Dicey pushed the forks around on the table, as if she was still setting it.

"So we'll have to go shopping tomorrow too," Cousin Eunice said.

"Thank you," Dicey said.

"I don't know how much things for children cost."

"Neither do I. I'm sorry," Dicey said. "Maybe I could get work?"

"I don't think so," Cousin Eunice said. She was stirring the noodles with a long-handled fork. "I was talking with my girls and they said someone your age could only get babysitting jobs. I don't know anybody who has small children. We might advertise in the paper I suppose, but who would take care of the housework then? The girls said—you know how silly some people are—that I was a saint to take you in, that anybody else would turn you over to social services. But I said, I can't do that, they're my own flesh and blood. Which in a way you are, you know."

"Yes," Dicey said. Then she added, because she knew it was true even though she didn't feel that it was true, "You are being awfully kind to us."

Cousin Eunice nodded and smiled her foolish smile.

"James is excited about school," Dicey told her. "Maybeth and Sammy are enrolled in day camp."

"That's nice. And you dusted?"

"Yes. Everything." Dicey was glad to be able to answer yes to one of the cleaning chores. "Are those your photograph albums in the bookcase?"

Cousin Eunice nodded as she put a colander in the sink.

"May I look through them?" Dicey asked.

"I guess so," Cousin Eunice said. "I didn't keep the albums. They're Mother's work. Some of the pictures are very, very old. You'll be careful, won't you?"

"Yes," Dicey said. "Will you be late coming home tonight?"

"After ten. There's no need for you to wait up. Mother never did. I expect you'll all be in bed by the time I return. There's a television in my bedroom you can watch. As long as you don't play in there. Children like watching television, don't they?"

Dicey answered with more enthusiasm than she felt.

"And tomorrow we'll have to remember to have a key made for you." Cousin Eunice sighed and drained the noodles.

CHAPTER 11

Something about Aunt Cilla's house (even though she knew it belonged to Cousin Eunice, Dicey still thought of it as Aunt Cilla's house, and still regretted her lost dream of it) made Dicey's brain slow down. Maybe it was trying so hard to please Cousin Eunice that had that effect on her. Maybe it was the routine of every day, with meals, cleaning, times to drop off the little children and pick them up, shopping, mending and ironing, having the cup of tea ready for Cousin Eunice at precisely twenty of six. Maybe it was just fatigue after her long journey there. Or maybe it was that nothing seemed to happen, except the same thing happening over and over again.

Even that was not precisely true. Sergeant Gordo called up one morning when Dicey was alone in the house. He asked her to come down to the police station, and gave her careful instructions for getting there on the bus. She took just enough change for her fare from shopping money and rode the bus down to the old stone building, with bars on the windows of the second and third stories. There she sat in the midst of a large, busy room to look at some pictures of women who might be Momma. None of them were. All of them, Sergeant Gordo told her, were dead and unidentified. They had found the Tillermans' car, he told her, and the Peewauket police could sell it and send the money to Dicey. He didn't expect she would get very much for it, he said.

"Does that mean Momma's not dead?" Dicey asked.

"I think we can assume that," Sergeant Gordo said. "Now, I'll start checking hospitals. Part of the problem is that we don't know where to look. If you'd reported her missing right away, we'd have a better chance."

"I'm sorry," Dicey said.

"Fat lot of good that does now," he answered. His phone rang then, and he waved her away. "I'll be in touch if anything turns up."

Dicey didn't have much time for thinking about her family. James, she knew, was perfectly happy. He studied at night and went through the heavy wooden doors into the school at a run, every morning. Now and then he would report some amazing fact to Dicey. One time he told her about Alaric's treasure, that disappeared long ago when Rome ruled the world and America wasn't even discovered. Nobody had ever found the treasure because Alaric hid it so well. He diverted a river, then buried the treasure in the river bed, then rerouted the river back to its old path. The treasure was somewhere there, in Italy. Only Alaric had known where. He even killed all the men who had worked to hide it, so they couldn't tell. James pored over the maps in his history book, trying to think out where the treasure might be. James was always willing to tell Dicey what he was learning, even though he seemed to have no interest in discussing other things with her.

Sammy, on the other hand, demanded more and more of her attention. He ran up to her every afternoon, grabbed her hand and pulled her away from the gate where she waited with Maybeth silent beside her. "Let's go," he said. "Let's play ball. Will you play catch with me? Can we race on the sidewalk?" He wanted to wrestle with her after dinner and needed her to tuck him in every night.

Maybeth was Maybeth. Silent and peaceful, she went off to church with Cousin Eunice on Sundays dressed in a frilly pink dress Cousin Eunice had bought her, wearing a little straw hat with flowers on the brim and white gloves. She even had a little white purse. Cousin Eunice had taken a great liking to Maybeth.

Dicey wondered if she was losing touch with her family.

Dicey had looked through Aunt Cilla's photograph albums. She didn't know what it was she was looking for, just something. There were only two pictures of Aunt Cilla's childhood, before she met and married Mr. Logan and lived in Bridgeport.

The first picture was a posed photographer's picture, badly yellowed, of a man with a long beard and a woman with long hair piled on top of her head. The woman held a baby on her lap. Beside her stood a girl with curling blonde hair and a silly smile. Underneath this picture Aunt Cilla had written in her lacy handwriting: *Mother, Father, Abigail, and myself.* Dicey thought Abigail must be the baby, since Cousin Eunice said Aunt Cilla was twelve years older than her sister.

The other picture must have been taken at a birthday party, because there was a cake with candles at the center of the picture. A pretty young woman in a white summer dress held a knife to cut the cake. Beside her, on one side, stood her parents, the man's beard turning white and the woman grown fat. On the other side stood a girl with wildly curly dark hair and a sour expression. The three adults were looking at the photographer and smiling. The little girl scowled down at the cake. Her hands were behind her back. Dicey would have bet that her fists were clenched.

Dicey recognized the older daughter as Aunt Cilla. The younger girl was Abigail. The sour one. Her grandmother.

One afternoon Dicey went early to meet James. She went early on purpose and entered the school building rather than going around to the playground to where James usually waited for her. She found Father Joseph in a small office, sitting behind a wooden desk correcting papers.

"We're very pleased with James," he said to her. "Sit down." He pulled out a chair. "How is everything going for you? You've been with your cousin for about two weeks now, haven't you?"

"Yes," Dicey said.

"Is something wrong?" he asked her. Then he seemed to recall something that had slipped his mind. "I've been wanting to talk with you anyway and haven't gotten around to it. I'm glad you came in. Shall we deal with your business first, and then get on to mine?"

"But you said you were pleased with James," Dicey said. She was alarmed. "He's happy here. Awfully happy."

"James is fine, fine," Father Joseph said. He closed up his grade book, folded his hands and looked at her. "What brought you to see me?"

"I wondered if you had heard from your church in Crisfield," Dicey said. Her mind was working furiously. Was something wrong about Maybeth? Or Sammy? Or both of them? She knew something was wrong with Sammy at camp, she'd known that all along.

"What do you know about your mother's family?" Father Joseph asked.

"Nothing. Momma never talked about them, never at all. Except Aunt Cilla. And that wasn't the truth—but Momma didn't know that. I found a picture of my grandmother in Aunt Cilla's albums, but she was only a girl, Maybeth's age. Cousin Eunice doesn't know anything. Did you find out something?"

"A little. The family is not Catholic, you know."

Dicey nodded. He kept bringing that up.

"So they aren't parishioners. If they were parishioners, then we would know a great deal about them. But—your grandmother. Her name is Abigail Tillerman."

"I knew that. There were names under one of the pictures."

"She lives alone on a small farm, outside of Crisfield. She lives absolutely alone there. Her husband died some years ago."

So Dicey didn't have a grandfather.

"They weren't Catholics, but Crisfield is a small town, where everybody knows everybody else. So—the priest asked some questions of his older parishioners. They had known the Tillermans. None of them had been friends—the Tillermans didn't seem to have friends—but they knew about them. He told me there were three children in the family. A boy, John, named after his father. People say he is in California. Nobody has heard from him for years, not his mother, nobody—twenty years or more. A second son died in Vietnam. Do you know about the war in Vietnam?"

Dicey nodded. Well, she had heard of it, and James would be able to tell her about it.

"Then the daughter, your mother. She ran off when she was twenty-one, they say, to join a merchant mariner she had somehow met, a man named Francis Verricker."

"My father?" The man who had swung her to his shoulder and named her his little only.

Father Joseph rubbed his hand over his eyes. "Yes. At least, that is the name on the birth certificates from Provincetown. I have no reason to think he was not everyone's father. The police are trying to trace him for me. They had searched for him some years ago. He seems to have disappeared."

"I don't mind," Dicey said.

"I do." Father Joseph's voice was sharp and angry. That surprised Dicey, and, sensing his concern, she was grateful to him, for the first time in all the time in Bridgeport, truly grateful.

"Do you mind hearing unpleasant truths, Dicey?"

"Yes. But I'd rather know the truth than not, if that's what you mean."

"I thought so. The Tillerman home—it must have been unhappy. Do you know what that can mean?"

"I think so," Dicey said. "I mean, we were happy. We were—whether you believe it or not . . ."

"Oddly enough, I do believe it."

Dicey smiled at him. "You see, there were kids at school—they hated their parents or they hated other people so much that you knew—it wasn't just being angry, it was hating. I can't explain what I mean, but I could feel the unhappiness."

"I see that James doesn't have all the brains in the family," Father Joseph said.

Dicey was flattered. "He's the smart one. I'm just—practical."

"Well, the Tillermans seem to have had that kind of unhappiness. The priest—or his informants—seem to blame her parents, especially the father. Remember, this is conjecture, not fact. It may just be gossip, you know. This is just what someone told him and he told me. Your grandfather seems to have been a stern man. An unbending man. Over-righteous perhaps. Perhaps cruel. Nobody knows anything certain. Your grandmother always let him have his way. Nobody can say what she thought. She never spoke of it. He had his boys do a man's work, from the time they were eight. He used a whip for disobedience, a real whip. He did not tolerate disobedience of any sort. He quarreled with his neighbors. He was angry—probably hate-filled too. She—your grandmother—was apparently the kind of woman who sticks faithfully to her husband's rule. She may have thought he was right. Or something else."

"It doesn't really matter which, does it?"

"In effect, no. You are practical."

"I haven't had much choice."

"Speaking practically then, your other uncle is dead, your mother has disappeared, and I don't think your uncle John wants to be found. Which leaves your cousin Eunice."

What was wrong with her grandmother? Dicey didn't ask aloud. She sat silent for a while. "What a family," she finally said.

"You shouldn't judge unless you've been there and known what actually went on," Father Joseph said.

"Come on," Dicey protested. "And Momma's—but she gave us a good home in Provincetown. She took good care of us, as good as she could."

"Yes, I think so, in some ways. One wonders," he said carefully, his light brown eyes resting on Dicey's face, "if there isn't a strain of—mental weakness."

Was he reading her mind?

"Your grandmother's isolation—she has no phone, so the priest drove out from Crisfield to talk with her. She wouldn't let him into the house. She apparently screamed aloud so that she wouldn't hear what he was saying."

Dicey remembered Momma's strangeness and James's idea that craziness was inherited.

"I mention this to you because I want to tell you that, if it can be inherited, you have probably *not* inherited it. In my opinion," Father Joseph said.

"Are you sure?"

"No, of course not. But remember, you've already been through more trials than most people endure in a lifetime. You and James, you two at least, seem to have the strength and resilience to go on. Isn't that what sanity is?"

"I don't know," Dicey said. She rose to go, her mind filled with what he had said.

"But we *are* concerned about your sister. She is—so far behind her age group. She doesn't speak. She can't read or work with numbers."

This again.

"She can," Dicey sat down again. "She can do all that. She isn't—she doesn't in front of strangers. Her teachers always said she couldn't do things, but at home, with me or James, she could. You don't believe me."

"No, I don't."

"You didn't believe me about our father being the same," Dicey reminded him.

"That's true."

"You just have to give Maybeth time."

"How much time? There's Sammy, too. The brothers report that he is not mixing in well. He is hostile to his peers and hard to direct and control. He plays alone, because the other boys avoid him."

Dicey sighed. "It was hardest on Sammy when Momma left us. And before it was hardest because she paid so much attention to him. James told me on our way here that in Provincetown Sammy had it hardest of anyone. Because of coming after Maybeth. And the things people said about Momma."

"How did you and James manage?" Father Joseph asked.

"James is smart. He'd think his own thoughts and ignore people. I guess I just fought back too hard for people to want to tease me. But Sammy wouldn't. I mean, he'd fight, but he's not as fierce as I am." Father Joseph smiled. "When he was a baby, he was always happy and friendly. That's the way he really is. He can still be that way. Sometimes, on the way here, you could see it, you could see him getting to be more like himself."

"Sammy is a difficult child," Father Joseph said. "But I suppose his hostility isn't surprising when you think of causes. He needs a warm, loving home."

So do we all, Dicey thought. She looked quickly at Father Joseph. "I love Sammy," she said.

"Of course you do. You must consider, however, the effect of these burdens on your own life. I think you must. I think you must give some thought to adoption and foster homes. Sammy, despite his behavior, may prove the easiest to find a home for. It will be hard to place Maybeth. A retarded child—"

"She's not!"

"She has the symptoms," Father Joseph answered gently. "And you, an older child. You also would be hard to place. Your cousin—I don't know what her plans are now."

Dicey had no idea what he was talking about. She shrugged her shoulders.

"James also is old for adoption, but he would easily find a permanent home here at the school, or he might stay with one of our families. His academic promise makes him most desirable."

Dicey could think of nothing to say.

"You should think of these things," Father said, still gently. "I know you don't want to, but you must think them through and be ready. Think of yourself also. You are still a child yourself."

A child? Dicey felt a hundred years old. Or more.

"I'm not asking you to decide. Just to open your mind to other possibilities."

Dicey nodded. She knew she should thank him, but she couldn't. So she just walked out of the room, without a word.

That afternoon, in the mail, Dicey received a check from the Police Department of Peewauket, for fifty-seven dollars. The receipt with it said "Profits from the sale of one 1963 Chevrolet sedan, less costs." Dicey looked at the check and smiled, for the first time in days, it felt. She could give it to Cousin Eunice and that would make her cousin feel better about taking the Tillermans in. Or she could buy some blue jeans for herself and Maybeth, which would make them feel better. Or she could hide the money away, for what purpose she didn't know.

Dicey knew what she should do. She should give the money to Cousin Eunice. Instead, she cashed the check at the grocery store, where the man knew her, and put the money into the box Maybeth's church shoes had come in.

Having money made a difference. It woke Dicey up. She began to think of how she could earn more during the day when everybody was gone. She could easily spend less time on housework if she pushed herself to be faster and more efficient. If she did that she could have some time for earning. Dicey felt like her old self again.

Because she was young, Dicey couldn't get a regular job. Over the next few days, she thought hard about what she could do to earn money. She could wash windows, she knew how, she'd done it. She decided to try that. If that didn't work, she would try something else.

The first place Dicey asked for work was the grocery store. The manager-owner, Mr. Platernis, liked her, so she figured she'd try him first.

Dicey suggested to Mr. Platernis that she wash his windows three times a week, for two dollars each time. He studied her.

"I've only got two windows," he said.

"They're plate glass, and big. I'd do them inside and out, and then I'd restack the canned goods and dog food," Dicey countered.

"You'd need some special equipment," he said. "A long-handled washer, a bucket, cleanser."

"If I knew I'd be using them I'd buy them," Dicey said.

He considered this. Dicey enjoyed the bargaining. He enjoyed it too. "I'd buy them here," Dicey added. "I'd buy all my supplies here too."

"You going into the business?"

"I might be."

He thought some more. "Two dollars is a lot of money."

"A store with clean windows is more attractive to customers. Especially a grocery store. More people would come to shop here."

"I can do the windows myself."

"Three times a week? They get pretty dirty."

"I know, oh I know. How about a trial period of a week?"

"Two weeks," Dicey said. "It'll cost me that much to get the equipment."

He laughed at her. "All right, two weeks. And I'll call some other people who might be interested, some other store owners in this area. We'll see if they would like to employ your services."

"Would you, Mr. Platernis? You won't be sorry." Dicey grinned at him.

By bargaining this way, before she knew it, Dicey had six regular jobs, washing the city grime off the windows of neighborhood stores. She had two grocery stores, one hardware store, one shoe store, one pawn shop and one dress store. The dress store was her best job—they had four big windows they wanted washed three times a week, so she earned twelve dollars a week from there. That, added to the six dollars weekly from Mr. Platernis and four apiece from the other three stores, made a total income of thirty dollars a week. Her supplies, once she had made the original purchase of bucket and long-handled squeegee, cost her five dollars a week. Mr. Platernis let her store her equipment in the closet with his own cleaning equipment and supplies, just to keep an eye on her, he said. He didn't need to worry—Dicey liked her work, she liked making money.

The money in the shoebox began to mount up. Dicey's spirits mounted with it.

She was working hard, but she seemed to have more energy than before. The July heat thickened and deepened, but Dicey wasn't slowed down by that. Mr. Platernis couldn't get over her high spirits. "You must have been raised in the tropics," he said, mopping at his face with a cloth handkerchief. He often stood outside and talked with Dicey while she worked. He would help her replace the soup cans and bags of dog food she had to move before she could wash the inside windows.

"I like having something to do," Dicey said.

"I'd think you have enough to do keeping house for Miss Logan and your family. Since you arrived I haven't seen her, except passing by. You're doing all her shopping, and the rest of it too, I'm guessing."

"That's not the same," Dicey said.

"You don't like housework," Mr. Platernis concluded.

Dicey didn't contradict him, though she knew that wasn't it. She didn't mind housework. She'd always kept house in Provincetown, although Momma wasn't nearly as fussy as Cousin Eunice. But it wasn't the same when you always had to remember to feel grateful.

Dicey bought herself three maps: one of Connecticut, one of New York and New Jersey, one of Maryland and Delaware. She found Crisfield easily enough, way down at the end of Maryland, facing the Chesapeake Bay.

One night at dinner Dicey tried to find out something about her grandmother. "Did you ever visit your mother's family?" she asked.

Cousin Eunice looked up in surprise. "Of course not. Mother said she didn't want to go back, and she wouldn't have me going near the place. Sammy! What are you doing? Sit up! Don't lie on the table! Bring the fork to your face, not your face to the fork."

Her eyes, sulking behind the glasses, went back to Dicey. "I don't know why you children can't work on your manners yourselves, instead of worrying me with them. Don't you think I have enough to do?"

Dicey cast a quick eye around the table. Maybeth put her left hand into her lap and straightened her back. Then she met Dicey's glance with a silly smile, half worried, half apologetic.

"I have enough to do," Cousin Eunice went on. "And added to—" She hesitated and seemed to remember something. "Sammy? Is that a cut on your hand?"

Sammy chewed and nodded.

"How did that happen?" Cousin Eunice asked.

Sammy stuck his jaw out. He did not answer.

"Answer me," Cousin Eunice said.

"I don't remember," Sammy muttered.

"That is a lie."

"How do you know?"

"I know because I heard about how you got cut, that's how I know."

"Then why did you ask me?" Sammy demanded.

Maybeth bowed her head lower over her plate. Dicey looked at Sammy, trying to will him to be cooperative. Or at least quiet.

Cousin Eunice spoke through stiff lips. "Don't be fresh. Don't you ever be fresh with me. You hear? The reason I asked you is because—because—because I wanted to hear what you would say," she finished lamely.

"I didn't say nothing," Sammy said.

"What was the fight about?" Cousin Eunice asked.

"Nothing," Sammy said.

"Sammy?" Dicey interrupted. "Cousin Eunice wants to hear your side."

"I can't remember what it was about," Sammy said stubbornly. Dicey could have picked him up and shaken him.

"Who won?" James asked.

"James!" cried Cousin Eunice.

Sammy lifted his head. "Me, I did."

"That has nothing to do with it," Cousin Eunice said.

Yes it does, Dicey said to herself. It does to Sammy.

"I don't want you to fight anymore," Cousin Eunice announced. "I want you to promise me that you won't."

Sammy chewed silently. He kept his eyes on his plate. At least, Dicey thought, his mouth was closed.

"Sammy—" Cousin Eunice warned him.

He shook his head.

"Then you will go to your room. Right now." Cousin Eunice's voice sounded angry, and tired. "And you will stay there for the rest of the night. You tell lies. You won't promise not to fight. I won't have you at my table."

Sammy got down from his chair and trudged out of the room. They heard his slow footsteps going up the uncarpeted stairs. They heard the door slam behind him.

"I don't know. I just don't know," Cousin Eunice said. She shook her head and the sausage curls on it bounced. "At least I hear some fine things about James. James seems to be making quite a good impression." She smiled at him.

James wavered between saying something rude and being flattered. Dicey watched him nervously. "James is smart," she said, trying to tip the scales.

"It's not only that," Cousin Eunice said. "James conducts himself well, too. He is a credit."

"It's a good school," James finally said. Dicey let out her breath. James looked across at her, waggled his eyebrows the way Windy had, and kept on talking. "When you think of all there is to learn, in order to understand things. Like history and science—there's so much to learn. The fathers say that part of man's purpose is to increase his knowledge, so that he can understand better how great is God's work. A lot of people think knowledge is dangerous. But they're wrong. Did you ever think of that, Cousin Eunice?"

"Yes, of course," Cousin Eunice said. "God wants children to study hard and behave well in school."

James answered slowly. "I guess you could say that. But that's not the way the fathers talk about it, about learning. They don't treat it like a duty. They treat it like a gift. Like grace."

"I don't think you can be right about that," Cousin Eunice said. "Not grace. That's not what the Gospels say, is it? Nobody's ever told me the Gospels say that. I've always understood that duty is the most important, even the best."

James shrugged. "Maybe learning's just that way for me. Lucky for me, isn't it?"

Cousin Eunice smiled at him. The tension was gone from the table. But Sammy hadn't had much dinner and he was up in his room. Dicey tried not to think about that. It was his own fault anyway, for being so stubborn. But Dicey had never talked about her fights when she got home—you just didn't do that. That was squealing. Momma never asked about them. Why did Cousin Eunice have to ask?

After the dishes were done and Sammy was asleep and Maybeth was tucked into her bed and James was settled down to homework in the living room, Cousin Eunice called to Dicey to join her in the kitchen. Dicey saw that a cup of tea had been made for her, and for some reason that made her nervous.

"Sit down, Dicey," Cousin Eunice greeted her. She was wearing another one of her black dresses. Dicey had never seen her wearing colors. Her eyes looked out at Dicey from behind polished glass. "I was talking with Father Joseph today."

"I didn't know that," Dicey said. She wondered what was wrong now.

"He took me to lunch," Cousin Eunice said. "Well, I was surprised when he asked me. I wasn't sure it was right—but he insisted that it was. We didn't go to a real restaurant, but it was a very nice cafeteria, everything as clean as you could want. I had a fruit salad. There's something I haven't ever told you, you see, and Father Joseph thinks I should."

"What is that?" Dicey asked.

"Before you came, you and your family, I had certain—ambitions," Cousin Eunice said. Her voice was very soft and she stirred her tea thoughtfully. "Father Joseph knows of these, of course. He approved of them, with certain reservations. And since he had approved, I was sure it was the right thing."

"What was?"

"To enter a sisterhood. To become a nun. I was going to be a nun before . . . and Father Joseph had made the preliminary arrangements for me. It's a useful life. I have a substantial savings account, which would make up my dowry, that and the house. So you see, I could have managed well."

"It sounds—" Dicey tried to think of what she should say. "Nice. You'd make a good nun."

"Do you think so? I had hoped so. However, that is out of the question now." Cousin Eunice's eyes filmed with tears, and she shook her head. "Because of you children. You need me more, Father Joseph says. It is God's work, just as much, caring for the abandoned children." As she spoke, she looked over Dicey's shoulder at something Dicey couldn't see, something Dicey suspected wasn't there at all, and her eyes shone. "That is my duty. You will be my family now." Her soft voice vibrated with the pleasure of resolution and sacrifice.

"Are you sure?" Dicey asked.

"It is God's will," Cousin Eunice said, bowing her head.

Dicey sipped tea, which she had never liked, and thought about this. "That's awfully kind of you."

Cousin Eunice smiled at Dicey.

"You're giving up something you want," Dicey said.

"You are not to speak of that," Cousin Eunice said. "I wasn't going to tell you at all, but Father Joseph said that you and I especially must understand one another. So that if sometimes I grow sad . . . you will know why and sympathize with me rather than feeling you've done something wrong. Perhaps Maybeth is meant to be a nun, perhaps she has a vocation, and it will be my place to guide her to it. Perhaps she will be my purpose in life."

Dicey wanted to get up and run, but she made herself sit still.

"Father Joseph suggested that I adopt you, so that I will be the legal guardian."

"What if Momma comes back?"

"Surely she has shown herself unfit to raise children," Cousin Eunice answered. Her lips pursed.

Dicey couldn't answer that.

"However, Dicey, you and I must deal with Sammy. He's causing some trouble at camp. Not just today—constantly. Father Joseph said he had spoken to you about this. Sammy has to be brought into line. I couldn't adopt a child who will bring nothing but trouble. Could I? You saw how he behaved at supper. Sammy has to understand that his behavior is unacceptable."

"But—" Dicey said, and then changed her mind. "How would you do that?"

"I'll talk with Father Joseph. He's not sure that my house is the best place for Sammy, but he feels we should try it for a while, to see if we can keep your family together. He's concerned about Maybeth, too, he told me, but I could assure him that we would do well, Maybeth and I. But Sammy—I don't know. I'll see. Father Joseph knows about disciplining boys. James, fortunately, is biddable. Sammy has to be brought into line, so he doesn't shame me."

Dicey stayed absolutely still. She didn't even blink. She didn't trust herself to speak.

"I do feel better, now that we've talked. Don't you?" Cousin Eunice looked happy. Her curls bounced on her head. "You will be like a family of my own. If I'd had a daughter, she might be just your age. You'll grow up and have children of your own. So that when I'm older, I won't be alone. Just as Mother wasn't alone. In a way, I'm glad about this. Aren't you? And you children will have a good mother."

We already have a good mother, Dicey said angrily to herself. Hold on, she said to herself. This was what Father Joseph had decided. It might be for the best. The Tillermans would be able to stay together—maybe. They would have a home. Dicey knew she should feel grateful to Cousin Eunice. But she didn't. She felt like crying.

CHAPTER 12

August choked the city. The morning sun had to burn its red path through low-hanging hazes and clouds of industrial smoke. The streets steamed, as concrete reflected heavy sunlight. The temperature climbed until one in the afternoon, and then continued climbing. When it rained, fat gray drops plopped down upon the roads, then bounced up, as if in a half-hearted effort to escape. At evening, darkness gradually smothered the sun, until night fell upon the city.

Dicey rose early every morning, cooked the breakfasts, cleaned the kitchen, walked her family to their daily activities and hurried back to pick up her equipment and wash whatever store windows were on her schedule for the day. Then she completed whatever housekeeping chores Cousin Eunice had assigned before she went to fetch her family, played briefly with them, prepared dinner and made Cousin Eunice's cup of tea.

Weekends were a little different. For those two afternoons, the Tillermans could go off to a park or a public beach after they had completed the morning chores, or after Maybeth had returned from church with Cousin Eunice.

Sometimes it was more convenient for Dicey to meet Maybeth at the church, if they were going to picnic at the park, or if Cousin Eunice had friends she wanted to visit with. Dicey would wait outside the big brick building, waiting for the heavy doors to be opened from within. The steeple stretched tall up into the sky. There was a gold cross on top of the steeple, and from below it looked like the tip of the cross scratched the bottom of the sky.

When the doors opened, Dicey watched carefully for her sister. Lots of children went to church with their parents, all of them dressed up. The girls wore organdy dresses and party shoes and ribbons in their hair, or hats. The boys wore real suits and ties. Cousin Eunice always walked out slowly, surrounded by a group of women who could have been her sisters. They dressed alike. They all wore those high-heeled shoes. They all had curled their hair into sausages.

These women made a pet out of Maybeth. She would stand in the middle and they would tell her how pretty she was, how lucky she was to have naturally curly hair, and what a sweet, quiet girl she was. "You're going to break some hearts for sure," they said, giggling.

Maybeth listened to this and smiled foolishly.

"An angel like you—nobody will be good enough for you. She's a treasure, Eunice," they said.

"Don't I know it?" Cousin Eunice answered smugly.

"A doll, a perfect doll."

Dicey put her hands behind her back and clenched her fists, waiting for Cousin Eunice to see her.

When Cousin Eunice called her, the women stepped back and smiled primly at her. Maybeth put out her hand for Dicey to take. Her eyes were wide as she looked at Dicey, wide and pleased with the attention. The silly smile stayed.

Sunday afternoons the Tillermans chose to go to a small park nearby because on summer weekends it was less crowded than the beach. There were trees there, and grass. Several times Dicey saw Mr. Platernis in the park, who greeted her warmly with:

"How's my go-getter today?" Nobody commented on this, except James, but Dicey abruptly changed the subject.

She found a time, soon after her talk with Cousin Eunice, to try to explain the situation to Sammy.

"You've got to be cooperative at camp," Dicey said.

"I don't like them," Sammy said.

"Don't like who? The boys? Or the teachers?"

"Don't like any of them."

"Why not?"

"They're all bossy."

That was all he would say. His little jaw stuck out, and he pulled at blades of grass as they sat by the sandbox.

"We've got a problem, Sammy," Dicey said. "We have to please Cousin Eunice. The way for you to help is to cooperate at camp. Act more friendly."

"Why?" Sammy asked.

"So we can all stay together with Cousin Eunice," Dicey said.

"When Momma comes we won't have to. And I don't want to anyway."

Dicey sighed. She didn't much want to herself. She daydreamed about Crisfield and a farm; but she had learned her lesson about believing in daydreams, learned it from Cousin Eunice and her house that wasn't a big white house by the ocean.

"Would you do it for James and Maybeth and me?" Dicey asked him. "Would you try, for us? I know it's hard. I know you get angry. But we need you to try. When we were on our own, you stopped quarreling and helped. Remember?"

Sammy nodded.

"You liked that, didn't you?"

Sammy nodded.

"All I want you to do is be more that way at camp. Can you try?"

Sammy nodded. "You sound like Momma," he said.

"What do you mean?"

"Well, you do. When she'd ask me to be gooder, that was the way she'd talk."

He ran off to join Maybeth on the swings. Dicey watched him catch a flying swing and leap onto it, then pump furiously with his sturdy little legs. When he caught up with Maybeth, he cheered for himself.

Day succeeded day in slow procession. Cousin Eunice treated Dicey differently since their talk. She wanted to sit with Dicey in the kitchen every night, with cups of tea, which Dicey could never completely drink, and talk about religion and serving God and how when she was a girl she had wanted to be a nun. But her mother said she wasn't strong enough in spirit, didn't have a real calling, should wait to see if she got married.

Dicey listened. She began to feel sorry for Cousin Eunice, who had lived all of her life in this city, who had gone off to work every morning along the same gray city streets. Dicey didn't like the sound of Aunt Cilla. She had lied to Momma in her letters. It seemed to Dicey that Aunt Cilla had tried to keep Cousin Eunice all for herself. And then, Dicey thought to herself as the soft voice droned on about service and prayer, just when Cousin Eunice was about to do what she'd always wanted, the Tillermans turned up to tie her down again. Poor Cousin Eunice.

If that had happened to Dicey, she'd be angry. Cousin Eunice wasn't angry at all, just sad sometimes. As if this was the way her whole life had to be, not getting what she wanted, always giving it up for the sake of someone else.

Maybe she enjoyed giving things up for the sake of someone else. Some people liked that feeling. But even if that was the case, Dicey knew her cousin would rather have been a nun. That was what she really wanted.

It wasn't very much to want, and she didn't have even that.

The money in Dicey's shoebox increased slowly, day by day. Sixty-five, seventy, which, with the fifty dollars she had left from the car, made one hundred and twenty, then one hundred and forty dollars, one hundred and fifty.

Maybeth came home from camp with a note addressed to Miss Tillerman. The note requested Dicey to come to camp the next afternoon at two, an hour before the children went home. Somebody named Sister Berenice wanted to talk to her.

Dicey didn't want to go. She knew what the sister would say. She read the note and reread it. She considered throwing it away and pretending she had never gotten it, as Momma had done. She ripped it up into little pieces and dropped them into the wastepaper basket. She didn't want to hear whatever the sister had to say, about Maybeth being retarded and needing a special school.

James was no help. He seemed convinced that the fathers, and the nuns too, couldn't make a mistake. "Go and talk to her. Maybe she knows something we don't. Maybe she knows something that can help Maybeth. Just plan to learn from her, about whatever she has to say. You've got to keep an open mind, Dicey. You've got to leave a door open so understanding can get in. That's one thing I've learned."

"It's not just minds," Dicey said. "You all think it's just smartness that counts. But Stewart didn't think that. And I don't think I do, either. I don't want to go."

"Suit yourself," James said. "I'd go."

"I'm not you," Dicey said.

But she kept the appointment, wearing one of the secondhand dresses that made her feel stiff and awkward because they never fit properly. She wore sneakers, because they were the only shoes she had. She held her chin high and a little angry—she knew Maybeth and this woman didn't.

Sister Berenice waited for Dicey in one of the classrooms next to the camp playground. It was a room for very small children. All the chairs were small. The tables didn't even come up to Dicey's knees.

Sister Berenice rose from her desk when Dicey came into the long room. The sister was very tall and very thin. She wore a black suit with a longish skirt, and her face was framed by the cowl she wore. She had pale blue eyes and her mouth looked stern. When she pulled up one of the little chairs for Dicey to sit on, Dicey saw with surprise that she wore a silver wedding ring on her right hand.

"You're a child," she said. Dicey nodded. "I asked Maybeth," Sister Berenice said, sounding cross, "I asked her who her guardian was and she said Dicey, her sister. I asked if you were married and Maybeth said no. Well, actually, she just shook her head. It is the longest conversation we have had. I didn't think to ask Father Joseph how old you were. Who is the person legally responsible for Maybeth?"

"Our cousin Eunice, I guess," Dicey said. "Until they find our mother."

"Miss Logan," Sister Berenice murmured, in apparent disbelief.

"She took us in. She didn't have to do that," Dicey said. "She'd never even heard of us." She wanted Sister Berenice to appreciate what Cousin Eunice had done. She wanted to appreciate it herself.

"How old are you?" she asked Dicey.

Dicey's temper flared. "I'm thirteen. How old are you?"

A smile bent the corners of Sister Berenice's pale mouth. "Fifty-three, old enough to recognize spirit when I meet it. Tell me about your sister, Dicey."

Dicey stared at her in surprise. For a minute she couldn't think of anything to say. Usually, people told her about Maybeth, and she tried to explain that they were wrong. Nobody had ever asked her first.

"She's shy," Dicey said. "She almost never speaks to strangers. And people always want to speak to her, because she's pretty. Usually, she stays stiff and quiet and stares, with big eyes. She doesn't even talk to us much. But when she does, it's always the right thing to say. Not right-polite, right-true."

Sister Berenice sat listening, with folded hands. So Dicey went on.

"I don't know why Maybeth is the way she is. But she's always been that way. From the time she started school, her teachers thought she was stupid. I guess I can understand that. She would be so quiet that you'd think she didn't know anything. She stayed back one year, in first grade. Then the teacher wanted to keep her back this year, or at least that's what I think. Momma never opened those notes."

"You said she almost never speaks to strangers. That means she sometimes does. Who did she speak to?"

Dicey told her how Maybeth had talked to Stewart and sung with him. "She sings—it's lovely when she sings. She learns songs fast, music and words. She couldn't be retarded and do that, could she?"

Sister Berenice just smiled.

"And she *can* read," Dicey said. "Not like James, but as well as Sammy. She used to read to me at home when I asked her to. And she *can* add and subtract." Dicey thought. "She's not quick, but she can work the problems out. It just takes her a longer time to learn school things, and she's too shy to say what she knows. When she plays, she builds gardens and castles and makes up stories about them." Dicey had never before defined so exactly just what Maybeth could and could not do. "I guess she's slow at school, but I don't think she's retarded. Or anything like that."

"Would you go look out the window at the children?" Sister Berenice asked Dicey. Puzzled, Dicey obeyed.

The playground was surrounded by a tall fence. Little groups of children were gathered about, playing or reading or listening to one of several nuns who were out there with them. Dicey's eyes searched for Maybeth among the many little girls.

She found her, sitting in a circle around a nun with a guitar. Maybeth sat behind the group. Her dress, like Dicey's, was long and dark. Her face was round and sad. All the other little girls were singing and clapping their hands, but Maybeth was staring at the nun's hands as they played on the instrument. She was not singing. She was not clapping.

The nun stopped playing and said something, at which all the little girls jumped up and ran to different parts of the playground. Maybeth didn't move. The nun bent to speak to her and she looked up.

"But she looks frightened," Dicey said. "Why does she look frightened?" She heard the rude, demanding tone of her own voice.

Sister Berenice didn't answer.

"I see what you mean," Dicey said. Maybeth did look different from all the other little girls. Dicey watched her sister walk slowly over to the swings. She stood there. Several girls were swinging energetically. There were some unoccupied swings, but Maybeth didn't get onto one. The other girls paid no attention to her.

It was as if Maybeth wasn't even there, not even to herself. What was wrong with her? She looked—empty.

"But she isn't that way," Dicey started to say.

"I wonder," Sister Berenice said in a voice that suggested doubt. Sister Berenice didn't believe Dicey. Why should she?

"Father Joseph said that you were unusual," Sister Berenice said to Dicey.

"He did?"

"Yes." The rich voice assured Dicey that this was the truth. "To keep your family together, and fed. But I wonder if you have faced the truth about Maybeth. I think you may be fooling yourself." This, too, Dicey recognized, was the truth.

Maybe she was, maybe . . .

"Do you know the kind of special schooling available to a child like Maybeth? Not through us, of course, but the state maintains excellent facilities for disabled children. There is much they can learn and do, such children, if they are properly taught. Is it fair to Maybeth to deny her the opportunity, just because you don't want to face the facts?"

"No," Dicey said. The word burst from her.

"I didn't think you wanted to do that to Maybeth."

"No," Dicey said again. "Those aren't the facts."

"Oh, now," the nun said. She sounded disappointed in Dicey.

Dicey sighed. "I'm sorry," she said. "I don't mean to be rude."

"Are you thinking of Maybeth or of yourself?" Sister Berenice asked quietly.

Dicey didn't know, and she didn't care; she was too tired and discouraged to think of an answer. This nun had already made up her mind anyway. Dicey didn't want to think about Maybeth anymore. She was arguing more from habit than conviction. "You just don't know," she repeated.

"I think I probably know better than you do."

Dicey was finished arguing. She just wanted to get out of there and take Maybeth with her. "Can Maybeth come with me now? It's almost time."

The nun stared at her for a long time. Finally she answered, "Yes, of course." But her voice said more, it told Dicey that the sister was sorry she had asked Dicey to come in. Well, Dicey was sorry too. She nodded, and left the room.

Dicey entered the playground through the tall iron gates. She started to walk over to where Maybeth was, but a young nun came and asked her what she was doing there. She sounded important, as though she was accustomed to being obeyed without question. Dicey explained who she was. She said that she had been meeting with Sister Berenice and had permission to take Maybeth home. The young nun looked back at the windows behind them and stood aside.

Maybeth had seen Dicey. She smiled at her, but did not come running as Sammy would have. Dicey smiled back and hoped the way she was feeling didn't show in her face. "Let's go get Sammy," she said, holding out her hand.

Sammy had a cut on his forehead that someone had covered with a big Band-Aid. His lip was swollen. "Oh Sammy." Dicey could not keep the worry out of her voice. "You said you'd try."

"I did."

"You were in a fight," Dicey said. "And a pretty bad one."

"He said—"

"Who? Who said?"

"Johnny. I don't know his last name. And I don't care. He's a big kid. He's in fourth grade. I made him cry and I didn't cry."

"What did he say?"

"He said I was going to a foster home because nobody here likes me. He said he heard the fathers saying it. It's not true, is it Dicey? So I fought him."

"What did the fathers say?"

"Johnny's the one that heard them. He said they didn't know he could hear."

"No, no. I mean when they stopped the fight. They did stop it, didn't they?"

Sammy nodded. They were walking to James's school. Dicey held one hand of each of the little ones. There was too much bad news in this day.

"They didn't say nothing. We didn't tell 'em nothing."

"So they think it's all your fault, don't they?"

Sammy nodded. "I have to stay inside alone tomorrow. All day."

"Oh Sammy. Why didn't you tell them what Johnny said?"

"Because they try to find out everything. What's a foster home?"

"You didn't know? And you fought about it?"

"It's not good is it? I could tell that. From how he said it."

Dicey sighed. "A foster home is where somebody not your own family takes you into their home to live. And somebody gives them an allowance, to pay for you."

"You wouldn't let them do that, would you, Dicey? I told Johnny and he said you couldn't stop them."

Dicey felt helpless, absolutely helpless, with the two little ones holding her hands. She knew how Sammy felt. She wanted to fight somebody herself. Or to run, fast, not waiting for lights to change. But she had the two little ones holding on to her.

"There's James now," she said to Sammy. Sammy ran to meet his brother. James was walking quickly, a huge smile on his face. At least one of us is happy, Dicey thought.

Dicey called the bus station and found out that it cost twenty-six dollars to get to Crisfield. Fifty-two dollars there and back. She would still have some money, so she wouldn't be dependent. She would stay in a hotel or something, for a couple of days. It was only for a couple of days, until she took a look at this grandmother, to see for herself.

She purchased a small overnight case at the Goodwill store. She located the bus station in Bridgeport. There, she picked up a bus schedule and found out that if she left Bridgeport at ten o'clock in the morning, she would have to change at New York for Wilmington. At Wilmington, she decided by looking at a map, she could get a bus to take her down to Easton, then Salisbury, then Crisfield. Easton and Salisbury were yellow on the map so they were big towns. There would be sure to be buses.

This was on a Thursday. She thought she would go the next Monday, so that the little ones would be in camp during the day while she was away. James could take charge, for four days. That was all she'd be gone for. They would just have to get along without her for four days. There was no way she could take them with her. Just as there was no way she could tell Cousin Eunice she was going.

That evening, Cousin Eunice came home late from work carrying a bakery bag. "Father Joseph called me at work. He is bringing a friend by after supper, after the children are in bed," she said. "I got a cake on my way home. Did you get the living room done today? It's Thursday."

Dicey nodded.

"Father Joseph said you have already met this man, a policeman. I have not. Did you wash the windows?"

Dicey had forgotten that. She lied. Well, it wasn't an entire lie, since she had washed windows that day. She just hadn't washed the windows Cousin Eunice meant.

"And a good vacuuming? I don't know—the house gets so dirty with all you children. I don't know how you manage to collect so much dirt and bring it inside." She fluttered about the kitchen, fussing over one thing and another, looking in the icebox for lemons, in the cupboard to be sure her good teapot was clean and there was sugar in the sugar bowl.

It could not be good news they brought. Dicey knew that ahead of time. If it had been good news, the sergeant would have called her up right away, or Momma would have called her up, or Momma would have appeared at the house.

Father Joseph and Sergeant Gordo arrived late. The two men and Cousin Eunice sat in all the chairs there were in the living room. After she had passed around the teacups, milk, sugar, lemon and cake, Dicey sat on the floor. She was wearing one of the stiff dresses Father Joseph had brought. Cousin Eunice twittered as she poured tea, then fell silent.

"We have located your mother," Sergeant Gordo said. He held a teacup in one hand and a plate with cake in the other. He could neither eat nor drink, because he had no free hand. He looked around for a table to set the plate on. Cousin Eunice made a little *Oh* sound at this news.

"I thought so," Dicey said.

"I don't have anything good to tell you," Sergeant Gordo said.

"I didn't think so," Dicey said. She made her face expressionless.

"You're a smart kid," the sergeant said. "Your mother is in a state hospital in Massachusetts. She was found in Boston. She—do you know the term catatonic?"

Dicey shook her head.

"It means the patient won't respond to anything. Your mother—well, she doesn't do anything, doesn't speak, doesn't seem to hear what's said to her, won't feed herself, won't move at all, not even to go to the bathroom. When they found out about her family, the doctors tried talking to her about you. No response. No response at all. Nothing. They think she's incurable."

Dicey nodded. "Are you sure it's Momma?"

"Her fingerprints match the ones the hospital took when you children were born."

"Why did they do that?" Dicey asked. She didn't know why she asked. She didn't care what he answered.

"So the mothers and babies can be sure they go together. They do the baby's feet. So nobody gets mixed up."

"Oh."

"And I've got a picture."

Dicey took the photograph. She looked at the vacant-faced woman lying in a bed, her hair cut off short and her hazel eyes staring at the camera without any expression, as if the camera and photographer were not there. Her face looked so flat and empty, so far away, as if it hung miles above the earth and could not be bothered by anything happening on the little planet below. "They cut her hair," Dicey said. "Are they sure she's incurable?"

"These head-shrinkers are never sure of anything. But they're as near to sure as they can be."

"I could go see her," Dicey suggested.

"I wouldn't do that, little girl. They'll get in touch with us if there's any change, and then maybe it might do some good."

"It would be best to forget her," Father Joseph said.

"What if I don't want to?" Dicey demanded, angry.

"I didn't mean that, child. I meant, it is better not to have false hopes."

Dicey clamped her mouth shut.

"Poor Liza," Cousin Eunice said. "She's only five years younger than I am. Do you know that?"

Cousin Eunice poured out more cups of tea, which Dicey passed around. The adults talked around her and above her, about adoption procedures and welfare applications. "Sammy is on trial here," Cousin Eunice said to Father Joseph.

He nodded. "As is Maybeth," he answered. Cousin Eunice shook her head but didn't say anything. Dicey walked out of the room. She heard Cousin Eunice start to call her back and Father Joseph say to let her go.

Maybeth was asleep and so was Sammy. James wasn't. Dicey undressed and lay down on her cot. Her mind was blank.

"What about Momma?" James whispered.

"How'd you know?"

"That policeman . . . they came in a police car."

"Momma's gone crazy," Dicey reported in a flat voice, "and they don't think she'll ever get better. She's in a mental hospital. She was in Boston. How do you think she got to Boston?"

James sat up. "What kind of crazy?"

"A kind where you just lie in bed and don't do anything. James, do you think Maybeth's like Momma?"

"Yes."

"Do you think Maybeth could go crazy like that?"

"Yes. If—if she had to. You know? Momma had four kids and no job. Our father walked out on her."

"But we were happy, weren't we? When we were in Provincetown. We were, I know it. Momma wasn't crazy then."

"Maybe. I don't know, Dicey. Does that mean this is our home?"

"Yeah. I guess so. I don't know, James. Would you like that?"

"It's a good school," James said. "I've never been in a school like this, where the teachers all know so much and they like it when you ask questions and they keep giving you more work. Nothing bothers the fathers, you know? Oh, swearing and things, those. But they're so sure they have the answers, they don't mind you asking questions. In this school, I'm really glad I'm me. I can learn anything—do you know how that feels, Dicey? The fathers show me how and I learn. You better believe I'm happy."

"Should we tell Sammy and Maybeth?"

"About Momma? I guess so, sometime. Not right now. Or is right away better?"

So they woke the two younger children and told them the bad news. Maybeth just nodded and sat closer to Dicey on the cot.

Sammy stuck his chin out. "She'll still get better maybe," he declared. "How do they know so much anyway. I don't care what they say. I won't believe them."

Dicey grinned at him, unable to stretch her mouth wide enough to let out all the feelings his silly stubbornness let her feel. Then she began to cry. "I'm sorry, Dicey," Maybeth said.

"Me too," Dicey said, burying her face in her sister's hair. "I'm sorry too."

Now she had to go on Monday and find out fast what Crisfield was like. What their grandmother was like. Cousin Eunice would flutter and flitter, and before they knew it the Tillermans would be adopted. Or something worse.

It was not that Dicey was ungrateful. They might end up here. Cousin Eunice's house might be the best place for them. Even for Sammy and Maybeth. It might be the best they could do, even if Sammy and Maybeth had to go somewhere else. But Dicey had to know that for sure.

That weekend she took the family to the beach. She was especially careful to pay attention to them. She laughed at Sammy's jokes and turned cartwheels on the sand with him and tossed him up over her shoulders into the water until he was exhausted. She built castles with Maybeth, decorating them with bits of shell and colored stones, telling stories about princesses and giants. She talked with James about history and science, listening with all her brain, so her questions would show that she was really interested.

Monday morning, she walked them all to camp and school.

Sammy hesitated at the gate and said, "I wish it was always the weekend."

Dicey ruffled his hair.

Maybeth let go of Dicey's hand and walked slowly over to where the little girls were gathering. Her dress was too long for her. She looked clumsy.

Dicey asked James to pick up the little children. "I'll leave the door unlocked. I've got something to do," she explained. "Can you get them at the end of the day? And don't be late—Maybeth worries."

James smiled happily over his pile of books. "Sure thing," he said. He ran up the steps to the doorway and turned to wave before he went inside.

Dicey hurried back to the little gray house. She had already told her customers she was taking the week off. She pulled the overnight case out from under her bed, put underwear, toothbrush, clean shirts and shorts into it. She put in the shoebox with her money the bus schedule and her map of Maryland. She would wear a dress for traveling.

Downstairs, Dicey wrote a hasty note to James, asking him to take charge until she got back, telling him where she was going, saying she was sorry but he would have to tell Cousin Eunice. She put her house key into the envelope and sealed it. She wrote James's name on the front and left it on the kitchen table. Suitcase in hand, Dicey opened the front door.

James sat on the stoop.

"I thought so!" he crowed, laughing at her as she stood, openmouthed, the suitcase in one hand, the door knob in the other. "You can't fool me!"

"I left you a note," Dicey said. "I've got to hurry or I'll miss the bus."

"The next bus doesn't leave Bridgeport until ten," James

answered. "You've got a whole hour." He smirked at her.

"James!" Dicey cried. "You've been snooping in my things."

"And here comes Sammy, right on schedule," James said. "I told him, when I found that money box. Besides, there was that man at the park, the grocer. I'd make a good detective. We're going with you."

"I don't have enough money," Dicey said. "What about Maybeth?"

"You'll think up a way," James said. "Where are we going anyway?"

"But what about your school?" Dicey asked. "I mean, you're the one who's really happy here. I will come back, you know that."

"How do I know it?" James asked her. "I know you mean to—but what if you can't, or don't?"

"I wouldn't do that!" Dicey protested.

"How do you know? How does anybody know? I don't want you to leave me behind. Besides, school—well, Dicey? Listen. It's me that makes the school so good, my brain. Other kids don't like it as much as I do. So, there are books all over the world, in libraries. The fathers help me, an awful lot—but there must be other schools with good teachers. Even if there aren't, I'll always be me."

"Are you sure, James?"

"I'm sure I want to go with you. And so does Sammy."

Dicey couldn't think clearly. She couldn't think at all.

Sammy marched up to them. "I crossed four streets with lights," he announced. "Hi, Dicey. I didn't believe James, but he was right."

Dicey didn't even try to argue further. They all went back inside. She sent the boys upstairs to get changes of underwear for everyone, and shorts and shirts. She changed into shorts herself. She wrote another note, to Cousin Eunice this time, a note much harder to write. Dicey knew that Cousin Eunice wouldn't understand, no matter what she said.

"We are going to Crisfield," she wrote. "I don't want you to worry about us, because I will take care of everyone. I don't know what will happen there. When we find out, I'll write to you." Dicey chewed on the end of the pencil and tried to think of some way to let Cousin Eunice know that they were grateful to her. "No matter what happens to us, I think you should go ahead and become a nun because it is what you really want to do," she wrote. "Your cousin, Dicey Tillerman." Once again, she put the house key in the envelope and sealed it.

Dicey went alone to fetch Maybeth. The boys waited at the corner, with the suitcase.

Dicey walked right into the playground. Groups of little girls ran around. The young nun approached her. Dicey took a deep breath. "I've come for Maybeth Tillerman," she said. "I'm her sister. Sister Berenice said I should pick her up now," she lied.

The nun hesitated. She squinted her eyes at Dicey.

"You can go and ask Sister Berenice if you like," Dicey said. "But then we'll be late for Maybeth's appointment and she'll be angry."

The nun called Maybeth from the sandbox where she was playing alone. Dicey took the little girl's hand and walked slowly out through the gates. She had to hold herself back from running.

"Where are we going?" Maybeth asked.

"We're going to see the place Momma lived in when she was a little girl," Dicey answered.

"All of us together?"

"All of us together," Dicey said. "That's the only way the Tillermans travel."

PART TWO

CHAPTER 1

The motor rumbled like hunger in the belly of the bus. The fumes that floated in through the open windows were swollen with heat. They were on their way. Again.

Dicey leaned back in her seat and tried to make herself relax. They had until evening, when Cousin Eunice got home. Unless the camps wondered why all the Tillermans were absent and called Cousin Eunice at work. She didn't think that was likely.

James leaned toward Dicey. They were the only people sitting in the back of the bus. Nobody would hear them over the sound of the motor.

"It's like a prison break, isn't it?"

Dicey knew what he meant. Even so, "That's not fair," she said. "Cousin Eunice wasn't a jailer."

James shrugged. "Whadda you think?" he asked out of the corner of his mouth. "I think, if we can get to New York without being caught—we'll be home free."

Home, Dicey thought. She remembered the inscription on the tombstone: *Home is the sailor, home is the hunter.* Until she died, Dicey wouldn't expect any place to be home. Home was with Momma—and Momma was in a hospital where the doctors said she'd always stay. There could be no home for the Tillermans. Home free—Dicey would settle for a place to stay. Stay free.

Cousin Eunice's house wasn't free; it was expensive. The price was always remembering to be grateful. And there was danger to Sammy and Maybeth, of being sent to foster homes or special schools; danger to Dicey and James of forgetting and saying what they thought before wondering if it would sound ungrateful. At Cousin Eunice's house, they were kept busy so they wouldn't be a bother, couldn't get in trouble.

Dicey had lowered her sights. She no longer hoped for a home. Now she wanted only a place where the Tillermans could be themselves and do what was good for them. Home was out of the question. Stay might be possible, if this grandmother could be persuaded. . . .

Dicey stopped thinking. She wanted to keep it simple. Get to Crisfield and see, that was her plan. That was all of it.

"Anyway, they know where we're going," Dicey told James.

"How could they know that?"

"I said so in the note I left."

"Dicey! Why'd you do that?"

"I don't think it would be fair to leave her to worry."

"She'll worry anyway. She likes worrying."

"I can't help that, James. I can't help what she's like. I can only help what I'm like."

"You've ruined it," James went on. "We can't be running away if they know where we're going."

"We're not running away—we never were running away," Dicey said. "We're just going to see."

James shook his head. "I'm running away. Before—we were always the ones who were run away from. This time I want us to do it. What's your plan?"

Dicey didn't answer.

The road flowed under the wheels. They were back on Route 1. Maybe it was her doom, always to get back on Route 1. She squeezed Maybeth's fingers. "Maybeth? What's the matter? You scared?"

Maybeth looked at Dicey and nodded.

"So am I, a little," Dicey said. "We'll just wait and see. That's all we can do."

"I don't want to go back." Maybeth spoke in a small voice.

"I thought you liked it," Dicey said. "The church, the pretty dress you wore there, all the attention."

"I did," Maybeth said.

Dicey decided to tell the truth, now. "We might have to go back. Do you know that?"

Maybeth nodded.

Well, Dicey thought. She had underestimated Maybeth. She'd been fooled, like the nuns were fooled and Maybeth's teachers. She'd been fooled into thinking Maybeth wasn't who she knew Maybeth was.

"Look, Maybeth," Dicey said, "if we do have to go back I'll go with you to church, and we'll both talk to the nuns. To Sister Berenice. I won't leave you alone so much."

Maybeth smiled, a tenuous little smile, and turned back to the window.

Smog made the air seem thick, like light, yellowed fog. In the heavy traffic the bus stopped and started, stopped and started. Buildings soared up higher than Dicey could see out the window. She twisted her head down to see their tops.

The bus turned onto a new street and headed east. Dicey felt as if they were in a maze and would never make their way out. Cars honked. Lights changed. They traveled down a narrow channel over which other roads crossed on high bridges. All the traffic, all the people, the tall buildings—Dicey felt scared, and exhilarated. There was so much life, all here in one place, teeming, whirling about her. More than at the crowded summer beaches in Provincetown. It was like a pot of vegetable soup boiling on a stove, everything moving. A restlessness and excitement came into Dicey with the air she breathed. Anything can happen, she thought.

At last the bus turned off into a huge warehouse. It followed a ramp, up and around, then fitted itself into a slot before a wall of glass doors. It became one of a row of buses.

The Tillermans stood up. Dicey led them to the front of the bus and down the steps, one after another, onto the sidewalk before the doors. Everyone was hurrying. Everyone acted as if he or she or they knew exactly where to go.

"What now, Dicey?" asked James.

"An information booth," she answered briskly. "Then bathrooms, and maybe something to eat."

They entered a huge, hollow hall lined with benches and ticket windows. Emptiness hung high over their heads although the room was crowded with people. The information booth was in the center of this hall. Dicey stationed her family by a water fountain and went up to stand in line.

When her turn finally came, she couldn't think straight. The girl behind the glass window spoke without looking at Dicey: "Next? Little boy?"

Dicey gulped. "When's the next bus to Wilmington, Delaware?"

Without speaking, the girl handed her a schedule.

"Where are the bathrooms?" Dicey asked.

"Lower level, on the street side."

"Where can I buy a ticket?"

"Upper level, any window with a yellow or green light."

Dicey fled, dragging her suitcase.

"She thought I was a boy," she said to James.

"So did Louis and Edie," he answered.

Dicey put the suitcase down and opened the schedule. They had forty minutes to wait. She would play it safe. "Okay, listen,

James. Take this money"—she gave him a ten dollar bill—"and go get two tickets for Wilmington. That ticket window over there with a green light."

"Why not four?"

"Just in case," Dicey answered. "Two and two is not the same as four."

James looked at her.

"Not in this case," Dicey said. "In this case, it is but it isn't."

"You can say so," James said. "And I'll do it. And I see what you mean. But you're wrong. Two and two is always four."

When they had all four tickets, Dicey started walking along the concourse. She found the escalators leading down. "Now we go to the bathroom."

The women's room could have held Cousin Eunice's house in it and had room to spare. Lines of women waited before each closed door, old, young, medium, some alone, some with friends, some with children, one with a tiny baby that rode in a pouch on her chest. The air smelled of perfume and cleanser. Maybeth and Dicey entered the cubicle together, because Maybeth didn't want to go in alone. Dicey protested, "But you're nine." Maybeth just shook her head.

They took turns, Maybeth first. Dicey set the suitcase on the floor and opened it. She took out shorts and a shirt for Maybeth and her shoebox of money. She put twenty more dollars in her pocket. As they left the room, they tossed Maybeth's rolled-up dress into the trash.

When they emerged from the women's room, Dicey could not see James and Sammy. People hurried past, some carrying suitcases, some shopping bags, some just purses or newspapers. You could get lost here in this crowded station. You could get swept away. Or grabbed by somebody.

"Maybeth? If we get separated—" Maybeth caught Dicey's

free hand. "Just in case," Dicey said. "We'll meet back by that information booth I went to first. Remember it?"

James and Sammy joined them. They had a hot dog apiece, standing up at a counter, and a glass of orange drink. Dicey looked at a clock—only ten minutes until the bus left. The air hummed with voices, distant motors, and the muffled droning of the loudspeaker announcing what buses were leaving for what cities. If they could get on the bus all right, and out of the city, then they were on their way. And they might make it.

James and Sammy went onto the bus first. Dicey dawdled by the gate, with Maybeth beside her. Maybeth went first up into the bus. Dicey followed, pulling their two tickets out of her pocket and handing them to the driver.

He looked at her with a grimace. "What is this, kids' day out?"

Dicey tried to look as if she didn't know what he was talking about.

"Never mind. But I'll tell you what I told them. We've got a long drive and I don't stand any horsing around."

"We won't," she said.

"I know, I know. You're angels from heaven. Go on back."

After a few minutes, the driver closed the door and turned on the engine. He backed out of the parking slot. With every turn of the wheel, Dicey felt her stomach loosen and her muscles relax. By the time the bus entered a tunnel, a smile was beginning to turn up the corners of her mouth. She felt her back relaxing into the back of the seat. Beside her, Maybeth hummed softly. The bus zoomed out of the tunnel and into the light. Dicey stretched, smiled, yawned—and fell asleep.

When Dicey opened her eyes, she saw the sleek, straight lines of the rectangular interior of the bus. Out the windows, on both sides, lay farmlands. Fields of corn ripened under a bright sun. The corn swayed in the wind, like dancers with scarves.

Dicey wasn't tired anymore. She was relaxed inside and out. She felt lazy and unworried. The bus rolled along.

It was as if, during that nap, Dicey had traveled days away from Cousin Eunice's house in Bridgeport. That time now felt like a distant memory, something so far behind them that they didn't have to concern themselves with it, not anymore.

She looked past Maybeth's head, out the window. Fields, farmhouses, trees, sky with clouds; her eyes roamed lazily over them all. Her thoughts roamed lazily too, over memories and ideas. She rode outside of time and place.

She thought about Momma, and it seemed to her that she almost understood why all of this had happened to them, to the Tillermans, all this sadness and running away. She thought about the long walk from Peewauket to New Haven, and the grandfather who had tipped them two dollars and Stewart with his blue-gray eyes; then her mind switched to the journey ahead of them, as if the future were a road stretching ahead, twisting and turning. What did it matter where they were going, as long as they were going?

Sammy was asleep on James's shoulder. Dicey leaned over to ask softly where they were. James told her the last stop had been Trenton.

Dicey took a map out of her suitcase. She unfolded it halfway, to show Wilmington and the Chesapeake Bay. Beneath her, the wheels rumbled on the road.

Sammy woke up. He punched James. James hit him back. Dicey quelled them with a glance and instructed them to play odds-and-evens while she thought. "But I'm hungry," Sammy argued.

"I can't do anything about that," Dicey answered.

"Why not?"

"Because I'm not a hot dog tree," Dicey said.

"Why not?"

"Because if I were, then you'd be one too because you're my brother. Only you'd be a pickle tree," Dicey said, turning back to her map.

"Pickle tree," Sammy repeated, trying to repress his giggles, not wanting to laugh at Dicey's joke.

Dicey studied the map. Just below Wilmington, the Chesapeake Bay drove up like a wedge between two sections of land. The eastern shore of Maryland, where Crisfield was, was on the land between the Bay and the ocean. It looked about two hundred miles from Wilmington to Crisfield. So it might be a lot farther. Maybe as much as thirty days of walking. Too far. But there were some cities that must have buses running to them: Salisbury, Cambridge, Easton.

They'd already spent too much on bus tickets. Money was always the problem. Dicey wanted to have money left over, so they could get back to Bridgeport, if they had to. She figured they'd have to walk part of the way anyway, and she wanted to have some tools for camping. A jackknife, one with a can opener on it. A pan of some kind. Ponchos, for when it rained. She let her mind wander on briefly to other things, to a backpack and bedrolls, to a portable stove. No, those would be silly; but fishing line and hooks would be useful. There was a lot of water around, so there must be fishing.

They had another choice: they could go down the western shore, to Baltimore or Annapolis—it would have to be Annapolis because that was near the only bridge over the Bay. That would leave them about half of the distance to Crisfield still to cover. Maybe two weeks of walking.

They would have to get over the bridge if they did that. The map said Toll Bridge, so they probably couldn't walk over it. They might hitchhike, but Dicey didn't like that idea. She didn't like being in somebody's car and not able to run away. Besides, who would pick up four kids? They might have to take another bus.

Definitely, then, the eastern shore was better. At Wilmington they would get on a bus going south. How far they went would depend on how much it cost. That was easy enough. She folded up the map and returned it to her suitcase.

The bus made its way through Philadelphia and then south through more farmland, more small cities. After another hour, after a bridge like a section of roller coaster, they came into Wilmington.

The Wilmington Bus Depot was a one-story building, a single room with wooden benches, a lunch counter, lockers where you could store your suitcases, six windows where tickets could be purchased and at its center an information booth with a clock on top of it. Three forty-five. Dicey told James to stay with Maybeth and Sammy by the door. Only one bus stood waiting, now that the one they had ridden on had gone on to Baltimore. That bus, she saw by the sign above its front window, was going to Annapolis.

Inside, Dicey picked out a schedule from the assortment at the information booth. The first thing she did was to see if Crisfield was there, at the bottom of the list of towns. It was. After Salisbury, Eden and Princess Anne, came Crisfield.

Her eye went back up to the top of the list, found Wilmington and traced the buses leaving for the eastern shore. There were several, but most went no further than Cambridge. Only one went down to Crisfield, a morning bus.

Then Dicey saw that the last afternoon bus heading south to Cambridge left Wilmington at two thirty. The only bus after that didn't leave until nine at night.

Nine. By nine, Cousin Eunice would have been home for

almost three hours. By nine, she could call Father Joseph. By nine, they might be able to trace the Tillermans, and maybe find them, and stop them. She didn't know Dicey had money, did she? She might think the Tillermans were walking. But Dicey couldn't count on that. She couldn't count on anything. She rushed up to the information booth and asked when the bus for Annapolis was leaving. The man put his hand over the microphone and told her, "Five minutes."

Five minutes, how could she think it through in five minutes? Dicey hurried over to a ticket window and bought four tickets to Annapolis. They couldn't just sit around the bus station for five hours, waiting to be recognized. Cousin Eunice would have to do something to find them; she would think it was her responsibility.

Dicey joined her family. "We missed the last bus until nine."

"Tonight? We better stay here," James said.

"No," Dicey said. "We can't. We'll go to Annapolis. It's the only bus."

"But Dicey—"

"Do as I say, James."

She wasn't thinking, she knew that. She wasn't thinking clearly. She hurried her family onto the bus just as the driver was closing the door. They sat at the back. Dicey chewed on her lip.

"Nobody will expect us to go to Annapolis," James said. "It was good luck that we missed the bus."

"I don't know about that," Dicey said.

The bus left Wilmington and headed south. This bus was air-conditioned, and you couldn't open the windows. The windows were smeared with grime, so you couldn't see out. The hour and a half to Baltimore seemed endless. At Baltimore, a lot of dressed-up people got on, commuters, Dicey guessed, going home from work. The bus grew crowded.

The circuitous route from Baltimore to Annapolis, where they kept getting on and off the same road to stop at little huts by the road and let off passengers, took another hour and a half. Dicey tried to control her impatience by reminding herself that if they had been walking it would have taken days and days. This was slow, but it was faster than walking. They'd be walking soon enough.

At last, the bus turned into a parking lot before a low brick building. The bus driver turned around and called, "Annapolis. End of the line."

The Tillermans hopped up and joined the few people waiting to get off the bus. Dicey just followed in the direction the majority took, turning left down a sidewalk, away from the bus station. Behind her, the sun lowered, so they were walking on their own shadows, heading east.

"Where we going?"

"We'll find a place to sit down and think," Dicey said. "I'm looking for a park."

They passed a drugstore and a finance company and three banks. They saw bookshops and card stores, clothing stores and a wine-and-cheese store. The road they walked along came up to a traffic circle. Cars and trucks whirled around it, circling a church that stood at its center.

Dicey led them around the circle. Streets led off, but none promised to go to a park, although one said it went to the hospital. At the top of one street, Dicey looked down and saw blue water with sails on it. She stood, staring.

It looked like the painted backdrop to a movie, not like anything real. The long main street went downhill and then fetched up at the water. On the blue water, boats sailed or motored as if they were in an entirely different world, and it wasn't clear, in the bright August light, where water ended and sky began.

They headed down the hill to the water, passing stores and shops and more banks. The street was crowded: parked cars lined both sides, while moving vehicles crawled bumper to bumper uphill and the sidewalks were crowded with people. At the foot of the street was another circle, around which cars traveled slowly, with a steady chorus of horns and many near collisions. Across this circle, a quiet finger of water, hemmed in by concrete, marked the corner of a narrow area where people thronged, eating, talking, sitting and watching one another. Dicey moved through the milling crowd and along beside the water. They passed boats crowded as closely together as the cars in a parking lot, motorboats, sailboats and old, worn fishing boats.

At the waterfront, beyond a huge parking lot jammed with cars, they found a public park. It had no grass, just trees in wooden boxes. The ground was covered by wooden flooring. Benches, however, there were in plenty. The benches right at the water were all full, but one beneath a sparsely leaved young tree was empty. The Tillermans sat on that.

"It's hot," James said. His face was red. Sweat plastered his hair to his neck. The air hung moist and heavy over the park. A slight ripple of a breeze came off the water, but that did little to relieve them. Everybody seemed slowed down by heat. Nobody walked briskly, everybody sauntered. A lot of people were licking ice cream cones. Dicey's mouth watered.

"What time's it?" James asked. Without waiting for an answer, he hopped up and asked the same question of a man moving by, who held his suit jacket over his shoulder. "It's seven thirty," James reported. "Time for supper."

"How about ice cream for supper?" Dicey asked. She didn't know just how much money she had in her pocket, not enough for a real dinner.

"We passed a hamburger joint," James countered.

"Ice cream," Sammy said.

"Hamburgers," James said.

Sammy stuck his jaw out.

"Ice cream's cheaper," Dicey said. "Double dip?"

"Can I have seconds?" James asked.

"We'll see how hungry you are," Dicey said.

James agreed.

"But first I've got to figure out a couple of things, okay?"

"Like what?" James asked.

"Like where to sleep, and how to find an army-navy surplus store. And how to get across the bay."

"Get across the bay? Why?"

Dicey pulled out the map again and showed him where they were. Then she pointed out Crisfield.

"Oh, Dicey. What are we doing on this side?"

"I told you, we missed the last bus."

"Yeah but—" James caught a glimpse of Dicey's face and stopped speaking.

"I know. I know. But if we can just get across, we'll be much nearer."

"How can we do that? Okay, we're here. We need a place to sleep tonight, right?"

"I guess. The army-navy store will be closed, wherever it is."

"If there is one."

"I'm sorry, James," Dicey said. "I panicked. When I found out we'd missed the last bus—"

"It's okay, Dicey. I just thought you had it all planned."

"I did. For me to go."

"Are you angry at us?" Sammy asked this. It sounded like the beginning of a quarrel.

"No. Well, yes, a little, but that doesn't matter. I'd rather be all together. Really, I would. I'm just confused still because I didn't have any plan for all of us. Can you understand that?"

Sammy didn't answer.

"I was going to come back," Dicey said to him.

He looked at her, with the question in his hazel eyes. "Really?"

"Really. Really and truly. Don't you trust me, Sammy?"

"You said you didn't trust anyone."

"I didn't mean any of us. I didn't mean you. Would you leave me behind? Or James or Maybeth?"

"No!"

"Well I wouldn't leave you, either. I feel the same way."

"But you were going to leave us behind," Sammy said stubbornly. Dicey sighed.

They rose to find the ice cream store. James got a double-dip chocolate-nut cone, explaining that nuts and chocolate were both rich and filling. Dicey got a scoop of chocolate and a scoop of butter almond. She noticed a pile of maps of Annapolis on the countertop and took one. Maybeth wanted pink sherbet and green, but Dicey told her to get real ice cream because of the milk. She chose two scoops of strawberry. Sammy asked for strawberry ripple ice cream topped with peanut butter ice cream. "Ugh," Dicey said, listening to his order. He grinned at her.

They sat at a small table to eat. The ice cream tasted rich and smooth and cold. You could tell that it was made from real cream, it was that rich. Dicey studied her map while her tongue made valleys in the ice cream and then smoothed them out. The cone was crunchy and sweet.

"There's a college," Dicey said. "Let's try that, okay?"

James had a single-dip cone for seconds, another scoop of chocolate-nut. They walked out and onto the crowded sidewalk. What were all these people doing? It was like a carnival.

The college lay in summer twilight, set back from the road by a long, sloping lawn. It was brick and very old. Everything looked old about it, old and tended, the smooth brick sidewalks, the many-paned windows, the little dome on top of the main building. It had trees—huge, tall trees, with branches too high for climbing—all about on its lawn. There were plenty of people. Students lay scattered about, reading. Watchmen wandered around on the brick paths. Families were eating picnic suppers. Children ran everywhere.

The Tillermans stood on the sidewalk, separated by a brier hedge from this scene. "No good," Dicey said. "Too many people."

She did not move on, however. It looked—so quiet and solid; the air over it was lavender in the evening light, and mysterious. She wished . . . she didn't know what she wished.

Resolutely, she turned away.

Her map showed only something called the Historic District. They had walked through some of it. All the houses crowded up onto the sidewalk, close to one another.

Dicey moved on. The suitcase weighed heavy on her shoulder muscle and banged against her legs. The map showed the Naval Academy in one direction, closed in by a wall that ran all around it. She turned the other way and led them back toward the first circle they had seen. She chose the road leading to the hospital, and they walked on, past that large building.

The houses were bigger here and had front lawns. A residential area. A rich residential area.

She walked on.

They saw one vacant lot that had no cover to conceal them from the surrounding houses.

She walked on.

The air grew darker, gray-violet now. The heat did not abate. Sweat ran down her back.

She walked on.

On her left, she saw a long, narrow stretch of grass in the middle of a kind of courtyard of houses. On both sides of the stretch ran roads, and houses stood facing one another across the grass. At the end of this stretch, with all its many windows dark, stood a house larger than any other on the street. Dicey headed down toward it.

They walked down the middle of the grass. There was one broad clump of bushes the little kids could hide in, if it came to that.

When they stood before the large house, Dicey noticed oddly shaped piles. Old radiators had been dropped here and pipes and slate shingles from the roof and even a bathroom sink. They were piled up right by the front porch.

"Let's go around back," she said quietly. "I think it's empty. It looks like somebody's fixing it up. If anybody calls out, don't run. Tell them we're looking for Prince George Street. Tell them we're lost. Don't look guilty."

Their feet silent on the unmown grass, they stepped around the side of the house.

A silver pool of water glimmered at the end of the long lawn. The back of the house was as dark as the front, and Dicey breathed easy. She put her suitcase beside one of the overgrown bushes that grew by the screened porch, and they all walked down to the water.

A long-fingered willow swept the top of the grass at the water's edge. Two towering pines stood silent guard. On the silver pool, which was part of a river, some sailboats floated.

There was a bulkhead at the end of the lawn made out of railroad ties. They sat on that and dangled their feet over the water.

Dicey's stomach had butterflies of excitement in it. "Remember that first house?" she asked James.

"Yeah. Think it's empty?"

"I think so. Let's risk it."

No other houses were visible, although patches of light from windows showed through high hedges or trees. It was a private lawn.

"No fires," Dicey said.

A sailboat, its sails down, motored up the river. It made little waves that streaked the silver with black and lapped gently against the bulkheading.

Dicey turned to look at the house behind her. Its windows were comfortingly blank.

"We'll have to be quiet and get out early," she said.

Her family watched out over the water with dream-dazed eyes. They nodded. The river was narrow enough to swim easily. Across it, houses looked back at them.

Dicey smiled. Sammy drummed at the wood with his heels, quietly. James lay back and looked at the sky. Maybeth hummed, a tune Dicey half-recognized. "What song is that?" she asked.

"Stewart's song," Maybeth said. "'Oft I sing for my friends,'" she sang softly. "Remember?"

Dicey shook her head. "We can't sing—but I sure feel like it," she said. "I don't really know why."

"Yes, you do," James said, but said no more. He was watching the first stars emerge in the gray sky.

And Dicey did. They had money and a good place to sleep. She had a map. They were together alone again, themselves again. The night air was warm, and the willow whispered behind her, and the water whispered before her.

"Okay," she said, rousing them, rousing herself. "Let's go up and get to sleep."

CHAPTER 2

Safe as she felt, Dicey woke early. She rolled over on her back. The lightening sky arched over her. Behind her, the empty house stood like a protecting wall. From the water came the cries of gulls. Their quarrels cut through the quiet slapping sound ropes and rigging made against masts. Dicey stretched lazily and sat up.

James lay sprawled on his stomach, one arm flung out. Sammy had curled into a tight ball. Maybeth lay on her back, her arms folded over her stomach.

To the east, the sky showed a lake of clear blue into which the sun would rise. It was a particular blue, made of light and darkness mingling, clear as glass, smooth as glass, as much like water as sky. Dicey stood up and went around the far corner of the house to pee behind a large evergreen bush. She decided to let her family sleep awhile longer. Even men eager to get started while the day was cool wouldn't come to work this early. Dicey returned to the bulkheading and sat.

The boats rocked at their moorings. The houses beside her and across the river from her slept. Quiet as kittens, the water lapped at the boats and the bulkheads. In the east, that first blue lake increased to an ocean. The sun rose.

The air shimmered in golden light. Water reflected and brightened the air. The masts and spars of the boats stood stiff and dark. The colors of the hulls became clear: whites, reds, yellows, greens and one burnished mahogany.

Dicey walked back through the long grass. She called each of the sleepers by name.

"James?"

He stirred, rolled over, sat up, grinned. "Hey. Good morning. Is it late? I'm starving."

"Maybeth?"

Maybeth's eyes flew open. She lay still for a minute, staring blankly, remembering herself.

Dicey crouched next to Sammy. She put her hand on his shoulder and jostled him gently while calling his name. "Sammy. Sammy. Time to get up."

He mumbled something and curled up more tightly.

"You've got to. Sammy?"

One eyelid struggled to open, then fell closed.

"Wake up, Sammy. We can't stay here."

He opened both eyes. "Okay," he said. He closed both eyes.

"That's right," Dicey encouraged him. James grinned at her. "C'mon, Sammy—time to get up. Gotta go to the bathroom and get out of here."

He stumbled to his feet. He and James walked together to the bush, James holding Sammy's arm to keep the little boy from falling.

Dicey pulled her suitcase out from under the bush, opened it again and took out twenty more dollars. She wondered how much money she had left. She could worry about that later in the day. For now, she wanted breakfast and a phone book.

They returned to the circle with the church at its center and to the steep main street. Once again Dicey was surprised to see the backdrop of water that lay at its foot. Something was peculiar about the perspective here, she thought. It looked as if two photographs of two different places had been jammed together. The town looked as though it fell into the water.

Her eyes searched eastward, across the water. "I can see something," she said. She could see a distant looming of land, low and flat. "Do you think that's the eastern shore?"

"How should I know?" James asked. "Can we eat in a restaurant?"

"If one's open. It's pretty early."

Early as it was, no more than half-past seven, the water was already dotted with white sails. Everybody here must sail, Dicey thought. Everybody must have his own boat. "Did you ever see so many boats?" she asked James, as they descended the main street.

He paid no attention to her. He was looking for a place to eat. They passed three closed restaurants before they found one open. Its single narrow room wasn't air-conditioned, but the cool morning air came in through the open door and was moved around by big ceiling fans. They sat down in a tiny booth.

Dicey read the prices before she read the menu. "Pancakes," she said. "Maybeth, Sammy and I can split an order. James, you can have one to yourself, if you'll give me half of a pancake. Is that okay? And milk." James was too hungry to argue. Dicey realized that they hadn't had enough dinner the night before. She would have to be careful about that.

The counter was filled with people drinking coffee and reading papers. The little room hummed with activity as waitresses whisked about taking orders, bringing food. When Dicey paid the bill, she asked the man at the cash register where an army-navy surplus store was. He told her it was out beyond the bus station, and he took the time to be sure she understood his directions, even though there was a line of people behind her waiting to pay.

Fast and relaxed, that was what it was like in that restaurant.

It was that way out on the street, too. The temperature was climbing up, and the sky was bleaching yellow with heat. People were entering the little stores that lined the streets or standing in groups before the doors of the several banks. The working day was about to begin. But almost all of these people turned, before they entered, to look down the hill to the water and boats, and then up the hill to the church within its ring of trees, as if they could take their own sweet time going in to work. Some of them smiled at the Tillermans. Some wished them a good morning.

At the army-navy store, Dicey studied the shelves of goods before she made her purchases. It was like a library in there, tall stacks of rods, shirts, hats, pants, shoes and jackets, and tennis rackets and inflatable rafts lining the narrow aisles. Dicey picked out a one-quart aluminum saucepan, four ponchos in children's sizes, a packet of hooks and the smallest, lightest reel of fishing line she could find. After some thought, she chose a red canvas bookbag and went to the front of the store.

The jackknife she picked out of a glass-fronted case was the most expensive thing she bought. It had two blades, one large and one small, a gadget to open cans with, a little screwdriver and a file. The bill came to seventeen dollars all together, seventeen dollars and twenty-four cents to be exact. Dicey sighed, but paid. She asked the salesman to put everything into the canvas bag, except the jackknife. She slipped the jackknife into her pocket. It felt heavy and good there.

Outside again, Dicey waited until they were out of sight of the store, then she transferred everything from the suitcase to the canvas bag. She gave James the empty suitcase to carry and slung the bag over her shoulder, holding it by the rope that pulled its neck closed. It was much easier to carry than the suitcase, so much easier that she wondered why she had bought a suitcase in the first place.

Dicey went into the small bus station and set her empty suitcase down by the door. She went out to rejoin her family. She was entirely pleased with herself.

"Now what?" she asked them.

"What do you mean?" James asked.

"What do you want to do now?" Dicey asked.

"Get going," Sammy said.

"I don't know how yet," Dicey answered. "I haven't figured that out. Are you tired?"

None of them was tired.

"Let's just wander around then, okay? I think better while I'm moving."

They walked the morning away. They stayed away from the hospital and their sleeping place and stuck to the historic section on the map. They wandered down narrow streets lined with narrow houses and up broader streets where the houses were grander, where the street-level windows rose from floor to ceiling of the rooms within. People in Annapolis, Dicey decided, must like bricks. The sidewalks were brick as were many of the houses and public buildings.

Dicey also decided that she liked brick. It was so sturdy looking and symmetrical, in the first place. And then, when it was very, very old, it achieved a gentle, mellowed look, like old photographs or long-burning fires or a pair of blue jeans you've had for so long that even when you take them off they still have the shape of your body in them. When brick aged long enough it could look soft.

They spent some time on the college lawn, watching other people wander about. They spent some time on the main street, walking down to the foot, where the crowds were just as thick as they had been the night before. At a stall in an open market, Dicey bought little sandwiches made of flat sausages in biscuits.

Nobody stared at them. There were lots of kids messing around, and almost everybody, adults and children alike, wore jeans and shirts. Not full, but no longer hungry, the Tillermans sat by the water and stared. Lots of bare feet and long hair, like Provincetown. But also lots of gold watches and big diamonds in rings. Boys and girls together, men and women, with arms around each other's waists.

"Too much lovey dovey stuff," Sammy announced.

Dicey noticed something else. Most of the young women wore no bras. Their breasts went jiggle-jiggle as they walked. Finally, she could hold her tongue no longer.

"James—the girls aren't wearing bras."

He turned red. "I noticed."

"Do you see how they all go jiggle-jiggle? No, look—see the one with the long red hair? The pretty one, with eye makeup? Jiggle, jiggle, jiggle—see what I mean?"

James giggled helplessly. Dicey joined in. Then she noticed a bridge, down the river, leading over to another part of the city. From where they sat it seemed that this other part was given over entirely to boatyards and docks.

"Let's go over there," she pointed. "Let's go look at some boats."

"Do you think the jiggling hurts?" James asked her. "I'd think it would."

"How would I know, James? I don't have bosoms."

"Yeah, but you will."

"I'll tell you about it if I do," Dicey said. "Do you want to go look at the boatyards?"

"Could we row it?" James asked her.

His brain, Dicey thought, must work twice as fast as hers. It had taken her all that time sitting there to think of the possibilities of a boatyard.

"I don't know," she said. "First, let's see what's there. It might be twenty miles across—I'll check the map later."

"We couldn't possibly row twenty miles, could we?"

"Let's worry about all that later, okay?"

They followed the water around to get to the drawbridge. Everywhere in Annapolis fingers of water would appear at the ends of streets or around corners, unexpectedly. Back in Provincetown, there was a belt of sandy beaches all around the town, except for the harbor side, where houses were built out over the water. Here, the town crowded down onto the water, trying to get as close to it as possible, all the time, at every opportunity.

They threaded their way through crowds of tourists. They passed countless cars, with license plates from many states, locked and empty.

The drawbridge humped over the water. The air around it was a little cooler, so they stood for a while, leaning against the railing, looking down at the busy harbor. There were no working boats, just pleasure craft.

The boatyards hummed with laboring. Some boats were up on racks, and men and women worked over the hulls, sanding, scraping, painting. One hull hung from a huge crane, ready to be returned to the water. Most of the boats were moored at docks that stretched out into the water. Many had people sitting on them, eating, reading. Others were empty, their sails furled, their hatch covers locked. The only rowboats the children saw were locked onto storage racks or tied on top of the cabins of the boats they belonged with.

Nobody stopped the children or asked them any questions. Many people seemed to be wandering like them, just looking at the activity. More were at work on their boats, polishing brass, sitting on deck splicing ropes, hosing down the sails.

Dicey led her family out to the end of one dock. The bag over her shoulder had grown heavy, so she put it down. They all sat, staring out across the water. The afternoon sun reflected off the water onto their faces and arms and legs. Next to them, two boys were scrubbing down the deck of a sailboat. They wore only bathing suits. Their bodies were tanned and their hair was bleached by the sunlight. They looked as if they spent all summer outdoors in bathing suits, on boats. One of them, the heavier one, whose stomach had ripples of fat on it, jumped lightly onto the dock to pick up a hose that was coiled there. Dicey watched him lazily.

He turned on the water, then leaped back onto the deck and rinsed off the suds their brushes had left.

Dicey knew what he would do before he did it. It was inevitable. It was what anybody would do with a hose in his hand and a friend who wasn't looking. He picked up the head of the hose, put his thumb over it and sprayed his friend.

The friend charged him, his hands up before his face. The heavy boy stood and sprayed him, holding him off at arm's length. The friend looked younger, because he was so much lighter and smaller. He spluttered and turned under the shaft of water, but he didn't stop trying to get it. Then, he stamped on the heavy boy's foot and grabbed the nozzle during that moment of distraction.

They wrestled for the hose, spraying one another, shooting the water over onto the dock, laughing and cursing each other. Neither of them could take the hose away from the other. Great, heavy arcs of water shot out from the boat, spraying everywhere.

"Hey!" Dicey yelled. "Look out!"

The two wet faces turned to her. The heavier boy spoke immediately. "I didn't see you," he said. "You really wet?"

"You could say so," Dicey said, wiping her hair off her face. "But it's a hot day and the water's cool."

"That's true," he said. "But still, come on up and dry off. Jerry? Doesn't your dad keep towels onboard?"

The slimmer boy swung down out of sight. He reappeared with two large towels. "It's okay if you want to come onboard. It's my dad's boat."

James looked at Dicey. Sammy was already standing by the bow. "Why not?" Dicey said.

The boys pulled on the bow mooring line until the boat was only two feet off the dock. "Can you jump?"

Dicey could, and did. She reached out a hand and helped Maybeth over. James swung over on the hand of the heavy boy. Sammy refused help. He stumbled as his feet hit the deck and fell on his face. Jerry leaned a worried face over him, but Sammy came up smiling. "I said I could do it," he said proudly.

"My name's Jerry," the slim boy said, "and this is Tom."

Dicey introduced her family.

They were given a tour of the boat, above and belowdecks. It was small, only thirty-two feet, but it had everything possible onboard, and everything tucked away into its own place. There was even a shower in the head, and the walls and floor of the tiny space sloped down, following the curve of the hull, to a central drain.

"You could live on a boat," Dicey said.

"Lots of people do just that, especially in summer," Tom said.

"I've tried to talk Dad into letting me live on her," Jerry said. "He just says I should be grateful he lets me have a key to her. Grateful . . ." He grinned at Tom. "I do enough work for him."

"Let's take some Cokes up with us," Tom suggested. They were in the cabin at the end of their tour.

The icebox was a two-level locker holding a huge chunk of ice. Tom pulled out six cans of Coke and shut the heavy wooden door. Dicey took a last look around the cabin. A table was hinged so it could be pulled up flat against the wall and clamped there. This enabled the berth, which served as a sofa during the day, to pull out into a double bed. There was storage space behind and below the berths. The efficiency of it took Dicey's breath away.

After they had seated themselves around the cockpit, back in the blazing sunlight, Dicey asked, "Do you work on this boat?"

"Yeah. We're free labor right now. Next year, when we're sixteen, he'll have to pay us. Or we can get work at one of the yards. I know a lot of people," Jerry said.

"Can you take the boat out sailing whenever you want?" she asked.

"Well, I've gotta ask permission." The two boys exchanged a glance that Dicey could read—it meant they often didn't ask permission.

"You must be a pretty good sailor," James said.

"I guess you'd say so," Jerry answered. He stretched out his legs and admired his tanned feet.

"Do you sail too?" James asked Tom.

"Not like Jerry does. I just hack around."

"Are you brothers?"

"Naw," Tom said. "We're old friends. Since first grade."

They drank their Cokes silently for a bit, basking in the sunlight.

"Does your dad sail the boat?" James asked.

"On weekends," Jerry said. "During the week, she's pretty much my own."

"Gee," James said, admiration in his voice. He looked at Dicey, hard.

Dicey got the feeling there was something James wanted her to understand, but she didn't understand it yet. She tried to help by talking about the same topic. "What does your dad do?"

"Works in Washington." Jerry's voice had pride in it as he said that.

"Gee, is he a senator?" James asked.

"Not so important," Jerry said. "Just a representative—you know what they are?"

"House of Representatives," James said quickly.

"Yep. He's the representative from Ohio, third district. It's his first term."

"Gee," James said again. He looked significantly at Dicey again. She didn't pay any attention because she had sensed it was a lie. She was busy wondering why this boy would lie about his father's job and why his friend would go along with it without saying anything.

"We live over here because my mom doesn't want to get all caught up in political circles. She says it's no good for kids. She's a regular hawkeye, my mom."

"She only wants to keep her baby boy as long as she can," Tom remarked.

Jerry flushed and bit his lip. "At least she cares about her kids."

Tom laughed. "You can't get me that way, old friend. My parents care about me—but I've made my declaration of independence, and they were smart enough to accept that. I've got my freedom."

"And I don't?"

"Not yet, old buddy. When you're ready, when you want it bad enough, you'll have the nerve to fight for it. But what the hell—it's summer—nothing's worth worrying about in the summer, is it?"

Sammy had lost interest in the conversation and was lying on his stomach on the deck, trying to dabble his hand in the water.

"Do you ever go to the eastern shore?" James asked Jerry.

At last, Dicey understood what James was driving at. She nodded her head at him briskly. He raised an eyebrow at her, as if to say, "Well, it's about time."

"Go there?" Jerry asked. "I've spent almost as much time there as over here. When you sail the Chesapeake you learn all about the eastern shore. Why?"

"We gotta go over tomorrow," James said.

"Yeah? Where?"

"Easton," Dicey said quickly. "We're visiting an aunt for a couple of weeks. Our parents sent us down from Wilmington. To get fresh air," she said, trying to sound disgusted.

"What are you doing in Annapolis?" Tom asked.

"There's this old lady my dad knows, from when he was a kid and his father was in the navy," Dicey said. "She always says she's dying to see us—I guess because she never had any children of her own. We're spending the night with her first. But she sleeps all the time. She told us to go run around while she slept. She's awfully old. I dunno," Dicey said, "I think she'd rather just invite us and not have us come. But Mom says she really enjoys our visits, as long as we don't hang around the house too much."

"Where is this?"

"Over on Prince George Street—you know where that is? Everything in her house can't be touched. It's hard on Sammy."

The boys seemed to believe this.

"So, you're making the great trip to the eastern shore tomorrow," Tom said.

"On a bus," Dicey said. "It's crazy. My aunt and her kids aren't even going to be there until dinner, because she works and they go to some camp. I told our parents we should wait until tomorrow and take a late bus to Easton, but they said—you know how parents are."

"Man, do I know," Jerry said.

"It's too bad you can't sail over," Tom said to Dicey.

"It sure beats the bus," Jerry agreed.

They didn't sound like they were offering, so Dicey played it low. "Yeah. But it's a short trip. We'll survive."

"Yeah, it's too bad," Tom said to her. "We'd offer to sail you over, see, but Jerry would have to ask permission, and . . ."

Dicey nodded, as if she understood. Well, she did. She understood what he was up to.

Jerry studied his feet.

Dicey stood up. "We gotta get back now. Thanks for the Cokes."

"Wait a minute," Jerry said. "Would you really like to sail over?" he asked. He was looking at Tom, not at them, as he spoke.

"Gee, yes," James said.

"We could get back by dark, you know," Jerry said to Tom. Tom just smiled. "I'll tell my mom I'm having dinner at your house. Do you think we could? Get over and back?"

Tom looked doubtful.

"I'd like to try it, wouldn't you?" Jerry insisted.

"Oh, I'd like it, you know that. I'm always game for something out of the ordinary. But *I* don't have to be home by dark. *I* don't have the mother who has to know where I am every minute of the day."

"Cut it out, okay? Lay off that stuff. I mean what can they do to me after all? Lock me in the attic? Beat me with wet noodles? Send me away to school?"

Tom shrugged.

"Gee, I don't want to get you in trouble," James said.

"Trouble," Jerry said, as if there was no trouble he couldn't handle. "Let me worry about that. I'm game for a day's hard sailing. Think you can do it?" he challenged Tom.

"Anything you can do I can do," Tom answered.

"We'll see," Jerry said. "You kids get back here early

tomorrow—eight o'clock. Can you be here that early?"

"I think so," Dicey said. "I think there's a seven o'clock bus we could say we were taking. It sure would be fun to sail over."

"It's not easy," Jerry warned her. "You have to keep out of the way."

"We can do that," Dicey said.

"And the little kids—can they swim?"

"I can swim good," Sammy said.

"Okay, then. Okay?"

"Okay," Dicey agreed. They left the boat quickly. She picked up her bag from the dock and hustled everyone ahead of her down the dock. When they were well out of sight, she slowed down and turned to James.

"Gee, James," she said—and burst out laughing.

James joined in.

"I want hamburgers for supper tonight," he said.

"You deserve them," Dicey answered.

"I thought you'd never catch on," he said. "I thought that Jerry'd never catch on. You know, Dicey? We made them do what we wanted them to do."

"Tom really did it," Dicey said.

"Yeah. Why did he? Does he want to get his friend in trouble?"

"I dunno," Dicey said. "Is that what friends do?"

"Don't you know?"

"No. I never had a friend like that, a best friend from first grade. We never had many friends, did we?"

"I guess not." James thought about that. "None of us did. Maybe Tillermans don't."

They ate dinner at Burger King: hamburgers, french fries, milkshakes. It tasted good to them, after weeks of Cousin Eunice's frozen dinners and pot pies. They wandered around again until evening had settled in, milling with crowds of people who seemed to have nothing else to do but saunter down the streets and look in store windows, or peer at the little houses.

When they had drifted back to their own empty house, the little children fell asleep almost at once. Dicey and James sat for a long time down by the river. Occasional boats motored up and down. Voices floated across the water. The air was humid and hot. Altogether Dicey felt satisfied.

"What do you know about our grandmother?" James asked her.

"I think she's poor," Dicey said. "And maybe strange."

"Strange? Like Momma? Crazy?"

"Strange like all the Tillermans," Dicey said. "She lives all alone on a farm."

"Why do Tillermans always live alone?"

"*We* don't. We live together."

"Together, but all alone together," James said.

"Maybe every family feels that way," Dicey said. "Maybe that's what families are."

"I don't know," James said. "I don't think so."

Before she went to sleep that night, Dicey counted her money, peering at the bills in the dim light. She had forty-seven dollars left, and some change.

It had cost them a lot to get to Annapolis. Dicey decided that forty would be the amount to keep in her pocket. Once they got across the bay, they'd have to stop spending. They'd have to fish for food, and get clams; or something. And she'd have to earn money if she could. Seven dollars could go a long way, if it had to, if you made it. She'd make it go as far as she could, all the way to Crisfield. If she could.

CHAPTER 3

When Dicey awoke, she was cool and damp, and even a little chilly. The morning air lay moist over her. She turned her eyes from the gray sky to her family.

Sammy wasn't there.

She sat up, peering toward the bush they used for a bathroom. She waited, long enough, she judged, but he did not appear. She jumped to her feet and looked around.

His little figure sat huddled on the bulkheading at the end of the lawn. In the mists rising from the water, he could have been a woeful little bush planted between the willow and the pine.

Dicey went to the bathroom, then walked down to join him. He knew who she was without turning his head. "What got you up?" she asked.

"I had to pee," he said. His fingers picked long splinters from the wood. "I was thinking," he said.

"You worried?"

He shook his head. "I'm not scared of sailing."

"I never said you were," Dicey answered. "You're not scared of anything, are you?"

Sammy looked at her then, his eyes questioning. "I had a dream that you were all on a bus and the door closed and I couldn't get on. I ran and ran after it, but it kept getting away."

Dicey nodded her head and watched the mists rising almost in straight lines, like rain going backward. In the east, the sky lightened.

"Dicey? Can I ask you something?"

"Sure."

"Tell the truth?"

"I always do."

"No, you don't," Sammy said.

Dicey understood him. "I'll tell the truth, Sammy, I promise."

Sammy asked his question: "Why were you going to go alone, before James caught you?"

The hulls of the boats were shadowy silhouettes on the water. Mist caught in the branches of the trees across the river. The mists would burn off, Dicey thought. There wasn't much wind.

"I don't know what we're going to find when we get there," Dicey said. "So I figured if I went down alone and saw what it's like, then I could come back and get you all. If it was okay. If it wasn't okay, I could just forget about it. Also, I had enough money to get there and back on a bus and stay on my own in a hotel. See, Sammy, I don't know what this grandmother will be like. I was trying to make things easiest for you all. Do you understand?"

"I guess so. I think so—like I fight when people say things, so they won't say them anymore. Are you sorry that we're with you?"

"A little, yes. It's harder with four of us. And more expensive. And"—since Dicey had determined to tell the whole truth, she did—"I kind of liked the idea of traveling alone—you know? With no one to look after. But I was wrong, Sammy, or at least I think now I was. I made a mistake not telling you."

"Why?"

"Because we do things together. The trouble was, we didn't do things together at Cousin Eunice's and that got me thinking the wrong way."

"How can something get you thinking the wrong way, if you know how to think the right way?" Sammy asked. But he was sitting up straighter and kicking his heels.

"They just do. I don't know how."

"I always thought . . . well, you didn't make mistakes."

"Everybody makes mistakes!"

"Not you—you didn't."

"Oh, Sammy. I made dozens of mistakes."

"Name one."

"Staying too long at Rockland. Not planning how to cross the Connecticut River. Not having any money in New Haven. Not telling Cousin Eunice what I thought, about you and Maybeth."

"Don't tell me," Sammy begged. "Don't tell me any more."

"But you asked me to!" Dicey protested.

The sun was rising, turning the sky and air a rosy gold color. Gulls wheeled through the air. A boat motored quietly down the river, the people on it dark figures.

"You did," Dicey insisted. "You did ask me." She reached over and tickled Sammy under his arm. He squirmed. She reached her other arm over and wrestled him down to the grass, tickling, crying, "You did, you did, you did. Say so."

Sammy screamed with laughter and wriggled under her hands. "All right, I did!"

Dicey stood up. She brushed her hands briskly together. "Let's get going," she said. They raced back up the lawn.

They were early down to the boat, early and hungry. James grumbled that he wanted breakfast but Dicey ignored him. She didn't want to spend any money until they got across the bay. She wanted everything to stay just as it was until they were actually on the other side.

The Tillermans sat on the end of the dock waiting. All around them, the boatyards came awake. Water traffic made many little waves. A slight breeze blew now, and little boats sailed down to the mouth of the river and the bay.

Time passed slowly. Dicey sensed that it was after eight o'clock. Cars streamed over the bridge, going toward town. People going to work, she thought. Her hunger mounted. She had been sure, at first, that she could wait to eat until they were across.

"Tonight," Dicey announced, "we've got to wash our underwear. And put on clean. Maybe shirts too. Okay?"

"Do you think they forgot?" James asked. His head moved restlessly. "Or changed their minds?"

"Maybe," Dicey said. "Or they could have been lying to us."

At this, James smiled: "That would serve us right, wouldn't it?"

They had to eat. If Dicey was hungry, James must be starving. She went back to a gas station and bought crackers with peanut butter from a machine. Then she put in two more quarters and got chocolate bars.

When she returned, the two boys were there, busy working with sails on the deck. They were dressed just as they had been the day before. Dicey wondered if they slept in their swimming suits. She looked at James and raised her eyebrows. She handed out packets of crackers and offered some of hers to Jerry and Tom. "No thanks," they both said. "We just ate. You kids stay in the cockpit, okay?"

It was like sitting in a booth without a table, with the four Tillermans, two to a side, knees hitting knees, stiff and watchful. The boys spent a long time putting on the jib. Jerry came back and stood by the base of the mast. He pulled down on a rope. The jib rose slowly and hung flapping at its stay. Jerry told Tom to fend off from the bow while he backed out of the dock.

When Jerry returned to the cockpit, he looked at the Tillermans. "Ready to go?"

"You bet," Dicey answered.

"Drop your bag on one of the bunks below," Jerry told her. "Then I think you and your brother James had better go sit on the cabin. I need room for play on the tiller, and Tom'll be back here, handling the sails. You ever sail before?"

Dicey thought of lying and then thought better of it. "No," she said.

Jerry considered this. His face was thin and his hair was bleached to a metallic tone that matched the gold in his eyes. His mouth looked soft and sulky, but his body was lean. "Okay," he said, "listen carefully. We're going to have to tack out a ways, then we can reach over to St. Mikes. Tacking means we zigzag, going as close to the wind as possible." His hand sketched a zigzag motion in the air. "At the end of each tack, I'll call, 'ready about.' The boat will rotate, about sixty degrees, and the mainsail and boom will swing from one side to the other. The heel will reverse too."

"What?" James said. "I don't understand."

Jerry held his hand out stiffly, slanted one way, then reversed the slant. "That's what the keel does when we tack and come about," he said. "On a reach we'll ride pretty flat. All you have to do is hang on when we come about. There's no danger. I want you to sit where you're put, and sit quiet. But if I tell you to move, or give any order, you've got to obey right away. Got that?"

"We can do that," Dicey said. "All of us."

She leaned down and tossed her bag onto a bunk below. Then she and James went up forward to sit on the roof of the cabin. They could lean back against the mast, or slip down to the deck and lean against the cabin wall.

Jerry started the motor. Tom uncleated a heavy line with a

floater tied on its end and dropped it into the water. James looked at Dicey: "I hope they know what they're doing," he said.

The sun was toasting warm. The water danced beneath the keel. The motor hummed. The boat slipped out into the river and turned east. The jib flapped.

Waterfront buildings glided slowly by, boatyards, condominiums with great glass windows looking out over the water, an occasional small house in the middle of a green lawn. Theirs was one of many boats headed out to the bay.

The motor stopped. Dicey turned her head. She smiled to Sammy and Maybeth, sitting straight up and still, one on each side of the cockpit. Tom stood up, holding the tiller. Jerry jumped up behind them to raise the mainsail. When he had it cleated, he jumped down into the cockpit and hauled in on a line.

The mainsail stiffened, then puffed out. The boat responded, surging forward underneath them.

Tom returned the tiller to Jerry and pulled in the jib. It was not the kind of jib Dicey knew. At Provincetown she had seen little, narrow triangular sails. This jib was long. It curved back around, halfway down the length of the cockpit. Dicey turned her head back and yelled, "What kind of a jib is that?"

"It's a genoa," Tom answered. He seemed to be enjoying himself. His eyes squinted into the sunlight, and his smile showed big, square teeth.

The wind blew firmly against the sails. The water jostled the boat, wave after wave. When Dicey looked at the water, they seemed to be traveling quite fast. But when she looked at the shore, now falling away beside them, they seemed to be going very slowly.

Under the protection of the shore, the boat heeled only slightly. Jerry brought the boat about, and Dicey and James had to do no more than protect themselves from the genoa as it flapped across the bow in front of them. Dicey saw a shadow of shoreline, across the bay.

She also saw three huge tankers, moored one behind the other, lying across their path, like tall buildings. Jerry approached them, then passed between two, where there was much more room than there had first seemed to be. The metal walls soared up above the little boat. Some crewmen waved down at them, and Dicey waved back. The tanker came from Athens, from Athens across the Atlantic and down the length of the Mediterranean Sea.

Dicey looked up the bay to where Baltimore was. Two bridges, twin spans, crossed the bay in long arcs. They looked like something from the future, slender silver ropes flung over the broad water, beautiful and strong.

Dicey's eyes moved out, across again. Jerry brought the boat about, and—after shifting her weight to compensate for the heel—she found she could no longer see the far shore, for which they were headed. They had left most of the other boats behind, and now passed only an occasional fishing boat, rocking at the end of its anchor line.

The wind hummed in her ears, the sun poured over her face and arms and legs, the waves knocked against the keel, and the boat pulled forward. Like everything else in Annapolis, the movement was both lazy and fast, at once. She turned back and saw Sammy staring at Tom. Jerry sat with the long wooden tiller in his hand, his eyes on the sails.

Dicey slid down onto the deck and leaned her back against the cabin. The sky was clear, the sails shone white against it. She closed her eyes.

In the darkness behind her eyelids, Dicey felt part of the boat itself, riding the wind over the water. It was easy work, this. It was silent and serene. Her thoughts loosed themselves from their everyday moorings and wandered. Nothing mattered out here. Nobody talked and nobody listened. The waves went past them, maybe each different, maybe the same wave over and over again. Who knew which? Who cared?

Dicey opened her eyes. They had never sailed in Provincetown. They had never been asked. She had rowed in dinghies and been out once or twice on large fishing boats. But they were nothing like this quiet harnessing of wind and the sharp keel cutting through silken water.

Out here, there was salt on the wind itself that fell on your skin like rain. You could taste it. Out here the sun heated and the wind cooled, and the waves sang their constant song.

Dicey wished she could stop breathing and give herself entirely over to the movement and the being still. Maybe she could learn to sail. Maybe she could go to sea, somehow. A boat could be a home. The perfect home that could move around, a home that didn't close you in or tie you down: and a sailor would always be at home if he was on the sea.

Maybe life was like a sea, and all the people were like boats. There were big, important yachts and little rafts and motorboats and sailboats and working boats and pleasure boats. And some really big boats like ocean liners or tankers—those would be rich or powerful people, whose lives engulfed many other lives and carried them along. Or maybe each boat was a kind of family. Then what kind of boat would the Tillermans be? A little one, bobbling about, with the mast fallen off? A grubby, worn-down workboat, with Dicey hanging on to the rudder for dear life.

Everybody who was born was cast onto the sea. Winds would blow them in all directions. Tides would rise and turn, in their own rhythm. And the boats—they just went along as best they could, trying to find a harbor.

Dicey didn't feel like finding a harbor. She knew she needed one, and they needed one, but she would rather just sail along, dreaming, not caring where they were going or when they would get there or what they would do there.

Couldn't you live your whole life without going into harbor? The land would catch you at the end. *Home is the sailor.* But until then, you could keep free. And even then, even when you died, you could die at sea and your body would roll with the underwater currents until your flesh peeled off and you were white bones rocking in the waves on the sandy bottom of the ocean. Always part of the changing.

Dicey smiled to herself. The ocean at Provincetown had always sung at her too. As long as I'm near the water, she thought, that'll be enough, even if I'm on land. Because life wasn't really an ocean, and she wasn't really a little boat bobbling about on it. There were James and Maybeth and Sammy, for one thing. But for now, she was content to sit still and silent.

The sun beat down hotter, and her skin started to run with sweat. She was getting sticky, uncomfortable. The sails fell lifeless and quiet, flapping morosely. The boat no longer thrust ahead, slicing the waves; now it rolled from side to side. She crawled back over the cabin.

"What's the matter?" she asked.

The two boys were leaning back, drinking beer from cans. "Wind's died down," Tom said.

"That happens," Jerry added. "Especially in the middle of the bay. No worry. The only deadline we have is I've got to be back in Annapolis by dark."

"Yeah, or the ghosties and boogies will get him."

Jerry frowned, but ignored his friend. "We can always let you off and head right back."

"I've got some friends in St. Mikes," Tom said.

"We know about your friends in St. Mikes," Jerry answered.

"It beats sitting around watching TV," Tom answered. "Doesn't it? Your mom's not here, Jer, you can tell the truth."

Dicey interrupted. "Could I steer? I mean, we're not going anywhere—"

"We are, but not far," Jerry corrected.

"Go ahead, let her," Tom urged. Jerry agreed.

Jerry slid down toward Sammy and put Dicey's hand on the long tiller. The wood was smooth and warm. It responded to every vibration in the hull and every flapping of the sails. Dicey's hand seesawed gently back and forth. The tiller let her feel the boat under her hand. She grinned at Jerry. "I like it," she said.

He grinned back at her and taught her how to head up, into the wind, and point down, away from it. He showed her what changes in the mainsail to watch for. He pointed to the glassy water just ahead of them and then to a patch far ahead where little ripples danced in the sunlight. "There's wind up there," he said. He leaned back and drank from his can of beer.

"I'm going below for a snooze," Tom announced. He climbed down the ladder and disappeared.

Sammy went up to sit with James.

Jerry moved over to Tom's seat. "He doesn't like sailing," he said.

"Who, Sammy? I didn't notice."

"No, Tom."

"But—"

"He's got nothing better to do." Jerry shrugged, then smiled a little. "And he likes getting me in trouble."

"What about you?" Dicey asked.

"I need some help getting in trouble. I'd never dare do it on my own. You know? Rebellion is necessary for the development of character."

Dicey wondered about that.

"Most men lead lives of quiet desperation," Jerry said. "Somebody said that. He was right. So—I get in trouble, now and then—so I won't be like most men."

"You're going to lead a life of noisy desperation?" Dicey asked.

He laughed at that. He gave himself over to laughter and enjoyed it. Dicey decided she liked him after all.

"At least that much," he said. "More if I can, but at least that."

They sailed on, if this odd, rolling progress could be called sailing. Then, under her hand, Dicey felt the boat stir. She looked at the water and the sails. They had reached the ripply patch of water. The sails bellied out.

Jerry was watching her. She offered him the tiller, but he shook his head. His smile teased her. He pulled in on the genoa line and held it. The long sail lay nearly flat. The mainsail line he had already cleated down. "Watch the genoa," he instructed.

Dicey did. She watched the sail and the water ahead. She rested her hand lightly on the tiller, letting the boat tell her where it wanted to go. She sat alert, her body tuned to that gentle pull on the tiller.

Boat, waves, water and wind: through the wood she felt them working for her. She was not directing, but accompanying them, turning them to her use. She didn't work against them, but with them; and she made the boat do that too. It wasn't power she felt, guiding the tiller, but purpose. She could not stop smiling.

The wind built up, and Jerry took back the tiller, giving Dicey the genoa line. She played it, without being told, letting it out a fraction, pulling it in two fractions, responding to the pull of the wind in the sail.

They didn't talk, sailing the boat. They didn't talk at all until Jerry pointed out the land approaching. Dicey saw short, narrow beaches, a few trees, some big houses.

"Another hour," Jerry said.

Dicey nodded.

"How old are you?" he asked.

"Thirteen," Dicey answered. "I turned thirteen in June."

"That's too bad," Jerry said. "If you were fifteen, or even fourteen . . . You really take to it, don't you? I've never seen anybody take to it like that. I never thought a girl could. You've got good hands, Dicey. And you're not scared."

"Thirteen isn't too young to sail," Dicey pointed out.

"No, it isn't," he agreed. He leaned his head down and called Tom awake. "We've got to come about and make the approach to St. Mikes."

Dicey nodded to show she understood, and she thought she did understand what he had said. She was too young to be a girlfriend. Her cheeks grew warm with the thought. Of course she was, much too young, and besides, she had more important things to do. She was surprised at herself, though, for the nice feeling it gave her. Maybe because she'd been so often taken for a boy.

She joined James and Sammy. Maybeth said she didn't want to move from her seat nestled up against the cabin wall, where she had sat silent for the whole trip. So Dicey returned to the foredeck. The boat heeled a little now, in the afternoon wind. She and James kept Sammy sitting between them. "I sailed it," Dicey said.

"I saw," James answered. "What was it like?"

Dicey couldn't explain. "Great," she said.

They watched the shoreline close them in as Jerry negotiated the channel into St. Mikes. This was low land, with large houses standing on bright green lawns. Buoys slipped by.

Jerry let down the mainsail and gathered it in, wrapping it around the boom and looping a line around it to hold it. Tom turned on the motor. Jerry loosed the genoa halyard and showed Dicey how to pull it down and hold it in at the same time. Great armloads of material surrounded her. She couldn't see anything.

Jerry's voice, muffled by the sail he was packing into a sail bag, assured her that she was doing just fine.

They pulled into the front of a long dock, and Tom took a line from the bow and wrapped it around one of the posts. Jerry tied the stern. He held the boat close to the dock while the Tillermans climbed out.

The steadiness of the land under her feet felt strange to Dicey. She felt as if everything was reversed. On the boat, the deck had been unsteady and her leg muscles had worked to keep her balanced. On land, the ground was so steady that her leg muscles took up the motion of the boat. It was crazy.

Her family stood back while she thanked Jerry. Tom was talking to him about calling some people. "We got beer on the boat," he was saying.

Jerry hesitated.

"Just an hour. You can call your old lady and tell her where you are, if you're worried. Or better yet, call her and tell her you're here and can't get back before dark. She'll be mad at you for sailing over, but glad you called, so it'll be all right. Jerry? You wanna? Man, we're over here with the boat and beer—we can really have a party."

Jerry laughed, a light, high sound. He turned the idea over in his mind. "I don't know," he said.

Dicey knew. She knew also what he would decide. "We gotta find a bus," she said. "Thanks an awful lot."

"That's okay, kid," Tom answered.

Dicey waited for Jerry to say something. Finally he noticed. "It was fun," he said.

"Yeah, it was. It really was."

"See you around, yeah?" he said.

"Probably not," Dicey said. She held out her hand and he shook it.

"Yeah," he said, but he wasn't paying attention to her. He was looking at Tom, and a smile was creeping over his mouth. Dicey picked up her bag, slung it over her shoulder, took a last look at the boat and walked off fast.

St. Michael's was a small town huddled around its waterfront. It was like Annapolis, but without the hurrying quality of the city across the bay. It was pretty, but Dicey was not cheered by that as they walked out of town on the one main street. She felt vaguely sad. To make herself feel better, she vowed that she would sail again, and often, if she could. Crisfield was on the water. People there must sail.

The midafternoon sun pounded down on them. They walked two abreast on the side of the road, Dicey with Maybeth, James with Sammy. Dicey carried her bag over her shoulder.

Little town houses, with handkerchief lawns, gave way to fields where corn and soybeans grew. Driveways led off the highway. Sometimes you could see the roofs of houses back among the trees that began at the far ends of the fields. Some of the mailboxes had the names of houses on them, Windward, Petersons Landing, Oakwood, Second Chance.

They came to a wooded section, mostly pines, and walked at its edge, as far from the traffic as they could get. In the midst of this section, a driveway went off. Like the other driveways they'd passed, this was a dirt road. But this road had a name, Overview Circle, and a bunch of mailboxes clustered at its beginning.

Dicey peered down the highway and saw a small store ahead, with a gas pump out front.

"You all wait here," she said, putting down her bag. "I'm going up to the store to get some food, and we'll see if there's a place to camp down this driveway. I figure, these are big estates, and probably on the riverfront. Okay?"

"It's not dark yet," James objected.

"It's getting late and we've got to find a place. This looks like there might be lots of privacy," Dicey explained.

"Okay, if you say so," James said.

"And if I'm wrong there'll still be time to find another place," Dicey said.

They sat down within the first row of trees. Dicey walked on, scuffing her feet, to the store.

Dicey entered the store through the screen door. She saw mostly cans and dried foods. There was one small icebox that held milk, butter, eggs and cold cuts in plastic packaging. She picked out a can of chicken noodle soup, a quart of milk, a loaf of bread, a bar of soap, a box of safety matches and four tomatoes from a bushel basket. It cost two dollars and ten cents.

The storekeeper stood beside her while she made all these selections, watching her carefully. He didn't say a word. He was a bony man, with short grizzled hair and long, nervous fingers. When Dicey had piled everything on the counter, he said, "That be it?" and rang up her purchases on an ancient cash register.

Something about his voice was familiar, but Dicey couldn't put her finger on it.

Outside Dicey recognized what had been familiar in the man's voice. He had Momma's way with the sounds of letters. They sounded, just a little, like Momma. Dicey smiled and rejoined her family.

The dirt driveway led off the road straight for a quarter of a mile before it began winding among the trees. At the turns, driveways entered. Dicey walked down one and saw a large house, white shingled, and water beyond it. Dogs barked at her, so she turned back.

The third house was silent, although a car waited in the long garage. The Tillermans skirted the trees at the edge of the property and cut down to the water when they saw it. They found a marshy beach, nestled back against the piney woods. It was not ideal, but it was private and, except for birds and frogs, quiet.

Dicey built a small fire and opened the soup can with her jackknife can opener. It was hard work, but it did the job. She mixed a can of milk into the condensed soup in the pan. Then she told everybody to strip and put on clean underwear. James stood in the muddy water and washed out their underwear, using the cake of soap. He brought it back for Dicey to inspect. "I dunno," she said. "The water's muddy, not like a laundromat."

Maybeth spread the wet clothing over some bushes. They sat around the small fire and took turns drinking soup from the pan, soaking it up with flabby slices of bread. They passed the milk container around, and Dicey halved the tomatoes. They ate these eagerly, even Sammy who didn't ordinarily like tomatoes. They were red, firm, juicy. They tasted fresher than anything Dicey had ever eaten before.

After supper, Dicey put out the fire ("We don't want to attract attention.") and set Sammy fishing in the quiet river. After a while, James joined Sammy, holding his own line and hook.

The sun set quietly, flaming in the water. The boys caught five small fish, which they killed and then left lying in the water, so they'd be fresh for breakfast.

When the sun was only a band of burning red seen through the trees, Dicey took out the ponchos and spread them on the ground, rolling on them to crush the undergrowth beneath. Nobody wanted to go to sleep, however. They sat with their knees pulled up under their chins. Maybeth began to sing, and they joined in without thinking. They kept their voices down, just in case, but they sang eagerly. When darkness had fallen over everything, and the stars burned bright in a moonless sky, they went to sleep.

CHAPTER 4

They slept late the next morning and were awakened by the roar of a racing motorboat as it headed down the river to the bay. They were all, even Sammy, shoved out of sleep into the hot morning, like falling out of bed.

Dicey raised her face from the poncho. Her cheek was damp with sweat. Her thighs stuck to the rubber. She rubbed at her eyes.

The woods rested behind them. The water and the opposite shore lay before them. Between these wandered the narrow river. The sun was high in the sky, high and hot.

They all peed in the woods and then gathered fuel for a small fire. Dicey pulled the five fish out of the water. With the jackknife, she gutted them and scraped off some of their scales. Then she and James threaded them onto supple branches. Nobody spoke.

They ate the fish and finished the milk and bread. James experimented with toasting the bread on a stick. He got a patchwork piece of toast, splotches of white, splotches of black and various shades of brown. Dicey gathered the underwear, almost dry, from the bushes where they had been hanging all night. James taught Sammy how to put out a fire properly; how to cover it with dirt and then stamp on it and wait, to be sure no telltale smoke rose from the ashes.

Maybeth helped Dicey fold up the ponchos and pack them into her bag. They gathered all their garbage into the brown grocery bag.

Dicey knew it was time to go, but she didn't want to start, not yet. She pulled out her map and studied it. They would go through Easton and then loop west. Dicey would have preferred to stick to the water's edge, to follow the shoreline down, but this countryside had too many fists and fingers of land that reached out into the water. If they followed the shoreline, they would travel many miles more than they had to, winding in and out along the points of land.

At the sound of another motor, they all froze. A small boat, really just a rowboat with an outboard, chugged downriver. Three boys were in it, all about James's age. They were tanned by the sun; all wore cutoffs, T-shirts and sneakers. Their hair looked shaggy, as if it hadn't been cut all summer. They trailed lazy hands in the water as they moved slowly, aimlessly, down the river and out of sight.

"You know," Dicey said, "they look like us. Don't they? James?"

He nodded. His eyes followed the wake the little boat left behind.

"Do you think we're like most of the kids over here, in the way we look?" Dicey asked.

"Natural camouflage," James said.

Dicey looked at them. They were all tan, and her day in the sun yesterday had caught her up in brownness for what she'd lost during hours inside at Bridgeport. Their hair was scruffy, and Maybeth's curls looked tangled. But they didn't look out of place, or unusual. They looked like kids running a little wild during the summer.

They returned to the road, hurrying down the dirt driveway. James carried the bag of trash and dumped it into a garbage can near the little store Dicey had shopped in the afternoon before. The clock within the store read ten. Late.

The children walked on beside the highway. This was Route 33, heading east. In Easton, they would change roads to go south. Traffic was light on this hot summer morning. They walked two by two on the shoulder of the road. Fields of corn hedged them in. Insects buzzed among the rows. Dicey wondered if they could take a few ears for supper. Her pan wasn't big enough to hold a whole ear of corn, but you could scrape off the kernels. Her curiosity was aroused by these fields, so unprotected from the road. Anybody could go in and steal the corn. There were no fences to stop them. Maybe that was why she didn't want to do it.

As they neared the town of Easton, they began to pass shopping centers and development houses, little, low one-story ranchers with sprigs of new grass and one or two puny trees. At one of the large markets, Dicey bought a pie on sale and four bananas. They cost ninety-two cents. She told her family that they would stop to eat after they had passed through Easton.

Sammy wanted to stop before the town. "It takes all day to get through a place."

"Not a little one like this," Dicey said.

"Are you sure?"

"Pretty sure," Dicey said. "Wanna bet?"

They wagered an hour's fishing time. If it took too long to get through Easton, Dicey would have to fish for an hour, while Sammy had free time. If it didn't, then Sammy would have to fish an extra hour. Sammy liked this. Either way, he won. He walked eagerly on.

Dicey won the wager, of course. As she said to herself, if she couldn't read a map by now, she'd be a pretty sore fool. The streets of Easton, even the main arteries that they walked on, were sleepy, treelined roads. The tallest buildings reached only four stories. Stop signs outnumbered traffic lights.

Their roads took them around the town rather than through its center. They passed by a long pond that ran behind the YMCA and then down across abandoned railroad tracks to where a big highway joined up with 322.

Here, Dicey took out her map again: Route 50—a four lane highway with a grass divider. Trucks, cars, campers, buses, vans, pickups, motorcycles, all thundered down the highway, hard on one another's heels, traveling fast. Dicey wanted to get off this road for two reasons. First, it was too heavily traveled, and the air was thick with fumes and noise. Second, Route 50 went due south, to Cambridge, before bearing east to Salisbury. It would be quicker to take a road that followed the third side of the triangle formed by Easton, Cambridge and Salisbury. A river lay across that route, the Choptank. It was broad down by Cambridge, but narrower up above, and would be easy to cross she guessed, remembering the little river they'd camped by. She decided to turn off the main highway and cut cross-country.

A quarter of a mile south of Easton, she took a turn onto River Road. That had the right sound to it. They crossed the highway at a run. They raced across the southbound lanes, then had to wait several minutes before they could dash safely across the northbound traffic. Dicey saw fields ahead, and a few houses. Twenty yards from the highway, they were back in open countryside.

It was James who sighted the circus ahead, set up on a fallow field. He saw the ferris wheel. "Let's go there and eat," he said.

"We can't spend any money," Dicey said.

"That's okay, I like to look," James answered.

They ate the bananas as they approached the circus. They came to it from the rear, from behind a big tent. A short midway with a ferris wheel and carousel and a dozen booths for games and food stands led away from the tent entrance. People were hurrying around, setting up games, carrying boxes marked with the names of soft drinks; a man tinkered with the engine that drove the ferris wheel. Dicey stopped by a trash can. She broke the pie into four pieces and handed them out. They dropped their garbage into the metal barrel. They stared for a while at the activity on the midway and then drifted back to the tent from which music and voices issued.

"Do you think they have elephants?" Sammy asked Dicey.

"It doesn't look big enough," she said. "I don't see any place where they'd keep animals, do you, James? It doesn't look like much of a circus."

James peered into the tent, standing in the doorway. "There's a tightrope," he reported.

"Out," ordered a sharp voice from the dimness within the tent. The Tillermans backed away. "You heard me." A woman stepped out into the hot sunlight.

She had bright red hair and wore a man's shirt over tight blue jeans. She wore sandals with very high heels. She carried a whip. Three terriers, like little white mobilized mops, swirled around her feet in eager circles. Somehow, she managed not to step on them or trip over them.

"What're you kids doing here?" she demanded. She sounded angry, angry at them.

"Nothing," Dicey said.

"Tell that to the Marines," the woman said. "You know we don't open until six."

"No, we didn't," Dicey said.

"You do now," she answered. She put her hands on her hips and glared at them. The whip dangled down, and one of the little dogs, the one with a pink ribbon on its head, jumped up to grab it out of her hand. The woman rocked on her heels and the dogs ran off in a row, the other two chasing the one carrying the whip.

Dicey started to smile.

"You heard me," the woman said. "Or should I call the police?"

"I don't think so." A slow, thick man's voice spoke from behind the Tillermans. Dicey turned to face this new person. He was a tall black man, with eyes so dark brown they looked almost black beneath thick eyebrows. He was clothed entirely in black, a black shirt and black pants and high black leather boots. His tightly curling hair was cut short, and he had a narrow, short beard along his jawbone. His face looked relaxed, as if nothing could upset him.

Maybeth moved closer to Dicey. James stood where he was, his mouth open. Sammy was poised to run.

The man spoke again. "Relax, kids, she won't hurt you. Claire? What is this?"

"They were snooping around," the woman told him. "This one," she indicated Dicey, "he said they didn't know we're closed until six."

"You go back to work," the man told her. "I'll take care of this." They waited while she whistled for the dogs and then stalked off, back into the tent.

"We are off-limits until the show opens," the man told the Tillermans.

"We really didn't know," Dicey said.

"Then you're strangers around here." His eyes studied her.

Dicey nodded. Looking at his calm face, with its studying eyes, she said what she was thinking: "Strangers about everywhere."

He looked quizzically at her.

"She had no cause to be angry," Dicey said.

He nodded. "I apologize for that. Claire's got a bad temper—but that's no excuse. Believe it or not, she's a good friend. A good person to have on your side."

"We owe you an apology, too," Dicey answered. "Even if we didn't mean to, we did trespass."

"I'll see you out," he said. "You came through the back? Where are you going, if you don't live in Easton?"

"South," Dicey said.

"Where you from?"

"North."

The man stopped two strides ahead of them and turned to look at them all. His leather boots creaked a little. The Tillermans stood in a row, facing him.

"Are you okay?" he asked.

"Yeah," Dicey said.

"You're not a boy," the man said, walking beside them now. He had a little smile hovering around his mouth.

"No, I'm not," Dicey agreed.

"Do you own this circus?" James asked.

"Yep," he said.

"Why?" James asked.

"It's my living. Name's Will, by the way. I like moving around, following the good weather."

"I wouldn't think you'd make any money," James observed.

"Why not?" Will asked.

"It's so small."

"That's right enough," Will agreed. "Still . . ." His warm voice drifted off without finishing the sentence.

At the road he said good-bye. "Good traveling," he said to Dicey.

"Thanks for rescuing us," Dicey said.

"You didn't need help," he answered. "Take care."

"You too," Dicey said.

"Oh I do, you can believe I do," he said. He turned back with a wave. The Tillermans walked away.

They were silent for a long time, each thinking his own thoughts in the steamy afternoon. The road wound through farm country. Here the farms were large. Several fields separated one farmhouse from another. The fields were flat. The farmhouses had only a few trees near them. Big barns and many sheds lay behind the houses. They were prosperous farms, you could tell, because the barns gleamed with fresh red paint and the houses often had swimming pools out front.

Finally, James broke the silence. "She probably figured she could be angry and mean to us and get away with it," he said. "Because we're kids."

"She didn't get away with it," Dicey reminded him. "Sammy? You were ready to run, weren't you?"

"I didn't know what she'd do," Sammy explained. "She said she'd call the police."

"That was smart," Dicey said.

"But—" James started to say, and then he stopped.

They walked on and sang as they walked.

They passed fields and more fields. Some of them had been picked bare. Some of the farms had a cardboard sign posted at their mailboxes: PICKERS WANTED.

At a crossroads, Dicey went into a general store and bought potatoes and tomatoes, a quart of milk and another loaf of bread. She also bought two Cokes in cans, because she was thirsty. All these cost two dollars and thirty-five cents. Except for the forty dollars she didn't want to spend, she was almost out of money.

They shared the Cokes. "We could pick for a day or two," Dicey said to her family, "and get some money."

"Do we need money?" James asked.

"Of course," Dicey said. "I've got some set aside, in case we have to go back to Bridgeport. I don't want to spend that. So we're not out of money, but we need more."

"Would they hire kids?" James asked.

"We could try," Dicey said. "Are you game to try? Could you pick for a day, Sammy?"

"Sure," Sammy said.

Dicey grinned at him. "I believe you could," she said.

"I'll try," Maybeth volunteered.

"I guess so," James said.

"Not today though," Dicey said. "Today—there's a creek up a ways, or down a ways. I thought we'd camp by that and fish. Somebody has a couple of fishing hours owed us. I will not say who."

"It's me!" Sammy cried. "Because I lost the bet. It's me!"

As they approached the creek Dicey had seen on the map—only the map called it a river—the land developed a few gentle rises. These were not hills like they'd found in Connecticut, not high, sharp hills. They were gentle roundings, mere ripples in the land. In contrast to the flat land all around, however, they stood up. Here, there were hardwood trees, sycamores and maples and oaks, as well as the pines that grew everywhere.

The road went over the little creek, and the Tillermans turned off the road, following the creek's dry banks until they judged they were far enough from road and farmhouse. Sammy dug a few worms and set himself to fishing. James and Dicey gathered wood for a fire. Maybeth spread out the ponchos under the green trees, as best she could. There wasn't room for more than two of them, because of the roots and bushes and the creek bank.

When everything was ready and they had only to wait for Sammy to catch something, Dicey and James and Maybeth went downstream to wade and wash. Sammy watched them go without a word. He stood very quiet in the center of the narrow creek, letting the water splash at his hips, holding the fishing line out from his hands.

The late afternoon wore away into early evening. Dicey came back and started the fire. Sammy had caught nothing and reported no nibbles. He was not quite ready to quit trying, he said.

Dicey shoved the potatoes into the fire. The skins would burn, maybe, but she didn't think she could get a pot of water boiling on the small fire she felt safe building.

They ate potatoes, tomatoes, and bread for supper and passed around the carton of milk. There was enough food to fill them, and they kept back some bread and milk for breakfast. James put out the fire, using dirt not water, because water would make more smoke.

The sun was going down, then. It grasped at the land with long yellow fingers and made the mottled trunks of sycamores look like people's skin. Flocks of birds made their evening journeys home, twittering to one another. Far off, an occasional motor sounded.

The Tillermans lay sprawled around with the creek at their feet and the slight hillside behind them. Clouds strayed across the darkening sky.

"You know," Dicey said, "we don't have to go anywhere. We could always travel like this, following the warm weather, like Will said he did. We can take care of ourselves."

"Yeah, but what's the point?" James asked.

"There doesn't have to be a point," Dicey said. "Just doing it. Like sailing."

"We have to go home," Maybeth said.

"Home? We don't have a home," Dicey said.

"I thought we were going to Momma's home," Maybeth said.

"Is that our home too?" Sammy asked.

"I don't know," Dicey said. "That's what we're trying to find out, I guess. Oh, well," she said, "I guess you're right, James. I mean, you have to go to school."

"So do you." He grinned at her. "So do we all. We're going to grow up. We have to."

"I know. I know," she said.

"If it was Momma's home, it has to be ours too," Maybeth said.

"We have this grandmother there," Dicey answered. "But we can't tell—what she'll think of us. What she'll want. Momma never talked about her," Dicey pointed out.

"Yes, she did," Sammy said, "but it made her sad. She'd cry."

"Is that right? What did she say?"

"I can't remember, only the sadness. I'm sorry, Dicey."

"That's okay. I didn't know Momma ever said anything about her. I just don't know what to expect there."

"Whatever," James said, "we can take care of ourselves. Wherever."

"'I know an old lady, who swallowed a fly,'" Dicey chanted. They sang all the silly songs they knew until darkness had gathered around them. Then they lay down close together and went gently to sleep.

CHAPTER 5

Early the next morning, after they had buried their garbage in the soft soil and washed briefly in the creek, they set off. By the time the sun had fully risen, the four children were back on the road.

The morning air tasted cool and clean. At a fork in the road Dicey headed south, because the Choptank River lay to the southeast. This road narrowed and ran straight between fields of tall, ripening corn. They passed farmhouses, barns and an occasional weathered gray shack raised off the ground on piles of bricks. Most of these shacks were guarded by thin dogs that yapped at the children from the shade under the houses.

Many of the fields were being harvested. People moved up and down the rows gathering corn, squashes, tomatoes or cucumbers into bushel baskets. Their heads were wrapped with bright red and blue bandanas. They stooped, squatted or stretched. Even from the road their fatigue was evident.

"Hard work," James remarked.

"We need the money," Dicey said. "But I'm not sure the little kids can do it."

"We don't really need the money, do we? You have extra."

It was hot. The sun burned high. Dicey was thirsty and impatient. "I don't want to be stuck in Crisfield, James. I don't know how things will go there. We've got to have some extra money. We may need it."

James considered this. "What's our grandmother's name?"

"Abigail. It was in the album."

"Do you think we could go back to Bridgeport? Do you think Cousin Eunice would take us back?"

"I dunno, James."

They passed no stores, no gas stations, just farms surrounded by outbuildings and old pickup trucks.

"The map shows towns across the Choptank," Dicey said to her family. "So even if we don't get lunch we can eat after we cross it."

"Does this road go over it?" James asked.

Dicey shook her head.

"Then what are we doing? How're we going to cross it?"

"Swim. Or wade if it's shallow."

"Do you know how wide it is?"

"How could I know that?" Dicey demanded. "Stop asking questions."

"Why?"

"You're driving me crazy with them, that's why."

James quieted, but his eyes held doubts.

At midday, they saw another sign that said: PICKERS WANTED. Dicey looked down a long dirt driveway that ran between fields of corn turned to the color of August sunlight. Trees lined the driveway. No house could be seen, although a circle of trees was visible beyond the tops of the corn. "I say we try it," Dicey said. Without waiting for an answer, she turned onto the driveway. They followed her.

The driveway ran straight for about half a mile, then curved to the east. The air was thick and hot. It hummed with the activities of insects. Dicey shifted her bag onto her other shoulder and trudged on. With her free hand she slapped at bugs.

The farmhouse sat within the circle of trees they had seen from the driveway. It was a two-storied building covered with pale green asphalt shingles. It had a discouraged look to it.

The Tillermans approached the house slowly. A large, windowless barn, sided in silvery corrugated metal, made one side of the farmyard. The house made a second. Some small sheds made a third. Tall wire cyclone fences lay on both sides of the house itself. The yard was a three-sided cage.

A dog growled and barked, snarled and leaped angrily up against the fencing on the right side of the house. This must be a kennel. This dog needed a kennel. It was a large gray-and-brown creature, bigger than a setter, with a huge slavering mouth. Its teeth hung long and sharp. It charged against the fence, setting up a clamor that would rouse anyone in the house, Dicey thought. She couldn't make herself step any further toward the screen door of the house, not with that dog there, not even to make money.

The screen door opened and a man holding a napkin in his hand stepped out. As soon as he appeared, the dog stopped barking and crouched, fawning and whimpering. The man started toward the children.

He was short and slender. He wore overalls and heavy working boots that laced up the front. The shirt under his overalls was dark blue with fancy red and yellow flowers printed all over it. His face was square and blunt; he had gray hair that he brushed back off his forehead and thin, straight eyebrows over cold eyes. He moved toward the Tillermans without hesitating, without hurrying, and stood silent before them. His skin was tanned and leathery. Deep lines ran across his forehead. He reached his napkin up and wiped his mouth.

"Yeah," he said.

Dicey spoke. "You have a sign out front, pickers wanted." She hesitated, but he didn't say anything. "We—my brother and me—we'd like to apply." She motioned James to come stand beside her.

The man didn't speak. He studied them, through hard gray eyes.

"We can work hard," Dicey said.

She waited. He didn't speak.

"What do you pay?" she asked.

"Fifty cents a bushel."

You could pick lots of bushels in a day. That would be okay. "Will you hire us?"

"Yes," he said. "What about the smaller ones?" he asked Dicey.

"They'll come with us and help," Dicey said. "They won't cause any trouble."

"Name's Rudyard," he said. "What's yours?"

"Verricker," Dicey said quickly. That seemed to be all he wanted to know. Except, "What's hers?" he demanded, pointing at Maybeth with his head. "Maybeth," Dicey said.

Something was wrong here, something she couldn't put her finger on. Well, it wasn't her problem; they would work an afternoon and take their money.

He told them to get up into the back of a dusty old pickup truck the color of canned peas. He drove them on a flat dirt road that led around the barn and behind it before heading straight up a slight incline, through an overgrown field, to another field. This was a long field of tomatoes. The plants were crowded with weeds, grasses and low vines. You could barely see the rows they had been planted in. But the tomatoes had grown red and plump. They shone out from the weeds like bulbs on a Christmas tree. At one corner of the field, a mound of bushel baskets waited. The Tillermans scrambled down.

Mr. Rudyard didn't even get out of the truck. "I'll be by at dark," he said. He backed the truck around and drove off. Dicey watched it go into the distance, back to the barn, then around it and out of sight.

"Creepy," James said.

"You can say that again," Dicey agreed. "Maybeth, you okay?"

Maybeth nodded, wide-eyed.

"How long do we have to stay?" Sammy asked.

They all felt uneasy. Dicey tried to reassure them. "Just this afternoon. Then we'll take our pay and get out of here. Okay?"

They got to it. Because they were hungry, Dicey decided they could each eat two tomatoes. That was fair enough, she figured. Then they all worked together, pushing or pulling weeds away from the tomato plants. One would hold back the overgrowth, and the rest would reach in for tomatoes, wresting the fruit from the stems. Their legs and hands and faces were scratched. They had bug bites on every part of their bodies. Dirt was smeared across their faces and arms and legs. They left the filled baskets where they were when they finished with them.

After an hour they had completed one row. Two to a basket, they carried the bushels down to where the pile of empty baskets waited. They had six baskets. "Three dollars," Dicey said.

Dicey's back ached from bending over. Her hands stung where small scratches had accumulated. She had never felt such heat before, an air that closed down over her and made it hard to breathe.

"Hot," James said. "It's too hot, Dicey."

"You two take a break," Dicey said to Sammy and Maybeth. "Go off and explore a little. Stick together though. When you're rested, come back and help. Remember our name?"

"Verricker," Sammy said. "What's that?"

"Our father's name," Dicey said.

"That right?" James asked. "How do you know that?"

"So what," Sammy said. "I like Tillerman better."

Sammy and Maybeth wandered off down the edge of the field, going away from the house and the dog. Dicey and James got back to work.

This row took longer. James grew sloppy and Dicey had to nag at him to keep at it and find all the ripe tomatoes that grew on the plants and on the long vines that crawled along next to the dry earth. "My back hurts," he protested. "I'm hot." His face was streaked with dirt and sweat. His eyes wavered between anger and self-pity. He crouched unwilling by her side.

"It's only for an afternoon," Dicey snapped at him.

Sammy and Maybeth returned before they had finished the row. "There's another field," Sammy reported. "And a river. I wanted to go swimming but Maybeth wouldn't."

"The Choptank," Dicey said.

"Could we swim across it?" James asked Sammy.

Sammy nodded. Dicey shot a triumphant glance at James. "It's not wide," Sammy said. "I could swim it easy."

"Can we go now, Dicey?" Maybeth asked.

Dicey almost said yes. They all looked at her, waiting. She shook her head. "Not before we get paid," she said grimly. "Don't worry, we'll be all right. As long as we're together."

At late afternoon, when the sun was beginning to lower and the mosquitos were beginning to rise, the green pickup truck returned. The children went eagerly to meet it.

Mr. Rudyard had the dog in the front seat with him. He climbed down and pulled on a long rope to get the dog to follow him. The Tillermans crowded together. The dog snarled at them.

"There's a bag in the cab," Mr. Rudyard said to Dicey. "The missus said I had to feed you something." He walked off, down to the far end of the field.

"What's he going to do?" Maybeth whispered.

"I dunno," Dicey said. Fear climbed up from her stomach to her throat. A sour, metallic taste was in her saliva and she swallowed it down. She made herself climb up and get the paper bag from the seat of the cab. Mr. Rudyard had left the keys in the ignition.

Mr. Rudyard tied the dog to a tree, using the end of the long rope. When he came back, Dicey had decided what to do.

"We can't pick anymore," she said. "We have to go now," she said.

He looked at her out of cold eyes. Then he said, "If he runs against that sapling it'll snap." He got back into the truck and leaned out the window. "I keep him hungry," he remarked. He backed the truck around and drove off.

In the silence, Dicey could hear insects humming. "What does he *want*?" she demanded.

Nobody could answer her.

"We might as well eat," Dicey said. They all sat down. Mrs. Rudyard had packed a tall thermos of milk and a package of tall biscuits slathered with butter and bright strawberry jam. They passed the thermos around. The biscuits looked delicious. Dicey took a bite of one, and her stomach closed against it. She put it down on the wax paper.

Even James couldn't eat. They looked at one another. "I'm sorry," Dicey said.

"Well, I don't care, I'm not picking anymore," Sammy announced. He threw his unfinished biscuit into the pile and they scattered around, like fallen blocks. "And you can't make me," he said to Dicey.

Dicey couldn't help smiling at him and that made her feel better. "I won't try," she said. "James? What can we do?"

"I'd like to kill him and hit him," Sammy said. "He scares Maybeth." Maybeth had big tears in her eyes.

"There's the dog," James said, "and the man." Absentmindedly, he picked up a biscuit. He took a bite, then tossed it down again. "He's crazy, Dicey."

"Bad crazy," she agreed. "Don't get on that truck again, no matter what."

"He wants us to be scared," Maybeth said. "He wants to hurt us."

Dicey nodded. Her mind was working and working, and she couldn't think of anything. James just stared at her. She picked up her maroon bag from where she had put it beside the bushels. She took out all of the money and jammed it into her pocket, with the jackknife. (With a jackknife, if she had to, she could try to fight the man or the dog.) She stuffed the map into the waistband of her shorts.

"We're going to have to run," she said. "When he comes back for the dog. James, you take Maybeth. Maybeth, no matter what, you stick with James." Sammy could take care of himself. "Go for the river."

"What about you?" James asked.

"I'm not sure," Dicey tried to keep her voice normal. She had gotten them into this mess, and if anyone got caught it should be her. "I'll do something. You just keep ready to run."

It was deep twilight, shadowy and still, when the truck returned. The Tillermans sat where Mr. Rudyard had left them. The headlights shone on them briefly. He backed the truck so that its back section was where the filled bushel baskets waited and its nose pointed almost straight down the road to the farmhouse. He got out and looked at them.

"You're not much use," he observed. Maybeth grabbed Dicey's hand as his eyes rested on her. "I'll just have to teach you. Now, load up," he ordered. He walked down to the dog, which barked a greeting.

"How does he know we're alone?" James wondered.

"Quiet," Dicey said. She looked into the cab to see if the keys had been left there. They had. "Okay, now listen. When he's to the dog, tell me. And when I say run, you run, all of you, as fast as you can. You hear?"

They nodded. Dicey got up into the truck. She tried to forget about the man at the far corner of the field. She looked for the key and found it. She turned on the engine. Nothing happened. She looked at the transmission box. A needle pointed to *D.* Quickly, she shifted it to *N.* "Now, Dicey," James whispered.

She turned the key again, and the engine caught.

Dicey looked back over her shoulder. Mr. Rudyard ran toward them, his mouth open in a yell. The dog ran ahead of him, at full cry, but held back by the rope that his master had looped around his shoulder.

"James," Dicey yelled. "Now. Run."

She shifted into *D,* and turned the wheel so it would head straight down the road to the barn. If she got it started, she figured, the incline would keep it going. She pushed on the accelerator and threw herself out of the cab.

The ground surged up to meet her and the cab door slammed against her shoulder. It hurt, but she didn't have time to worry about that. She rolled onto her feet and looked to see her family, waiting, watching her. "Go!" she shrieked.

Dicey led them into the middle of the tomato field, away from the man and the dog. It was harder running, especially for Sammy with his short legs, but it would be harder for Mr. Rudyard too. She let James and Maybeth pass her and slowed until she was behind Sammy too.

They weren't going to go without her. She didn't have time to know how she felt about that. She glanced over her shoulder.

Mr. Rudyard was already letting the dog's rope fall from his shoulder as he ran after the truck. He would catch it easily, but how soon? The dog looked after his master for a second and then bent his head to the ground, snuffling something. Probably their scent, Dicey thought, turning her head back and making a burst of speed to catch up.

Across the tomato field, and then across the next field, where young corn made a narrow path for them to follow, they ran. Dicey tried to listen for the sound of the dog behind them, or the sound of the motor coming out of the darkness. But she could hear only their labored breathing and the stamping of their feet. She charged through the row of brush and small trees that separated the second field from the river, grabbing Sammy's hand, pulling him with her. The earth fell away from beneath her feet and she tumbled into water.

Water closed warm over Dicey's head. She shut her eyes. She held tight on to Sammy's hand. How deep was it?

Her toes touched muddy river bottom and she pushed up. She shot out of the water. It was only up to her chest.

"James? Maybeth?"

"Here," James spoke just beyond her.

"It's warm," Sammy said.

In the distance, a truck motor roared.

"Straight across, then right, downstream. Okay? Stay close."

They set out into darkness, paddling quietly across. Through the gentle sounds of water, Dicey could hear their breathing. Dark water was all around them, and the dark land behind, and the dark land ahead. Every now and then she lowered a tentative foot to touch bottom.

The river was no more than fifty or sixty yards across, and it wasn't long before Dicey saw the opposite bank rise over her head, capped by a tangle of undergrowth and trees. She put her foot down again. It sank into mud.

Dicey and James were tall enough to touch bottom, but the water was over the heads of the smaller children. So Dicey and James each carried the weight of a younger one floating beside. They made their way cautiously, silently, quickly, downstream. They didn't speak, not even when they heard the man breaking through the bushes behind them upstream.

Sounds of someone walking hastily through underbrush across the river.

James moved doggedly on. Dicey followed him. They were near enough to get out and run, if Mr. Rudyard dove into the water to pursue them. They could hide in the bushes on this side. He didn't have the dog with him.

The sounds ceased, as if someone were standing still to listen. James stopped too, but she pushed him on with an impatient hand.

The water gurgled around them.

The crackling sounds began again, hurrying away.

The darkness around Dicey lifted, as if a blanket had been taken off her head. There was no actual change, of course. Only, the night seemed cool and empty, and the clear dark silhouettes of bushes and trees above them seemed to move back to give her more room, and the broad river seemed to float peacefully beside them.

They kept silence for another half hour, working their way downriver. At last, Dicey spoke. "Let's get out—James? Can you lift Sammy? Sammy? Do you mind being first?"

"'Course not," Sammy said.

James hoisted the little boy up onto the bank. Sammy reached down to help Maybeth scramble up. Dicey pushed James from behind, and he turned around to pull her up, while her feet slipped against the muddy bank, searching for firm holds. They sat, huddling together, shivering but not from a chill.

Dicey turned to look behind them, where flat farmlands stretched off. No windows shone, but she could see a pair of headlights, far off, moving on a straight line. There must be a road.

"Not him," Dicey said. She kept her voice low. Danger lurked all around them, always, she knew that now. "It couldn't be him. There aren't but two bridges over the river and they're miles away."

"What about the dog?" Sammy asked.

"Dogs can't track through water," James said.

Dicey remembered the dog, snuffling at the ground for their scents. Then she began to giggle. "It was eating the biscuits!" she cried. "He couldn't get it to chase us because it was hungry. Doesn't that serve him right."

This set them all giggling, even Maybeth. They kept their laughter low, and after a while they lay back on the grassy bank and slept, close together.

CHAPTER 6

At the first signs of dawn, the first pink glimmers, the first watery bird songs, Dicey opened her eyes. She lay on her back with James on one side and Maybeth curled against the other and Sammy on his belly beside James. Her eyes looked up through the delicate leaves of trees into a depthless sky. She smiled, and her eyes closed.

Later, when they opened again, the sun was fully risen. Faint voices floated to her across the fields that lay behind them. James had rolled away from her. The sky had blued above her. Dicey sat up.

The Choptank danced at her feet, deep and clear. It looked cleaner than any water she had seen. Grasses grew up its banks, and a musical silence stirred in its depths. She followed its path with her eyes to where it wound out of sight, going west.

When they were all awake, even Sammy, and when Dicey had pulled out her jackknife and dried it thoroughly on her shirt and counted her money (handling it delicately so that the damp paper wouldn't rip apart), she gently spread the map before them.

"We're about here," she said. She pointed to a place on the southern bank of the Choptank. "Let's head for that town." Her finger traced a path to a place named Hurlock.

James protested: "Secretary's closer."

"Hurlock's bigger. It's in the right direction," Dicey said. "If he comes after us—"

"You think he will?" Sammy asked.

"I don't know, but I don't want to take any chances."

"It'll be easier to hide in a bigger town," James said.

That was what Dicey was thinking. She was also thinking what a long, unknown way lay between here and Crisfield; and that Crisfield too was unknown.

They cut across fields. The ground underfoot was dry and crumbly, and although they tried to hurry, it was difficult because the furrows rose up to trip them. Walking across fields was like having one leg shorter than the other.

One of the fields they had to cross was being picked. Pickers were scattered among tomato plants that rose up from the tops of furrows. Weeds had been kept down in this field, and the plants had been trained up stakes. It looked like a painting, the ridges of brown earth, the tepees of dark green tomato plants with their bright red fruits, the bent figures of the pickers and the blue sky overhead.

Dicey led her family single file along the edge of this field. She set a brisk pace, so that anyone who saw them would think they had someplace to be and the right to be where they were. Nobody paid them the slightest attention.

After the field they came to a road. Dicey turned right on it. She wasn't sure of her direction, except that she wanted to go south, away from the river.

So began another morning's march. This part of the journey was often interrupted because at the faintest sound of a motor, the Tillermans ducked into the bushes at the side of the road and hid. Dicey didn't have to tell anybody this.

No green pickup passed them. He would have to search both sides of the river, Dicey thought. If he searched at all.

Their road made a fork with another road, and now they walked on a gravel shoulder. After an hour, they came to a crossroads that had signs. Hurlock was one and a half miles straight ahead. Dicey found herself looking at the houses they passed (whether the buildings were run down or cared for, whether they were small or large, close to the road or set far back) with questions in her mind. Every house was a secret place, a fortress, within which anything might be going on. Every house was perhaps a trap.

They bought a cantaloupe from a boy at a roadside stand. Dicey cut it up with her jackknife. They pulled the seeds out with their fingers. The juices ran down their chins as they took huge bites of the warm fruit. It was mild, sweet and chewy. When they had finished it, they heaved the rinds into an empty field and continued on.

An hour later, they reached the outskirts of Hurlock, a dusty, sprawly little town, with one stoplight at its center. The windows of the stores were crammed with notices of church suppers and house tours. One poster advertised a circus and showed a lion jumping through a hoop. Hawkins Circus, it announced. Admission, $1.50 for adults, $.75 for children. Taped to the bottom was a hand-lettered notice that said that the circus would be in town for two nights only, on the grounds of the elementary school.

Dicey went into the second market, just after the stoplight at the center of town, and bought milk, peanut butter and bread. When she emerged, she saw James studying the circus poster.

"That's nothing to do with us," she said. He followed her down off the porch. Sammy and Maybeth stood up from the curb.

A dusty green pickup drove by them, driven by a square-faced man. The head and shoulders of a large dog were visible sitting beside him. The man and the dog looked straight ahead. The truck headed out of Hurlock, past the stop light, back toward the Choptank.

Dicey's heart jumped. She clutched the bag of food to her chest.

James watched the back of the green truck. "He didn't see us. I don't think he saw us," he said. "What can he do, anyway?"

Dicey couldn't imagine what Mr. Rudyard could do, but she was afraid he would do something. "Let's run," she said. The elementary school might be on the far side of town. They hadn't passed it coming in. "Come on."

"He didn't even turn around," James protested.

"A circus is here now. There'll be people and if he does turn around and try to do something, we can get help. Call the police, or something."

"They wouldn't believe us."

"Stop arguing, James!"

Dicey grabbed Maybeth's hand and began to run. James and Sammy followed.

They ran along uneven sidewalks in front of stores, then houses. Nobody paid any attention to them. They cut past two women who were meandering along, talking. At corners, Dicey looked quickly up and down, for a building that might be an elementary school. It had to be in the town. When she didn't see it, she dashed across. She couldn't go as fast as she wanted because Maybeth's legs were shorter than hers.

At last she saw a modern building that nestled against the ground, down a low sloping hill. Behind the building rose the hoop of a ferris wheel.

The sidewalk they were on went beside a playground, then up to the front door of the school. As the Tillermans, breathing in gasps, were passing the playground, a dusty green pickup swung into the road that circled before the school entrance.

Dicey swerved onto the grass. "James! Go around behind!" She grabbed Sammy's arm and pulled him. He struggled to keep his balance at Dicey's pace. Ahead of her, James and Maybeth ran side by side. Maybeth's legs pumped frantically.

Around the corner of the building, Dicey caught sight of the big tent. She pulled Sammy up even with James and Maybeth. "Into the tent," she gasped. They dodged around the base of the ferris wheel. Dicey heard footsteps behind her now and the familiar snarling of a dog.

She turned her head. Mr. Rudyard was jogging along easily, pulled by the dog, which he held on a short chain. The rest of the chain he carried looped over his shoulder.

At the open space before the tent, Sammy tripped. He stumbled and fell, rolled over and sat up. Dicey stopped. She turned to face their pursuer. That would give Sammy time.

James and Maybeth had run into the tent. Dicey heard noises from within, voices and the yapping of dogs. She backed toward the entrance. Mr. Rudyard slowed his pace to a walk. He took the loops of chain down from his shoulder and began to play them out. The dog strained toward Dicey. She could see the yellow eyes and the saliva dripping from its tongue.

He was going to loose the dog on her.

Dicey put the paper bag up over her chest and throat, ready to jam it down the dog's teeth if he should leap. Dogs went for the jugular. "There are people around here," Dicey panted. Her voice was hoarse. "You can't get away with it."

He didn't seem to hear her. He was intent upon her face and her slow backing away.

Suddenly, Dicey's legs were shoved from behind. Her knees buckled and she fell on the ground, flat on her back. She dropped the bag. Up she sprang to her feet, still facing Mr. Rudyard. He was not the kind of man you could turn your back to.

Three white terriers had charged out from behind her, bowling her over in their excitement. They yapped and yipped, happily. They ran up to the big dog, holding their tails up like little flags. The big dog snarled, growled and dove into their midst. A cacophony of noise burst out of the mass of tumbling dogs.

Claire rushed out from behind Dicey. She laid into the dogs, cracking her whip. The terriers danced away. Claire played her whip around the ears and eyes of the big dog, forcing him backward until he stood at Mr. Rudyard's side.

Dicey turned around then. She saw a ring of people, with Will at the center and James beside him. Two men were dressed as clowns; three more large, muscular men in jeans and workshirts inched forward with clenched fists; a girl in ballet tights stood tensely beside an older man who wore glasses and chewed on a fat cigar.

Claire looked Mr. Rudyard in the eye. In her high heels, she was six inches taller than he was. "Hold your dog," she said.

His hand took the leather collar. Dicey edged toward James.

"Where you going?" Mr. Rudyard's voice demanded. He surveyed the group. "They're my kids, foster kids," he said.

"No, we're not," Dicey said. She turned to Will. "We're not, you know that."

"You in charge?" Mr. Rudyard asked Will. He sounded surprised.

"I am," Will said. He stepped up beside Dicey.

"They gotta come back," Mr. Rudyard said. "I got papers."

"What kind?"

"Legal papers."

"Show me," Will said.

"I've got them back home," Mr. Rudyard said.

Dicey looked at James. She saw Maybeth and Sammy standing in the gloom just within the tent entrance. They could still run, maybe. How did Will know what was true? How could he possibly know they were telling the truth? He seemed to be thinking about what Mr. Rudyard was saying. Nobody knew the Tillermans, except back in Bridgeport, nobody even knew they were alive. Why should anyone care what happened to them?

And how was Dicey going to keep them safe?

"I want them kids back now," Mr. Rudyard said.

"I'd need to see those papers first," Will answered slowly. He took a couple of steps forward. His boots creaked.

Dicey's legs felt watery.

"I said, I'll take them now." Mr. Rudyard's voice was steely and he didn't bother to disguise the threat.

"I don't think so," Will said, still slowly. "Not until I see the papers."

Mr. Rudyard loosened his hand on the dog's collar.

"I wouldn't," Will said, still slowly. "Claire here—she's got one nasty temper—and a good hand with a whip. That so, Claire?" Claire smiled. "And I've been chased by dogs myself often enough not to be overly scared of them. Animal dogs or human dogs."

"Nigger!" Mr. Rudyard hissed the word.

Will didn't move a muscle of his face or body, but the three big men behind him did. Claire, however, was the one who attacked. She moved smoothly, like a snake. She cracked her whip before her, at the dog's feet and chest, at his head. The dog whined and growled and backed away. Mr. Rudyard was forced to move with him.

Claire moved steadily forward. She cracked the whip again, at Mr. Rudyard's feet, then at his knees, then at his hand where he held the dog, then at his shoulders. He was wearing another fancy shirt, red with long white fringe hanging from the shoulders. Claire snapped the whip at one shoulder then the other, back and forth.

He backed steadily away from her. His eyes burned cold at her.

"Get out," she said. She didn't shriek it, she hissed it. "You make me sick."

Mr. Rudyard looked as if he wanted to say something. Instead, he spat into the dust at his feet. Then he turned his back to them and walked slowly away, the dog at his side. Claire lifted the whip and snapped it sharply against his fanny. He leaped forward.

Dicey held herself stiff until she heard the motor of the truck start, and then longer, until she saw the truck pull up the long slope before the school building and turn back to town. Then she let her legs collapse underneath her.

The people drifted away, leaving Claire, Will, the Tillermans and the three terriers, who ran happily in circles.

"Well, Claire," Will said.

"Well, Will," she answered, looking him straight in the eye. Her cheeks were red.

"I always said you've got quite some temper."

"You could use a little of it," she said shortly. "I'm going back to work."

Will turned to the Tillermans. "Why don't we talk this thing over?" He sat down beside Dicey. James, Maybeth and Sammy joined them. Dicey kept trying to speak, but her voice caught in her throat and she couldn't make words come out. The others waited for her to say something first.

"What's in the bag?" Will asked. "Food? Lunch?" Dicey nodded. "Go ahead and eat. If you've got enough, I'd like something too. I seem to have a bad taste in my mouth."

Making the sandwiches relaxed Dicey. It was such an ordinary thing to do. She spread the peanut butter with her jackknife, then wiped the blade clean on her shorts. She made everybody one sandwich and two for James. She opened the milk and set it on the ground.

"We're not foster kids," James finally said. "That's the truth.

He—it's so crazy I wouldn't blame you if you didn't believe it—we took jobs as pickers and—"

"He never paid us!" Dicey realized.

Will chewed contentedly on his sandwich. "Happens I do believe you. That was one mean man."

"Boy, was he," Dicey said. Her voice had returned. "We—thanks, you know?" He waved that away with a hand.

"My idea is you ought to stay with us awhile," Will said. "We're going south to Salisbury for our next shows, then Berlin. After that down to Virginia. Where are you headed for? You ought to tell me. Don't you think?"

"We can work," Dicey said. "We can help out. We could pay you, too."

"Let's start somewhere solid," Will said, smiling. "Like names. I'm Will Hawkins."

Dicey introduced them. She picked up her sandwich and began to eat. Between bites, she told their destination, as briefly as she could, not about Momma and the journey to Bridgeport, nor about leaving Cousin Eunice's house, but about Crisfield and the grandmother there they'd never met and about needing some kind of home. He listened, nodded, asked no questions and made himself another peanut butter sandwich.

"We've got two nights here and then we break. We'll be a week in Salisbury," he said. "What say you stay with us and we run you down to Crisfield one of the days in Salisbury. That okay?"

"That's fine," Dicey said. "That's great. But do you have room for us?"

"It's a bit primitive. We live in trailers—you could go in with Claire."

"Wouldn't she mind?"

"I don't think so. I'll have to ask her, of course. But she has all those dogs in there, I don't see four kids would make such a big difference."

"We can sleep anywhere," Dicey said. "As long as we're together."

"We'll have to think some what to do about him," Will said. "But not now. I've got work to do now. Stick around—hear me? He might come back."

"I know," Dicey said. "We'll stay close."

They stayed near the tent all that afternoon. Sammy hung around Claire until she finally let him help her by holding hoops and moving the little stools the dogs perched on. James went to watch the man with the cigar who operated the ferris wheel. Soon, he too was working busily, passing tools and squirting oil. Dicey and Maybeth cleared away litter from the midway. They ate supper back where the trailers were parked, at a campsite that had only three trailers on it. Each of these had a picture painted on its side of a lion jumping through a flaming hoop and the words Hawkins Circus spelled out in bright letters. "But there aren't any lions," Dicey said to James. He shrugged.

At dinner, Maybeth helped with the serving and clearing. Dicey wanted to help too, but the cook, a tiny black woman with her hair grown out into an Afro, said the two of them were just fine and she didn't think she'd ever had a better assistant. When Will asked them, James told how they met up with Mr. Rudyard. "We were walking down the road," James began, "feeling pretty good." Everybody listened. Dicey sometimes forgot to eat because she was so interested, as if this was a story that had happened to somebody else.

That night they went to the circus with Mattie, the cook, who was married to one of the big men Dicey noticed earlier, a man named Samson whose head was entirely bald even though he wasn't at all old. Dicey insisted on paying for all their rides and games, as if they were real customers. She was through worrying about money. While she had it she didn't need to worry. When she ran out, she would earn some more. They sat in the front row for the show. They clapped for Claire, who looked like the Snow Queen in the fairy tale, white and glittering. They smiled at Will in his black cape with red lining and a tall hat he swept off his head. They gasped when the tightrope walker fell off into a net and cheered when she climbed right back up to try again.

The Tillermans slept in Claire's trailer, James and Maybeth on the second bunk, Sammy among the nestled pile of terriers, Dicey on the floor. When Dicey awoke the next morning, she saw filmy shadows, as if the inside of the trailer was swathed in veils. She awoke to the quiet sounds of seven creatures deep in sleep. For a while, she lay and listened.

James turned restlessly, uneasily, and the sheets rustled around him. Maybeth was still. One of the dogs yipped gently: Dicey raised her head and saw his little legs moving as he lay on his side with his eyes closed. What did dogs dream? Sammy had an arm around another of the dogs. All that Dicey could see of Claire was her hair spread out on the pillow. She snored gently, like the waves on Long Island Sound, soft and regular.

Making no noise, Dicey slipped out to sit on the metal trailer steps. Animals stirred, birds and squirrels, two timid rabbits. Distant motors stirred beyond Dicey's sight. The branches of the tall pines stirred in a rain bearing wind. These pines were not like the thick, cone-shaped trees of New England. On these pines, the needles hung like pompoms in sparse clusters along lank branches. As the trees grew taller, the lower branches fell off, so they grew into giant lollipops. Loblollies, Will called them, and it was a good name for them.

Mr. Rudyard could have caught the Tillermans so easily. Were they just more stupid and helpless than most people? And what about this farm they were going to, their grandmother's farm. When you walked down a road, you could be walking to anything. Anything. What if this grandmother, too . . .

Well then, Dicey thought, they would beg to return to Cousin Eunice, and Dicey would know enough to be grateful, really grateful, for someone who took them in and meant to take care of them. Cousin Eunice wasn't perfect, and she wasn't Momma, but they could work things out with Cousin Eunice.

If she would. Maybe she wouldn't take them back. Maybe, maybe, maybe.

A squirrel up in a tall oak tree set up a terrific chittering. He was furious, frantic. His tail thrashed up and down.

What good did it do, worrying and making plans, and more plans, if the first plans failed. It was like money. If you had it, good. If you didn't, then you had to find a way to earn it. There was nothing to be gained by fretting over maybes.

Dicey took a deep breath, which tasted of dampened sunlight and moist earth. They were living with a circus for a day or so. For a day or so they were safe. Something would happen after, but that was after. You had to keep alert and watchful, she'd learned that. You had to be ready to run. But if you wasted every day worrying about the next . . . And you never knew what was coming, anyway.

After breakfast, Will took Dicey into town. "To get some stuff," he said, "and see someone." The stuff, as it turned out, was clothing for the Tillermans, underpants (three new pairs each, because they came in packets of three), T-shirts, and shorts. Will also got toothbrushes, toothpaste and a comb. They dropped the packages in the windows of Claire's big white station wagon. Then Will insisted on buying Popsicles, which they ate as they walked to visit the somebody, a friend of his who was a reverend. Will explained to the reverend about Mr. Rudyard, and Dicey listened. The reverend said he thought he could speak a word to the sheriff about it. He asked Dicey if she was sure she didn't want to speak to the sheriff herself. "She can't," Will said, and the reverend didn't ask any more questions.

As they walked back to the car, Dicey said, "I used to think that everyone was the same, pretty much like us. They're not though, are they?"

"Not a bit of it," Will answered. A minute later he added, "Everybody's different, and everybody thinks everybody else is the same and they're the only one different." He smiled at Dicey then. "We've done the most we can, just about," he told her.

Back at the circus, Sammy dashed up to tell Dicey that he was going to be in the show with Claire, helping, as long as they stayed with the circus, that Claire thought he would be funny and he thought so too, that Maybeth and Mattie were making him a costume with spangles on it, like Claire's. James was busy with the machinery that ran the carousel. Dicey spent the day drifting around. She had passing, lazy conversations with people. After a conversation, she would walk away slowly and sit somewhere private to think over what she'd heard. She would sit and watch the people moving about, like characters on a TV screen with the sound off.

She was alone all afternoon. The sky got heavier with rain, but no rain fell. It was a gray afternoon, the kind of gray that darkens and deepens the greens of leaves and grasses. She had nothing to do, and she didn't want anything to do. Her thoughts whirled among bits of information and ideas that crowded into her brain, and blew about there, like dry leaves in a storm.

Sammy came to find her late in the afternoon. She was sitting in the grass by the playground, pulling out the blades and looking at them. But she wasn't seeing them, she was seeing the windy dunes at Provincetown and all the days they had lived there.

"Time for supper, Dicey," Sammy said. "What're you doing?"

"Thinking." He hadn't entirely awakened Dicey from her reverie. He stood in front of her, and she saw him and did not see him.

"Thinking what?"

"About Momma."

"We gotta go now." He tugged at her hand. He had already forgotten about Momma, Dicey thought, and probably that was better for him.

"I dream about her," Sammy said, hurrying Dicey back to Claire's station wagon. "A lot."

So he hadn't forgotten: and Dicey knew that, whatever anyone wiser or smarter might say, she didn't want him to forget. "What do you dream?" she asked.

"Nothing special. She's just there, in the dreams." He ran ahead.

That night, the tightrope lady fell off the wire in the same way, and the audience gasped in the same way and applauded with the same enthusiasm when she climbed back up the tall ladder. Dicey realized then that the fall was part of the act. The fall was as flawless as all the rest of the steps. It was a fake. Like the lion on the poster and the glittering costumes that made everybody look beautiful. Like the way everyone laughed at Sammy because they thought he was making mistakes with the dogs, when it was really part of the act. Like the way Maybeth looked like a princess when she circled under the cascading lights of the carousel. Fake.

Dicey looked at James. He shrugged his shoulders at her. He didn't care. But Dicey did, she discovered. It wasn't that she minded, exactly. Not exactly—because she had done too much lying of her own to mind about this. But—they didn't need to lie, did they?

The circus days floated by. They drove through the rain to Salisbury and set up the tent and booths in the rain. Dicey didn't do anything much, she didn't even go to the shows after the second night. James and Maybeth and Sammy were busy and contented.

Contentment was too small a word for what Dicey was feeling. They had food and a warm place to sleep, and Dicey had money in her pocket. They were traveling and had purpose and destination, but no conclusion. Dicey had nothing to worry about. Nothing except what lay ahead, in Crisfield, and she didn't want to think about that anymore. She had thought all she could about that. You couldn't know what lay ahead. How could you know that? How could Dicey expect herself to know what this grandmother would be like? She couldn't; she realized that at last. She would have to wait and see. That part was easy, the waiting and the seeing.

These circus days drifted slowly. It would be something to live in a circus, Dicey thought, always moving around, always heading for somewhere new. If it was Dicey's circus, she would go everywhere. She planned it out to herself, alone in Claire's trailer at night, with the noise from the fairgrounds behind her. First, all around the United States, then up to Canada and down to Mexico. She would make her circus get famous and get jobs in Europe, and maybe even China or Japan. They'd have trailers for land travel and a ship of their own for sea travel. She would have real lions.

Day after lazy day, night after long dreaming night passed Dicey by.

CHAPTER 7

Late one morning, as Dicey stood in a blazing sunlight where the tent had been the night before coiling up the long ropes so that Samson could stack them evenly on the truck and find them when he needed to stake down the sides of the tent that evening in Berlin, James and Maybeth and Sammy approached her.

"Hey," James said.

"I don't need any help," Dicey told him. "Go on and do what you like."

"Are we going to go to Crisfield?" James asked. "We're all ready. We packed our things into a paper bag and your map too. Will says he can take us now, in Claire's car."

"Is it time?" Dicey asked.

"Will says so," James said.

"Let me just finish this, okay?"

More good-byes, Dicey thought to herself, coiling up the last rope into a dark brown hoop, piling loop upon loop. "I am unfond of good-byes," she said to herself. All of their good-byes lay like the coiled ropes on the ground, connected and unconnected, curling silently, finished things.

But the kids were right, and Will was right. It was time.

Dicey took a deep breath. Time to get moving.

She sat beside Will in the front seat. James and the little kids sat behind them. Dicey took out her map. Time to put the circus behind them.

The circus people stood around and waved and made jokes. Dicey looked around at them, gathered together there in the fairground, their hands held high, their friendly wishes for good luck floating around the car still, like cherry blossoms blowing down to the ground. The car pulled out of the fairgrounds. "Good-bye," everybody called. "Good-bye, good-bye."

After a while, Dicey turned to the map. There was nothing to look at on the road. It was just like Route 1. "What route are we on?" she asked Will.

"Thirteen. We follow that to just south of a place called Princess Anne, then get onto Three-thirteen," Will said. "How do you figure to find her?"

"Look up the address in a phone book," Dicey answered. "Then we'll ask directions."

"We've got lots of time," Will assured her. "All I have to do is go back, pick up Claire and the beasts and the trailer and make it to Berlin in time for supper."

"Are you going to take us right there?" Dicey asked.

He didn't turn his head. His profile was smooth lines, slightly curved except where his nose jutted out and his beard jutted out at the end of his chin. His skin was smooth and brown, like silk. He didn't answer, he just nodded.

"But why?" Dicey asked.

"To make sure you're okay," he said.

Dicey looked out the window. City clutter had fallen behind and now there was country clutter, junkyards, a trailer park, billboards advertising dog food and faraway hotels. Beyond these the land stretched away to low, flat country. The fields and woods all had shallow ditches dug around them to drain away water. Most of the land was being used for farms, interspersed with patches of loblollies and other trees.

"Crisfield's a small town," Dicey said to Will. "We'll be okay."

"You don't want me to take you right there, do you?"

Dicey leaned toward him. "It's not that. It's—she doesn't know about us. Not only that we're coming, but she doesn't even know we exist. We didn't know about her until our cousin in Bridgeport told us we had a grandmother. And—I don't know how she'll be. There was this priest in Bridgeport. He had somebody here come to see her and tell her. She wouldn't let him in, or listen. He said she screamed so she couldn't hear what he was saying. So I don't know how she'll act. Momma . . ." Her voice faded away.

"There's a lot you haven't told me, isn't there?" Will asked.

"Yes." Dicey thought. "It gets so complicated."

"I'll tell you what," Will said. "How do you want to do it? I'll go along with you if you'll make me one promise. You keep your promises?"

"Yes."

"If you'll promise me that you'll come to me if you need help. We'll be in Berlin for a week, four shows and then three days off on the beaches. The police can always find me if you call. Will you promise?"

Dicey thought about that. "But what could you do?"

"Who knows? What do friends do for each other? Something. Whatever. Will you promise?"

"Okay," Dicey said. "I promise."

"We'll be coming by again in eight months—but anything can happen in eight months. I can't just dump you kids off. Not and forget about you. I can't do that. But I can let you do it your own way if I know you'll call me if you need to—if it's not working out."

"Why?" Dicey asked. "I mean, why should you bother? You have your own life."

"You're a little bit of my life now. You can't get away, and I can't get rid of you. That's a fact."

Dicey understood. A lot of people had little bits of her life now, and they were tied to her now, or she was tied to them. To some of them, she owed something that she hadn't paid yet, like Windy and Stewart, or Cousin Eunice. You didn't just let people go, that's what Will meant. You always did what you could.

Dicey leaned back into her own corner by the door. Well.

"What I thought was," she said, "we'd go downtown and find out where she lives. Then just go out there." That was almost the truth.

"And you want me to leave you off and drive away," Will said. Dicey had no idea what he was thinking. "Are you scared?" he asked her.

"Some."

"Why?"

"It's a last chance for us," Dicey said.

"I don't know about that," Will said slowly. "You could say all of life is a series of last chances."

"Okay," Dicey said, "but inside of houses—no matter what they look like from outside—even that one"—the car sped past a tall brick house, surrounded by old elm trees and seeming serene and wise, as if it had stood there for so many years that nothing could surprise or hurt it—"you can't tell what's inside. You can't tell what might happen. How do you know who to trust when you meet people? How can I tell about this grandmother? I know I can always run, but when there are four of us . . ."

"Wouldn't it be easier if I stuck with you?" Will asked.

Dicey shook her head. "Well, yes, of course it would. But I have to know by myself, for us."

"Okay," Will said. "Okay. You can have it your way."

As they neared Crisfield, entered the town limits, followed the main street, they all fell silent. Dicey could almost hear the worries that nobody said aloud. The air inside the car grew thick with them.

The road ran straight and broad until it came to the water. They looked around. Docks, most of them vacant now on this summer morning, stretched out into the bay. Sheds lined the land's edge. Piles of small wire boxes were everywhere, and oyster shells had been scattered like a layer of earth. A few people, mostly old men, sat in the sunlight, looking at nothing.

"Well," Dicey said.

"We'll meet again." Will turned to her. "One way or another. Okay?"

"Okay!" Sammy said.

The Tillermans climbed out of the car. They stood at the road's end by the water's edge. Will backed the car, turned it around, looked out the window to give them the thumbs-up signal, and drove away.

Until the station wagon was out of sight, the Tillermans didn't move. Dicey held the grocery bag in one hand, and the other hand she held up in farewell, until she could no longer see the square back of the car.

They were on their own again.

"Okay," Dicey said. She passed the bag to James. "You wait here. I'm going to find a phone book." She didn't wait for anything, not even to study the flat expanse of blue water. She walked back along the docks to the sidewalk and entered a grocery store. There was a poster in its window advertising Will's circus.

The store was filled with darkness, dust and the smell of the food on its shelves. Dicey stood inside the screen door for a minute, while her eyes adjusted to the dim light. The only person in the store was a woman in a stained apron behind a glass-framed counter. Dicey walked up to her. The woman had thick, strong arms and her hands were mottled red. Her face was pale and thick with flesh. Her eyebrows were straight and bushy over little colorless eyes.

"Yeah?" she asked, leaning her elbows on the top of the counter. "What can I get you?" Her words came thick and slow, like molasses—again, something like Momma.

"I'm looking for a phone book," Dicey said. "Do you have one I can look at?"

The woman nodded. She plodded out from behind the meat counter and walked heavily down to the cash register at the front of the store. She pulled out a thin phone book from underneath the counter there. She watched Dicey open it.

There was a Peter Tillerman on a place called Deal Island, and a G. Ridgely Tillerman in Princess Anne. There was no Abigail Tillerman. There was no A. Tillerman, either.

Maybe their grandmother didn't have a phone. Or maybe it was listed under their grandfather's name. Only, there was no Tillerman listed for Crisfield.

Dicey looked at the page and chewed on her lip.

None of the Tillermans listed lived in Crisfield. Was her grandmother still here?

Yes, because that priest had gone to see her. He would have told Father Joseph if she'd moved or died. He knew where she lived.

"Something wrong?" the woman asked.

"I got work to do," the woman continued, to prod Dicey. She leaned down on the counter as if she needed the rest.

"I was looking for the telephone number for Abigail Tillerman," Dicey said.

"Why would you do that?"

"I was going to call her up. To see if she needed some help around the place," Dicey said.

"I've never seen you before," the woman remarked.

"We're new," Dicey said. "We just moved in."

"Ab won't hire you," the woman said. "She's letting the farm go."

"Selling it?" Dicey asked.

"Naw, she'd never sell that place. But she can't work it by herself."

"That's why I thought she might hire me," Dicey said.

The woman shook her head, closed up the phone book and put it away. "Besides, she hasn't had a phone since Bullet died. If you'd asked me I'd of told you. She came down and threw her phone through the telephone company window. You don't want to work for her."

The woman trudged back down the aisle to the meat counter. Dicey stood where she was, listening to the hum of a large refrigerator.

"Where is her farm, anyway?" she called to the back of the store.

"Down to the water, south," the woman answered.

"What road?"

"Landing Neck. It goes off South Main, half a mile inland. Maybe a mile. There's a bend on Landing Neck, and a new little house sits right on it. Next mailbox is Ab's. But it's seven miles. I wouldn't go out there. She's queer."

"Queer?"

"Crazy as a coot, that's my opinion. We leave her alone. You should too."

"Maybe you're right," Dicey said.

"No maybes about it."

Dicey left the store. She returned to her family. Their eyes held the same question.

Dicey sat on the edge of the dock, hanging her feet over the water. James, Maybeth and Sammy sat in a line beside her. You couldn't see the bottom of the water. It was muddy, so you could only see a little way down into it. The waves gurgled underneath them.

More bad news, Dicey thought to herself. But why didn't she feel bad? She looked around at the docks and the dozing men and the water and the shacks. She picked up an oyster shell and dropped it into the water.

The air smelled of salt and fish and motor oil.

"You know what this is like?" Dicey asked James. "It's like Provincetown. Isn't it? It smells like it."

"Yeah. What about our grandmother?"

"She lives seven miles out of town, on Landing Neck Road. She doesn't have a telephone."

"How do we get there?"

"I don't know yet. But I thought . . . James, I want to go out there alone. Just in case. I want you to stay here with the kids. And I'll come back for you when I know."

"Know what?"

"If it's okay for us there."

"I don't like that, Dicey. What if you get in trouble?"

"Better just me than all of us, right? Will said we could call the Berlin police to get him if we need help. So if I don't come back then you can call him. Here's the money, for lunch and anything. Can you keep an eye on Maybeth and Sammy?"

"Yeah, but I don't like it."

"I'm in charge, James. Remember."

"Okay. But . . ."

Dicey gave him the money she had left, nine dollars. She

leaned over to talk to Maybeth and Sammy. "You do what James says. You hear?"

They both nodded.

"That's all right then," Dicey said. She stood up quickly and hurried away, without looking back.

The business section of Crisfield lay next to the water, low buildings with big plate glass windows. The business section crowded as close as it could to the bay and looked out over the docks, as if that was where its real interest lay. Beyond that, residential streets branched out, circling around the town itself.

There seemed to be three kinds of houses. There were lots of churches, even on the one street Dicey followed out of town. These were mostly small stucco or clapboard buildings with short steeples. Then, there were the usual narrow clapboard houses on little handkerchief lawns, two stories high, two rooms wide. The third kind were large wooden houses with broad porches that ran around the buildings; they had odd shapes, round towers, octagonal bays, balconies. These houses had paint that had faded and peeled. Often, their screens were ripped or doors hung askew. But they spoke clearly of what they had once been: once they had been homes for large, rich families; once the spiraled pillars that held up the veranda roofs had gleamed with white paint; once the tall windows of the ground floors had opened into rooms crammed with plush furniture and oriental rugs, and the large trees in the yards had swarmed with climbing children. These were the kind of houses that might have treasures in the attic, or ghosts in the cellar. These were the kinds of houses that could burst with life. Now they rotted quietly, neglected, sad, but filled with mysterious memories.

Dicey walked on, walking fast. She turned at the second stop sign and found herself on Landing Neck Road, in farm country, where broad fields burgeoned with corn or barbed wire contained cows and horses, where chickens and ducks wandered around the yards. The farmhouses sat next to the road, quiet and clean, secretive.

How would she know if their grandmother's house was safe for them? What questions did you ask a person to find out if you could like one another? If she could be trusted?

Dicey's sneakers made no noise on the roadway. No cars overtook her. There was no sound at all, except the occasional distant barking of a dog or lowing of a cow. The silence wrapped around her like a quilt, a silence made up of trees growing and corn ripening, of the bright sky glowing and the distant water following its tides. This was not an empty silence.

Six miles outside of town, Dicey came to the expected bend in the road. A low, one-story white house looked out from a stand of pines. Behind it were stables. Two pastures, where long-legged horses grazed, came next.

Half a mile down the road, Dicey saw the mailbox, dented, rusted, its post awry; *llerma* was all that remained of sloppily painted black letters. The little door hung open, like a dog's tongue. Two or three old leaves lay inside, and a plastic glass with a straw sticking out of its cover.

Across the road, where the farm itself lay, overgrown fields stretched back to meet a thick woods of pine trees, oaks and tall, topheavy loblollies. The fields had small trees scattered over them, pine and maple saplings, and the grass was thick and tangled, as tall as Dicey's waist.

The driveway ran straight between the fields. It too was overgrown. You could barely make out the ruts where car wheels would fit.

The sun had risen high into the sky. Dicey turned into the driveway, walking slowly now, even reluctantly. She did not look ahead, but at the ground before her feet. Abandoned, that was the word this farm said to her.

She couldn't even see the house until she had passed under the pines, walking now on a thick carpet of needles that seemed never to have been disturbed. The air under the pines was thick and shady.

The house sat behind a small orchard, and beyond it, a barn was slowly falling down. The house was faded white clapboard, two stories high, and had a screened porch all along the front that ran around the sides. The roof, gray slate, slanted down in four directions from a central peak. Two chimneys stuck up through the roof.

The house was silent, vacant, neglected. Long weedy grass grew up, as high as the porch floor. Honeysuckle spread over the screens of the porch, and its long fingers reached for the trees in the yard. Most of the trees were short, heavily leaved. Some had tiny apples growing on them. They had the rough bark of fruit trees.

One larger tree grew right up in front of the house, hiding the front door, shading the lawn. This tree looked like an umbrella, held overhead by four trunks that spread out from their common source. Its broad leaves made a green canopy against the sunlight. It wouldn't be a good climbing tree, Dicey thought, walking up to it and past it, but you could make a platform tree house to rest on the four trunks and build steps out of pieces of wood to go up one trunk. Then, you would have a house like a boat, almost floating on air, and the long, leafy branches stretching above like sails.

Dicey pushed her way through the long grasses to the steps leading to the porch. The grass tickled her knees. Grasshoppers leaped aside to let her pass.

The steps were rotting away. The screen door hung from

broken hinges. The sun couldn't penetrate the honeysuckle leaves, so the motionless air on the porch was as dark as twilight.

Dicey knocked on the door. It was a wooden door, once painted white. A rusted nail stuck out from its center, over Dicey's head.

Nobody answered. She knocked again and listened. She heard faint noises, like some night creature scurrying. But the noises did not come toward the door.

Somebody was in there, of that Dicey was sure. She knocked again, three loud raps. No voice called out. Dicey turned the knob and pushed against the door. It was locked.

She went back across the porch and down the steps. She walked around to the side of the house.

The side looked just like the front, except that it had no steps or door. There were two windows on the second floor and four on the first, which were barely visible through honeysuckle. The honeysuckle here had not grown as fast as that on the front of the house. The porch, she noticed, continued around the back. The whole house was surrounded by a broad porch.

All the second story windows had their shades down. Nobody could be seen inside, nor any light. Dicey went on, around to the back.

She saw the woman the moment the woman saw her. The woman sat on the bottom of some steps facing out, over more fields (only these had crops growing in them) and the distant dull green of marsh grass. She wore a shapeless blouse over a long, shapeless skirt. Her feet were bare.

Her dark eyes looked at Dicey angrily. Her skin was tanned. Her hair had been hacked short, so its iron gray curls burst helter-skelter all over her narrow head.

Dicey stood where she was. She swallowed, twice. Her throat was suddenly dry.

"Mrs. Tillerman?" she finally asked. Her voice squeaked.

"You're trespassing," the woman said. She had a thin, stiff voice, not like Momma's at all.

"I thought I heard—when I knocked—I didn't know if—" Dicey stepped forward. "The fact is, I wonder if you would hire me to work for you." She stood right in front of the woman now. Her grandmother.

Her grandmother's eyes seemed big for her face as she stared at Dicey. But maybe that was just because her face was small, the skin stretched tight over its bones. Her eyes, now that Dicey was closer, were not brown but dark hazel, browns and greens without any yellow to give them sparkle. Fine lines sprayed out from around her eyes.

These were the eyes of the girl in Cousin Eunice's photograph album. The rest of her was all different, but the eyes were the same.

"The fact is you're trespassing," her grandmother said. "Who told you to come here?"

"Nobody. I heard you were alone—so I thought I'd try."

"I don't know you, do I?"

Dicey shook her head. "We're new here."

"Why aren't you in school?"

"It's summer."

"Not for long."

Her grandmother stood up. She walked up the steps and through the screen door, without looking back. The back door stood open, and she went straight into a kitchen.

Dicey followed her.

Her grandmother opened a glass-fronted cupboard and pulled down a can of spaghetti. She took a can opener out of a drawer and opened the can. A saucepan waited on the stove. She opened another drawer, took out a big spoon and scooped the stiff red and yellow contents of the can into the saucepan. With a match, she lit a fire under the burner. She dropped the match into an ashtray and turned to take a bowl out from the cupboard.

Dicey might just as well not have been there.

Her grandmother waited by the stove, stirring in the pan.

"I didn't say come in," she said.

"You never said if you want me to work," Dicey answered.

Hazel eyes studied Dicey. Dicey studied the barefooted woman. Her feet were caked with earthy dirt.

"How do I know you're not going to rob me?" her grandmother said.

How could she know? Dicey thought. The people in the houses were in just as much danger as the people outside the houses. "I'm not," Dicey said. "It doesn't look like you have much to steal anyway."

"You have family?"

"Yes," Dicey said.

"Where do you live?"

"In town. I can work hard. Your barn needs painting, and the screens and the steps, and the lawn. I could take off the honeysuckle."

"I'm not too old to do that."

"I can pick and weed."

"So can I. So can anybody. You better get down a bowl, since you've invited yourself for lunch."

Dicey did as she was told.

They sat down at a long table, big enough for ten people. It was made of wood and had been scrubbed to a pale, smooth finish. Dicey sat across from her grandmother. She spooned the canned spaghetti into her mouth. After the first bite, she ate quickly, trying to fill up her stomach without tasting anything.

"You like my spaghetti?" her grandmother asked.

"No," Dicey said. "But I'm hungry. Do you like it?"

"It's easy to fix. You know what I sometimes think?" Her grandmother looked straight at her, her mouth chewing. "I sometimes think people might be good to eat. Cows and chickens eat corn and grass and turn it into good meat. People eat cows and chickens. In people, it might turn into something even better. Do you ever think that?"

Dicey shook her head.

"Especially babies," her grandmother said. She swallowed thoughtfully. "Or children. Do you have brothers and sisters?"

"Yes."

"Who told you I was alone?"

"A lady in the grocery store."

"Millie. She's the butcher. Can you imagine that? A lady butcher."

"Why not?" Dicey asked.

"I guess you might say so. Millie is one, and that's a fact. Facts are facts. What did she say about me?"

"Nothing much."

"Did she tell you I was crazy?" Her grandmother wasn't looking at her.

Dicey didn't answer.

"Maybe I am. You know? When you die all the gases build up in your body for weeks, like yeast in dough. And you swell and swell. Then, things start exploding. That's where the stink comes from. After that, you're fresh as a daisy and the worms and maggots have you. What do you think?"

Dicey put her spoon down. She was through eating.

Her grandmother's mouth twisted. "What do you think about death? Don't be smart with me, girl."

Dicey was puzzled.

"Or don't you think?"

"I saw a tombstone. *Home is the hunter, home from the hill and the sailor home from the sea:* that was what it said. As if"—Dicey tried to explain her thoughts—"that was the quiet place at the end of things."

"It's not quiet," her grandmother said. "Not for the worms."

"I wouldn't care about that if I was dead," Dicey said.

"Maybe I am crazy," her grandmother said. "You know?"

Dicey was beginning to think she might be.

"Maybe not. Do you feel sorry for me?"

"Why should I?" Dicey asked.

"Old, alone, crazy—the farm falling down around me. My husband dead these four years and more."

"I'm sorry," Dicey said.

"I'm not. I'm happy since he died."

"Why?" Dicey asked.

"He kept wanting his shoes polished. He never did polish them himself. First thing I did, I bought myself a washing machine. Do you play the piano?"

"No."

"Too bad," the woman said. "I've got one. Haven't played it myself, I never had time. My children did. They all died too, and that was a relief."

Dicey stood up. She didn't even feel bad. She didn't feel anything, except maybe glad she had come out here by herself.

"You're going," her grandmother said.

Dicey nodded.

"You didn't offer to help with the dishes. No, don't bother. I know what children are like."

"Okay," Dicey said. It didn't matter. She'd go back and get her family, and they'd call Will.

"Don't you want to know if I want you to work for me?" her

grandmother said. She was still sitting in her chair, but she had turned around to watch Dicey leave. "Well, I don't. I couldn't pay you anyway."

Dicey nodded and turned her back to the room.

The woman's voice spoke from behind her: "I know who you are. You hear me? I know who you are, and you can't stay here."

CHAPTER 8

Slowly, Dicey turned. She looked all around the room before she answered. She didn't know what she should say. Why should she say anything? She'd been told to go away.

Sunlight poured into the kitchen through the door and windows. (So, her grandmother had kept the honeysuckle down on this side of the house.) It was a long bright plain room, the kitchen. Everything in it looked old and scrubbed, like the top of the table. Wooden counters, wooden cupboards, wooden chairs, wooden floor; only the refrigerator, sink and stove were porcelain. A single light hung down over the table. It had a pale yellow glass hood over it.

Her grandmother sat without moving, staring at Dicey.

"Then who am I?" Dicey asked.

"I knew the minute you knocked on the door. That's why I came outside. A polite person would have gone away." Her grandmother waited to see what Dicey would say.

Dicey didn't say anything.

"Oh, I know who you are; you're the oldest one, I can't remember your name. There's a foolish letter here, somewhere. It has all your names in it."

This wasn't good enough. "You don't know who I am," Dicey said.

"You're Liza's daughter. Some ungodly name she gave you, her and that Francis. I liked him, I did."

"Who's the letter from?" Dicey asked.

"Connecticut," her grandmother answered. "Where are the rest of you? One's retarded, the letter said. Maudlin, simpering fool. Can't blame her though. Her mother simpered, simpered and looked in mirrors, all her life. She's dead now. My sister Cilla—she's dead too. Is she retarded?"

"No," Dicey said. "Not that it concerns you."

"You're right. It doesn't concern me one whit. Did you ditch them somewhere?"

Dicey could follow her grandmother's thoughts easily now, now that she knew what the woman was talking about.

"They're waiting for me in town. We've got a place to go."

"Back to that one?"

"Maybe," Dicey said. She was angry now. This—grandmother. Dicey wouldn't give two pins to satisfy her curiosity. If this grandmother had known all along.

"A polite person wouldn't have pretended not to know me," Dicey said.

"Never said I had good manners. Never had any manners to say anything about." Her grandmother seemed pleased.

"My name's Dicey," Dicey said.

"That's right," her grandmother said. "I remember now. It was in the letter. I'm not crazy."

"I know," Dicey said. "I'm going now."

"Suit yourself. Where you all sleeping?"

"We're moving on. We don't need a place to stay."

"Don't you lie to me, girl. If you didn't need a place to sleep you wouldn't have traipsed out here this morning. You wouldn't have come around back to find me. You wouldn't have asked Millie—did you tell her who you were?"

"No," Dicey said. Her anger flamed up again. "No, why should I? We can't stay here, you said so. So there's no point in hanging around. I've got my family to get back to."

"I said sleep. There's no reason not to sleep here, is there?"

"Yes," Dicey said. "I think there is." Why should James and Maybeth and Sammy have to be disappointed.

"I'm family too," her grandmother said. She took the bowls from the table and walked over to the sink. "And I can hear what you're thinking, girl."

Dicey hoped she couldn't.

"So you'll sleep here. All of you. Because you have no place else to go."

"We do too," Dicey said.

"Then why did you come here? Can you answer me that?"

Dicey's lips were tight. Her grandmother's lips were tight. They glared at one another across the kitchen. Neither one of them faltered.

Then her grandmother's lips twitched and spilled out laughter. She cut the laughter off quickly, dried her hands on her skirt and said to Dicey: "Two of a kind we are. Poor Liza. Two of a kind."

It was the laughter that undid Dicey. How could you be angry at someone who was laughing. "Okay," she said. "But—"

"But what? Be nice to them? Nicer than I was to you?"

"Yeah," Dicey said.

"I'm not promising anything," her grandmother said. "Let's get going."

She led the way out to the back. Dicey turned toward the dilapidated barn, where the truck must be. But her grandmother headed straight off to the fields. Her feet must have leather soles, Dicey thought as they crossed through the vegetable gardens on a dirt path.

"I don't have a car," her grandmother said over her shoulder. She moved like a young woman, long, strong strides, her arms hanging easy at her sides. "Not since he died. I always hated them. I never learned to drive."

The path crossed between two long, well-kept fields (mostly tomatoes and corn, but other crops too, squashes and beans) and entered the marsh grass. Dicey followed her grandmother. However bad the rest of the farm, the barn and the house looked, her grandmother had worked on these fields. A steady wind blew, causing the grasses to bow and whisper among themselves.

Ahead, Dicey saw open water. The bay lay at the farm's edge.

The path led up to a dock built of weathered gray wood. At the end of it was tied a long open boat. It had an outboard motor and four seats. It was at least fifteen feet long and painted a bright red, inside and out. The boat looked taken care of too.

Dicey jumped in and sat on the center bench. Her grandmother untied the painter, pulled the boat around until its stern was near the dock and jumped in herself, dropping the line into Dicey's lap.

"Coil that," she said, and turned to the motor.

She pulled once on the starter, the motor hummed, and she headed the boat out into the bay.

They couldn't have talked over the noise of the motor without screaming at one another, so Dicey didn't try. She sat with her back to her grandmother and watched the prow of the little boat cut through the quiet water. She felt the fine spray the boat threw back, inhaled the salty air, and looked out to a horizon made only of sky and water.

They followed the coastline, which was mostly marshes. Dicey saw few houses. Then they came into Crisfield harbor, which was hidden behind a point of land. Shacks, bleached white by sunlight, leaned against one another. Piles of oyster shells made small pointed hills beside the shacks and behind them and in front of them.

Dicey turned around and leaned toward her grandmother. "They're on the farthest dock over," she called.

Her grandmother nodded and yelled something back. Dicey couldn't hear her. They didn't speak again.

They chugged into the dock, tying up at the far end. Dicey scrambled out and hoisted herself up onto the boards. Her grandmother climbed up the wooden ladder.

The dock was empty. There was no shade on it at this time of day, so not even the old men remained.

At first, as her eyes searched for her family, Dicey didn't worry about the dock being empty. Then she did.

Where were they? She'd told them to stay there. Where were they? What had happened? Her eyes searched up the street to see three small figures.

Nobody moved on the sidewalks.

They were gone.

Dicey felt cold, despite the heat of sunlight reflected off water. It was not the gentle breeze that cooled her. It was fear that froze.

Not thinking, not caring whether her grandmother wanted to help at all, Dicey turned to her. "I don't know," she said. "You go up that side. Look in stores and restaurants. I'll go up this side."

Dicey didn't wait to see if her grandmother started off. She ran, her heart pounding painfully.

As she reached the end of the dock, she heard her name called. She swiveled around and saw Sammy running toward her from the shade behind one of the shacks across the harbor.

Dicey's grandmother was right behind her. "It's okay," Dicey said. "That's Sammy."

She was so relieved to see him that she ran across the crushed oyster shells to meet him and caught at his hand. He let her hold it briefly, then pulled away. "I told James," he said proudly.

They walked back together.

"Told him what?" Dicey asked. "I didn't know where you were. I'll tell you, I was scared."

Sammy ignored that. "Told him you'd be back."

"Where is he? Where's Maybeth?"

"They walked out to the farm. James said we should have all gone together anyway. He said you were wrong about that. We waited and waited. Then he said it was time to go. And I said no. And he said he'd thought it all over, and there was no good reason for you to go alone. He said I had to do what he said. And I said no. He said you said to. And I said you said to stay here and do what he said, not go off because he said to. So he took Maybeth."

By this time, they were back to where their grandmother waited. She listened, watching Sammy, watching Dicey.

"Sometimes I get so mad at James," Dicey said to Sammy. "But I'm glad you stayed—how would I have known where they were? He thinks he's so smart"—she turned to her grandmother—"and he is smart—but I told them to stay here. I told him." She scuffed her foot in the shells. How was she going to catch up with James and Maybeth? What should she do now?

"Are you the grandmother?" Sammy asked.

Their grandmother nodded.

"What am I s'posed to call you?" Sammy asked.

Dicey hadn't even thought of this. Neither, apparently, had their grandmother. She didn't answer Sammy. She pretended she hadn't heard him. "Let's get back," she said.

"What about James and Maybeth?" Dicey asked. "I can't just leave them."

"You already did," her grandmother said. "They'll make their own way. It's what James wanted, isn't it? He'll find you."

She headed back down the dock to the boat.

Dicey followed. When they got back, if James and Maybeth weren't there, she'd walk back toward town. James wouldn't get lost. He'd listened to the directions, so he'd be on the right road. He didn't forget things.

Sammy jumped down into the boat and climbed to the most forward seat. Dicey sat in the middle again, facing her brother. Behind her, she heard her grandmother untie the line and lower herself carefully from the ladder to the boat. "Hold on to the dock, girl," she said to Dicey.

Dicey stood up and reached out for a firm grip on the wood. As soon as the motor started she pushed the boat away from the dock. Sammy leaned to her. "Where is it?"

Dicey pointed south. "A ways off," she said.

"What's it like?" he asked.

"Run down."

"Are we going to stay?"

Dicey shook her head firmly. "Just tonight."

"That's okay, Dicey," Sammy said.

They were silent the rest of the way back to their grandmother's dock. The two children climbed out there. Dicey took the line and tied it around one post. Then she sat on the edge of the dock and held the boat steady with her feet while her grandmother lifted the motor up and rocked it into a resting position inside the boat. The metal propeller blades dripped water into the bay, like sullen raindrops.

Their grandmother led the way back to the fields and farm. Sammy walked behind her on the narrow path. Dicey came last, looking around over the waving fields of grasses, savoring the salty, muddy air.

When they got past the fields, Dicey broke into a run. She sprinted around to the front of the house, hoping to see James's skinny figure sitting on the steps, with Maybeth quiet beside him. They weren't there. Sammy had followed her. Their grandmother had not.

"I'm going to find them," Dicey said. "Do you want to come or stay?"

"Stay," he said.

"She's not friendly," Dicey warned him.

"Neither am I," he said. "Besides, I'll stay out here. James'll be all right, Dicey."

"I hope so," she said. She loped down the long driveway without looking back.

As Dicey emerged from the pine woods, she saw the two figures standing far off, across the road by the mailbox. The brown grocery bag was on the ground between them. Dicey raised her hand in greeting and slowed to a walk.

James picked up the bag. Dicey stopped. Let them come to her. She had a few things to say to James.

His narrow face looked worried and relieved and ashamed and glad, all at once. He was too smart not to know all the things that could have happened. "Sammy's alone downtown," James said, before he said anything else. "I'll go back and get him. If everything's okay?"

Dicey forgave him, without a word, without another thought. "Everything's not okay, but Sammy's here. She doesn't have a car, she uses a boat. That wasn't very smart, James."

"I thought it was, when I started out."

"Well, don't worry. She doesn't want us to stay, but we can sleep here tonight."

"Then what?"

"I dunno. Let me think about it. Why didn't you come in? Were you there long?"

"We couldn't see any house," Maybeth said. "We didn't know what it would be like."

They walked back together. As they came up to the house, Sammy called to them from up among the leaves of the big tree. "I was right, James, wasn't I? We went in a boat."

"How'd you get up there?" James asked.

Sammy descended, with a shivering of branches. He slid down the curve of one trunk and stopped himself just at the bottom, where all four trunks came together. His legs were scratched.

The Tillermans stood together at the base of the tree. The house was before them, overgrown with honeysuckle, dark-windowed, looking abandoned. Off to the right, Dicey saw the lopsided barn. It had once been red, but the paint had weathered, faded and peeled, until it looked pink as a bad sunburn. The tin roof was rusted in large patches.

"Anyway," Dicey said, "this is where Momma lived."

"It's beautiful," Maybeth said.

"It's a wreck," Dicey answered. "The fields out front—and look at that barn. It's gone to ruin. She hasn't taken care of it."

"But it's big," James said. "Big enough for all of us. Is it near the water?"

"There's a marsh first," Dicey said, "a long, empty marsh. Then the bay. There's a path, but the water's at least a quarter of a mile away. Not like Provincetown. Anyway, who cares? We won't be staying."

"True enough," her grandmother said from the side of the house. "But you'll be here for supper so there's work to be done. I see you found them." She stared at James. "James," she said.

He tried to smile but her face discouraged him.

Her eyes flickered over Maybeth. "And Maybeth." She looked away quickly, as if nothing about Maybeth could interest her. The little girl moved closer to Dicey.

"I've got crab pots set down by the dock," their grandmother said. "Who'll fetch the crabs?"

"I will," Dicey said.

"Me too," Sammy said.

"James and Sammy will," their grandmother announced. "It's after four. I eat early, and so will you. I put a basket by the back steps."

The two boys ran off.

"You two come with me. I'll show you where to sleep."

She strode around to the back of the house. Dicey picked up the grocery bag and followed her. Maybeth clung to Dicey's hand.

They saw James and Sammy heading off down the path to the water. James carried a bushel basket by its two metal handles.

Their grandmother led them through the kitchen and into a dim hallway. "That's my room," she said, pointing at a closed door, "and my bathroom," pointing to the closed door next to it. They turned left down the hall and ascended a narrow staircase.

Upstairs, they saw a long, U-shaped hallway with five closed doors around it. A window at one end looked out over the front yard, through the leaves of the big tree. Their grandmother stood on the top step and let them go past her. "That's the bathroom at the far end. Sheets are in one of the bureaus. I can't recollect which."

Dicey went to look out the window. "What kind of tree is that?"

"Paper mulberry," her grandmother answered.

Dicey noticed from above what could not be seen from below. There were strong twisted wires running around the tree. "Why is it wired?" she asked.

"Because paper mulberries are fragile," her grandmother answered. "It's the way they spread out at the top, it's the way they grow. If you didn't brace it, the weight of the leaves and the growing branches would pull the tree apart. Like families." She went abruptly downstairs.

Dicey and Maybeth stood in the dim hallway. "Cripes," Dicey whispered. "It's like a ghost house."

The air was warm and old, as if the same air had been up here for hundreds of years. The closed doors looked like so many secrets.

Maybeth's eyes were round and frightened.

"Look at it this way, Maybeth, it's only for one night. And besides, this was Momma's house, when she was little. Isn't that right?"

That didn't make Maybeth feel any better, but it made Dicey feel better. She forced up the old window to let in fresh air. She braced it with a piece of wood lying on the sill. Their grandmother wasn't going to take any trouble for them, but Dicey would show her.

Dicey opened the nearest door and stepped boldly into the room. This was a bedroom with a plain iron bedstead overlaid with a thin white quilt. The pillow had no cover on it. The room held a dresser, a desk and chair and a wardrobe, all of plain wood. Dicey went to a window and snapped up the shade. This room faced the big tree. She snapped up a shade on the other wall and found a window that looked out to the barn. Between them, she and Maybeth got the four windows up, and braced them with pieces of wood. Fresh air filtered around the room and light came in.

The smaller room across the hall was almost identical, except the quilt was faded blue instead of white. On the front of the wardrobe somebody had painted a picture of Indians coming out of the woods, carrying bows and arrows, wearing warpaint and bright headdresses. It was a kid's painting with blobs of green paint for leaves and the sun a yellow circle with lines coming out. Dicey liked it. They opened this room too and returned to the hall. With two doors open and the sunlight and the clean air, the upstairs seemed more friendly. Dicey walked down the wooden floor to the opposite end.

First she opened the door opposite the hall window. This was a bathroom. It had a toilet with a wooden seat and a wooden box above the seat from which hung a long, wooden-handled chain. The bathtub was raised off the floor by four stubby legs that ended at four feet with claws on them. The sink stood on a tall pedestal. Above it was a shelf where you could put soap and toothpaste.

Dicey and Maybeth both went to the bathroom. They pulled on the chain to flush. When you flushed, you could hear the water gurgling down the pipes from the overhead box.

Then Dicey opened the window and looked out.

From this window you looked over the roof of the porch, over the backyard, over the planted fields, over the long stretch of marshes—to the water. The band of water lay blue and sparkling, out and away. A boat, tiny at this distance, moved up the bay, maybe heading back to Crisfield with its day's catch.

Dicey hurried into the room on the right. Here there were some small differences. There was the same iron bedstead, and the quilt was multicolored, faded but still cheerful with reds and blues and greens and yellows. The bureau and wardrobe had been painted white. The desk and chair were plain wood. A picture hung on the wall, a childish picture of a little boat sailing on blue water. Fish swam in the water, and crabs ran about the sandy bottom. Gulls wheeled in the air and rode, with folded wings, on the waves. Dicey snapped up the side shades and held the windows while Maybeth put the braces under them. These windows looked to the barn. But the other two windows, as she had hoped, gave out over the marsh and to the bay.

The last bedroom had a ruffled quilt and pictures of ladies in old-fashioned dresses on the walls, pictures cut out of magazines and pasted on a white background. The childish painter had put a picture on the wardrobe here too, of a castle and town and a queen, wearing an impossibly tall crown, walking in the garden.

Dicey hurried to open the windows, one over the backyard, and two to the piney woods that closed around the house.

She turned to Maybeth. "Well. This isn't bad, is it?"

Maybeth smiled quietly.

"It's only for a night. Let's each take our own room. Which one do you think was Momma's?"

"This one," Maybeth said.

"Then you'll sleep in this one. Okay?"

Maybeth nodded happily. They found the sheets in one of the front bedrooms and made up the beds together, folding hospital corners, plumping up the pillows. For herself, Dicey chose the other back bedroom, because it looked to the water.

There was nothing in any of the rooms to show that they had ever been lived in by anyone. But they must have been lived in by the three children, Momma and her brothers. None of their personalities had been left in the rooms, except for the two paintings on the wardrobe doors, the lady cutouts, and the little picture of the boat.

None of the children had wanted to stay here. They had all left home, one way or another. Except the one who had died, maybe. You couldn't be sure. He might have wanted to come back.

They went downstairs. Maybeth followed Dicey like a shadow. The kitchen was empty. Their grandmother was out in one field, wearing a broad straw hat, picking tomatoes into another of the bushel baskets.

"We can do that," Dicey said, coming up behind her.

"And so can I," she answered without looking up. "They're coming in too fast. They always do this time of year. Gotta start canning again. Can she pick beans?" She nodded toward Maybeth, without looking at her.

"Can you?" Dicey asked Maybeth. Maybeth didn't answer. "Sure, I guess so," Dicey said.

"Over there then," their grandmother said, jabbing with her head to another side of the field. "Bring 'em back here to me. Take the biggest. You"—this to Dicey—"go into the barn. There's a bin of potatoes up against the far wall. Get as many as we need. Keep your shoes on. I don't know what-all's on that floor."

Hedges of honeysuckle—twisting, strangling vines—had grown over what must once have been a split rail fence between the house and barn. The big barn door was pulled half open. Bits had rotted out of the wood at the base of the door, as if someone had kicked at it in unappeasable anger.

Dicey stood for a minute, letting her eyes grow accustomed to the darkness. A large shape loomed in the center, and lofts lay in high darkness along both long walls. She brushed cobwebs away, waiting until she could see enough to go on.

Empty stalls lined one side. The smell of dry hay was in the musty air. The center shape grew smaller as she found her twilight vision. The thing seemed to hover in the air above the packed dirt floor.

Something rustled in the lofts. Many things rustled there. Where the boards had fallen away at the sides of the barn, honeysuckle grew in. Dicey stepped into the dim darkness.

The first thing to do was to define that shape. Whatever creatures were living in the barn were probably more frightened of her than she would ever be of them, even if they panicked and touched her.

Dicey approached the shape. It was something long, slightly curved, and resting in a kind of saw-horse cradle. It was about shoulder height to her, with a flat back.

She approached it with her hands behind her back.

Dicey almost didn't dare name it, even when she knew

what it was, even after she had raised herself onto tiptoe to peer inside and seen there a long mast, tied down around the sides, surrounded by tangled ropes and projecting over the bow.

A sailboat.

It was small, only fourteen or fifteen feet. It had an open cockpit, without any seats in it. It had a slot in the center of the cockpit, beside which rested a long centerboard.

Dicey reached her hand into the cockpit. Cobwebs. She touched the long arm of the tiller, resting against the stern. Where were the sails? Would it still float? Whose boat was it?

She rushed to the back of the barn. There, three large bins had been built. She opened one, and little creatures scurried at the bottom. The lid of the second revealed a mound of potatoes. Dicey put her hand in. The potatoes had begun to sprout. Each eye of the potato she held had knobbly, pale growth on it. But when she squeezed it with her hand, it felt firm enough. Dicey took out a dozen potatoes. Of these, she selected the seven largest (four kids and one woman, and James could eat two or three), cleaned off the sprouts with her fingers and tossed the remaining five back into the bin. Her arms were full of potatoes as she hurried back out of the barn.

Their grandmother was coming in from the field, carrying the basket. Maybeth trailed behind her.

"There's a boat in the barn," Dicey cried.

"I know that. It's been there for years. Don't put those potatoes in the basket. Take 'em to the sink. Don't you know potatoes have to be scrubbed?"

Dicey hurried ahead. She was so full of questions about the boat, she didn't care how her grandmother felt about them. She dumped the potatoes in the sink and turned on the water.

Her grandmother put the basket on the table. She took a

china platter from the cupboard. "Can she take the ends off beans?" she asked Dicey, referring to Maybeth.

"Sure," Dicey said.

Maybeth stood across the table from her grandmother and snapped the ends off the green beans. She worked carefully, wasting little of the vegetable, making a neat pile of ends on the table before her. It was as if she knew how suspiciously the woman was watching her.

"Whose boat is it?" Dicey asked.

"Mine," the woman answered.

"I know that, but whose?" Dicey said.

"My boy built it," their grandmother said. "He built it and he sailed it."

"Where are the sails?" Dicey asked. She knew she shouldn't be asking. "Will it still float?"

"He kept them on the boat, up forward under the bow," their grandmother said. "They're still there, far as I know. I don't know if it's seaworthy. It doesn't concern you."

Her voice was cold and final. Dicey, standing with her back to the room, the cool water running over her hands as she scrubbed the dirt from potatoes, heard that coldness and that finality. Her back stiffened. "Oh doesn't it," she said to herself. Here was the place, a farm with plenty of room and plenty of work for them to do, and the bay just beyond the marshes, and a sailboat in the barn. She wasn't about to let this grandmother keep them from it.

"I can hear what you're thinking," her grandmother said.

Dicey swiveled her head around to meet those dark hazel eyes, the sullen, angry eyes she had seen in the photograph Aunt Cilla kept. Could her grandmother know what she was thinking? And so what if she could?

"Maybe you can," Dicey said, not dropping her glance. She'd think of a way. She's been thinking up ways to get them in and out of trouble all summer long. As if she had been practicing for this occasion, warming up for this last struggle. Her grandmother didn't know Dicey. Her grandmother didn't know the kind of thinking and planning Dicey could do.

A fleeting expression that might have been unaccustomed mirth, or might have been a twinge of pain, went across her grandmother's face. For a second, the face came alive around the eyes. Then it was all gone.

Dicey turned back to the sink. She didn't want to be distracted. She had thinking to do.

They had crabs for dinner. It had taken the boys a while to learn how to shake the crabs out of the pots into the basket. The first pot they'd just opened, and the crabs had fled sideways in a turbulence of muddy water. Sammy had tried to grab a couple and been nipped for his pains.

"You should have seen them," he cried, telling the story. His cheeks were pink and his eyes shone. He was too pleased to let his grandmother's stony silence quiet him down. "They looked at the door and looked at us and then"—he thrust his arms straight out and waggled his finger—"gone! I didn't know things could go sideways so fast. Boy are they smart."

James spoke to their grandmother: "We closed the doors and set the traps back where they were. Is that right?"

"Right enough. What did you use for bait?"

"I didn't think," James said. "What should we use?"

"Fish. You have to catch the fish."

"Good-o," Sammy said. "Can I go down after dinner? Do you have any line?"

"No point to it," their grandmother said. She was checking the boiling water in a huge pot on the stove. The potatoes were in the oven, the beans in a covered pan, the table set with forks and a platter of sliced tomatoes and glasses of water.

"So what?" Dicey answered quickly. "I'll go with you, Sammy. We like fishing," she said defiantly to her grandmother.

The woman didn't answer, but instead lifted up the basket and poured the teeming mass of crabs into the water. She slammed the lid down on top of them. You could hear them scrambling around inside the metal pot, scrabbling up to escape the steam. Their grandmother stood with one hand holding the lid down, staring at the children.

Maybeth ran out of the room. Dicey felt like following her—she could imagine how those crabs felt, and she had had that feeling herself at times—but she wasn't going to back down before those eyes. So she stood, and pretty soon there was silence in the pan. She knew they were all dead then.

They ate the crabs from a big plate in the middle of the table. They were served individual plates with potato and beans on them. There was no butter for the potatoes, but there was salt.

The Tillermans had never eaten crabs before. They learned how to rip off the legs first, then lift back the top shell. Then you broke the crab in half, like a turnover, and picked out the meat from between sections of cartilage. Each crab had two larger chunks of meat in it, and an awful lot of stringy little pieces.

It was hard work getting full on the scraps of crabmeat. It took a time to get even a mouthful ready, once you'd taken out the two chunks. But it was a good dinner for talking at, if you wanted to talk. Everybody's hands were busy, and almost nobody's mouth was full.

Their grandmother seemed to want to talk, or seemed to want them to talk. She asked questions.

"Where's your mother?" she asked. She sent the question out to the middle of the table, as if she was asking the platter of crabs.

The children looked to Dicey.

"Momma's in a mental hospital in Massachusetts," Dicey said. "She doesn't recognize anybody. She doesn't do anything. They don't think she's ever going to get well."

"Who don't think?" her grandmother asked.

"The doctors," Dicey said.

"They don't know," Sammy said. "She might. Isn't that right, Dicey?"

Dicey nodded.

"So you know better than the doctors," his grandmother said to Sammy.

Sammy's jaw went out and he didn't answer.

"And you ran away from this silly chit in Bridgeport. You ran away from someone who was willing to take you in and take care of you. Why'd you do that?"

They looked to Dicey again.

"It wasn't right for us. Especially not for Sammy and Maybeth."

"Because Maybeth's retarded?"

The cruel question lay before them.

Dicey looked at Maybeth. Maybe she hadn't understood. But she had. Well, that was good because if she hadn't understood that would mean maybe she really was retarded. Maybeth's eyes filled with tears.

"She's not," Dicey said.

"What is it? Can't she speak for herself? Can't you?" Her grandmother glared at Maybeth. Maybeth sat staring at her lap. "Can't you?"

"Yes," Maybeth said softly.

Dicey fumed. She felt like throwing her plate at her grandmother.

"You keep out of this, girl," her grandmother said. "You, Dicey."

Maybeth looked up. Tears rolled out of her eyes, but she stayed at the table. "I don't think I am," she said. "I don't know just what it means, but if it's such a bad thing to be—why do you want to know?"

Their grandmother nodded once, briskly. She asked another question. "You do a lot of running away. Where's your father?"

"He's been gone for years," James said. James's voice was tight. "Six years. Longer. Since before Sammy."

"I remember him," their grandmother said.

"The police in Bridgeport tried to find him and couldn't," Dicey said.

"He was the kind of man who always sailed close to the wind," their grandmother said.

"What does that mean?" James asked. "What do you mean? Did you know him?"

"He used to come around here, whenever he was in the area, when his ship was in Baltimore," their grandmother said.

"What was he like?" James asked. "Only Dicey remembers him—I don't. What did he look like?"

"Slim, dark-haired. He was a quick, nervous, darting kind of man. Not steady, but lively. The kind who might cheat at cards if luck wasn't running his way. And he'd bet too much too, that would be his way. She should have come back here when he ran out on her."

"She didn't want to," Sammy said.

"How do you know?" their grandmother said. Then, before he could answer, she said, "What does it matter anyway?"

"Momma matters to me," Sammy said, his chin stubborn.

"She went off and left you," their grandmother said.

"She wanted to come back," Sammy said.

"How do you know that," their grandmother said. She didn't ask it, she said it.

"Because she loved me. Didn't she, Dicey?"

"Yes, she did. She loved all of us," Dicey said.

"Humph," their grandmother said, reaching for another crab.

The Tillermans had won that battle. Dicey knew it. She knew it as close to her bones as she knew that Momma did always love them. Dicey tried not to grin. It didn't do to grin when there was still the whole war to win.

The children washed the dishes while their grandmother watched them and told them where to put things away. When everything was finished, and Maybeth had scrubbed the wooden tabletop with mild soap and a stiff brush, Dicey announced that they would like to go down to the dock, to fish for crab bait and to swim.

"Can Sammy swim?" their grandmother asked.

"We can all swim. We were raised near the ocean," Dicey said.

"Suit yourselves," their grandmother said.

At the dock, they took turns fishing and swimming. They stripped down to their underwear and dove into the quiet water. The bay had no waves and no undertows. It was as calm as a swimming pool. You could swim miles in this quiet water.

Dicey swam out, away from land, in a slow crawl. Her mind was working fast. There was a way, if only she could see it. Sammy and James took the few bony fish they had caught and baited the crab traps. Maybeth jumped off the dock into the water, then climbed back onto the dock to jump again. When she hit the water, waves surged up around her and the water she sprayed out turned golden in the setting sun.

Evening fell across the water, toward them. The sky turned twilight purple. A molten pink band flowed across the horizon, where the sun had been.

The children dashed back to the house, trying to outrun the

mosquitoes that swarmed up from the marshlands. Their grandmother sat in the same chair in the kitchen. They wished her good night, and she nodded her head but said nothing to them.

Dicey showed James and Sammy the rooms they could have. She unpacked the toothbrushes and toothpaste and comb into the bathroom. She put each one's underwear and clean clothes into his own room.

They gathered in Sammy's room, the one with the picture of Indians on the wardrobe, and sat on his bed. "What're we going to do tomorrow?" James asked Dicey.

"I dunno yet, James," she said. "She doesn't want us to stay. She said so."

"Well, neither do I," Sammy announced. He was in bed but sitting up. His hair was damp. "Even if it is fun."

"What about you, James?" Dicey asked. "People say she's crazy."

"Crazy like a fox," James said. He dismissed that question, without hesitation. "It would be okay here. It's sure big enough."

"Maybeth?"

Maybeth didn't answer. She looked down at her hands and across at Sammy. "You want to," she said to Dicey. "Don't you?"

"*That* we'll talk about in the morning," Dicey said. "How about a song, how about Peggy-O."

They sang softly, in case it might bother their grandmother, sitting alone downstairs at the empty kitchen table.

CHAPTER 9

Dicey woke herself up early the next morning, before the first gray signals of dawn, when the air outside lay black over fields, marshes and the glistening water she could just see from her window. For a time, she sat by the window and thought out the plan she had gone to sleep considering.

It all depended on what their grandmother was really like, inside herself where she was who she really was. Not outside. Dicey knew about the difference between outside and inside.

You could assume that everybody wasn't just the way they seemed. The question was, in what way was their grandmother not what she seemed. Did she really want the Tillermans to go away?

Dicey was sure that she didn't want the Tillermans to stay. But Dicey wasn't sure she wanted them to go away. Their grandmother was a Tillerman too, which made everything contradictory. If she wanted the Tillermans to go, then she wanted herself to go—in a contradictory way this was true. Dicey's job was to see through the contradictions and find out where they made sense together.

Why had their grandmother gone outside to the back when Dicey knocked? She could have stayed inside and not been found. Why had she asked all those questions at dinner? Cousin Eunice's letter would have explained about Momma. And what did she mean when she said to Dicey that she knew what Dicey was thinking? Unless it was what she herself was thinking.

Besides, their grandmother had taken the boat to town to find James and Maybeth and Sammy. That was something she wouldn't have done if she'd really wanted them to go away.

Maybe their grandmother didn't know just what she wanted. Or maybe she didn't really want anything, except to be left alone. Four kids, they were an awful bother. Cousin Eunice said so, again and again. And an expense.

Dicey could manage the bother and they'd figure out a way to cover the expenses. She was sure they could do that. They could leave their grandmother pretty much alone. It was the place Dicey wanted, the big house, the acres of farmland, the barn, the water and the boat. It didn't have anything to do with the woman.

The sky lightened. Over in the east, behind the house, the last star would be fading as the sun surged up. Above the marshes, a pale quarter moon waited in a light blue sky, with mares' tails clouds brushing against it. Time to get moving.

Dicey woke James and Sammy and Maybeth. They all met in Dicey's room over the kitchen, so that any noise they made wouldn't waken their grandmother. Dicey explained her plan:

"We have to get started on something useful before she wakes up. That way, she'll keep us here today. Or if she tells us to go, we can say we will, as soon as we finish the job."

"But—" James said.

"But what?"

"What if she means it?"

"She does mean it," Dicey said. "That's the trouble, isn't it? I figure, if we get her to put it off she'll get used to us and forget that she wants us to go away. We pretend we're not even thinking about staying here. But every day we do something that needs to be done so it's worth her while to keep us."

"She could call the police," James said.

"She doesn't have a phone. But if she does then we will go, I promise. If she really means it. Can't you tell? She doesn't want us to stay, but she doesn't want us to go, either."

"I don't think she likes me," Sammy said.

"That doesn't matter, Sammy. It's not her I'm thinking about. It's us."

"She's mean," Sammy said. "She's not like Momma at all."

"That doesn't matter," Dicey repeated. "Besides, she's not really mean, not like Mr. Rudyard. Is she?"

"How do you know?" Sammy demanded.

"Remember when James took that money?" Maybeth asked him. "Remember how Dicey's face got all red and hot and she told us we had to go, and she told James he had to obey. Remember? That was like our grandmother. Mr. Rudyard was cold."

Sammy subsided. Dicey took advantage of the moment to announce their project for the day: honeysuckle.

They dressed quietly, used the bathroom quickly and tiptoed down the stairs into the dark hall. The kitchen lay in shadows.

They began with the honeysuckle growing up around the front porch. It had formed a massed wall that wove around itself and clung to itself with tiny tendrils. The tendrils looped and looped around anything that would hold them up.

The Tillermans had no plan. They just reached into the plants and pulled. The honeysuckle vines emerged in long stringers, unwoven from the mass.

By the time the sun had risen and only the shadow of the paper mulberry tree kept an early morning coolness over the yard, they had a large mound of honeysuckle branches at the foot of the lawn. Dicey didn't know how they were going to get rid of it. In some patches, she could see the screen on the porch, but they hadn't gotten a quarter of the growth yet.

Maybe it would burn, but she doubted that; it was lush summer growth, tensile vines and green leaves.

"I'm hungry," James said. "This is going to take all day."

"I hope so," Dicey grunted, jerking back on a fat vine. "Anyway, let's see what there is to eat."

They trooped around the side of the house and across the porch. At the kitchen door, they stopped. Their grandmother was up. She was at the stove, making pancakes on a griddle so large it covered two burners on the stove. She turned around when she heard them coming in.

"Wash your hands. I see that you don't make your beds."

"I'll do that," Dicey offered.

"No, you'll each do your own," their grandmother said. She turned her back on them. She was wearing another shapeless blouse over another long, shapeless skirt. Her feet were bare and clean. She had set the table.

When the children sat down, two platters of pancakes waited for them. There was no syrup or butter, but quart jars of strawberry jam were set out. Their grandmother didn't say a word. She just served herself two pancakes and spread jam over them.

The pancakes looked normal, but they tasted curiously flat. The jam, however, was delicious and the children ate with good appetites.

Finally their grandmother spoke. "I like that honeysuckle." She looked at Dicey.

Dicey's heart sank.

"That honeysuckle's been there a long time. It's the kind of tenacious plant I have to respect," their grandmother said.

"Honeysuckle is parasitic," James announced. "It can be trained and kept back, but when allowed to proliferate without controls, it chokes out other growth. It's begun to climb over the small trees out front."

His grandmother studied him. James ignored her and slathered jam on his seventh pancake.

"Where'd you learn a word like proliferate?" she asked him. His mouth was full so he couldn't answer. "The honeysuckle will take you all day, at least," their grandmother said.

Nobody answered. Dicey tried to look unconcerned with what her grandmother would say next.

"You can't just leave those vines piled up. They have to go out on the marsh," was what she said.

Dicey chewed hard, to keep herself from smiling. This was just a skirmish, not even a real battle. She looked up to meet her grandmother's eyes and swallowed hastily.

After the dishes were washed and the beds made, the children went back outside. The temperature had gone up and they stripped down to just their shorts. This meant that as they pulled the vines or piled them up they got mightily scratched, all over their arms and chests and legs, but it was cooler.

They sang as they worked, sometimes in harmony, sometimes all singing melody.

Dicey showed Maybeth how to wrap a long vine around her arm and pull back on it, with all her weight, taking the strain in her shoulder. Sammy used both his hands. Half the time he jerked so hard that he fell over backward.

The overgrowth gradually gave way to a thin layer of the oldest, thickest vines. These had to be worked out of the screen netting, because if you pulled hard on them, the screen ripped out.

As they stood, patiently unravelling coiled tendrils, Dicey began to sing the song about the wide river and the small boat. She liked the way the melody held its notes and lingered over its phrases. This was a song they all sang together, but each of them sang it his own way, holding the notes and words he liked best.

The voice came from behind them: "Where'd you hear that song?"

They turned, wiping back sweat-dampened hair. Their grandmother had a cantaloupe cut up into thick slices. She had arranged the slices on a metal cookie sheet.

"Momma sang it," James answered her. "Is that for us?"

"I don't have lemons for lemonade," she said. "Don't have milk, eggs, butter—it's melons or nothing."

"Melons are fine, thanks," Dicey said quickly.

"Did you sing to our momma?" Maybeth asked.

"I don't recall," their grandmother said. She walked away from them, back around the house.

The children ignored her and fell upon the melons. As they sat and ate, Dicey looked at what they had accomplished. "We can finish the front and clear away around the trees. Then we'll eat lunch, okay?"

They agreed.

"And after that we'll move that pile of vines down to the marsh. I guess it might be safe to burn them there. And after that—how does a long swim sound?"

A long swim sounded fine.

When they went into the kitchen for lunch, their grandmother was not there. They couldn't call out to her, because they didn't know what name they were supposed to use. It sounded funny to say "Mrs. Tillerman," and it sounded just as funny to say "Grandmother." Dicey knocked on the closed door of the downstairs bedroom, but there was no answer.

Because Dicey didn't feel right about going into the refrigerator or the pantry, they ate tomatoes and cucumbers from the garden. As soon as they were finished, they jumped up to carry huge armloads of tangled vines out to the marsh. Dicey decided that the pile should be a good way into the marsh, but next to the path so they didn't have to tramp through the wet grasses. It made quite a hill, big enough to slide down if it had been hay.

Dicey didn't want to light a fire without checking with their grandmother. She didn't feel sure of what would happen when the leaves caught. So they left the vines and ran down to the water, single-file along the narrow path.

They tossed their shorts and sneakers on the end of the dock and leaped into the water. It was cool and cleansing. It washed the sweat off their bodies. They stretched muscles that were taut and tired from pulling and carrying. Dicey swam underwater, looking at the muddy bottom. The water soaked through her hair and cooled her head. She rolled and floated under water, as if she were a piece of seaweed.

After a while, she climbed out and sat on the dock. It was then she realized that the boat was gone. What was their grandmother up to?

The children lay on the dock, letting the hot sun dry them.

"We ought to trim back that honeysuckle by the barn," James said. He was lying on his back in the puddle made by the water dripping off of him. His eyes were closed tight against the bright sunlight. "She said she likes honeysuckle, didn't she? If we trimmed it, it would make a kind of hedge, and it wouldn't harm anything."

"We don't have anything to cut it with," Dicey said.

"You could ask."

"No, I can't. Don't you see? We can't ask, we just have to do things. We can't give her a chance to say no, because if we do then that's what she'll say. And we've got to get back to work. There are still the side porches. I've got to look in the barn for tools because the next job is to fix the screens on the porches." Dicey sprang up and put on her shorts. She hurried her family along.

James and Maybeth and Sammy pulled at the honeysuckle on the side near the barn, while Dicey explored the cobwebby barn inside. She forced the doors wide apart, so she would have enough light to see. She found a small workshop opposite the empty stalls. The tools looked clean and well-oiled, saws, hammers, pliers, axes, mallets, planes, drills, screwdrivers, a level. No cobwebs had been spun around the workbench, so she figured her grandmother kept it in order. Nearby, garden tools hung on the wall and lay on a long shelf, clippers in four different sizes, shovels, hoes, stiff metal rakes and long-fingered leaf rakes. A tiny cupboard with three dozen small drawers held nails and screws of every size.

Dicey did not let herself linger by the boat. The boat was the prize. Unless they could stay, she wouldn't think about fixing it up or sailing it. She hoisted herself up onto the side and checked under the bow to be sure the sails in a canvas bag were there. Then she picked out the two largest pairs of clippers and ran outside.

James and Maybeth began the slow task of trimming back the honeysuckle hedge. Sammy didn't want to. He enjoyed tearing down the vines, grabbing at them with both hands and holding hard, as his hands slipped down, ripping off the leaves. Then, when his grip held, he would lean back on the vine and swing his weight against it. He grunted as he pulled. He braced his sturdy little legs against the ground. Sammy was hard to stop once he'd made up his mind to do a job.

Dicey saw their grandmother walking through the vegetable fields carrying two large grocery bags. She called to James to go take them, or at least one, and continued pulling. The next time she looked, her grandmother was walking along, still carrying two bags, and James was nowhere in sight. Dicey let go of the vine in exasperation and ran to help.

She met her grandmother at the end of the lawn. She didn't

even ask, she just took a bag. "Front must be clear, by the size of that pile out in the marsh," the woman said.

Their grandmother came around the side to inspect the work. Sammy decided he should show off. He leaned back and grunted, to show how hard he was working. He jerked his arms. His whole body pulled back against the vine.

The vine snapped free of the roof.

Sammy tumbled backward onto his fanny. His feet flew up in the air. The vine came after him and wrapped around him, as if it had a life of its own, as if it was a boa constrictor attacking its dinner.

Their grandmother laughed, a thin, rusty sound. Sammy struggled to free his head and arms from the snaky leaves.

"What's so funny?" he demanded.

"You are," his grandmother said.

And Sammy laughed too.

James came up from the marsh, carrying two more bags of groceries.

"Can she use clippers?" the woman asked Dicey when she saw Maybeth. "Is it safe for her?"

This irritated Dicey. "Ask her yourself. She's not deaf. If you can't see for yourself."

"Well, you'd better rub the tools down carefully with the tack cloth before you put them away. Or they'll rust. I have groceries to put away."

They swam again before dinner. They came to the table with wet heads and shining faces. Their grandmother had fried pieces of chicken in a thin cornbread batter. She served mashed potatoes with butter in pools on the top, and green beans. She even had dessert, a store cake with stiff, over-sweet chocolate frosting, and a bowl of apples and bananas. By each child's place stood a tall glass of milk.

"You did a good day's work," their grandmother said. "I suppose you'll be moving on tomorrow."

Dicey took a deep breath. "There's still honeysuckle to be pulled."

"Don't know why you carried it so far into the marsh," their grandmother said. "You could leave it up to the near end, and it'll rot away by spring. James, you look like you could use another piece of chicken."

It was not what she said, but what she didn't say, that Dicey heard. The Tillermans had won another day.

After supper, the children washed up the dishes and their grandmother went out to the fields. As Maybeth soaped and rinsed, and the boys dried, and Dicey put away the glasses, dishes, knives, forks, pots and pans, they sang. Maybeth scrubbed down the wooden table and Dicey polished it dry. Maybeth sang the song about the man who sang for his dead friends. The others had forgotten the words, so she taught them again. Their voices blended in the yellow kitchen light, and filled the empty house as the world outside darkened into twilight. "'When I come to the cross of that silent sea, who will si-ing for me?'"

They let the echoes of melody fade away before they moved again.

"I'll give you this much," their grandmother said from the doorway. "Your momma taught you how to sing." She stood with darkness behind her. Dicey couldn't read her expression. "Where'd you hear that song?"

"A friend taught it to us. Someone we met when we were going to Aunt Cilla's house," Dicey said.

"Stewart," Maybeth said.

"Stewart who?" their grandmother asked.

"I don't know," Dicey said. "It was at a college."

"What were you doing at a college?" their grandmother asked.

James told her about their time in New Haven. He started with the rain and the hunger. He even told about stealing the money. He finished it at the beach in Fairfield.

Their grandmother had stood silent in the doorway while he told it. "You're not helpless infants," she remarked. Then she added quickly, "If you want to wash anything, tonight's the time. I'm canning tomorrow and the next week."

Dicey washed out their dirty underwear in the sink. She stumbled through the dark outside to the far side of the house, the side they hadn't yet pulled honeysuckle from, to find the clothesline. Mosquitoes bit at her, but she lingered outside anyway, listening to the wind in the pines and the frogs croaking across the marsh. Overhead, between the branches of the trees, stars shone. Clouds drifted across the moon's partial face. When she returned to the kitchen, it was dark and empty. She ran up the stairs two at a time to join her family.

That was how the first day went.

On the second day they pulled down the rest of the honeysuckle on both sides of the house and gathered all the piles together near the edge of the marsh. In the afternoon, James and Dicey started patching up the holes in the porch screens, where the screens had pulled out of the wood or just ripped.

Their grandmother spent the whole day in the kitchen, canning batches of tomatoes and carrying them out to cool on the back porch. Sammy and Maybeth emptied the crab pots for supper, and they ate at the trestle table on the porch. Some crabs were left over. Even James couldn't fit any more in. So Maybeth picked out the meat and put it in a bowl in the refrigerator, for lunch the next day.

"I guess you'll be moving on tomorrow," their grandmother said again.

"There's still screens to be patched," Dicey said.

"Did you bait the traps?" the woman asked Sammy and Maybeth. They had.

That was how the second day went.

On the third day they finished the screens and James set to work mending the front steps, with Maybeth to give him an extra hand. Sammy and Dicey mopped and waxed the floors inside. They even went into the dark dining room (which had a big table and eight chairs, and a fireplace at one end) and the living room. Dicey snapped up the shades and looked around there.

This room too had a fireplace, and a sofa in front of it, and a huge wooden desk and walls full of books. Dicey called James in to see it. A few of the books he'd read. Some he'd heard of. The rest he stood and looked at. "You could read for years," he said.

"Who wants to?" Sammy asked him. "Hurry up, so I can go swimming."

At dinner, James asked their grandmother about the books.

"My husband was a reading man," she said. "For all the good it did him."

"What do you mean?" James asked.

"He got all of his answers out of books," their grandmother said. "Books don't change, and he liked that. They made him feel right."

"What's the matter with that?" James wanted to know. "You can study books and think about what's in them. People put down what happened before you were even born, and you can understand and not make the same mistakes. Like history."

"The past is gone," their grandmother said.

"But it shouldn't be forgotten," James said. "Should it?"

"Sometimes," their grandmother said. "Sometimes it's better. My husband used his books to build a wall to keep things out. Oh I know." She cut off James's answer. "I know it doesn't have to be that way. But that's the way it was."

"Books let things in," James said.

His grandmother studied him. "I guess they could. For some. They didn't, not for him. But he knew a lot about history and ideas and the way things should be." James was listening carefully, but she changed the subject. "Will you be moving on tomorrow?"

"When the front hinges are set in," Dicey said. "Your mailbox needs bracing, and there's some patching to be done on the barn. You do have lumber in there, don't you?"

"It's going to rain," their grandmother said. "There's storms brewing."

Dicey's heart fell.

That night, Dicey was awakened by thunder roaring about the house. Lightning snaked down out of a black sky. She started counting at the end of the thunder, and barely got to two when the lightning flashed again.

Maybeth entered her room. "Dicey?"

"Climb in."

"It's right over our heads," Maybeth said.

It certainly seemed to be. Thunder growled just outside the window, trying to get in. Lightning flashed down and cracked like a whip. Dicey reached for Maybeth's hand and they tiptoed down the hallway and down the stairs.

In the kitchen, Dicey turned on the light. Maybeth stood by the door, pale. "Come on. Sit down," Dicey urged her. "I didn't know you were afraid of thunderstorms. Don't worry. Lightning goes for the highest thing, so it'll hit a tree or one of the chimneys. Not us." She reached out and pulled at Maybeth's right hand.

The little girl winced and turned paler. She pulled back and rubbed at her arm, up by the elbow. The arm hung down by her side, as if it were a broken wing.

"Maybeth?" Dicey asked. "What's wrong with your arm?"

"It hurts. It hurts when I close my hand into a fist or try to hold something. Sometimes it just hurts when I don't do anything. It woke me up. I don't know what's wrong, Dicey."

"Maybe it'll go away by itself," Dicey said. She poured Maybeth a glass of milk and got one for herself. They sat and drank quietly. Maybeth held the glass awkwardly in her left hand.

The sky outside exploded with rain. It pounded on the tin roof of the porch. After a while the two girls went quietly upstairs again.

There was a bar of light under their grandmother's bedroom door. Dicey wondered if she was afraid of storms. Momma wasn't.

The morning of the fourth day dawned low and dark. The thunderstorm had passed, but the rain poured steadily down. It drummed on the roof, it splattered on the ground, it rattled softly among the trees. Dicey stood by the window, looking west. A low gray mist covered the marshes and you couldn't see the bay.

They couldn't work outside in the rain. But surely their grandmother wouldn't ask them to leave on a day like this. But then why shouldn't she? What did she care? Dicey stood, watching rain fall in sheets. The barn. They could clean out the barn.

She woke her brothers and sister. They dressed quietly. Quietly, they went to the bathroom and washed the sleep from their eyes and brushed their teeth. Quietly, they went down the stairs and into the kitchen.

Their grandmother, already dressed in shirt and skirt, stood by the sink. She was running water into a canning pot. Glass jars stood on the draining board. A bushel basket of tomatoes was on the kitchen table. The woman's hair was damp and curled wildly. Her feet were caked with mud.

Caught, the children could only wait.

"You can help me," the woman said. Her eyes were bright, but her face sagged with fatigue. "I need the ripe tomatoes picked, and the squashes and cukes that are along the ground. Drainage is so bad they'll rot if we don't get them in."

The children took off their sneakers and shirts and left them by the porch door. Dicey and James carried a towering pile of bushel baskets. They stepped out into the rain.

The drops of water hammered down on them, like a shower on at full force. They bent their heads and ran for the field. The long grass was wet and cold against their legs. They were soaked before they reached the field. Dicey told James and Maybeth to tackle the tomatoes. She showed Sammy where the cucumbers were and went back to the squashes herself.

Mud oozed up through her toes as her feet sank into the earth. She worked as fast as she could, around the mounds where zucchini and yellow squashes spread out. The squashes were hidden under leaves larger than her hand. Dicey knelt down into the chilly mud and picked them out. She tossed them into the basket beside her. The rain beat down on her bare back. Her wet shorts chafed against her waist and thighs. They might as well have taken off all their clothes, she thought.

In spite of her discomfort, she worked fast. Once she looked over to see how James and Maybeth were doing. When she checked on Sammy she saw that he had taken off his shorts and underpants and was standing stark naked over the cucumber plants. Sometimes, she thought, he has more sense than any of us.

Dicey carried the two baskets she and Sammy filled back to the porch, without going inside. She ran to help finish the tomatoes. Sammy's fanny gleamed white in his tan body as he stooped over to pick beside Maybeth. Maybeth was using only her left hand. She held her right arm stiff by her side.

James and Dicey carried the full baskets back. Maybeth ran ahead inside. Sammy didn't want to go in. He ran about in the long grass of the lawn. He turned cartwheels and the rain droned down around him.

When Dicey came up with the last basket, she saw him rolling about in the long grass, like a dog. His face was bright, entirely happy. She looked past him and saw their grandmother standing to hold the porch door open for James, who struggled up the steps with a basket of tomatoes in his arms. The woman was watching Sammy with a smile in her eyes. Their grandmother seemed to have a smile as sudden and complete as laughter.

Dicey called Sammy in. Maybeth had dressed and sat quietly at the table, nursing her arm. Dicey ran the boys upstairs to dry off and change clothes.

The table was set for breakfast when they came down. The huge pot steamed and rattled as the glass jars boiled, to be sterile for the day's canning. Their grandmother served them bowls of hot oatmeal with brown sugar and milk to put on it.

Dicey sat beside Maybeth. "It still hurts?" she asked. Maybeth just nodded. She held the spoon in her left hand and ate sloppily. Dicey realized that she shouldn't have let Maybeth come out picking with them. She didn't know what could be wrong. What was it like when your arm was broken? How could Maybeth have broken her arm?

Maybeth reached across the cereal bowl for the pitcher of milk. She tried to pour it over her cereal, but it splashed onto the table.

Their grandmother stormed up from the table and threw a dishcloth across at Maybeth. "Can't you even feed yourself? Mop it up."

Maybeth mopped at the milk and knocked at her bowl. Dicey caught it before it spilled.

"What's the matter with her?" their grandmother demanded. Maybeth's face was white, and she stared at her cereal. Dicey mopped up the spilled milk. She touched Maybeth softly on the left shoulder, to let her know she wasn't angry.

"Answer me," their grandmother said. "Or is this the way she usually is, and it's all been an act until now."

"Something's wrong with her arm," Dicey said.

"What something?" The woman sat down and began eating again.

"I dunno," Dicey said. "It hurts."

Their grandmother turned her attention to Maybeth. "How long has it hurt?"

"Since yesterday morning," Maybeth said.

"Why didn't you say?" Dicey asked, exasperated.

Maybeth shrugged. Dicey subsided, because she knew why Maybeth hadn't said anything.

"What does it feel like?" their grandmother asked.

"It hurts. It feels burny and achy. When I close my hand and try to hold something, it's like a fire going up around my elbow." Maybeth swallowed. "It's getting worse, not better."

Their grandmother stormed up from the table and out of the room. The Tillermans looked at one another, surprised. "Maybe she doesn't like people being sick," Dicey said.

But the woman returned with a jar of ointment and a broad roll of gauze bandaging. She rubbed the ointment into Maybeth's elbow and down her forearm. Then she made a tight bracelet around Maybeth's wrist, ripping off the gauze with her teeth and tying it into a knot. She made another such bandage above the little girl's elbow.

"Probably a tendon," she announced. "Does that help?"

Maybeth nodded. "It sounds like you've pulled a tendon in your arm. Pulling down that honeysuckle—it doesn't surprise me. You'll have to take it easy with that arm for weeks. The bandages will ease the strain on the muscle."

"Thank you," Maybeth said.

"You should have spoken up sooner," her grandmother answered. "No need to bear pain unless you have to."

Maybeth nodded. "I was afraid it wouldn't ever feel better," she said.

"Tendons can be pretty bad," their grandmother answered. "What are your plans for the day?" she asked Dicey. There was a challenge in her words.

"Clean out the barn," Dicey said.

"Not without sunlight. It's dark as the tomb in there," the woman answered. She waited, her eyes snapping.

"We'll wash windows," Dicey said.

"In the rain?"

"It's not raining inside."

Her grandmother nodded. "I could use some help in the kitchen."

Dicey washed off the tomatoes. James cut them up and Maybeth ladled them awkwardly into jars with her left hand. Sammy got down some old towels and ripped them into cloths. Their grandmother put the tops on the jars and set them into the canning pot.

"You know those old houses in town," James said. "Who owned them?"

"Rich people. There was a time when Crisfield was a boom town," their grandmother said. "People made fortunes in oysters and crabs and built big houses."

"What happened?" James asked.

"The usual," his grandmother said. "There was a lot of

money and a lot of crime—gambling and drinking and people killing one another one way or another. So the town tried to clean itself up. They passed a law against whiskey and that had the usual result."

"Bootlegging? Moonshining?" James asked. She nodded.

"And the oysters had a few bad seasons. So there were no more big fortunes to be made here, legally or illegally. So people left. The trains stopped running. When I was a girl, this was quite a town. Not like it is now."

"Did you know any bootleggers?" James asked. "On the water, with boats, there must have been a lot of it around here."

"I suppose I did," their grandmother said. "But, they'd been doing it for so long—"

"Prohibition didn't last that long," James said.

"Around here it did. It started in 1875—and that was before my time, long before, in case you think of asking. There were families that had been bootlegging for two or three generations."

"Why did it start so early?" James asked. His eyes began to gleam and Dicey knew that he would pick information from the woman's brain as long as she would answer his questions. Dicey filled a bucket with water and ammonia and took Sammy upstairs with her to wash windows. They soaped the glass down with sponges and dried it with the pieces of towels. By midafternoon, Sammy's restlessness had grown too large for the house to contain him. Dicey had worked slowly, dragging out the chore, but Sammy didn't see any sense in this.

At two o'clock, by the clock that ticked on the mantel in the living room, he was ready to quit. Dicey told him he couldn't, he had to be useful.

Sammy thought for a minute, then ran down the hallway to the kitchen. Dicey had polished dry all the windows before she wondered where he was.

He'd been gone an hour. He wasn't in the kitchen. He wasn't upstairs. Dicey ran out to the barn, but he wasn't in the gloom there, either.

She came inside again. Only her grandmother was in the kitchen, sitting with a cup of tea at the table, while two canning pots rattled on the stove. A huge bowl of cut squashes stood ready to be canned next. "Did you see Sammy?" Dicey asked.

"He ran through a while back, more than an hour. The other two are in the living room." Dicey heard the faint notes of the piano.

"I'm going down to the dock to look for him," Dicey said. "He's been gone too long."

"Didn't he say where he was going?" her grandmother asked. Dicey shook her head. "That boy needs some controlling, doesn't he? Your cousin said that."

"She didn't approve of us," Dicey said. "She—she wanted Sammy to be like James, only James isn't like what she thought, either. She just liked him because people praised her about him. And Maybeth—she wanted her to be a doll, a dressed-up doll to take places. Sammy wasn't easy enough for her, that's why she said that."

"What about you?" her grandmother asked.

"I dunno," Dicey said. "I never thought about it. I was busy."

"Busy sneaking out to earn money and never saying a thing about it to her."

Dicey bit back her anger. "She thinks we're not grateful enough, doesn't she?"

"Something like that. She says it's her duty, though, to take care of you. I've never seen such a foolish letter. She wrote me another one when her mother died."

"You didn't answer it."

"I couldn't answer such silliness. I'll have to write her now."

Dicey stared at her grandmother. She wasn't going to ask any questions. Her grandmother looked tired. "You were awake during the storm," Dicey said.

"So were you and Maybeth. Were you scared?"

Dicey shook her head. "Maybeth's arm hurt and it woke her up. Were you scared?"

"There's nothing to be frightened of in a thunderstorm. I was thinking. With four children in the house, the only time you can feel alone is at night."

Sammy burst into the kitchen. His hair was plastered down over his forehead. His shirt and shorts were sodden. He dripped onto the floor.

"Where have you been!" Dicey demanded. Before he could answer, she ran to get towels.

When she returned, her grandmother was in the middle of a lecture. "—running off without telling anyone where you're going. Your sister was worried."

"You weren't, were you?" Sammy said. His grandmother shook her head. "Then why are you yelling at me about it?"

His grandmother stared at him. Sammy's jaw stuck out and he stared right back at her.

Dicey handed him a towel. "Don't be rude, Sammy," she said.

"But it's the truth," he protested. She dried his hair for him, and his voice came out muffled from beneath the terrycloth. "I'm sorry, Dicey—I thought I'd break something if I stayed inside. I was down at the dock. I bailed out the boat, so the motor won't get covered with water. Then I checked the crab pots. The water doesn't have any waves."

"Because there's no wind," Dicey said. "Next time, tell me where you're going, okay?"

"Okay," Sammy answered.

Dicey knew Sammy. He wouldn't do things for politeness or

because he was told. He would obey if he loved you and knew you loved him. You could trust Sammy.

"Go get into dry clothes. And hang up the towels," she said.

Her grandmother was looking at her. "Doesn't he get punished?" she asked.

Dicey wanted to go along with her, so that she would like the Tillermans and let them stay on her farm. She wanted to agree so badly that she had trouble saying the words to argue. But she had given Sammy her word, and Maybeth. She had said she'd stand up for them. And she had learned that she had to do what she thought was right for her family, not what someone else thought.

"No," Dicey said. She made her voice as pleasant and unquarrelsome as she could. "Why should he? It was a mistake."

"You'll ruin him. He's willful and needs to learn."

"No," Dicey said again. "He doesn't need to learn to give in and give up. That's what you mean, isn't it? The way Sammy is—he's not perfect, but he's all right. Stubbornness isn't bad."

"He fights," she said.

"So do I," Dicey answered. "And I'm glad he knows how to."

That was the end of the conversation, but not of the battle, for this was a battle, not a skirmish. Dicey knew it. She wondered if she won that battle, would she lose the whole war?

CHAPTER 10

The next day, the fifth day, it rained again. Their grandmother continued with her canning. Dicey thought that the children should be out of the house (although James protested that he wanted to read and he wouldn't get into any trouble), so she made them all go into the barn. It was dark and gloomy in there, but after a while their eyes grew accustomed, and they could knock down the big spider webs and polish the tools with the tack rags and put the pieces of lumber into neat piles.

The rain splattered on the tin roof of the barn, like a drummer who was just learning how to play, uneven and off-beat. Dicey examined the places in the barn wall where the wood had been torn away, or had fallen awry. She and James worked on figuring out how to make patches. There was a tall extension ladder in the barn, so they could reach all the damaged places.

Late in the morning they heard the sudden, sharp call of a car horn.

At first, Dicey couldn't think of what it was, but when it sounded again she realized that there must be a car outside. You couldn't hear anything from the road this far back.

Dicey and her family went to the door of the barn. They couldn't see anything, so they went around the house to the front yard.

Claire's white station wagon, with two people in it, was stopped under the paper mulberry tree.

"We figured you were still here since we didn't hear from you," Will said, climbing out. "This sure is the boonies."

Claire had come with him. She wore her same high-heeled sandals and blue jeans, and a yellow rain jacket. She had tied a clear plastic scarf around her hair. "How is everything?" she asked. "Are you doing okay?"

Dicey nodded. "Okay," she said to Will, "but not terrific."

"Are you going to introduce us?" Will asked.

"I guess so," Dicey said. How could she introduce them when she never called her grandmother anything but *Umm-ah*?

"Something wrong?" he asked.

"Nothing's decided," Dicey said. "For us, I mean. She says we can't stay. But she hasn't made us go."

"Invite us in, okay, Dicey?" Will said. He and Claire looked at each other.

"Your feet'll get wet," Dicey said to Claire.

"Worse things have happened to me," Claire answered.

"Do the dogs miss me?" Sammy asked her.

"Of course," Claire said.

They waited on the broad back porch while Dicey called her grandmother from the stove. "I heard company," the woman said.

"Come and meet them," Dicey answered. "This is Mrs. Tillerman," she said. "Will and Claire, friends of ours."

Her grandmother shook hands with Claire, then Will, and asked them to sit down on the porch because the kitchen was so hot. She asked them if they wanted some lemonade and they asked what was wrong with Maybeth's arm. Dicey brought out a pitcher of lemonade made from a can and seven glasses. The children sat silent while the adults talked about who Will and Claire were. Will called their grandmother, "Mrs. Tillerman, ma'am," until she finally snapped at him to call her Ab.

"We had the devil of a time finding you," he said. "You don't have a phone."

"I know that," she said. "I took it out years ago."

"Why would you do that?" Claire asked.

"You have any children?" their grandmother asked Claire. Claire shook her head. "You wouldn't understand then. I used to. My boy, Bullet, he was in the army. . . ." Her dark hazel eyes clouded while she talked, and her face stiffened. "They called me up on the telephone to tell me he got killed. I had to do something. What I did was, I went downtown and took the thing and threw it through the phone company's window. They were surprised, I can tell you that. It didn't help, of course—but it was better than doing nothing."

Will threw back his head and laughed. Their grandmother smiled her sudden, surprised, smile.

"Did you hit anyone?" Sammy asked.

"All their desks were at the back," their grandmother said, "and there was a display shelf right by the window. I didn't aim to hurt anyone."

"What kind of a name is Bullet?" Sammy asked. "A nickname? What was his real name?"

"Sam. Samuel."

"Like me? Dicey, he had my name."

Dicey wondered if Momma had named Sammy after her brother because he was dead. How would Momma have known that? Maybe she had liked her brother Bullet.

"Claire," Will said. "The rain's let up a little. Why don't you take the kids out and show them what we have in the car?"

In the back of the station wagon were three bicycles, piled one on top of the other. A fourth was folded in behind the front seat.

James and Dicey had full-sized bikes, with three gears. Sammy and Maybeth had smaller models, but theirs too had gears and thin wheels.

"Oh," the children said.

And, "Oh," again.

Claire grinned at them. "They're not new. We're near Ocean City, right? And it's the end of the season there so the places that rent bicycles to tourists are selling off their old ones. Well, we all thought of you when we saw that. So everybody chipped in."

Sammy hopped onto his and wobbled for a few feet before he toppled off. "Did you see me ride?" he yelled.

Dicey and James had ridden on other kids' bikes in Provincetown, so they knew how. Claire took Maybeth aside to begin teaching her. Sammy needed no help, or so he thought. Dicey watched him for a minute and decided that he would manage on his own and that would be better than trying to get him to sit still and learn properly. She and James raced down the muddy driveway and back again. As they rode back, the rain intensified.

"We'd better get these in the barn," Dicey called over to him.

"If we'd had bikes I bet we could have gone twenty miles a day," James answered.

They took the bikes into the barn and dried them off with the tack cloth there. "If the rain lets up later, can I ride again?" Sammy asked. "I'm beginning to know how."

"Maybe," Dicey said. Claire had gone back to the porch. "We didn't say thank you," Dicey realized.

They quieted down when they came to the back porch. Maybeth went up to Will. "Thank you," she said. "It's more wonderful than anything. Will you tell everyone thank you?"

"I certainly will," Will answered.

"For me too," James said, and Dicey and Sammy added their thanks.

Will and Claire stood up then, while the rain poured down

beyond the wire screens, over the trees and garden and marsh.

"Do you have to go?" Dicey asked. She felt that when they did go she and her family would be further away from the circus than before, than just that morning. "Can't you stay for lunch? Can they?" she asked her grandmother.

Her grandmother looked hesitant.

"Perhaps you would allow us to take all of you to a restaurant for lunch," Will said. He spoke to their grandmother.

That seemed to decide her. "And pay good money for what we can make better ourselves? Nonsense. If James and Sammy will empty the crab pots and Dicey will get us some tomatoes, I think I can feed us pretty well here. If you don't mind eating out on the porch. If it's not too cold for you."

So they had lunch together on the back porch, while the rain faded away outside. They ate and talked. Will told their grandmother about how he first met the children, and how they turned up again with Mr. Rudyard on their heels. Then James had to tell about Mr. Rudyard again, because he told it best. Their grandmother picked crab meat and chewed and listened. She studied James's face as he spoke. She looked from one to the other of them, especially at Maybeth. At the end she raised her eyebrows a little and said to Dicey, "You ran a risk to hire yourselves out."

"I had to," Dicey said.

"I can see that."

Then lunch was over and it really was time for Will and Claire to leave. The rain had stopped by then and the thick masses of gray clouds were beginning to break apart. A golden bar of sunlight would occasionally slip past the guard the clouds had put up. But the mood as the children stood around Claire's car, saying good-bye, was still rainy.

"Well," Dicey said.

"Well," Will said. Then, like a bolt of sunlight he changed the subject from good-bye. "It's turning into biking weather, wouldn't you say, Claire?"

Dicey grinned at him then. "Don't lose touch with us," she said. He reached into his shirt pocket and pulled out a calling card, printed with the name of the circus and an address in New York City.

"My booking agent," Will said. "He always knows where we are."

Dicey reached up and kissed him on the cheek. His short beard scratched at her cheek as his arms hugged her, round and strong, for the briefest of times.

"You'll be okay," he assured her. "I don't know what that old lady will do—I don't think even she knows—but you kids, remember you can always call on us."

Dicey nodded, and tried to smile. What was the matter with her today? Wasn't she used to saying good-bye?

The white car drove off, splashing through puddles, its wheels throwing muddy water aside.

Sammy asked if he could ride his bike and Dicey gave him permission. Maybeth went into the house to help their grandmother clear up. James and Dicey worked out plans for mending the biggest holes in the side of the barn.

"Whadda you think, Dicey?" James finally asked. "Are we going to stay?"

"I think so," Dicey answered. "I think we've shown her we can be useful. And not too much trouble. I think she likes Sammy—maybe because he's named after her son—"

"Our uncle. Did you think of that?"

"And I'm pretty sure we'll be okay here. All of us."

"What about schools?"

"We can ride our bikes downtown and find out. Tomorrow. You want to?"

"Tomorrow's Sunday."

"Then the next day."

"That's Labor Day."

"Then Tuesday or next week. Why are you quarreling, James? Don't you want to stay?"

"I guess so. I like it, and all those books. Do you think our grandfather was smart? Do you think he went to college or just read? What do you think he was like?"

"I don't know anything about him except what she said. Would it be okay with you if we stayed?"

"Sure. It's a good place. But Dicey, why did all of her children leave her? She's not so bad."

"Do you think there's something we don't know? Do you think it's dangerous for us?" Dicey asked him.

"Do you like her?" James asked.

Dicey considered this. "You know? I could. I mean, she's so odd and prickly. She fights us, or anyway I feel like I'm fighting her and she's fighting back, as if we both know what's going on but neither of us is saying anything. It's fun."

"You're crazy," James said.

"Maybe. But she's a good enemy—you know? In that way. Cousin Eunice wasn't." Dicey thought some more. "So she might make a good friend," Dicey said finally.

"You are crazy," James said. He looked at her. "But you might be right. You're smart too, Dicey, do you ever think about that?" Dicey hadn't. It didn't seem very important to her, not the way it was to James.

Sammy had ridden out of sight, beyond the long driveway. He wasn't back in an hour and he wasn't back in two hours. The rain clouds blew away, leaving room for a bright red sunset, where fiery lights burned behind the clouds that gathered around the lowering sun.

They had cold ham for supper, and Sammy hadn't returned when they sat down. Dicey was worried. She didn't dare say anything though. They sat down in a troubled silence.

When she heard Sammy's feet on the steps of the porch, Dicey's appetite revived. He burst in the door to the kitchen, his cheeks red, his eyes sparkling.

"Wash your hands," Dicey said. She could see him and he was fine, he was safe and back again. Relief dissolved into anger then. She looked at her grandmother.

"When you've done that, go to your room," their grandmother said.

Sammy turned. "But I'm hungry."

"That'll help you remember. Did you tell your sister where you were going?" Sammy's jaw went out. He wasn't going to answer, not to tell a lie.

"Did he tell you?" Dicey shook her head. "Did he have your permission?"

"Sort of," Dicey said.

"Sort of?" their grandmother said in a sharp, sarcastic voice. "Sort of? How do you sort of give permission to disappear for hours at a time? What do you say? 'Okay, Sammy, go sort of run wild and sort of let people worry'? Are you stupid, girl?"

Dicey chewed her lip. Why did every adult send kids away from the table? Maybe because nobody sent *them* to bed hungry. Maybe they'd forgotten what hungry was. But it wasn't right. Dicey knew what hungry was, and so did Sammy.

"It's not Dicey's fault," Sammy said. "It's my fault. Don't yell at Dicey."

"I will yell at whom I please," his grandmother answered him. "I have told you to go to your room."

"No," Dicey said quietly.

"Dicey!" James whispered.

"It's not right, James," Dicey said. "It's not right to send him to bed hungry. I can't let that happen, and I was wrong when I let Cousin Eunice do it. Sit down and eat, Sammy," Dicey said.

Then she turned to try to explain to her grandmother. Her grandmother's eyes flashed. Her face was stiff and pale. Her lips were hard together.

"You," Dicey said. She wanted to call her by name, but she had no name to call her. "You don't understand, not what it is to be hungry. It doesn't serve any purpose to punish Sammy that way."

Her grandmother's fury burned behind her immobile face. Her hand clenched the handle of the fork.

Dicey was frightened, with a fear that swelled up deep within her. This fear had two heads, and Dicey was caught between them: she was afraid to speak and lose what they had gained of a place for themselves in this house; she was afraid to keep silent and lose what she felt was right for Sammy, for her family. This was more difficult danger than any she had faced before. It wasn't the kind of danger you could run away from, or fight back at. Dicey wasn't even sure she wanted to fight. She just knew she had to stand by her brother and her family.

"Whose house is this?" their grandmother said. "Whose food? Whose table?"

"You're right," Dicey said. "It's not our house, that's what you said from the beginning. But we're not your family, you meant that too, didn't you?"

Her grandmother stared at her.

"Sit down and eat," Dicey said to Sammy. James and Maybeth were staring at her. Everybody was staring at her. "But you're not to ride the bike again for two days."

"Aw, Dicey," Sammy said. He slipped into his chair and cut his meat.

"I mean it. No matter what. Will you obey?"

Sammy nodded.

"You have to say when you're going off," Dicey said. She ignored her grandmother, who was sitting at the head of the table in a silence of furious anger.

Sammy nodded again. "I know. I will. I'm sorry, Dicey," he said, with a weak smile. Then he turned to his grandmother. "I'm sorry to you, too. I didn't mean to make trouble. But it's my fault, not Dicey's."

"You're a child," his grandmother answered.

"So is Dicey," Sammy said.

"I will not have this talking back!" their grandmother snapped.

"But it's not talking back," James said. His voice was high and frightened. "It's explaining. We're trying to get at the truth." His grandmother stared at him before she answered, as if he had said something she didn't understand.

"You are in my home," their grandmother said. She looked around the table at the four pairs of hazel eyes, none as dark as hers. And none, except Dicey's, as angry as hers. "My home, not yours," their grandmother said.

We might as well have it out now as any other time, Dicey said to herself. She felt as if she had been running away from this for days, and she had only the last of her strength left. She had to turn and fight now. She took a deep, shivering breath.

"Are you expecting us to stay then?" she demanded. Her voice sounded thin and hard.

Her grandmother's mouth worked, and she looked surprised, as if she hadn't understood what it was they were fighting about this time. Her mouth formed words, but no sound came out. Finally she spoke:

"No."

The word ballooned out and filled all the air of the kitchen.

Dicey didn't even try to argue. She just nodded her head and ate her supper in silence and helped with the dishes, and when the little children went up to bed she went with them. The *No* filled the whole air of the house. Every time she breathed in she breathed in that *No.* Dicey wasn't even frightened anymore. She was simply defeated. She fell asleep suddenly and without any thought.

CHAPTER 11

Dicey awoke to a thick, black silence. She slipped out of bed and went to the window. Night smothered the land. A dark wind blew clouds over the face of the moon and over the little stars. This kind of wind blew in clear weather. So tomorrow would be a good day to begin traveling again.

They had only seven dollars left, but they had bicycles now, and Dicey had her jackknife and her map. What they didn't have was any place to go.

Back to Bridgeport, Dicey supposed, the long way back.

Will couldn't help them. They couldn't live with the circus. James had to go to school. And so did Maybeth, but for different reasons.

Could they hide out? Could they find the circus again and travel south and then pitch a permanent camp somewhere? Dicey thought they could manage that. She could lie to any school officials. She'd be eighteen in five years. She could say they lived back in the hills with their momma and their momma couldn't come in because she was working the farm. Nobody'd care enough to question, not as long as they showed up in school. There was a boy Dicey knew in Provincetown who ran away from home and he just kept on coming to school and nobody knew, not for months.

The plan was possible, Dicey thought. Only she couldn't get

excited about it. Having someplace in mind that you were traveling to was different from not having any place.

But it was a plan. She'd ask James what he thought. He might think they should go back to Bridgeport, and he might be right. One way or the other, north or south, they'd be moving on.

"Okay," Dicey said to herself. "Okay, that's what we'll do." She thought she'd go back to bed and sleep some more, if she could get to sleep again. She took a last look—seeing in her mind's eye the things she couldn't really see, the pines and the fields, the marshes and the bay beyond, the barn that held the sailboat like a buried treasure in its dark belly. Dicey belonged here. She belonged here; yet she was being blown away. Well, it wasn't her house, that was true. It was their grandmother's house and they were not welcome. They would stay together, at least that. She could go along with Cousin Eunice on everything except about that; she wouldn't agree to sending Sammy or Maybeth away. She'd say that right away.

Dicey noticed a yellow light, flowing onto the lawn below the porch. Had somebody left the kitchen light on? She went downstairs to turn it off.

Her grandmother sat at the kitchen table wearing an old striped cotton bathrobe. She had a cup of tea before her and a pad of paper on which she was writing. Her hair was all in tousled curls. She looked up at Dicey when Dicey came in.

"I couldn't sleep so I'm writing that silly woman, Eunice," she said.

Dicey stared. Her grandmother was pretty. Her face had delicate straight bones, and those wide dark eyes.

"What're you staring at, girl?"

"You. You're pretty. I never noticed," Dicey said. "Never mind. I saw the light from my window. I didn't know anyone was here. I'm sorry."

"Sit down," her grandmother said. "Get a glass of milk first. I wondered who'd taken that room when I heard you up there. Get your milk and sit—I've got something I should say to you."

Dicey poured herself a glass of milk and sat down. She had never really looked at her grandmother before, just at the enemy she had to trick, just at her bare feet.

"It's okay," Dicey said. "I'm not going to argue about staying."

"Wouldn't do you any good," her grandmother said. She put the cap on the pen and twisted it shut. "But I should apologize for yelling at you."

Her grandmother's mouth twisted in her sudden smile. "That Will seems a good man. Could you go to him? Would you rather do that than go back to this woman?"

"I was thinking about that," Dicey said. "I was going to ask James what he thought. He's the one, really, he should go to school. Well, Maybeth should too."

"Maybeth's not retarded," her grandmother said.

"I know that. She is slow though. Not as slow as she seems in school, but . . ." Why go over this again? "There was a lady, a nun, in Bridgeport. She might help Maybeth."

Her grandmother sipped at her cup of tea and Dicey drank at her milk.

"I want to explain," Dicey's grandmother said. "I've never explained before, to anyone, but I have to now. Because, in a way, I do want to keep you here. But I can't."

Dicey nodded. She could feel how true that was. Her grandmother went on speaking.

"I'm old. Not very old yet, but getting older. You can't tell what will happen. What if I fell sick, for instance. And I've very little money. When my husband died he left some insurance. Enough to live on if I live carefully. I don't mind that. But it's expensive with children." She smiled again. "I'm already going to have to die a month sooner than I planned, with the food this week."

"That's crazy," Dicey said.

"It's a joke, girl," her grandmother said. "I mean to explain that I don't have the money. Will said Social Security would give me money for you. But I never took charity."

"Momma wouldn't, either. That's why she was taking us to Aunt Cilla's house," Dicey said. "I understand about that," she said.

"There's more too," her grandmother said. "I don't know whether you can understand this now, but if not now there's always later. I was married for thirty-eight years and my husband just died these four years ago. Until then, until he died—when you marry someone you make promises. I kept those promises, love and honor and obey. Even when I didn't want to I kept them. I kept quiet when I had things to say. I always went his way."

"That's hard to believe," Dicey said.

"It is, isn't it. Since he died, I've been different. It took a while, but—it's my own life I'm living now. I had a hard time getting it. I don't want to give it up. No lies, no pretending, no standing back quiet when I want to fight."

Dicey thought of Cousin Eunice. She couldn't picture her grandmother like Cousin Eunice. It would be awful if her grandmother was like that.

"It's okay," Dicey said. "I understand."

"That's more than your momma could," her grandmother said. "She felt sorry for me—do you know that?"

"No. She never talked about you. Except to Sammy and he couldn't remember."

"Your momma stuck around here a long time just because she felt sorry for me. I was glad when she began seeing Francis.

He was handsome and cheerful. I thought, maybe she'll be happy, maybe she'll steady him down. But do you know what I said to her, just before she left this house? She was twenty-one then and her father couldn't stop her. I said—'We don't want to hear anything from you until we hear that you've been married.' He was right beside me then and I knew it was what he would say. So I was the one to say it, because I didn't want her thinking I wouldn't stand by him. I had to stand by him—he was my husband. Do you know what she said? She said, 'I'll never get married.' She wasn't angry. She never fought, not your mother. She was gentle—like Maybeth. Your father wasn't a fighter, either. I don't know where you get it from because you are."

Dicey knew where she got it from, but she had a more urgent question. "Why didn't Momma want to get married?"

"She had seen what happens. She didn't want to give her word, like I did. We keep our promises, we Tillermans. We keep them hard."

"But I don't understand. Can't you love somebody and fight with them? I fight with Sammy, and with James. I make Maybeth do things she's scared to do. But that's because I love them. If I didn't love them I wouldn't bother. And they fight back—like James walking out here instead of waiting, that's fighting back. It was okay too, because it was his own decision. I want him to make his own decisions. Didn't you love Momma?"

"Oh yes, I loved my children. I had a lot of love to give in those days, to my husband too. But it got turned around. I got turned around. I let myself get turned around." Her grandmother waved her hand, vaguely, to brush away the memories like you brush away cobwebs. "And it's all gone now and they're all gone now. So it's the past."

Dicey finished her milk. "Will you tell them about Momma

not marrying? I lied to them about it. It was better then, to lie. Now it isn't; at least, I don't think so. I'll tell them if you won't, but if you would they'd understand better."

"Maybe. Maybe I'll try."

"I saw a picture of you when you were little," Dicey said. "Cousin Eunice had one. You looked angry."

"I was angry—most of my life," her grandmother said. "Not anymore—if you can believe that. Just crazy now, and that's an improvement. Not really crazy. Eccentric. But those years, morning to night. All that anger—you can choke swallowing back anger. And it still sneaks out, in little ways, and everybody knows although nobody says anything. So they left, every one. They couldn't stay here. All of my children, they ran as fast and as far as they could. My Sammy, he died of it, and that was hard. Hard. And your poor momma—they shamed me. And I shamed myself." She chewed on her lip. Then she looked Dicey full in the eyes and said:

"I failed them. I let them go. I told them to go. There were times I could have killed him. He'd sit chewing and the anger and shame were sitting at the table with us. Chew and swallow, so sure he was right. But I'd promised him—and he didn't know why they each left. I did. So, I'm responsible. I won't have that responsibility again. Not to fail again."

"Are you sure you'd fail?" Dicey asked in a low voice. "We can't stay here, I know. Don't worry about that. But I don't think you'd fail with us. We had Momma. And I wouldn't let those things happen." That was true, Dicey knew it. They were safe, safer than her grandmother, even though her grandmother had this big house and what remained of the farm to keep her fed.

Her grandmother nodded. "You've got determination," she said.

"Momma said it was in my blood," Dicey answered. "I never knew what she meant before."

"Your momma was a kind child," her grandmother said. "But she never forgave her father."

"Did you?" Dicey asked.

"No. Yes."

Somehow, this made sense to Dicey. It let her know that she would be all right, and her family would be all right. They wouldn't be children forever. They didn't have to have a place, they just had to have themselves. She yawned, fighting it off and losing.

"You'd better get back to bed. I'll finish this letter to that Eunice now. I'll try to tell her about Maybeth—but she's such a silly woman I doubt she's got two ounces of common sense rattling around in her head. Your cousin doesn't care much for you."

This didn't surprise Dicey. "That's okay," she said.

"Well, I do," her grandmother said. "I care for all of you. Now get to bed. I'll wash out your glass. Scat!"

Dicey ran upstairs. She ran into her bed and pulled the covers up over her head. Cousin Eunice didn't want them, but she would take them in. Her grandmother wanted them, but wouldn't let them stay. And they, she, James, Maybeth and Sammy—they were the losers. Dicey cried herself to sleep. She couldn't stop. She tried, but she couldn't. She didn't know if she was crying for her family, or for herself, or for her grandmother—or for all of them, all the Tillermans, Momma too, lost up in Massachusetts, and Bullet lost in Vietnam. They were all lost. Dicey promised herself this was the last time she'd cry, ever, and wept until her eyes were swollen shut and she slept.

Sunlight was pouring over the house and yard and through the windows when Dicey awoke the next morning. She pulled on shorts and a shirt and looked into three empty bedrooms before she came downstairs.

Her grandmother was alone in the kitchen. She was kneading dough. "What's that?" Dicey asked.

"Bread. I haven't made it for years. You slept late."

Dicey nodded, without apologizing. She looked at her grandmother. She had gray splotches under her eyes, and the fine wrinkles that came out from the edges of her eyes and her mouth seemed deeper this morning. This was not quite the same woman Dicey had talked with in the dead of night; but this was not a different woman, either.

Dicey poured herself a glass of milk and took an apple from the bowl of fruit. She stood by the sink, drinking and chewing, and watching her grandmother knead the pale dough. Push-pull, slap, push-pull. Her grandmother leaned into the dough with her shoulders, but handled it gently at the same time.

Her grandmother was contradictory. Except for the fatigue, her grandmother looked perfectly ordinary this morning. Only now Dicey knew better.

There was a warm feeling in her stomach, as if she had swallowed sunshine. At least now, everything was settled, she wasn't battling anymore. She liked her grandmother, her momma's mother. She liked her all prickly and contrary. She liked the way her grandmother said one thing and then the opposite, because it made sense to Dicey, the same kind of sense Dicey made to herself. She liked the way the woman had watched Sammy roll naked in the grass. She liked her bare feet.

This was a good way to feel to say good-bye.

"We'll be moving on today," Dicey said. "I wanted to thank you for letting us stay so long."

"Not today, you won't," her grandmother said. "You can't just bolt off like that. You've done enough running away, don't you think?"

Dicey couldn't see her face, but her voice sounded pleasant enough.

"I've written to your cousin. We have to wait and see what she answers. You'll stay here until then. I'll mail the letter Tuesday. We're going to town Tuesday, for food and to talk to the people at the school. What grade are you in?"

"Going into eighth," Dicey said. "But why?"

"Do you know how long it'll take that dithering woman to get advice from all the people she talks to and arrange to come and get you? You may, but I don't. Children should be in school. School starts Tuesday, or so James tells me and I have no reason to disbelieve him. Those bikes will give some trouble—I have no idea how to ship bicycles and I won't have them here, rusting in the barn."

"What if we don't want to go back to Bridgeport?" Dicey asked.

"First we find out if you can. For today, while the bread is rising, we might go take a look at Janes Island. It's all marsh and you can't land there. Don't know why they call it an island."

"Where are the little kids?" Dicey asked.

"Down by the dock, bailing out the boat. *They* have all agreed. *They* want to see the island." Her hands slapped at the bread. She poked at it with a finger, then began kneading it again. "I told them, what you wanted me to. Sammy"—she shook her head and slapped the dough down on the table—"he said I was lying and he said he didn't care. Then he said he was sorry, he knew I wasn't lying, but he still didn't care. Maybeth didn't say a word. But James—he told Sammy he did care, and if it was what your momma wanted then that was okay with him because she might have been crazy in some ways but she was never crazy when it came to loving her kids. I asked him where he got ideas like that and he looked me straight in the eye and said, 'From books.'" She laughed briefly. "Yes, I told them, I also told them they ought to think twice before they held that lie against you."

Dicey ran down to the dock. The bay was lively, with crisp-topped blue waves under a steady breeze. Her family had bailed out the boat and now they were swimming.

"What's going on, James?" Dicey called. He swam over to her.

"I dunno, Dicey. We'll be here a little longer, that's all I know."

"We're going to an island!" Sammy called. "It's okay about Momma. She didn't want to get married. Did you know?" Dicey nodded.

They motored over to the stretch of marshland just off the town shore. There, they dropped an anchor on the bay side. Birds lived on Janes Island, but nothing else could. One snowy heron soared down, folding its wings in at the last minute, returning to its nest deep in the marsh grass. A few ducks wandered along the muddy shore, in and out of the tall grasses. They saw flocks of gulls, gossiping, bickering, bobbling on the waves, flying in noisy swarms.

Their grandmother had packed a bag of fruit and some cold crab, left over from yesterday's lunch. As they ate, she asked them about their travelings, so James and Dicey took turns telling her. "Well," she kept saying. And, "That was a piece of luck." She didn't ask them about Bridgeport.

Back at the farm, Dicey took Sammy to the barn to begin patching, while James and Maybeth rode their bikes up and down the driveway. "You don't have to do that," their grandmother said to Dicey.

"I know," she said.

The patched places showed up bleak against the wasted pink paint of the barn. They would hold, Dicey knew; they had been nailed into place firmly and the edges were sealed against the weather. If she'd had time, she would have liked to paint the whole barn. Just so there would be something here to say, "Dicey Tillerman stayed here awhile and she made a difference." Dicey figured they had a week, maybe two, before they had to go back to Bridgeport, to the little house and the fussing and fretting. She planned to enjoy the time and not worry about the future. Her grandmother seemed to feel the same way. It was as if now everything was decided, they could both relax.

So they passed two quiet days, hammering, bike riding (except Sammy), swimming, weeding, picking, fixing the mailbox—just living together. In the evenings, they went onto the back porch or into the living room. Their grandmother found an old checkers set, somewhere deep in a closet. Maybeth picked out tunes on the piano. Some of the songs they sang, the songs Momma had sung, their grandmother knew. Some of them she had to learn, and she wasn't very good at it.

Yet, the feelings in the air were not all placid. Dicey disagreed with her grandmother whenever she thought her grandmother was being unfair. "Ah-ummm," she would say, because they still had no name to call their grandmother, "Cousin Eunice tried to do her best. Sure she's silly, but that's not her fault, is it?"

"Well, whose fault is it then?" their grandmother would answer sharply. "If it's not her own fault for what she's like, I'd like to know whose fault it is."

"Okay," Dicey would say, giving ground because privately she thought her grandmother was right, "but she's not bad."

"Who mentioned bad?" their grandmother would say. "James? Did I? Maybeth, did I say bad? I said silly and I meant silly." Their grandmother would rush on before they could answer. "And there's an end on it."

"Dicey's the one who said silly," James would say.

"Aha!" their grandmother would say. "I told you, Dicey, it's all your fault."

Then Dicey would swallow her disappointment and enjoy this temporary haven. For these two days, she stopped thinking ahead. She learned how to put the bandage on Maybeth's arm, which Maybeth said was better, but their grandmother said should be supported for two full weeks, especially since Maybeth was riding her bike so much.

They took one long ride, James and Dicey and Maybeth. They saw several farmhouses. Some of them had cows and horses. All of them had chickens. Most of them had fields of corn and tomatoes.

Dicey made herself stop thinking about the sailboat in her grandmother's barn. That was to have been the prize, her prize, if they had stayed. She wouldn't go near it now. She knew that if she did she'd begin planning again, and she'd get it down to the water, somehow. Once the boat was in the water, they could take it away and sail south, and hide. But they didn't have any place left to go to. She had been beaten this time, down to her bones beaten. She had fought her hardest and her smartest, and she had lost. She could take that, and she could understand the whys of it. But not if the boat was in the water, and the sails fitted to the mast, and the wind blowing little clouds along the sky. So she shut the sailboat out of her mind, just as she shut out hoping and caring and the disappointment that waited for her to relax her guard so it could leap out and get its teeth into her. She just lived through the hours, taking them as they came, knowing they would never come again.

CHAPTER 12

On Tuesday morning, their grandmother started another batch of bread, then told them to take baths and put on fresh shorts and shirts. When the children came downstairs, their grandmother was waiting in the kitchen. She had combed her curly hair with water, but it wouldn't lie flat. She was wearing a dark blue suit, with her blouse tucked in, and lipstick, stockings and loafers.

"You're all dressed up," Dicey said.

"It's old," her grandmother said. "But I'm old. Or do you mean the shoes? I hope you children appreciate what I'm going through for you." But she said that as if it was a joke.

"I don't care if you have bare feet," Sammy said, very serious.

"Neither do I," his grandmother said, "but there are them that do."

Maybeth stood shyly beside Dicey. "You look different," she said to the woman. "Pretty."

Their grandmother blushed. The dark red came up under her tanned cheeks. "I'll be getting vain the next thing you know. And that's a vice I never had. Let's go." She picked up a worn black purse from the table. "I'm bound to leave this behind somewhere. Keep an eye on it, somebody. James, you're reliable, will you?"

"I'll try," James said.

The wind blew their carefully combed hair all out of order, and the salt spray covered their bodies, so they arrived at the dock looking as they ordinarily did, except their grandmother. She led them down the main street, and then down a side street, to a long, low building that had windows over most of its walls.

Inside, the air was noisy with children's voices. The halls were made of white-painted concrete blocks. A long dim, windowless hallway went down the center of the building, with classrooms on both sides. It smelled like a school, of chalk and children's sweat, and warm food from the lunchroom. A teacher told their grandmother where the registration office was. The sign over the door said *Guidance.* In the tiny office, they found a fat young woman seated behind a big wooden desk.

"My name is Abigail Tillerman," their grandmother announced. "These children will be in Crisfield temporarily and they ought to be in school until they go back. What's your name?"

Their grandmother sounded nervous.

"Mrs. Jenkins," the woman said. "I'm the guidance counselor." She told them to come in and sit down. The room was so crowded with filing cabinets and plants and her big desk, there was room only for two straight chairs for visitors. Dicey and her grandmother sat in those. James and Maybeth and Sammy crowded into the corners of the room.

"What do you mean by temporarily?" Mrs. Jenkins asked.

"For a short time. I'm not sure how long exactly," their grandmother said. "If I could tell you I would."

Mrs. Jenkins asked their names and ages, and Dicey told her. She asked for their address, and Dicey looked at her grandmother, who told Mrs. Jenkins. Mrs. Jenkins asked what the last school they had been in was; her grandmother looked at Dicey, and Dicey told her.

"Parents?" Mrs. Jenkins asked.

"Not noticeably," their grandmother said. James gave a short snort of laughter.

"What then is your relationship to them, Mrs. Tillerman? I assume you will be responsible for them while they are attending school here."

"I am their mother's mother," their grandmother said.

Mrs. Jenkins looked at her for a long moment. Dicey watched her write down, *grandmother.*

"All right then. I will call the Provincetown school to have your records sent to us. I think it would be well to do that now, before we assign the children to classes. Would you like to walk around the school for a bit? Come back, in half an hour, I think."

They trooped out of the office. All the classroom doors were closed, so they went outside. The playground was a huge field of short grass. Scattered over it were jungle gyms and tall swings, sandboxes, slides and a baseball diamond. It was empty now, with the children inside. The equipment gleamed, as if it had never been played on.

"It looks brand-new," Dicey said. "The whole school does."

"I should think it is," her grandmother said. Sammy and Maybeth ran off to the swings.

"Who pays for it?" Dicey asked.

"Me," her grandmother said.

Dicey stared at her.

"Taxes, girl."

"Do you pay taxes?"

"Indeed I do. Taxes on land, taxes on my house, death taxes, life taxes. I even pay taxes on the money I keep in the bank."

Dicey hadn't known that. "No wonder you're worried about money," she said.

"But with a farm, there must be ways to get money," James said. "Did you ever think of growing trees?"

His grandmother just looked at him.

"No, Christmas trees, on those front fields. There are pine seedlings already there."

Dicey chimed in. "It shouldn't be hard to grow them and people always buy Christmas trees. Even we did, in Provincetown."

"Why should anyone buy what they can walk outside and cut down for free?"

"In many places," James said, as if he were talking to somebody a little stupid, "like Annapolis—there they can't just walk outside and cut down a tree."

"How would I get trees to Annapolis?"

"There must be ways." He dismissed that problem. "You could earn money that way. Or you could sell land—"

"No," their grandmother said.

"Or chickens—why don't you have chickens? A lot of other farms do."

"I don't care for the company of chickens."

"Maybe," James said. He leaned toward her, earnestly trying to explain his ideas. "But you can sell eggs. You could sell some of your vegetables, too, if you had a stand out front by the driveway. Or you could rent out your fields to some other farmer who wants more land. Or butter." His ideas dashed on. "People will pay for good butter, won't they? You'd need cows, but you've already got stalls in the barn. What about pigs?"

Their grandmother was looking at him, with a contradictory expression, half amusement and half interest.

"You've got to be careful with money and earn it whenever you can," Dicey said.

Her grandmother shook her head, as if Dicey didn't know

what she was talking about. Maybe she didn't, Dicey thought. But maybe she did.

"I know what you're thinking, girl," her grandmother said.

"Then you know I might be right," Dicey answered.

Her grandmother humphed.

"She is," James said. "With inflation, and if you're on fixed income—you could lose the farm if you can't pay taxes."

"Could you?" Dicey asked. "Could that happen?"

"What's that to you?" her grandmother demanded.

"I guess nothing. But if we can't be there I want you to be. So it matters something. And you can't change that."

Her grandmother humphed again.

When they returned to Mrs. Jenkins's office, the counselor was waiting for them. She had papers on her desk, and a pad with notes all over it. She waited until they were all in, all five of them, before she said anything.

The first thing she said was "You're in the wrong school, Dicey. You should be in the junior high. I've called and they'll expect you tomorrow morning. Mr. MacGuire will be your guidance counselor. Can you find the junior high?"

"She can," their grandmother said.

Dicey hadn't thought that she'd be in a different school.

"James will go into the accelerated section of fifth grade. We have some special programs for the gifted student. They should suit you, James. Your teacher will be Mr. Thomas."

James looked at Dicey and grinned. She knew what he was thinking: a man teacher. There weren't any men teachers in the elementary school in Provincetown, not one.

"Sammy will be in Miss Tieds's second grade."

"Okay," said Sammy. "I don't care."

"James and Sammy," Mrs. Jenkins said, "I want you to meet your teachers today. If you go to the principal's office, they will come there when the recess bell rings. That will be in ten minutes. It's the third door on your right, as you go down the hall. You may go now."

The boys left together. James walked eagerly, but Sammy dragged his heels. James turned at the door. "Don't forget your purse," he said to their grandmother. She waved him away.

Mrs. Jenkins gathered her papers into a pile.

"What about Maybeth?" Dicey asked. She got herself ready to fight for Maybeth.

"I'm coming to that," Mrs. Jenkins said. Maybeth sidled over between the two chairs Dicey and their grandmother sat in. She didn't say anything.

"Your records—Maybeth, are you listening to me?" Mrs. Jenkins asked. She spoke without emphasis. Maybeth nodded. "Your records show that they wanted to hold you back in second grade. That would be the second time you have been kept back. Did you know that?" She turned to their grandmother. "Their recommendation is—most strong."

"But—" Dicey began.

Mrs. Jenkins cut her off, to say: "Our school, however, has a policy not to put brothers and sisters in the same grade. Do you want to be in Sammy's grade, Maybeth?"

Maybeth shook her head, no. She looked at Dicey.

"Why not?" Mrs. Jenkins asked.

Maybeth waited. No one else said anything. "Because I'm bigger than he is," she whispered.

"I thought so." Mrs. Jenkins smiled. When she smiled, with her short dark hair and bright cheeks, she looked like a kid herself, Dicey thought. She was as fresh as apples.

"I thought that would be the case. If you want to go into third grade—and mind you, I'm not promising anything—but if you want to try, you'll have to take some tests for me."

"What kind of tests?" their grandmother asked.

"A quick IQ, then reading and math, achievement and aptitude. They're short and not precise, but they'll give a fairly good idea of where Maybeth can be put in school." Mrs. Jenkins waited for an answer.

"How long will it take?" their grandmother asked.

"An hour at the most. Will you do that, Maybeth?" Mrs. Jenkins kept talking to Maybeth. Maybeth looked at Dicey with wide eyes.

Their grandmother stood up. "We have errands to do, so if you'll tell James and Sammy to bring Maybeth and wait for us by the boat, I have no objections."

Maybeth's hand held on to Dicey's arm.

"But—can I stay?" Dicey asked Mrs. Jenkins. "It'll be better. You don't understand—"

"No," her grandmother said. "Maybeth will take the tests by herself."

"I would prefer that," Mrs. Jenkins said.

"Don't argue, girl," her grandmother said to Dicey, just as Dicey was opening her mouth to say she wasn't going to leave Maybeth there alone. Her grandmother spoke to Maybeth. "Maybeth? You've got two hard times coming. This, now, is the first. Tomorrow morning is the next. Nothing will make them easier. That's the way it is. Do you understand that?"

Maybeth nodded, but her hand stayed on Dicey's arm.

"Will you try?" their grandmother asked. "It'll take some courage, but I think you've got that. Do you have it?"

"I don't know," Maybeth said. "I'll try." She released Dicey's arm. "It'll be okay, Dicey."

Dicey wasn't sure.

"Come along," her grandmother ordered. "I'll see you tomorrow morning, Mrs. Jenkins. Mind you, she's ripped a tendon in her right arm so her writing won't be much."

"Yes, thank you," Mrs. Jenkins said. She stood up, and Dicey followed her grandmother out of the little office, leaving Maybeth behind.

When they stepped out of the building into the hot morning sunlight, her grandmother turned on Dicey. "You've got to let her make her own way."

"I know," Dicey said. "But—"

"But nothing. But hogwash. If she can't do that—"

"But she *is,*" Dicey argued. "She's doing it right now."

Her grandmother nodded her head briskly. "Yes, so she is."

They strolled back to the main street and entered the grocery store Dicey had gone into days earlier. The storekeeper and butcher, Millie, looked like she wanted to say something when she saw them, she looked like she had several somethings to say, but she didn't dare. Dicey didn't know how her grandmother stopped the questions, but she did, by the glitter in her eye and the lift to her chin. Dicey took part of their list and went around the store finding cans of tuna, jars of peanut butter, bags of apples, and all the odds and ends that go to keeping house for a family. The store was warm and dim. Her grandmother spent a long time at the meat counter.

When they were ready to check out, Dicey stood awkwardly aside. The bill came to forty-seven dollars. Dicey chewed on her lip. Maybe she could find work. Maybe she could find work here, dusting the shelves and washing the windows and making the place look brighter, cleaner, more like someplace where you wanted to buy groceries.

Her grandmother paid the bill. Millie took the money and gave her back her change without a word. She packed the groceries into four large bags.

Then the shopkeeper could hold her tongue no longer. "I see you found work," she said to Dicey.

"Yes," Dicey said. She said no more. She turned her chin up the way her grandmother's chin was held. It worked in just the same way.

"Tell me, Millie," her grandmother said, with a side glance at Dicey. "Do you get Social Security money?"

"Of course, since Herbie died. It's my due. I paid into it every month, all my working life. It's a widow's due, I tell you. I couldn't get through the month without it, not with what the store brings in. Widow's due, that's what I call it, and there's no shame. You take it too, don't you?"

"I didn't work to pay in," Dicey's grandmother said.

"No more you didn't, Ab Tillerman, raising three children and working on that farm. Your John did, too, every year in his taxes. It's for widows and their children, as much as for people older than we are, and helpless. So don't raise your nose at me."

"Ever buy a Christmas tree?" Dicey's grandmother demanded.

The abrupt change of topic flustered Millie. "What?" she asked. "What do you mean? For Christmas? Why should I do that, when I can get one cut for me just by asking? I know a lady in Cambridge that bought one, but I never did. What kind of a question is that?"

"How much did she pay?"

"How should I know? Ten, fifteen dollars, I think she said. And it was a scrawny thing, too, some poor relation of a loblolly. She had more bulbs than branches on the thing, trying to make it look right. You feeling all right, Ab?"

Dicey looked at her grandmother, glad because it meant her grandmother was thinking of putting in a cash crop, to repay herself the money she'd spent on the Tillermans.

"See if your family's around, girl," her grandmother said. "We're going to need some extra hands with these bags."

Dicey went out through the door.

Sunlight burned on the street. She saw James across by the docks, leading Maybeth and Sammy down to the boat.

"Hey!" she called. "Hey! James! Over here."

They turned and strolled toward her. They looked tanned, healthy and perfectly ordinary. Dicey tried to read in Maybeth's face what had happened.

"I thought you were at the boat," James said.

"There are bags to carry. Maybeth?" Dicey asked.

Maybeth nodded and her eyes gleamed. "I can go into third grade. I read for her, the most I could. Out loud. I tried to sound out the words I didn't know, just like they said at school. It was easier, because it was the story about the little goats that get left at home and the wolf comes and tries to trick them into opening the door. So I knew the story. I told Mrs. Jenkins I already knew it and asked her if she wanted to find another story to test me with, but she said it was okay. She said even if I knew the story I'd still have to read the words. I answered all her questions about it, but they were easy ones. I got two wrong on the adding and three on subtracting, and they don't start multiplication until third grade. But they know fractions already."

"I can show you fractions," Dicey said. "Was it hard?"

"Not as hard as I thought," Maybeth said. "Not as hard as tomorrow will be. But I think maybe I can do that too."

Their grandmother pushed the screen door aside. "What are you waiting for?"

Maybeth ran over to her and pulled on her arm. Their grandmother bent her gray curly head down to the bright yellow head. She listened to Maybeth and smiled at what she heard.

The children went inside. Sammy said he wasn't too small to carry a bag, but he was, so Millie divided one bag into two smaller bags, one for Sammy and one for Maybeth. Her eyes bugged out with curiosity.

"By the way, Millie," their grandmother finally said, "I don't believe you've met my grandchildren." One by one she introduced them. "Liza's brood," their grandmother said. "They'll be staying with me for a couple of weeks."

Their grandmother herded them outside before Millie could ask any questions. They walked together down the hot street and along the dock. Dicey got into the boat first. James handed the bags down to her.

Sammy had been thinking. "If you're our grandmother—I mean, if you say you are—I mean, you know you are but you never said so—now that you say so what do I call you?"

The boat was rocking under Dicey's feet. She wished they weren't going to be in different schools, even for this little time. In Bridgeport, there would be boys' schools and girls' schools, and they'd all be split up. She wished that here, just for this little while, they could still be in the same school. But it didn't matter. It was just another way things weren't working out.

"You'll call me Gram," their grandmother said to Sammy.

"Gram," Sammy repeated, trying it. He ran to the edge of the dock and wheeled around. "Hey, Gram!" he yelled. He ran back. "Gram?"

"Yes, Sammy." She sounded tired.

"You like us, don't you? You do, no matter what you say. I know."

"Never said I didn't," Gram said. "And I'm pretty proud of Maybeth at this moment."

"So am I," Dicey said.

"So am I," Maybeth said, with a smile at herself, a smile that had no silliness in it.

They all stood for a minute there. Little bright-topped waves rocked the boat gently on the way to pattering up against the seawalls. A salty wind blew from the land out over the water. The town of Crisfield lay in the sunlight before them, bleached white as the oyster shells scattered around the ground.

Dicey thought about the bread dough rising in the big earthenware bowl back on the scrubbed wooden table in her grandmother's kitchen. She was getting hungry. She looked at James. He was studying his grandmother, as if he was hungry too, but for something not food, hungry in a way that food could never fill.

It wasn't fair, not just for Dicey but for all of them. Well, Dicey said to herself, life isn't fair. Everybody said that to you. They had all tried, and they had lost, and they were going to have to make the best of it with Cousin Eunice.

She remembered the letter then. Gram hadn't mailed the letter. Dicey thought about not telling her grandmother; but not for long. What was the use of postponing it? When something bad was going to happen it got worse the longer you waited. If she didn't tell Gram, that would be like asking again. And Gram had said no. Dicey wasn't the kind to argue and beg when somebody said no.

"You forgot to mail your letter," she said.

Gram's face was surprised. She really had forgotten it. She was also surprised (Dicey knew this too) that Dicey had remembered and said something. She opened her purse and took it out.

Dicey looked down at the floorboards of the little boat. She looked at her sneakers, worn with all the traveling they'd done. Her big toes stuck out through the canvas. Those sneakers had come a long way.

Wasn't it worth it, having come such a way, to fight a little harder? A little longer? Being told no twice couldn't be worse than being told no once.

"Gram?" Dicey said. She looked up. She was almost as tall

as her grandmother, but now the woman loomed above her, standing on the dock. The dark hazel eyes stared down at her, forbidding her to speak.

"Well, you should," Dicey said fiercely. "You should let us live with you."

That was no way to ask.

"Would that suit you?" Gram asked Dicey.

Dicey was shocked into silence.

"I thought you were the one it didn't suit," James said.

"Well, it doesn't," Gram said. "But it will. I give up. I do, I give up. You've worn me out. You can stay, you can live with me. You hear that, girl?" she called down to Dicey.

"Do you mean it?" Dicey asked.

"I don't say what I don't mean. You should know that. You'll live with me and we'll see lawyers about adoption and take government money—and we'll plant Christmas trees and raise chickens, whatever we have to do, whatever ideas James cooks up that we can't talk him out of. But can we go now, please? My feet are itching me half to death."

But instead of getting into the boat, Gram held up the letter to Cousin Eunice and ripped it into little pieces. She tossed the scraps into the air. The breeze took them out and dropped them onto the dancing waves.

"I'll have to write to her again," Gram said, as if the idea gave her no pleasure.

"Gram," Dicey said. Her grandmother looked down at her again. "The boat, the sailboat in the barn. Can I fix it up and sail it? Can I have it?"

"Do you know how to sail?"

"No. But I could learn. Could you teach me?"

"Yes," Gram said.

"Yes, what?" Dicey asked.

"Yes to both—and no more questions; not until I get my shoes off."

Gram climbed down into the boat and held it steady against the dock while the little children jumped in. James threw the painter down to Dicey and leaped down himself.

"Ready to go home?" Gram asked Dicey. She was smiling.

Dicey just grinned back. "Ready," she said.